LIT

Giselle Green was brought up in Gibraltar and then moved to London to study science at university. She is now a full-time mum to six boys, including twins, and lives in Kent. Giselle is also a qualified astrologer, specialising in horary, a form of medieval astrology. Her debut novel, *Pandora's Box*, won the Romantic Novelists' Association New Writer's award in 2008 and has sold across Europe.

To find out more about Giselle Green go to www.gisellegreen.com

By the same author:

Pandora's Box
A Sister's Gift

GISELLE GREEN

Little Miracles

avon.

A division of HarperCollins*Publishers*
www.harpercollins.co.uk

Published by AVON
A Division of HarperCollins*Publishers* Ltd
1 London Bridge Street
London SE1 9GF

www.harpercollins.co.uk

This paperback edition 2018

First published by HarperCollins*Publishers* 2009

ISBN: 978-0-00-828250-9

18 19 20 LSCC 10 9 8 7 6 5 4 3 2 1

Typeset in Minion by Palimpsest Book Production Limited, Falkirk, Stirlingshire
Printed and bound in the United States of America by LSC Communications

For more information visit: www.harpercollins.co.uk/green

To Eliott, because we both believe in miracles . . .

The child with the long hair. It is him.

The moment I caught sight of him I knew he was mine. He had his back turned to me, bending over the flat grey stones he had been gathering along the seashore, but a mother knows such things. He has grown, of course. He is no longer the baby that he was. But that lock of strawberry hair that always curled just so, under his ear, it's still there. The way he holds his arms so close to his body, fists clenched, crouching over his stones, it is just the same and I know in my heart he is mine.

Oh, I have searched so long for him. The woman who he turns his face to, calling out to her, *Mama, Mama*; she would never know how my heart feels, to see my child again. I have waited so patiently and endured so many bitter tears for this moment of reunion; so why do I hesitate now?

I have sweeties for him. Gummy bears. He likes the red ones. After the memorial service this morning I went out and bought some because I knew, I *knew*, deep in the deepest part of my heart, that my boy was not really dead. I have never accepted it. I have prayed so hard that he might be delivered back to me. I have never given up faith. Even when all my staunchest allies and supporters gradually fell by the wayside, one by one, I never gave up believing. I never let him go.

And now I am vindicated, because he is here.

They will all see that I was right. I will have my child again, hold him in my arms again, touch the soft skin of his hands and smell the scent of his hair while he sleeps. Ah, how I have dreamed for that, longed for that.

So *why* do I hesitate now?

He turns, like an animal sensing he is watched. I have the dark sunglasses on, the ones I always wear so I may scrutinise others undetected. It's a habit that I've got into; it's been necessary. But he knows I am watching him. His unafraid eyes look directly into mine. He is secure within the boundaries of his own safe little world. His mama has marked out her territory in the usual way; the beach bags and the wind-breaker, the damp towels lining the sand, the children's playthings, buckets and spades and plastic starfish surround the periphery like guards on patrol around the central watch-tower where she sits, under the beach umbrella.

She has another baby in there. I can see that now. A newborn, judging by the size of the basket it's in. She's talking to it, singing a little, softly, laughing, touching the baby's face, and I see my boy get up to go and join her.

'*Helados! Helados!*' The man with the bright yellow ice-cream box passes near them and I can see her shaking her head, smiling, as the child pulls on her arm. *Later*, she seems to be saying; *I'll get you one later*, and I watch my son clap his hands in antici- pation, do a little jig.

The pang of jealousy that shoots through me right then, it feels like the sharp end of a sword. It feels as if this woman – this unknown woman, who has stolen *my* baby – she would kill me with her happiness. But it is all over for her. She will see. I will have him back and then she will know what it is to suffer as I have suffered. She will know what it is to be bereft of a child.

How could a woman do such a thing to another woman? She cannot know, she cannot, what she has done to me. How she has caused me to become twisted in such knots. I can scarcely breathe for thinking about it. I can scarcely force my feet nearer

2

to the place where her bastion lies, the place I shall soon enter to take back what is mine.

And I shall, too, because her attention is unevenly divided between the two of them. She lowers her face so gently into the basket, whispering sweet nothings while he, his mind back on his mountain of stones, is forgotten. In a minute he will venture a little further down along the shore to find another stone, and then another one. I know, I have been watching what he's been doing. Each foray takes him a little further away from the safety of her watch-tower. Each little trip for stones brings him closer to his real mama, back to me.

And I am feeling calmer, now. Much calmer than I ever thought I would be, considering what it is I'm planning to do. I have found courage from somewhere; the courage of a mother. Clearly, there is no way this woman will ever admit to what she's done, nor will she willingly give him back.

No, if justice is to be served, there is only one way forward. I just have to wait here a little bit longer and soon, very soon, my child will be back within my reach.

Julia

Everything is going to be all right.

It's going to be just fine.

'*Have you told him yet?*' Alys's text, engraved like the guilty secret in my heart, has just popped up on my mobile. My spirits sink right down to my toes and I know Charlie sees it because his eyebrows go up inquisitively.

'It's nothing.' I plaster a smile on my face, snapping the phone shut. 'Just Alys.' But from the minute we enter the arrivals lounge at Malaga airport, blinking like moles emerging from a tunnel into the bright Christmas lights, the urge to just come clean with him is overwhelming.

I want to tell him. I've *got* to tell him.

Sometimes you've got to do a thing just because it's the right thing to do. Even though the thought of doing it fills you with fear. Even though you know that the people you love most in the world might judge you for it; that you might lose them over it.

The longer I leave this, the harder it is going to get.

Any second now, all Charlie's family will be here to greet us. Not just his brother Roberto who is bringing the car, but the rest of them, too; his sister-in-law Eva and the kids.

'And my aunt Laura and her husband,' Charlie ticks them off on his fingers, 'and my *abuela* Agustina and her neighbour Pepi . . . there's going to be a whole crowd of them coming to pick us up.' He stops and gives me a reassuring squeeze around the waist when he sees my face.

'Why so many?' I swallow.

'They'll be curious to get a look at you, Julia; you *and* our son.' He grins at Hadyn who has one arm wrapped, koala-like, around my neck at the moment. The other, as ever, is gripping tight onto Bap-Bap, the white elephant.

'Moon,' Hadyn informs his father. He's been tracking the moon through the airport windows ever since we left the plane.

'Moon,' Charlie confirms. He's got that just-woken-up look, his rumpled fair brown hair falling into his eyes, a five o'clock shadow because he was up at dawn finishing off in the surgery. He's got creases under his eyes but I know it's the kind of rugged unkempt look that women of all ages can't resist sneaking a second look at.

Damn, I'm lucky.

Charlie grins suddenly, catching me admiring him. He makes my heart jump. I push my mobile phone down into the very bottom of my handbag. I'll deal with this later.

Now that our fellow travellers are slowing down, coming to a stop, I take a curious peek out of the windows myself. If I squint hard I can just make out the silhouette of some palm trees way in the distance.

'*Moon*,' Hadyn murmurs again, and I make an exaggerated show of looking up. Above the rows of planes parked on the tarmac a crescent moon rides high, much bigger and yellower than it seems back in England. When we stop again, the queue slowing down as people pause to get out their documents, Charlie's hand steals up to the hairgrip I've used to twist my hair into a demure bun, and pulls it out.

'*Charlie!*' My hair tumbles down in a mass of dark unruly curls about my shoulders.

'You look better like that.'

'No I don't!' Now I'm never going to look how I wanted to – poised and elegant for the relatives.

5

He silences me with a kiss on my mouth.

'You're going to love Spain,' he promises, and for one split second I forget about the bone of contention that is threatening to loom between us.

I haven't got out of the airport and I love Spain already. I love the sound of his abuela's villa up in the mountains. Charlie's told me about the prickly pear plants that grow there and the horses that run wild. I love the sound of the little round cakes covered with marzipan and pine nuts that they put out at Christmas. I love Charlie's description of the rough-hewn stone church of San José where he was christened; it backs out onto the cemetery where the bones of his ancestors have been interred for centuries.

I don't think my dad was buried with his forefathers.

I think what it must be like to have a place back home where all my ancestors were buried. It would be nice to think of them all being in one place; it gives a person a sense of stability, knowing that they've come from *somewhere*. Me, my dad's side were from Donegal and my mum's from Croydon, but the way I feel inside I might have been blown in on a Gulf-stream breeze, a milk-thistle seed that'll just set up store wherever it happens to land. At least Charlie has got roots.

Anyhow, that crescent moon – if I put my hand up to the window I can cup it in my right hand, so that means it is waxing, getting bigger. My Irish nan Ella would have said that means we are heading *towards* something. We're on a path that hasn't completed its course yet. My thumb slides automatically over the engagement ring sitting newly on my ring finger.

God, there is so much to look forward to, so much that I long for.

I am going to tell Charlie what I need to tell him; I'll do it tonight. Alys is right. I can't put it off any more.

'Is Spain going to love me though?' I bite my lip as Charlie nudges me.

6

'Spain will love you,' he reassures me solidly 'as much as I do.'

He's right. And I mustn't be scared of what's coming. It is what it is. If I can be matter-of-fact about it, then probably so will they. If only Charlie's time weren't so consumed by a million and one things then I probably would have brought it up before. There would have been the right moment . . .

'Julia, look over by the barrier. They're all over there!' Charlie's face creases into a huge grin. Now I see them, and there must be over twenty of them – a sea of tanned, beaming faces; lots of arms waving excitedly, '*Aqui*! *Aqui*!' *Here*, they call. Over the heads of the line in front of us I can just glimpse the children hopping up and down underneath the rope barrier, the greying heads of the aunties not looking our way at all, chatting to each other, dressed in ubiquitous black; I'm guessing that the well-dressed elegant lady must be Charlie's sister-in-law, Eva.

Which one is Agustina, though? The knot in my stomach returns with a vengeance. His grandmother is the one who matters most of all to him, I've picked up that much.

The suitcase in front of us gets picked up. The line moves on but Hadyn is wriggling down now out of my grasp. He runs back a few paces to examine the huge Christmas tree that stands to one side of our route like a sentinel. When I look at him I can't help feeling some of the tension drain right out of me. He looks so sturdy that he makes me smile. He's barely fourteen months old but has the determination to match any teenager.

'You coming?' I ask him.

He shakes his head, solemn. I changed him into his new cotton PJ top when we were on the plane, and only *now* do I notice you can see his tummy poking out the bottom. I give it a sharp downwards pull.

'Oh yes, you are. You're coming with me, mister.' He doesn't respond but his hand in mine feels solid and warm.

'All the people have come,' I tell him brightly. 'All your cousins and your aunties and uncles. All these people have come here

7

just to see us. Isn't that kind? Shall we go and say hello to them?'
Hadyn doesn't budge.

'Come on.' I need a bribe, quick. I don't want them to think
he's naughty or anything. I dig in my bag for his bottle. Out
comes my Spanish linguaphone CDs that I've been listening to
on the flight; out comes a large pack of baby-wipes and a spare
nappy; some polo mints, my sunglasses. Oh shoot, I didn't leave
the bottle behind on my plane seat, did I?

'Hey, J.!' Charlie has turned back, eyes shining; he's already
reached the waiting crowd.

'Come on, Hadyn. Your public awaits you.' I scoop my son
up in my arms before he can protest and hurry over to where
everyone is waiting.

'Julia, welcome to Spain. *Mira el niño, qué guapo!*' The women
crowd around me at once.

'So, how's *Dr Lowerby*?' I'm aware, out of the corner of my
eye, of Roberto slapping Charlie heartily on the back. The women
are all smiling at me, asking me questions, but I can't tear my
eyes away from the brothers. Roberto doesn't look like Charlie.
His eyes are typically Spanish, flashing, dark. His hair is spiked
short and still black. He must take after their late mother,
Conchita, while Charlie, with lighter brown hair, green-eyed,
looks more like their father, who's a Yorkshireman, Northallerton
born and bred. Something, though – I can't tell quite what –
something makes them brothers, places them in a common
bloodline.

Now the woman with the bright red lipstick – who introduced herself to me as my 'sister-in-law', Eva – is cooing
enthusiastically.

'Hadyn is a true Sanchez.' A murmur of approval and agreement goes round the crowd. 'Abuela is going to love him. She is
waiting in the car,' she tells me, 'because of her legs.'

'He looks just like Conchita,' she adds, and when Charlie
glances back at Hadyn now, I catch a glimpse of a certain

8

machismo pride in his eyes. Hadyn grins broadly at his aunt as she strokes the dimple on his cheek that apparently makes him the spitting image of Charlie's beloved late mother.

I wish I could catch exactly what it is they are saying. I've drawn back a little now and I can see they have broken up into little sub-groups. The men are walking slightly ahead with Hadyn, talking motorway routes and roadworks.

'There are long delays – road-works – on the E30,' Roberto is telling Charlie. 'You can't take the Costa road to Arenadeluna. We'll have to take the motorway.'

My attention is drawn back to Eva as we women all walk along together. Two teenagers are pushing our trolley ahead of them now, the younger children grouped around them. 'That's Giorge, my son,' she tells me with obvious pride. 'He wants to go and work in the City now he's left school, but we're trying to persuade him to find work here.' She nods encouragingly at me. 'And you, Julia, you have been to Spain before?'

'No, I've been learning Spanish, though.'

'*Hace bien*!' She nods approvingly. 'You'll soon pick it up. You'll be coming here many times now, no?'

'I hope so.'

'Charlie has a big family. We're a lot of people to get used to. Have you many people flying out for the wedding? The church isn't that big,' she warns with a wan smile. 'Sometimes people have to stand outside and listen to the service, if they have so many relatives . . .'

Ah yes, the church.

'You okay?' She looks at me curiously now.

Do I not look okay? Why did she have to bring up the *church*?

'Of course I'm okay.' I brush my hair away from my eyes and turn the corners of my mouth up a bit. *Why wouldn't I be*?

She looks away then as someone calls her and as we walk through the glass doors away from the cool processed air of the terminal the damp heat of Malaga hits me like a wet glove. It's so

9

hot it makes me feel sick. Outside in the car park I breathe in the sweet almond smell of the oleander bushes.

This is the place where I am going to be getting married to Charlie in September.

I try to work up some excitement that we're *here*.

'You okay, honey?' Charlie glances back at me as we reach Roberto's 4x4.

'I'm fine.' I blow the sticky hair out of my eyes. 'Just fine.'

'Oh.' Roberto looks a little frazzled now. 'I put the baby seat in here, Carlos, with Abuela. I thought there would be room for your wife, too, but now we've bought those groceries. . . . Eva's got room for you in her car, Julia, if that is okay with you?'

What is he saying? That I have to travel in the other car? I peer in through the window covertly, hoping to catch a glimpse of the old lady, but the glass is too dark. Is Charlie going to introduce me to her now? I feel the knot of fear in my stomach returning with a vengeance. 'Sure!' I realise with a jolt that Roberto's still waiting for an answer.

'Are you certain?' Roberto is saying to me, but not with much conviction. 'I could move the cakes . . .'

'No.' I give a shrug. It's nothing. I don't mind. 'Please, I don't want to be a bother. We'll go in separate cars.'

'We'll do the introductions back at the house,' he adds curtly, closing the door on Charlie as soon as he's climbed into the front seat. 'The longer we leave it, the busier the road will get, okay?'

I nod in agreement. What else can I do?

It's only going to take half an hour, maybe less. I can bear to be separated from my two for that long, can't I? I'm a grown-up, for heaven's sake!

The feeling of disappointment that wells up inside me now doesn't know that I'm a grown-up, though. Oh Charlie, I wish – just for a day or so, we could be alone together, just you and me. We're heading into the arms of a huge welcoming committee, your family are dying to see you again and to welcome us all – and that's lovely. But sometimes it seems we get such little time to just *speak*, you and I. And now that we're here, I know everybody is going to want your attention. Everybody always wants your attention, Charlie.

I look away regretfully. I know that's how it's always going to be.

I watch the young girl with the long brown hair who's been walking just behind us, pushing our trolley out to the car for us. Her body language is totally at ease. The way she strides across the car park is enviable – as if she owns the whole world. And of course she's got the safety and support of all her people around her; why wouldn't she feel like that? And then there is Roberto and Eva's son Giorge swaggering along beside her, looking totally bored.

The crescent moon winks at me a few minutes later as Eva's car speeds along the Costa road towards Fuengirola, Mijas Pueblo and then Arenadeluna. There was a moon just like this one the night Hadyn was born. I remember the nurse commenting on the tiny birthmark on the nape of his neck: 'Just like the moon in the sky tonight,' she'd said.

The beaches we pass along the way look dark and abandoned, but there is a stillness and a beauty about the little white crests of the waves rolling in. To the left, the white façades of the holiday villas remind me of lace runners against the brown table-tops of the mountains behind them. My nana Ella used to have lace runners just like that on her furniture in her cottage in County Donegal.

For a brief instant I feel her gnarled hands on my shoulder, the summer-holiday touch of her fingers stroking my hair. Beautiful Nan; silver-haired Nana; who knows what she might have achieved beyond the shackles of superstitious rituals that ruled her life? But she never went out, Nana Ella. For forty-five years, so they tell me, she never left her home . . .

The bright fluorescent lights of a casino break the spell, then.

11

Flashing lights promise big wins for punters, free drinks after midnight. I'm back on the Costa road.

The sky is blue-black tonight, bubbling with excitement once again.

Two weeks, and by the time we leave here the moon will be full; all the awkward introductory phase of getting acquainted with Agustina and the rest of Charlie's family will be over; they will know me and I will know them. I'll be on my way to changing my name to 'Mrs Charlie Lowerby' this coming autumn.

And then – just like the girl who walked by with head held so high in the car park – *I'll* be one of them, too.

Charlie

Agustina Pilar Avila de Sanchez. In the back of my brother's car, sitting beside my baby, she seems so frail and shrunken to me now, but when she leans forward, her work-worn hand on my arm, my *abuela* radiates the same strength of feeling towards me that she always did.

'Too long,' she says to me now in Spanish. 'Why have you left it so long, *hijo*? The years go by too fast for us old ones,' she keeps her tone jovial, light, 'and you young ones – you have forever, to come and go, or to stay away as you please . . .'

'I'm sorry, Abuela.' I reach my arm back to hug the woman who was my second mother. 'I know I have left it too long.' It's been just over five years. I never meant to. I never meant to abandon Spain. '*Lo siento.*'

'*Sí, sí,*' she waves her hand, understanding. 'You have to work very hard, yes?'

'Sure. Too much work.' And too many memories, I think.

'But I am happy,' she assures me. 'You have come and brought your *mujer* and your baby to me. Hadyn has brought you back to us, no? After all this time. I thought I would die and never see you again,' she says feelingly. '*Es un milagro!*' My grandmother laughs. 'He has made me prouder than the Queen of Spain!'

'A little miracle,' I agree. He is. We both look simultaneously towards my son's sleeping form. The streetlights flicker by outside us, momentarily picking out his beautiful face, his strawberry blonde hair. He is the son I never thought I'd have. His mother is the woman who has given me what I have most desired in my life; my heart swells with pride when I think of them both. They are the reason why I have come back to my birthplace this Christmas; because of them, I am prepared to leave all my bad memories and sorrows aside – so that I can share my heritage with them.

'They are all miracles, children.' My brother's voice is nasal. He takes a sharp left turn suddenly and I put out my hand to steady our grandmother. '*All* of them. I already have three,' he reminds us.

'Of course,' Abuela placates him. 'God gives them all. They all are.'

But Hadyn is more of one to me.

More than they will ever know.

Julia

'Like this!' Eva laughs; she's undoing a knot where the washing line attaches to a wooden pole up on the sunny terrace of her house. With a smooth movement, the washing line – a moment ago so high, beyond my reach – goes slack, and I can pull it down to hang out my few items; Hadyn's PJs (that got covered in the cocoa they gave him to drink this morning), yesterday's T-shirts, my undies . . .

Actually – I glance at what Eva's currently pegging out on the line beside mine – I think I'll take my frilly knickers and hang them up later on the shutters within the privacy of our own bedroom. Compared to Eva's and Abuela's, they look a little . . . scanty.

'The sun dries out the rope so the line goes higher,' she informs me. 'Is that all you've got?' She peers into my little plastic bowl and I cover my knickers with my hand.

'We only arrived yesterday.'

'Ah. But with *kids*,' she says in her perfect and only slightly accented English, 'there is always washing. Every day – *washing!*' She shakes out a huge white sheet with a quick flick of the wrist and the fresh laundry scent spreads out as it billows up gently in the breeze. 'We have a *máquina* here though, Julia. You don't have to wash things in the sink. Give me everything you have, while you are staying here. I will wash it for you.'

'That's really kind. I wouldn't want to give you extra work . . .'

15

but Eva waves aside my objections with a shrug and a wave of her hand.

'*De nada,*' she says. Maybe, I think, Eva *enjoys* being up here, hanging out the washing on such a beautiful day as this. I would. While I look out over the rooftops of the houses below, Hadyn picks up her peg-bag and carefully spills each and every one of the remaining pegs out onto the hot terrace surface.

'Oh, hell. Sorry.' I jump up but Eva is unconcerned. She smiles at him indulgently.

'They like the colours of the pegs, children. My girls always used to play with my pegs. They are all the same.' I sink back onto the wall and watch him crouching, sorting them out separately.

God, can it really be *Christmas Eve*? It cannot be. I glance at the date on my watch – a fruitless exercise, since I know full well that it is. The sun winks over the black tiles of the rooftops, baking the surface of the terrace floor where we're standing: how can it be this hot?

'Nearly time for *el almuerzo,*' Eva reassures me, mistaking the reason for my clock-watching.

Almuerzo. I think that's lunch. What, already?

'Abuela has prepared some tortillas. You like this?'

'That'll be great.' I give Eva a smile.

'We just have to wait for the men to come back.' They all eat together here, I'm beginning to learn. *Every meal.*

'Oh, I'm not hungry,' I assure her. We got up late today. I close my eyes, relishing the blissful memory of this morning; just lying there, awake, no pressure to get up because Hadyn was still sleeping. Charlie had leaned in towards me. I had him all to myself just for a few brief, uninterrupted moments. I lick my lips, remembering the taste of his kiss on my mouth before one of Eva's little messengers had knocked on the door, calling out to say that Abuela had prepared breakfast and we could go down 'whenever we were ready'. By the time we got down there they were all waiting for us. Nobody said anything, of course;

they are all much too polite. I saw that Eva's daughters had begun to nibble the edge of their *madalenas*, impatiently.

'It's nice,' I turn to Eva, 'that you all eat together, as a family.'

The surprise in her eyes betrays the unspoken question.

'Oh, *we* would too,' I assure her, 'but we don't all that often get the chance at home. Charlie's work is so . . . unpredictable.'

'Ah.' Eva returns to her basket. She's reached the end of the line and she's started on the shirts. They must be Roberto's. There seem to be rather a lot of them, all expensive, white linen. 'Carlos still has to travel so much?' she inquires sympathetically.

'He still does about half of his work in the country of referral. Mostly Africa.' I stand up, pulling the drawstring bag closed before Hadyn manages to tip any more of her pegs out.

'Still with the Esperanza project?' Eva pauses and turns to look at me, eyes widening in interest. 'We had assumed – with a little family – maybe he did less of that now? Is he still working with the children with the . . .' She grimaces, indicating the side of her face.

'The NOMA sufferers?' I go up to the last line where a row of towels, beautifully dried, are waiting to be removed. I pull off the pegs and hand them to my son, who puts them obediently in the bag. 'Yes. He's still working with them.'

'This NOMA – this rotting away of the face . . .' She's shaking her head regretfully. 'How does it happen? How do they get this infection?'

'It can be something as simple as gingivitis – just poor oral hygiene. You'd be surprised. It mainly affects little kids. They'll have had measles or something that's dampened down their immune system. The necrosis can happen in a matter of days – maybe as little as two weeks. The whole side of a child's face can be ravaged.'

'So soon?' Eva shakes her head, it's a shame, she seems to say. 'That must take up a lot of Charlie's time?' she muses, automatically folding the towels that I hand her. 'It can't be that easy on family life?'

17

'Well.' I turn away from her. Charlie's showed me enough pictures. He's made sure I know enough about his work that I could hardly begrudge those poor people – mainly infants – his time and attention. 'It does mean he's not around with us as often as he'd like. He almost didn't catch the flight with us out to Malaga yesterday. They were operating on a child whose jaw and half his cheek had been eaten away by necrosis.' Eva winces. 'The operation took just under seventeen hours. When Charlie left there he flew straight out with us. That's partly why –' I glance at her under my straw hat – 'we didn't get up quite so early this morning.'

Eva turns her attention back to her washing basket.

'And then – afterwards, Carlos still goes on to do the breast implants and the facelifts, eh?' She pulls a bemused face.

'I know,' I smile. 'Everyone finds that strange. But he still needs the Drapers Street practice to pay the mortgage. The private cosmetic work is how he supports his family.'

Eva nods rapidly.

'Naturally,' she says, 'he still has to earn money for himself. He's a good man, Julia.'

'And you?' she adds curiously, picking up my camera that I'd balanced along the top wall. 'You were a fashion photographer, yes? You still take pictures? Oh!' She looks startled as the flash goes off. 'What happened?'

'Only of Hadyn,' I admit wryly. Mine was another job with unsociable hours. 'Don't worry. You took a picture of us, that's all!'

She puts the camera down and hands me back the bale of dried, folded towels and we both glance at a yawning Hadyn, his face screwed up in the bright sunshine.

'If you're going in, could you take these towels in to Abuela for me?'

I take my son's hand and she adds, 'You're a lucky girl, you know. There are always going to be a lot of women interested

18

in a man like Charlie,' she says this last bit almost to herself. 'He's thirty-five now, at the peak of his career, a catch. But he needs someone who will understand the importance of what he does. You're a little bit younger than him, aren't you?' She looks at me frankly, pegging up the last of the laundry – my frilly knickers! – on the end of the line beside the white shirts.

'Twenty-seven,' I tell her.

'Still, I think that you do understand. I think you are honest enough to know what you're letting yourself in for with him.'

I hesitate and wipe away the hair from my eyes. I'm getting too hot and bothered up here. I've got to go down.

I think you are honest enough . . .

When I pick my son up and carry him down the shaded steps that lead from the terrace back into the main part of the house, Eva's words echo in my head for longer than I want them to. Am I so honest?

I *am* honest, I tell myself. If things between Charlie and me hadn't progressed so quickly, we would have had the time any normal couple gets, to fill each other in on all the little background details of our lives. I would have told him all that he needed to know about my past. He would have told me about his. We would never have come to this point that we're at now because . . . Well, because we wouldn't.

Back in our bedroom, I put Hadyn into his cot and stand on the cool balcony for a few minutes. Outside I can hear the sounds of Roberto's car pulling into the drive. He and Charlie are back. They come out talking loudly in Spanish, laughing and joking, and speaking so fast I can barely understand a word that passes between them. I am not part of this world, yet. Here in Spain, amongst his family, I have already once or twice caught a glimpse of a different Charlie. Just little things; like the way that, when he's out with Roberto, he walks with the ghost of a swagger. He laughs louder. Oh, it's nothing much. He catches my gaze, now looking down at him, and blows me a kiss.

19

I wave back and go inside to sit on the bed where Alys's text is still there on my phone, warning me to get on with it. *Have you told him yet?*

No! No I damn well haven't. I'll tell him today for sure.

I will.

Julia

I walk in to the cool walk-in pantry area and stop dead with disappointment.

He isn't here.

I could have *sworn* I saw Charlie walk this way just a moment ago; this house has too many doors, too many routes to the outside. I've just spent the best part of a nail-bitingly long lunch psyching myself up to come clean with my fiancé and I'm *still* not going to get a moment to do it.

I'm not alone in here, either.

'*Hola, hija!*' Agustina smiles broadly at me. The door to the pantry creaks closed behind me. If she wonders what on earth I'm doing in here, she doesn't show it.

'Is the boy still sleeping?'

I nod, smiling a smile that I don't really feel. Hadyn has slept right through into the early afternoon but I don't want to wake him right now. I feel a flutter of nerves. *I need to talk to his dad and I can't put it off any more.*

I'm about to ask Agustina if she's seen Charlie when she points to a box poised on a shelf above a crate of oranges.

'Could you help me, *hija*? I'm too –' she searches for the word – '*baja.*' She indicates her small stature with a hand gesture.

'Too short?' I lean over and pull the box down for her easily. Some loose bits clunk together inside as I do so and she pulls a face, warning me to take care. Whatever's inside it is clearly very precious to her.

'It's the Nativity,' she tells me. 'With the crib,' she adds by way of explanation. 'You have those in *Inglaterra,* yes?'

'I've seen them before.' We never had one in the house, though. I stand there awkwardly for a moment, holding the box, impatient to get away. But I can't. She is standing there, smiling so sweetly, and I'm well aware that – of all of them – Abuela is the one I've spoken least to, so far. If I try to make an escape now, she will think me so *rude.*

'Would you like me to . . . take this through somewhere for you, Agustina?'

She nods slowly, still smiling. I'm not sure if she understands what I've just asked her.

'I am very *feliz . . .* that you are here, Julia,' she announces feelingly. 'We are very happy to have you here. And to see Hadyn. It has made us all . . . very happy.'

'Thank you, Agustina.' I glance towards the door. Would it be okay to call her Abuela – Grandmother – just like the rest of them do? I'm not sure.

One thing I *am* pretty sure of is that I heard Roberto making plans over lunch to take his brother out again this afternoon. They have the important mission of procuring some fresh fish for tonight's meal. If I don't catch him now . . .

I shift over from one foot to the other, impatiently. I'll be happy to get to know his family better. I just . . . need to talk to Charlie first.

'He is a very good boy, you know.' Agustina's voice has taken on a sentimental tone. Who does she mean? Hadyn?

'We missed him so much when he left us,' her voice is quivering a little, remembering, 'so many years ago now. He was only little. We missed him.'

She means Charlie. I'm not going to get away just now, am I?

22

I set the box with her precious Nativity down on one side and give a quiet sigh.

'His father wanted him in England,' she reminisces now. 'So . . .' she looks at me with a shrug. She had no choice in the matter, she seems to say. 'He used to write me – how you say? – *cartas*, all the time.'

Letters. I nod. I'm not sure what to say in response.

'He's happy now in *Inglaterra*,' she gives me a narrow glance, 'but in those days he used to beg me to bring him home. In those days I would have given . . .' she shifts her weight from one leg to the other, leans a little further on her stick. ' . . . I would have given the whole world, to have him back.' She smiles sadly, remembering. 'But now – I think – he is happy.' I shift my gaze to the dark pantry floor. A line of ants has set up a delivery system along the near wall.

'I'll try and make sure that we visit you as often as we can,' I promise her. What else can I say?

A fly buzzes through the door and lands on the shelf beside the large drying ham. Agustina swats it expertly with an open hand.

'But, really, I am so *contenta* that Carlito has found someone like you,' she continues openly. 'Eva has been telling me about you. You understand very well the work that Carlos does, she said?'

'I try,' I confess. 'I'm not all that involved in it.' *He's involved enough for both of us isn't he?*

'You want to help me put this together?' she offers shyly. She's indicating the Nativity box with her head. 'It's a very important – how you say it? – a *costumbre*?'

'A tradition?'

'A custom. That's it.' She opens the box and gingerly pulls out one of the pieces, lovingly wrapped in newspaper for protection. 'Some of the pieces are very old. This one,' she holds up the

23

figure of a blue-clad Madonna to show me, 'this belonged to my great-grandmother. She is the *Madonna de Las Lágrimas* – of Tears. The Madonna of all those lost at sea. The women in my family have always handed it down. It would have gone to Conchita, Charlie's mother. If you have a girl one day,' she adds softly, 'it will go to her.'

'She's very . . . beautiful.' I take the little china piece from her and examine it more closely. The Madonna's little painted face has bright cherry-red lips. Her cloak is of the deepest blue, her robe a cloudy white. She's got a little chip on her toe, but apart from that she is perfectly preserved. 'Do you mind if I take a photograph of her, later?' The little figurine is such an iconic figure I can't help myself.

'Of the Madonna?' Agustina looks bemused. '*Si, claro.*' Be my guest, she makes a gesture with her hands.

'I'd love to help you put the Nativity together,' I add chival-rously, despite the fact it's not what I really *want* to do.

But I might learn some things about my reticent Charlie that he'd never tell me himself. I'd never realised just how much of a wrench his leaving Spain with his dad must have been for him. It would have been, if he was as close to his grandmother as she seems to imply.

'So, when your daughter Conchita died, and Charlie's dad decided to take him over to live in the UK . . .' I carry the box through for her and we set it up on the table in the hallway, 'was that something to do with his father's work with the World Health Organisation?'

Her face blanks over then and I realise I might be talking too fast.

'*¿Por qué no se quédo Charlie?*' Why didn't Charlie stay in Spain with you, I attempt, and I see her smile. 'I know that Charlie's dad used to travel about a lot with his work for WHO – a bit like Charlie does now. Why did they leave Spain?'

'*Demasiados recuerdos, yo creo.*' She taps her head. He had too

24

many memories. There's a small silence then and she takes in a deep breath; it's a breath full of long years of silence, of holding her peace. 'Charlie's father loved my daughter as much as his own life. I don't think he could bear to see us.'

'And Roberto?'

'He was older by then. Sixteen. He already had a girlfriend. He didn't want to go, you know how it is. Heh! They have cut the *electricidad* again!' She tut-tuts, flicking the switch to give us better light, but to no avail.

'No electrics?'

'No. It's the *trabajadores* – the men, working – they keep cutting it off.'

'You mean the work going on in the town – all those improvements they're doing in Arenadeluna at the moment?' Agustina pulls a face at the suggestion that they're making 'improvements'.

She brightens then, remembering something. 'They say there will be more *oportunidades* for young people here once they are finished,' she tells me, and I see the glint of a hope rekindled in her eyes. She hasn't yet given up on the idea that her Charlie will return to her.

We bring out Joseph and the three shepherds, leaving the three kings, – who have clearly come from a different set because of the resplendent colour of their garments – until last. I unwrap the figures, and Agustina wipes them carefully with a damp cloth. Now that they're all out: baby Jesus in his crib, the shepherd boys on their knees and the various animals dotted about over the gently undulating plains of papier-mâché that form the backdrop behind it all – I can see why the Madonna of Tears is the most special one of them all. Not only is she the oldest piece, she looks, to me, to be the most *loved*.

Agustina cleans a space for her in the stall behind the crib and looks up at me with her face beaming.

'Did Charlie *ever* talk of coming home?' I ask her now. It's clearly the topic uppermost in her mind. It's the one thing that this old lady would love to hear from me more than anything else – that I, as his prospective wife, would countenance the thought of maybe setting up a base here. The idea does not seem to me so very terrible, either. Maybe I could?

'Once, he did.' Agustina's voice goes very quiet.

'A long time ago?' I prompt. When he was still a child, stuck in his lonely boarding school, longing to return to the warmth of his family and Spain.

'Not so long as that.' We both look up as Eva joins us now, a very sleepy and slightly disgruntled Hadyn in her arms. Eva kisses my son on the top of his curly head. It's a kiss that lingers over the scent and the sleepy softness of him. 'It was – maybe – five years ago, that we thought he might return to Spain.'

'Really?' I hold out my arms to receive my son from Eva and he immediately rests his warm head on my shoulders. 'As recently as that? I never knew.'

'Of course!' Agustina says decisively. 'They were going to buy a house. Where was it, Eva, *cerca de Puerto Banús*, no?'

They were? Charlie and who else? I turn to Eva, confused. She speaks better English than Abuela. Maybe Agustina didn't mean 'they'? Eva coughs. She looks at Abuela but she doesn't say anything.

'I've changed his nappy for you,' she says at last, slightly out of breath.

'Thanks!' I hug him in closer and Hadyn perks up suddenly. He's just spied his bottle on the floor.

'Juice!' he demands.

'I'll get him some water,' Eva volunteers, but Abuela isn't finished with her yet.

'*Ay, dios mio!*' Agustina taps her head in frustration. 'Was it Puerto Banús, Eva?

'I think so, Abuela.' Eva is definitely uncomfortable. She bends down to pick up the bottle.

'If he had married Lourdes,' Abuela continues unabashed,

'they would have both come to live here in Spain and then I would have seen him nearly every day.'

I bite my lip.

I've heard of Lourdes, of course. He's mentioned her in passing. He never actually said they had plans to get married at one time!

So, I'm not the only one who has been holding some of my past back. I wonder why he never mentioned it. On the other hand, Lourdes was clearly history long before I ever met Charlie. I stare at the floor.

'I've made an appointment at the church for you, like you asked,' Eva puts in helpfully, clearly anxious to change the subject.

I try to hide my frown. I never asked her to make an appointment at the church. Things do move fast around here, it seems.

'Carlos and Roberto were talking about this yesterday,' she says, in answer to the bewilderment in my eyes. 'He didn't tell you? Abuela thought perhaps when you met the priest to talk about your wedding, you could arrange a date to christen the boy while you're in there?'

Yet another thing that Charlie and I haven't had a chance to discuss properly. Oh, he mentioned something about it last night I think, just before we went to sleep. I didn't pay him any mind at all, I was too tired. I put my hand up to my head, which is beginning to throb. This is *precisely* the kind of situation that I was hoping at all costs to avoid. All these church preparations. . . . I should have just come clean with them all right at the beginning but it seemed too hard. Charlie hasn't been available for me to talk to, not once. There have always been so many people around, not a moment of privacy. Why oh why didn't I just tell Charlie back in the UK, long before we ever got here?

Because, back in the UK, I remind myself, *none of this seemed like the huge deal that it does over here . . .*

'Juice!' Hadyn roars into the lull that ensues and makes a swipe at the bottle Eva has just placed on the table. I put my hand out automatically to try and redirect his – that bottle is too near the whole Nativity scene – but then the worst possible thing happens. How it happens I don't know, but my balance just goes and my hand comes down hard onto the table. They both look on in horror as the whole table wobbles and some of the little figurines topple over.

Including the *Madonna de Las Lágrimas*. She doesn't just topple onto her side. Maybe it's the chip on her foot that makes her less stable than the others; maybe it's just sheer bad luck, but the oldest piece in the set falls right off the table onto the smooth tiled floor, and, horror of horrors, breaks into two pieces.

There's a silence so thick you could walk on it.

'I'm . . . I'm really, *really* sorry,' I gulp.

Eva bends down and picks up the two shards, her face looking a bit red; she seems stunned into silence. Why did that have to happen, right now?

And why did it have to be *that* figurine? The extra-special pass-it-down to your daughters heirloom from the great grandmother that is clearly the most loved piece of all? Agustina is dumbstruck for the moment. The accidental breaking of that piece has struck right to the very heart of her. I can't even imagine how I am ever going to recover from this fall from grace.

'*Trae mala suerte!*' she says feelingly after a while. She shakes her head reproachfully at me. *Mala suerte*. What is that? I look at Eva.

'She is saying it is very bad luck,' she mutters, head down. I feel my heart skip a beat, ricochet back to my childhood for a second, to Nana Ella's house and the heart-stopping anxiety that could be induced in her by the smallest infringement of her 'luck' rules.

I feel my face flaming red in embarrassment. I'm sorry I broke the thing. I'm really sorry I broke it. But I'm not having anyone start laying all this 'bad luck' crap on me all over again.

At least it has stopped them talking about the church.

I shouldn't have put my hand down so clumsily; I should have taken more care. I was distracted by the sudden revelation that Charlie had a former fiancée. Now *that* I was not expecting!

I have to look on the bright side of this. It means I don't need to be so worried about facing Charlie after all. My 'little secret' is hardly much worse than his.

I know that all this church stuff is really important to them but they've got to stop making all these 'helpful' arrangements without checking it out properly with me first. This church wedding they're planning for me and Charlie isn't going to happen.

I have to tell them that it can't because once – eight years ago now; a lifetime ago – I was married to someone else. We were both still at college and we were both too young; we never thought it through properly. It was hardly a proper marriage at all – we were more companions than anything. I never felt for Sebastian the way I feel about Charlie. We got divorced.

But in the Catholic Church, once you're divorced, you can't be married in a church ceremony a second time. It'll have to be a civic ceremony for Charlie and me. I glance at Abuela and Eva uneasily as they fuss over the figurine, discussing whether it can be mended. They've all made so many assumptions. They've worked so fast, they haven't given me a chance to say . . .

But I have to tell Charlie about it, first.

Charlie

I had forgotten how Arenadeluna looks on a morning like this. The sun skims its silver shards of light across the choppy Mediterranean just as Rob and I used to skim stones from here, on the Playa de Luna. Rob used to dive in, over there, by those rocks. He had a harpoon back in those days. He'd bring *calamares* back for the women to clean and we'd eat them for supper. I wanted to go spearing squid with my big brother too but he'd never let me anywhere near that bloody harpoon . . .

It's been a long time.

I draw in the scent of sardines cooked over last night's open fires, the smell of the surf and the shingle that is bright with ozone. When I shade my eyes, looking further out, the sea is a duck-pond green this morning. The air is hot – topping twenty-eight degrees already – but the water looks cold. On a day when the mist clears over the water you can see right the way to the Rock of Gibraltar from here. And, once you get to Gibraltar, under the right conditions, you can see right over to the shimmering mountains of North Africa.

A picture of Ngosi Ontome flashes through my mind.

We did what we could, I remind myself. Now we have to wait; that's how it always is. Sometimes you just get – a *sense*, though, what can I call it? – a feeling of unease after a procedure. You can't worry about the patient. You just have to forget about them and wait.

'Heh, *extranjero!*' Rob claps his hands together, gets my attention back. 'You forgot your sunglasses, eh?' He hands his over magnanimously, his eyes automatically screwing up against the glare. 'Notice anything different?'

When I turn my eyes from the sea the rest of the beach all looks pretty much as I remember it. Except maybe – the sand looks different. It looks whiter than I recall. And then there's that wrought-iron balustrade, shiny and black, heading up the walkway to the beach. Makes me think of the ornate window-bars outside the tenements in the town. Who thought up that little detail, I wonder? I narrow my eyes, glancing at Rob, who can barely conceal his glee at all the improvements. It'll be his department at the town hall that'll be heading all these off, I remember.

But where's the crumbling sea wall, I wonder, the one we both used to vault over in our efforts to be the first one down here?

'Sure; the colour of the sand is different,' I tell him. My brother grins broadly.

'Imported. We got it from Tunisia,' he confesses proudly. 'It's nicer for the local people and, of course, better for the *turistas*! So, everyone's happy.'

I turn and scan the beach behind us now. The fishing boats, wooden and dilapidated most of them, are still lined up on the shore, just as they always used to be, waiting for tide and time. Arenadeluna has a fishing industry that goes back centuries. I had thought maybe this little corner of the Costa del Sol, tucked away amongst these rocky coves as it is, might have escaped the attention of the tourist industry, but it doesn't look like it.

'I take it the fishermen still set out from here?'

'*Claro!*' Roberto holds up his hands at the thought it could be otherwise. 'It's what people expect. And you have to let the old men keep their jobs – what else would they do? A lot of them take the tourists out fishing now, though,' he adds as an afterthought. 'More money in it for most of them.'

'And the cafeteria,' I glance behind him, 'it's gone.'

'We're building a bistro further up where the Solero used to be.' My brother rubs his hands together, impatient, because it seems I haven't noticed the one main change.

'The *playa*,' he indicates the beach all around us, 'it's *bigger*, can't you see?'

I see. I frown at him. I *think*. I can't really tell, can I? It's been a while.

'Quite a lot's different, isn't it, Rob? All your department's doing, I suppose?'

'Heh, you've left it a long time, *hermano*,' he shrugs.

'I had reasons why I didn't return to Spain,' I remind him.

'*Bueno*, but that's all over and done with now, eh?' He lifts his shoulders in a pragmatic gesture. We have reached the end of the beach. I see now there are signs up everywhere, warning of works in the imminent future. The shingle up here is more like I remember it, sharp brown stones that scrunch under my bare feet. Some kids kick a ball directly at us, and I lob it back to them. Rob shoos them away. 'You have another *mujer*. A good one, Eva tells me. She's a pretty girl, Carlos.' He winks meaningfully at me now. 'And good with the kids.'

'She's . . .' I give a low laugh, 'she's very good with children.'

'It's a virtue in a woman. You should give her lots of them, Carlos.' He smiles amiably. 'That's what it's all about, eh? In the end, everything we do – it's all for our family, right?'

'Sure.' I look away from him. Easy for him to say. I really don't know if Julia and I are going to be having any more kids.

'What?' He homes in on my reticence like a heat-seeking missile. 'Julia doesn't agree? You should make your wishes known!' My brother slaps his thigh. 'Modern women – they like the freedom of work too much, that's the trouble. We have the same problem here in Spain,' he says feelingly. 'All this business of having a career – what do they want with it? Their career is looking after the kids and they should be happy with that, I say.'

I give my brother a look that leaves him in no doubt of what I think about *that*.

'What? Now you're telling me she's full of ambition?' Rob insists.

'It isn't that. Julia's actually a stay-at-home mum. She's exactly where she wants to be right now and she couldn't be happier. I'm only grateful I can afford to support her in her choice. It's just—'

'Just do it while you're both still young,' my brother counsels. 'Older people don't do so well running after kids,' he laughs. '*Bueno*, you're back home now and that's what counts. I take it you've had wind of the *gran fiesta* that Abuela is organising in your honour for year's-end, no?'

Is she? I look at him in surprise. I was hoping she wasn't going to go in for any fuss. My phone buzzes in my pocket and I put my hand over it. If it's Julia she'll tail off after three rings so I know and I can ring her back. Otherwise . . . My heart sinks – *please don't let it be London.*

'Abuela insisted,' Rob blusters on, 'and you've got to let the older people have their way. She's had to wait long enough to see you, hasn't she?'

I should be grateful. At least he hasn't cast me as the prodigal son.

We need to get back.

Up along the street at the top, echoes of the procession of the *Madonna de Las Lágrimas* line our path in the form of coloured petals: roses, lilies and . . . what are those orange ones? Gladioli, I think. They carry a statue of the Virgin all along the beach front, so she blesses the fishing boats. Then the statue is taken up to the chapel where it stays for three days until the Christ child is born on the twenty-fifth.

I focus downwards on the petals in my path, remembering. I was in a procession just like this once. When I had my first communion. I remember Conchita dressed me all in white. All of us children had to walk two by two. I had to hold Maria Ortega's hand and her fingers were all sticky from the flower-petals she'd been scattering. They still do this, even now. Eva sends me pictures of the kids on their high days and holidays. Rob reminded me again yesterday that I need to get Hadyn christened. I'd never have thought of it myself. Back home in England it doesn't seem so important. Here, it is *everything*. I'll have to speak again to Julia.

'Hey, you have to . . . forget the past, *hermano*.' Rob mistakes the reason for my silence. 'Everything you have now – it's good, no?'

'Sure. It's good.' It is good. I swore I wasn't going to bring this damn phone out to Spain. I was going to have a holiday here. I was going to be away somewhere where nobody could contact me. If it had been anyone else, I might have done it, but when I left that little boy. 'I'm . . . thinking about my work,' I confess. 'I left a child we were working on at a critical stage, that's all.'

'Ah your work – well, at least it's still going great, Eva tells me.' Rob waves cheerily to some guy over the road. 'It's the new mayor,' he tells me. He can't catch the man's attention so I still have his.

'It's good but there are never enough hours in the day, are there?'

'Still doing the Esperanza work, I hear?' My brother kicks a cigarette butt away with the tip of his foot. 'All that *pro bono* surgery for the African children? God must love you, *hermano*!' he accedes graciously. 'You're a truly charitable man. I hear you barely made it out of London on time yesterday?'

I grin ruefully. I must apprise Julia of the fact that anything she mentions to anyone – anything at all – will get back to me within twenty-four hours in Arenadeluna.

'We were working on a four-year-old. Ontome is his name.' *Why did I say his name*? I must get that child out of my head.

'It's a terrible disease this NOMA – I've seen the pictures.' My brother pulls a face. 'It's a true miracle what you surgeons do.

I swear, I don't know how they survive.' He shades his eyes, looking out over the green sea from the head of the beach. Roberto was always squeamish, I remember now. He could never bear to see – or speak – of blood and guts. He likes things to look nice. To *be* nice.

'You'd be surprised just what it's possible for us to do. Nowadays we can use pedicled supraclavicular flaps to cover defects as large as half the face.' Rob looks at me blankly.

'We use skin grafts taken from elsewhere on the body, somewhere like the thigh. We take the living tissue, with all its blood supply . . .' Roberto's mouth twitches and as we duck under a freestanding rope barrier that blockades off the area where the 'works' are progressing I change tack.

'We do what we can, Rob. We put the rest into God's hands.'

'That is the way with so many things, no?' he agrees. He waves at the new mayor who's caught his eye at last. 'Hey I have to see this guy just for a second – you'll be all right, *hermano?* I need a private word with him. It's okay with you?'

'Sure, you go ahead.'

'I won't keep you,' he promises.

My phone goes off again. This time I pick it up. It must be Julia. But it isn't, and my heart sinks. It's from Angus.

Re: Ngosi Ontome; poss. team recall. Incorrect application of wound dressing has kinked the pedicle of the flap. On alert for flap necrosis. Be on standby. Sorry folks. Angus.

Damn it, *I knew it!*

Now I'm going to have to leave Abuela and the family before New Year's Eve and that'll break her heart. How can I go?

But how can I not go?

And Julia – I can just imagine – she isn't going to like this, not one little bit.

Julia

Oh, Hadyn has taken so long to sleep! I carried him up half an hour ago and we are already into the small hours. The Christmas Eve meal – like every meal here – went on for an age. If it hadn't been for the broken Madonna and the fact that I *still* haven't spoken to Charlie, I would have been happy to sit back and enjoy it.

Charlie knows something's up. He's been looking at me all throughout dinner, trying to catch my eye. He knows we need to talk. When I sneaked out onto the terrace at one point, knowing he would follow me, we had no time together at all before Agustina came out too. I heard his soft sigh when he saw her come out and I knew that he too had hoped for some time alone with me. *But we're here for them, aren't we?* His eyes on me in that moment seemed to say. We're here in Spain to spend time with the family. And now I know how much Agustina has longed for this, I mustn't begrudge them. I just never realised how few snatched moments would be left over for Charlie and me.

Charlie's here. I turn away from Hadyn's cot as he closes the bedroom door behind him. With his fingers he extinguishes one of the three fat candles that Eva has brought up for us to get undressed by: no *electricidad* again. The lights went out about 11 p.m. By the very minor irritation that seemed to cause, I get the impression the electricity must get cut off quite a lot around here. The flickering shadows of the last candle-flames against the stone walls make me imagine we could have been thrown back a few centuries.

When I draw aside the long linen curtains to let in the moonlight, the air is crisp and bright. Just as on any Christmas Eve night in England I might have looked out of the window as a child and thought – a good night for Santa to arrive? He doesn't arrive on the twenty-fifth over here, though, I remember. The Spanish children have to wait till the feast of the epiphany – the sixth of January – for the three kings to bring them their presents. That isn't the only note that throws this Christmas Eve out, for me. Outside on the terrace the stark white of a few jasmine flowers, tricked into flowering out of season, throw up their heady scent.

'I thought you might be in bed already . . . waiting for me?' By his low tone Charlie manages to convey the hint of disappointment, but I shake my head briefly.

'Why so nervous?' Charlie moves closer. When he catches me up against the dark bedroom walls the stone feels cool against my fingertips.

'I'm not nervous!' My high laugh betrays me. 'I just . . . wanted to . . .'

'You're not *shy* of me, are you?' There's a glint in his eyes.

'Hah!' I retort, but I cannot hold his gaze. He *makes* me shy. Because of his physical beauty. Because of his unshakeable self-assuredness. He moves in just a fraction closer and now I can feel him, the length of his body poised just beyond the reach of mine. 'You've given me a son already,' he reminds me in a low voice. 'You can hardly be shy.'

'No,' I manage. 'It's not that, Charlie.'

'I have something for you,' he murmurs against my ear. 'A present. Do you want it now?' He pushes me onto the bed.

I laugh. Does he mean my real present, or something else?

'I'd like that, Charlie. It's just that first I need to—'

'No?' He sounds surprised that I'm putting him off. 'You don't want my present? Is something troubling you?'

Oh Charlie, I just want to tell you something! But I fall silent, because by some strange magic, I find I cannot tell him. His face is so close to mine I can smell the sweet scent of him. I want to kiss him but there's something about him tonight . . .

'You're right,' I confess. 'I am feeling a bit *odd*. I'm not sure what it is, it's just being here with all your people, I think,' I stutter. 'And seeing how you are with them. You're not quite the same over here either, are you?' I add. 'You're . . . different. I don't know. More *Spanish*.'

He gives a low laugh at that. 'I've just spent the afternoon with my brother being reminded of how very un-Spanish I am. When I'm here, I'm neither one nor the other; neither English nor Spanish. There are so many things I have forgotten – you can't imagine it, Julia.' He bows his head and I catch a glimpse of the struggle going on underneath. 'I don't even remember how to speak Spanish properly any more, but I'd be lying if I didn't admit there is still something about this place that calls to me.' He looks up and smiles. 'When I hear Giorge playing the Spanish guitar, when I see Eva's girls praying at their rosaries – I'm rediscovering what I left behind.'

'Five years ago?' I breathe. Will he tell me, I wonder? He frowns.

'Much longer ago than that, *querida*.'

'I've been meaning to bring something up with you,' I get out now. 'Before, when we were at dinner, d'you remember, I went out onto the terrace and you came too but then Agustina came out after us?'

'Yes, I know.' He looks pained. 'I'm aware. We need to talk, don't we?' Charlie directs a glance towards the closed bedroom door. We are alone at last. *He knows?*

I'm confused now. How could he know? I haven't said anything to any of his relatives about Sebastian. Could Charlie have somehow picked up my phone and read Alys's text? Surely not! On the other hand, I *did* lend him my phone yesterday, I remember with a shiver.

38

'You've got something on your mind,' he tells me now.

'It's true.' I look at him unhappily. If he knew what my marriage to Sebastian was really like, if he knew why we hooked up in the first place – because there were no student flats available unless you were a married couple – and we'd thought of it as a solution, as a way round the problem.

'Is it Agustina? She can be a little – formidable, I know.' Charlie is silent for a few moments, reflecting. 'Could you try being open with her?'

'About what?' I look up sharply, heart thudding.

'About your fears, maybe.'

I give a little laugh, to cover my feelings.

'Maybe I'm terrified what her reaction might be,' I fence.

Charlie's face remains inscrutable but his eyebrows go up a bit at the word 'terrified'.

'If this is about the Madonna,' he shakes his head briefly, 'she's already forgiven you, J. It was old. She told me, when you rushed forward and it got broken, it was because you were trying to *prevent* an accident. These things happen. It was only broken in two pieces I hear?'

The Madonna. My heart sinks; is that what Charlie thinks this is about? He turns to lie on his back and I know he's turning things over in his mind too. 'It brings back memories, that Nativity.' We lie there for a while and I can hear him in the semi-darkness, brushing his hair away from his forehead.

'She was a beautiful lady you know, Julia. My mother Conchita. We made the Nativity for her.'

'I've seen the photographs'. I turn and lie on my side to face him. There are pictures of her everywhere in the house and she was beautiful, too; absolutely stunning. I know it hurts for him to see them. Charlie hasn't even *opened* the photograph album of old pictures that Eva had made up for him for his Christmas present. But I did. I looked at the pictures while he was out with Roberto. There are loads of photos of Charlie as a boy with his family. There's even a picture in there of Conchita as a child and it's true what they say about Hadyn being the spitting image of his grandmother.

It's a lovely album – full of memories of happy times; but there's something incredibly sad about it too because . . . Photos never really capture the whole story, I know. When you have someone and you love them, you think you're going to have them forever but you never do.

Charlie doesn't talk about Conchita. I know he lost her a long time ago when he was still a boy, but he never mentions her at all. I've never had even a glimpse, until this moment, how much he must still hurt over losing her.

'I'm sorry,' I say. I run my fingertips over the length of his arm, my touch as light as a feather, scarcely wanting to disturb him, but he pulls me towards him in a fierce hug.

'You lost your father too,' he reminds me.

'Yes.' I swallow.

'You know what it's like; to lose someone who meant the world to you.'

He doesn't know the half of it. I'm glad it's so dark, that he cannot properly see my face. I push away the discomfort inside and reach up to kiss the man who will become my husband.

'You're still fretting about something, aren't you?' He looks at me suddenly.

'I . . . don't know how I'm going to make amends to Agustina,' I make up quickly. 'When the accident happened earlier on I just—'

'You don't have to. Abuela sees you as bringing me back to her. The whole family are in love with you, Julia: you don't have to worry about that.' I swallow and he kisses me hard, making me silent. If I didn't love him so much, if he didn't have this ridiculously strong effect on every one of my senses, I would push him away right now and just say my piece.

Because it is not such a big deal, really.

My marriage to Sebastian was never a big deal. If it had been I would have told Charlie all about him. You can't be with someone for just over two years and not bring up little memories of past romances. The sad thing is that there were so few of those that Sebastian and I shared. And any there were I've probably just blanked out, just as I've blanked out how gutted he was after I decided to end our marriage after just three months. I don't want Charlie thinking I would take *our* marriage as lightly. That was eight years ago and I was a lot less wise than I am now.

'It's true, everybody loves you here,' Charlie traces the line of my jaw, brushes over my lips, 'but not as much as I do.'

And have you, I wonder with a sudden chill, *ever loved anybody else as much as you say you love me now?*

He's never told me about his fiancée, has he? He senses the – almost imperceptible, surely? – distance that thought puts between us.

'But we still need to talk, yes?' I breathe. 'Outside on the terrace, earlier . . .'

Charlie takes in a deep breath. He hangs his head slightly.

'There was something I wanted to tell you, yes. Something that I maybe should have told you about before. It was wrong of me not to mention it and I apologise in advance for not warning you because now you have every right to be mad at me.'

I stiffen, because I know it's coming. He's going to confess to me about her, now – *Lourdes, isn't it*? I should see the bright side of it – the fact that my way will then be clear to tell him about my meaningless marriage to Seb and bring up the fact that it's only significant now because Charlie and me won't be able to have a church wedding.

Go on, I lift up my chin a little, waiting for him to go first. Say her name.

'It's Ngosi Ontome,' Charlie breathes.

I shake my head, confused.

'Ngosi?' I frown at him.

41

'The little boy I was operating on before we came here. It's not confirmed yet, but I may have to leave Spain and fly back to London for him, Julia.'

'You *will?*' I sit up straight on the bed, disappointment zapping right through me. 'You'll have to go back?'

'It looks very likely. I'm sorry,' he mutters. 'I cannot begin to tell you how sorry I am.'

Nor I you, I think. Because you have something that you're still withholding from me and I from you. When bright tears spring readily to my eyes and he tries to wipe them away, I push him roughly off.

'So, we're going home then? When?'

'I have a feeling they'll confirm it by tomorrow. And . . .' He sits up beside me now. 'If I do have to go, I have a favour to ask of you.'

'Ask away,' I sniff. Oh, this is crazy! I haven't told him about Seb and he hasn't told me about *her* and it looks as if now we may have to leave Spain before getting anything sorted out for this wedding anyway.

'If I have to leave, I'd really like you and Hadyn to stay on.'

'What, here? Without you?' No; I don't want to. I shake my head at him.

'Why not?' he reasons. 'You still have the wedding plans to complete. They still have to be done, you need to be here. And –' *here comes the real reason* – 'there's Abuela to consider. She'll be heartbroken if you go now and take Hadyn with you. She's going to be upset enough about me leaving.'

You bet she is.

'Will you do that for me?'

'Sure.' I sit on the bed like a stone. Abuela. I have to consider Abuela and her feelings. What about my feelings? My feelings . . . have no basis in reason and rationality that's the problem. I cannot think of a single good excuse why Hadyn and I should not stay here to finish the end of the holiday so Abuela can have him around for a little longer. No, I can't think of *one*, but my stomach tells me otherwise, twisting in an unnatural fear at the thought that we will stay on. *Follow your instincts*, Nana Ella would have said. *Always follow your instincts.*

'I've disappointed you,' he apologises, 'and I . . . I don't know how to make that up to you, my love.' He does know, though. When he kisses me now he knows that I will not resist his caresses. I love him too much. And we will stay on, of course, because I don't want to let him down. And because there is always the possibility that my fear stems from nothing more terrible than the thought that I will *still* have to face this whole 'I can't get married in the church' thing. And I'd rather not go through that alone, without him.

We make love, and Charlie uses no protection, as usual. Not for the first time, I wonder – does he hope for another child? *That's another thing we have never spoken about* – is this not rather odd? He's never told me he hopes for more children and yet we don't use contraception either. Do we really manage to communicate so little with each other after all? It's never struck me before but it does now.

Julia

'Don't come to the airport with me, Julia,' Charlie whispers.

'Malaga's only twenty minutes away . . .' I start, but he puts a finger to his lips, shushing me. Six whole days have gone by since Charlie first had that text from Angus. At first the team in London hoped Ngosi would respond to an aggressive treatment of antibiotics; that they might not need to reassemble. Agustina has been praying to the Virgin every day that he would recover – not just for his sake, I suspect, but so that Charlie wouldn't have to go home early. Ever since Charlie announced he might have to go everyone's been a little tense and on edge because no one wants to upset Abuela. I would have told him about Sebastian if it had not been for this added complication.

How could I say my piece in the midst of all that? Charlie has so much else on his mind just now. He's worried about the little African boy too, I know. When the call came last night, saying that the team was regrouping, he couldn't book his flight fast enough.

'Take a look at the time,' he's saying now. 'Hadyn's going to wake up soon and he's going to want his mummy.'

I turn my head away so he won't see my disappointment. We came away precisely so we could be together, all three of us on holiday as a family for once. But okay, it hasn't worked out that way, that's all.

When he leans over our son's cot I catch a glimpse out of the window behind them, the moonlight sparkling off the dark Mediterranean and I think: it's not time yet, it's still night, you don't have to go yet. Please don't go.

I think that, even though I know full well that the little boy he is going to needs him more than we do. The fact that he can save people's lives means more often than not that our own lives must take a back seat. I know this, but he is still *my* man, and I want him here tonight.

At the moment he is oblivious to me. He's standing so still over Hadyn, watching him. I wonder what he's thinking.

'What are you worried about, J?' He turns and catches me looking now.

'Nothing.'

'Are you worried that I might meet some other glamorous woman on the plane and I won't come back to you?' He grins at me and his small white teeth look so perfect it sends a shiver right through my spine.

'Hey, maybe I'll meet someone else *myself* if it comes to that. One of your Spanish cousins, maybe a Scandinavian tourist . . .'

'You won't.'

'You sure about that?' For some reason his dead certainty about this leaves me feeling annoyed.

'Yep.' He nods in the direction of the cot. 'For one thing, you won't have the time. He'll keep you too busy. Secondly, you won't have the energy to go chasing any Scandinavians.'

I clear my throat.

'I'm going to miss you, Charlie, that's all.'

'I'm going to miss you too.' He comes and sits on the bed beside me. Already he is half-dressed, his skin damp from the shower, his hair wet. Roberto is giving him a lift to the airport.

'I don't want you to go.'

'I don't want to go either.' Out of habit, we're both whispering, trying not to wake Hadyn. Charlie nuzzles my ear; I trace the line of his arm softly with my fingertips. His mouth finds mine, suddenly hungry, and I hope, I *pray*, that the baby won't wake because I so want Charlie all to myself for the minute.

'Go back to bed,' Charlie pushes me back towards the white rumpled sheets and I pull him easily with me. When he slides my nightie off my shoulders I can feel my bare skin being cooled by the morning breeze. And then – because these doors in Roberto's house have no locks – Charlie pulls a thin white sheet closer to us. The baby shudders in his sleep and we both stop breathing for a minute. I think I can hear someone coming up the stairs but then the footsteps stop.

'I love you, Julia,' he breathes into my ear.

'Let's make another Hadyn,' I suggest. Have we got time? But he starts up at that. I notice that his hair is still wet. He smells of the freshness of shower gel but he is only half ready. He wants to stay here with me but he has the air about him of someone who is leaving. Charlie looks me solemnly in the eye.

'We've already got one of those,' he reminds me. 'You can't make another one of him.'

Someone else then, I don't mind. Let's just do it. This could be a good way to leave the old year behind, I think. If we do this now I could almost bear him to leave us for five days. If we do this now I could bear to face his grandmother all by myself. We have not much time today but he is not one to rush things, and this of all things Charlie never rushes. When he kisses my mouth again, slowly, I feel the tingle of his skin against my skin all along the length of my body. But now I can hear Roberto coming up the stairs. I *know* it's him, because he's got this thing about always being on time which means that if you ask him for a lift anywhere he will invariably get you there too early. Charlie hears him too, laughs good-naturedly, pulling himself away from me and reaching for his shirt.

'Tell him you're not ready,' I hiss.

'I *have* to be ready, Julia. I've a plane to catch, love, remember?'

He stands up to retrieve his clothes and even as he does I notice that there is no longer any remnant of night-time outside; the day has sneaked in cleverly and quickly, time moving without us noticing. The first rays of the day look bright. When I look through the window at the vista of roofs and verandas cascading into the town below us, I see the white cross above the church of San José catching the early rays of the sun.

And I remember: today is the day Agustina has scheduled in for me to meet the priest who is supposed to be marrying us. My stomach tightens at the thought of going it alone. I never asked her to organise it, but she went ahead and did it anyway. Now I'm supposed to be visiting the church with her this morning.

But I won't.

As Charlie dresses, I cock my head to one side, trying to read his expression. Maybe it's just regret that he's leaving that's making his eyes look even darker than usual?

'*What?*' I whisper when he catches my eye, wanting something. Maybe he's still thinking of telling Roberto to bugger off, they don't need to be there so early . . .

'Look after our son for me.'

What a strange thing to say. I always do, don't I?

'With my life,' I tell him with a dramatic gesture, hand on heart. He smiles, then leans down easily to pick up Bap-Bap off the floor where Hadyn has thrown it. He gives it a tender kiss before placing it in the cot beside its owner.

'It smells of him,' he says.

'You're nuts,' I tell him. But the thing probably does. Hadyn takes it everywhere with him. I know I need to wash it, but I'd have to have it dried and sorted before he noticed it was missing and that would be a neat trick.

'I never did give you your present the other day, did I?' Charlie offers suddenly.

I laugh, remembering Christmas Eve. 'I thought you did,

47

though?' When he comes back to sit beside me, I run my hands over his bare chest, but Charlie leans over to the bedside cabinet and fetches something out. Is it diamond earrings? I know he bought them for Agustina and Eva.

'Diamonds, Charlie?'

'It's something much more special. Close your eyes and hold out your hand.'

I do as instructed and after a moment I feel the coldness of a metal chain being dropped into my palm. Oh! I had expected something else. A box, maybe? It's not even wrapped.

I trace the shape of it with my fingers first. The links in the chain are quite large, coarse; it is not a delicate thing. Then, the heavy round shape of a medallion becomes apparent. The metal has some kind of relief on it – hell, is it one of those saints' medals I've seen the children wear?

'Open,' he says softly. So I do, and take a closer look at what he's just dropped into my hand.

'Well, thank you, Charlie.' I turn it over in my palm. 'It's a saint, isn't it? It's too dark to tell which one.'

'My father gave me this,' he says now, 'when I was just ten. Just as I left Spain to go to boarding school. He told me: Joseph is the quiet father. The one who's always there in the background. He's not God the father, the glorious all-powerful one. He's just a carpenter, but he provides for his family in his own quiet, practical way. Do you see?'

I'm not entirely sure that I do. 'Charlie, there is something we need to talk about.'

'Go on,' he kisses my nose.

'I can't take your dad's medallion,' I say brokenly. This isn't what I want to talk about. *Why can't I just come out and say it?* 'It must have meant a lot to you.'

'I want you to have it. I always said that one day I would give it to the woman I would marry. When my dad gave it me, he said, even though we weren't going to be together any more, I was still

48

important to him. He might not be so obviously in my life all the time but . . . he would still be there for me.'

'It clearly means a lot to you.' I clear my throat. 'Do you want to help me put it on?'

Charlie laughs.

'It might look a bit chunky on a little thing like you but I wanted you to have it. I wanted you to know I'm always going to be here for you, Julia, no matter what happens. Even though I'm going to have to be away a lot.' He stops. He puts his head in his hands and I know he's feeling the tensions between work and home that pull him in two directions at once.

'Are you disappointed I didn't get you diamonds, my love?'

I shake my head. I'm disappointed in myself, that's what.

'That's how I know that you're the one.' His lips on mine are ardent, sweet. 'You understand what matters in life. And it isn't pretty baubles, expensive bits of rock that somebody mined from the ground. It isn't that . . .'

Oh, God, and being honest with each other, I think, but I don't dare say it.

'Don't be so sad, Julia. I don't want you ever to be sad . . .' He breaks off. 'Julia, you know I'm not very good with words, but you'll always be the first person on my mind, wherever I am, whatever I'm doing.'

'That's the best gift you could have given me, Charlie.' The small thud of a prettily wrapped box hits my side of the bedclothes then. My fingers slide over the smooth silver wrapping, the opulent ribbon festooned into an elaborate bow and I'm happy not knowing what it is; because he loves me; because it reminds me there is so much more that we will give each other.

I want it still to be night-time, just like in *Romeo and Juliet*, but already the sun is rising over the rolling brown hills, the back of the slumbering dragon that is Arenadeluna. I want the birds to stop their singing and fly back into their nests, and the droning of the mopeds to stop coming up the hill, the rubbish trucks and the women moving downstairs in the kitchen all to stop, go back, back to the darkness and the night-time when I had Charlie all to myself, but everything rolls inexorably on.

'You go back and lie down,' he commands as he leaves, but his last urgent kiss on my mouth makes me restless, running on adrenalin, unable to sleep.

So instead I tiptoe out to sit on the balcony of Roberto's house. While Hadyn sleeps, I sit for a whole hour on the stone wall that looks out over the coarse grass of the lawn, the pool, the elegant urns spilling their tutti-frutti-coloured lantana at the sweep of the stairs. It is all so beautiful, but without Charlie it does not feel the same.

Without him I feel suddenly so much more exposed.

Charlie

It's an eleven o'clock kick-off on the Ontome procedure, Angus says in his text. That's a couple of hours yet. *Pre-op briefing at 9.45. Expected duration: two hours.* I reckon I'll make it to Drapers Street in good time, provided the traffic doesn't get snarled up. Two hours in surgery isn't too bad, either. I might – hey – I might even be able to catch a flight back to Malaga later at this rate. I didn't think of that. I could be back in Spain for New Year's! Still, better not get too excited. You never know how these things will go till you get there.

Man, it's cold. It's foggy and damp in London after Malaga. When you breathe in you get a lungful of it, and I'm just wearing shorts and T-shirts. Not exactly how Angus expects his consultants to dress, but the Ontome lad won't be complaining.

No word from Angus on the Esperanza project, I notice. I'm trying not to see that as ominous. Santos has been backing the project for the last eight years and I don't know of any reason why he wouldn't continue. The meetings they've been having over it – they're just a formality. Santos values what we do. He's been to Sokoto himself, hasn't he? That's more than most of our sponsor organisations do. I put the thought out of my head.

I need to focus on what Angus will be expecting from the team this morning. We'll have to remove the necrotising tissue of course. We'll have to attach some alternative blood supply, be it arterial or venous. The graft will never be successful without the living tissue having adequate means of support.

'Okay if I drop you off up this end, mate?' The Cypriot at the front of the taxi grins amicably at me. 'They've got double-yellows all the way down here and bloody cameras watching yer every move . . .'

'Here'll be fine, thanks.' The man's covered the distance quickly, so I tip him double. It's only 8.40 a.m. No one else here yet, I don't suppose. I let myself into the Drapers Street clinic and the familiar smell of it – clean and polished, luxuriously, *affluently* hygienic and efficient, washes over me in an instant.

I flick a switch and bright lights flood every surface. The desks at the front are all gleaming, spotless. The white sofas with their carved wooden legs in the reception area are plush and firm and opulent. I often wonder what the likes of Ngosi Ontome and his family must make of all of this when they first come here? It is such a world away from Sokoto. How do you begin to take such a contrast in? I got a snapshot of their world when I first visited northern Nigeria, not long after I graduated. The landscape that filled my eyes then was savannah, flat and endless and surprisingly green. The hugest sun I had ever seen rose on the end of the grassy plain. That day I felt closer than I had ever felt before to something vibrant – how could I describe it? – to the heartbeat of the world.

I wonder if they miss that, when they come over here?

The coffee machine in the corner will make you an espresso, a cappuccino or a skinny latte at the touch of a button. Clients get it for free, of course, but the price per unit to us is forty pence. Drink three cups of coffee and you've already spent enough to pay for the antibiotics that would have prevented Ngosi's condition from taking hold in the first place. This savage, life-destroying disease called NOMA can be halted and reverted completely in the initial stages, but the people who get it have no money to pay for treatment. And, like Ngosi, they have immune systems already compromised by mal-nutrition, measles, and poor hygiene.

The downstairs door opens now and I can hear the familiar tread of Angus's footsteps on his way up. He takes the stairs two at a time, efficient, brisk but light on his feet.

'Charlie!' There's the barest trace of his Glaswegian youth left in his voice. He's cut-crystal polished it over the years. He's had to. 'You made it. Good man!' He slaps me over the shoulders. 'I knew I could count on you.'

'How is he?'

'They're bringing him back from the recovery suite in half an hour.'

'Not recovering well though?' I pull a face.

'Just a blip, old man, a blip. We'll fix him up just fine today. We'll do it right this time. These things can't always be so finely controlled, can they? I'm pleased with the job we did. So should you be.'

'Who else will be attending?'

'Hughes, same anaesthetist – she has the best experience in fibroscopic intubation of children, we're lucky she came back – and the same two nurses.'

'Not Tan Yeo?' I gulp my coffee and he shakes his head when I offer to get him some.

'Not him.' Angus lets out a breath. *Thereby hangs a tale*, I think. 'I let him off. I know he was the one on the rota for emergency work and not you, but,' Angus glances at me apolo-getically, pours himself out a glass of water, 'I wanted *you* here, Charlie.'

I frown. Tan's a great surgeon. He's every bit as good as I am and at least as experienced. If he should have been on the rota, why was I the one who was called instead?

'What's going on, Angus?'

'Look,' Angus adjusts his collar. He's looking uncomfortable but resolute. 'We need to talk, you and I. Something's come up.'

'What?' We're walking back towards the briefing room. The others have started to arrive; we can hear their chatter as they make their way up the stairs.

'Later, Charles. We'll get a chance to talk later. It's Santos Enterprises,' he admits after a pause. 'I think you need to have a word with him. Lopez is here from Sokoto, and, well – we think you should go to Cambridge to speak to Santos. Hey – we'll discuss this more fully later, okay? Let's focus on what we need to achieve this morning and greet the team now. Good morning, ladies!'

Lopez is here? He's Santos's right-hand man and Santos is our biggest financial backer in Sokoto. Without all the funds that Santos Enterprises brings in, children like Ngosi wouldn't stand a chance. Something is up, obviously, but it'll be some administrative matter. Nothing as important as the work we're about to do here and now.

The nurses troop in. The two young ones are laughing and eager, their hair dampened by the fog. Judith, the anaesthetist, keeps them in check with her gravity. Our team is gathering; soon somebody will bring Ngosi Ontome up the road from the recovery suite, back to theatre. Where he is, little yellow ducklings blaze a trail up the lemon-coloured walls to a dappled green pond that's been painted on the ceiling. Fluffy white clouds drift by over their heads. The curtains at each bedside echo the scene. There, they play calming music. Everything is bright and soft and gentle, but soon he will be taken away from that and be brought back down here to go once more under the knife. We let him bring his favourite toy with him but, once he is asleep, we take the toys away and do our desperate job of trying to give him back the face that has been so cruelly and unnecessarily taken away from him. All because – I drain my cup – his parents could not meet the price of a cup of coffee.

Julia

'We are doing much beautification work here in Arenadeluna. You see all these diggers?' Roberto's voice cuts right through my reverie. Charlie only left four hours ago but already the temperatures are pushing twenty-seven degrees centigrade.

'I'm sorry?'

'They are widening the pavement along the beach front which will make the whole area a lot more attractive to tourists, but before *that* – ' he waves his hand expansively towards the mass of building debris to the left of us – 'we are reclaiming fifty metres of beach through the use of landfill materials which will enable twenty per cent more people to utilise the area.'

'That's very interesting.' I try to enthuse but I'm not properly listening to anything he's saying. My future brother-in-law has been pointing out landmarks and 'places of cultural interest' ever since I got into the car ten minutes ago. There aren't many, to be sure, but they're obviously a source of great pride for him ('This is the well where the King of Spain stopped to ask for water in the days before the civil war.').

'You are a photographer, no? You should take photographs, maybe?' Roberto's eyes narrow for a second, 'So that your son will know his father's birthplace?'

I smile at him but don't answer.

On a normal day his tales wouldn't exactly thrill me to bits, but I might at least be touched by how genuinely proud he is of his town's heritage.

Today isn't a normal day though, is it? I'm supposed to be meeting Eva and Agustina at the church in a few minutes and I have no idea how the hell I am going to blag it.

'You see, our little town of Arenadeluna – that means "sand of the moon" – was first settled by the Romans.' Roberto waves his hand loftily to the left as we coast in his Overlander down the hill. 'Over there, up on the tor, there still stands the remains of a Roman fort.'

He seems oblivious to the fact that I'm not interested.

'And the Roman fort is being relocated so it will sit in the centre of our new municipal park.'

'I suppose the *location* of the fort might have had some meaning historically, though?' I venture.

'Naturally it did. The Romans built it up high so they could see who or what was coming. But you see,' he pre-empts my next observation, 'the modern people of Arenadeluna have to look to see what is coming up for us. And the merging of the old and the new, this is the new way.'

I nod, but I can no longer drum up any pretend enthusiasm. I've got to get away from him. I've got to get out of this bloody meeting. I can't – I can't *breathe* at the thought of it. I don't understand it. I'm not agoraphobic like my nana Ella was.

'What? You don't like the *new ways*?' Rob persists. I didn't say that, did I? Maybe he is mistaking my silence for disapproval?

'I thought all you modern women *liked* progress?' I can't make out if he's being deliberately provocative or whether he's always like this: forceful and opinionated?

'Progress is good,' I concede. But whether what Rob and his team are achieving here can be considered progress is another matter. Okay, I don't know this place. But it seems to me it must once have been a quaint little fishing village. Now it's turning into the tourist's version of that.

'We have to do it,' Roberto puts in. 'We can't stay as we were. If we do, we die. Like the dinosaurs, no? We have to *evolve*.'

'I suppose so.'

'The *jóvenes*, they are all leaving otherwise. All the young people. Like my Giorge. He's twenty now. He wants to go. I told him no, you stay here and I'll find you work. It's the only way, you see.'

'Of course.' I'm not arguing with him. I can feel him just willing me to, though. I can feel it in his whole body, in the way he changes gear abruptly and we start to go down the hill.

I've got to find somewhere where I can just be alone and sit and breathe, and then I'll be okay. Is this what a panic attack feels like? I wish Charlie were here. I can't sit here any longer listening to all this heritage nonsense.

'Look, I . . . I need to check my emails.' I've just spied a *locutorio*, a call cabin along the road. 'Drop us here, please'

Roberto looks at me, frowning. 'Now? You will be late.'

I'm not going at all, so just leave me alone, I think.

'I'll only be – what, two minutes?'

He rolls his eyes in exasperation at the silly English girl who's checking her emails when she's got an appointment at church.

'If I leave you here, you'll walk down to the church, yes? I have to be at work.'

I know very well he has to be at work. He takes his position as architect for the town planning people very seriously. I've also sussed out in the last few days I've come to know him that – atypically for a Spaniard – he can't bear to be even a minute late.

'Here will be fine, Roberto. Thanks for the lift.' I scramble out with Hadyn and the buggy the second he stops the car and we're free of him in a minute. 'I know where it is from here.' I wave at him through the window. 'I'll be fine.'

Just *go* already!

I rub at the place just under my ribcage where a constricting band of pain is pressing in like a steel-trap. *Shit,* not this again. I haven't felt like this for years and years. I thought I'd grown out of this ages ago.

I'm not going back there now, either.

Not now that my life is finally going in the direction I want it to go.

Julia

'Your boyfriend,' the woman with the husky voice stops me, one cool hand on my bare arm, '*Carlos* – he is gone now?'

'I'm sorry?' I'm about to cross the road, which is extremely busy. After Roberto dropped us off, the cars backed up as a truck stopped in the middle of the road for unloading. Some people are beeping their horns but most of them are just staring out of their windows, faces blanked out by the heat.

'Sorry, what did you say?' She did just mention *Carlos*, didn't she?

'Carlos and I knew each other when we were both younger.' She's looking at me curiously and I wonder how she knows me. 'I saw him in town a few days ago with Roberto. We were going to meet up for coffee – but I hear that now he's gone?'

'He's gone, yes.' I set the front wheels of Hadyn's pram back onto the pavement. 'He went this morning, in fact. You knew him well?'

'I knew him very well,' she assures me. 'I know all his family, too.'

'Well. I'm Julia,' I tell her, though she clearly already knows that. 'And you are . . . ?'

'Maria,' she says simply, 'Maria Ortega.' As if the whole world must surely know that name. When I look at her properly now I can see just how pretty she is. Her waist goes in at the middle, an hourglass figure. Her hair is sleek and black, the ends of it brushing against her bottom as she nods her head at me.

'Charlie's never mentioned you,' I tell her slowly. I haven't had a chance to meet any of his old friends here, yet. He didn't mention meeting up with anyone for coffee, either, but at least this isn't – *Lourdes*. Maria smiles knowingly.

'Men! They always forget the important things, don't they? You are going to check your emails in the *locutorio*?'

'Yes. Oh! Darn it.' I bump the pram just that bit too hard as a break looms in the traffic.

'You okay?' she looks at me solicitously.

'I'm okay.' I breathe. 'I think one of the front wheels just came loose, that's all.'

'You need a lift somewhere?' she offers immediately.

'I'm fine, honestly.'

I'm going to have to check that wheel out in a minute. I'll wait till this woman goes, I think. But she doesn't go. She follows me across the road.

'I'm waiting here for my friend.' Maria folds her arms, smiling at me through narrowed eyes. Then she obligingly holds the door open while I pull the buggy through.

'Thanks. Sorry you won't be able to meet with Carlos this time. He left in a bit of a rush.'

'S'okay.' She shrugs nonchalantly, peers into her bag for her cigarettes. 'I hope they've got a good internet connection for you today.'

I do, too. I could do with hearing from Alys right now; I could do with some of that gung-ho, get-down-to-it, spade-is-a-spade advice that Alys is so good at. If I'd only followed her advice a little sooner I wouldn't be in this pickle right now.

I pay my euros for an Internet connection and squash Hadyn's pram up against the wall.

TheladyofShalott14 writes:

Hi Julia,
Went down to Harvey Nicks about the wedding list and
the dinner service us girls were putting together to buy
has been pretty much snapped up. Merde!

Anyway darling we're looking at a chandelier for your
hallway instead. Not on your list I know but I saw it and
it simply screamed buy me; jpeg-enclosed. What d'you
think? Ask Charlie. It'll look wonderful in the entrance of
Blackberry House, I'm certain. They only have two left and
the Tuscan artisan who makes them has gone out of business so you'll have to be quick.

Bye bye sweetie,
Alys.

A chandelier? What is she on about? Her email reminds me that
I do have a life beyond Spain, though. I let out a long, deep
breath and rub my damp hands together. Focus. Think like you
would do if you were back in England and stop panicking . . .

Okay, the chandelier. It's what Alys would have, I'm sure, but
is it really our style? Who knows. Maybe she's right? The hallway
at Blackberry House does look a little bare. And it *is* huge.

This is the sort of thing I need to be concerning myself with
right now. Wedding gifts and the dress and the cake. I haven't
got time to waste moping about just because Charlie's needed
to go off early. I have so many loose ends that I planned to tie
up whilst I was in Spain. I'll need to sort out a venue for the
reception for one thing – Eva's got some good ideas about
that. I dig in my bag for a bit and hand Hadyn his juice bottle.

I need to start getting practical and stop worrying. And all
this about *where* we get married – it's nonsense, really. I know
in my heart of hearts that Charlie would think so.

Maybe when he's here being *Carlos,* things take on a different flavour and importance, but back home in England he'll still be Charlie, won't he?

I press the reply button.

Alys,
Thank God you got in contact! Sweetie, I know it's nearly New Year's Eve and you'll be ever so busy but I'd SO appreciate a chat with you right now. I haven't told Charlie yet about you-know-what and now he's gone and I'm here on my own and in a right pickle . . .

If only Alys could be online right now, because if she read this she would get straight back to me – I know she would. No use me ringing her because her mobile is *always* switched off. But tomorrow's New Year's Eve and Alys is probably entertaining relatives or else she's out there going for a long bracing walk with the kids while I'm sitting sweltering in this heat.

When I look up I see through the glass window that whoever Maria was waiting for has arrived, because she's standing out there chatting animatedly with him. When she glances in and catches my eye, smiling, she indicates me with her head to her companion.

'*This is Carlos's* mujer,' she will be telling him.

Her companion peers in through the window unabashed, bright blue eyes matching his blue sun-cap. He makes a cheery thumbs-up sign at me. We've been as good as introduced, I guess? I look away as Maria wraps her arms around his neck, kiss, kiss, on either side of his face and now he's coming in here so my eyes flicker back to the screen.

Nothing. Alys isn't there.

If only I'd just *told* Charlie.

I could text him now, I guess. Except he'll need to have his mind on the little African child and that might distract him. No; I'll just have to pay the price of my stupidity and hold onto it for a little longer.

'Sorry, can you get by?' I push at Hadyn's buggy but I can't move it any further out of the way.

'I'm good.' Maria's friend takes the seat beside me, winking at the girl who's waiting to take a few euros off him for an Internet connection.

'Maria just pointed you out in here. You're English, aren't you?' He holds out his hand. 'I'm Blue.'

'Pleased to meet you,' I offer my hand primly. 'I'm Julia.'

The man's accent is English enough, but tinged with something that hints he has been abroad a long while. He leans forward towards me, picking Bap-Bap off the floor, and now I see that he's clean-shaven but not quite as young as I'd first thought – maybe late twenties like me – and he doesn't take his eyes off me as he does it. I'm suddenly very aware that my T-shirt is gaping a bit at the front because it got bigger when I washed it. I pull it down at the back, self-conscious.

'Yours?' The man offers Hadyn back his elephant. Hadyn snatches Bap-Bap and holds it tight to his chest. He gives the guy a stare that could petrify.

'The man wasn't trying to take it away from you,' I feel obliged to say. 'I'm sorry. Nobody else is allowed to touch the elephant . . .'

'It's special.' The guy shrugs, understanding. 'You've got sweat running down your face,' he adds after a while.

'Oh,' I wipe at my cheeks with the back of my hand. His directness takes me aback. 'Well,' I defend after a bit, 'it's *hot*.'

'It's snowing in London,' he says softly. When he looks through the window I catch a wistfulness in his eyes. 'What wouldn't you give to be back there right now?'

'In the snow?' I follow his gaze through the window and out on the shimmering road where the cars have lined up back to back again. This is the Christmas holidays, I remember suddenly. It was Christmas and we ate fish instead of turkey and Charlie's not here.

'It sounds ungrateful, but I wish now I *could* be having

63

Christmas in the snow,' I confess. 'I wish I could have had at least one mince pie. A Christmas cracker with an awful joke inside it.'

'A roaring log fire, endless repeats of Morecambe and Wise on the box,' he laughs. 'Welcome to the world of the ex-pat, my friend.'

'I'm not an ex-pat,' I tell him. 'I'm here because my boyfriend's family are here and we're spending Christmas with them. And you?'

'I haven't been home for four years, Julia. I don't suppose you'd call me a typical ex-pat either.'

'How so?'

He laughs. 'No sumptuous villa and no plans to own one; no snazzy car; no girlfriend and no money.'

'Oh.' *Sorry I asked.*

'Don't suppose *you're* looking for a boyfriend, are you?' His wide blue eyes are laughing, only half-joking as he locks his fingers in behind his neck, sits back in the chair.

'Do I look as if I am?' I just *told* him I'm staying with my boyfriend's people. Creep. I frown, annoyed that he's had the cheek to ask me.

'Sorry . . .' I push my chair out briskly now. '*We* need to make a move.' I click the Internet screen down. Alys hasn't got back to me and I can't hide out here all day.

Half an hour has gone by. They surely must have given up and gone home without me by now?

My phone gives a loud buzz then and I pick it up with a flood of relief. Thank heavens, that'll be Alys. She'll put it all into perspective for me, I know..

'Hello?' I turn my face away from Blue, smiling into the phone, and the line is remarkably clear, but the voice that comes back to me not Alys's.

'Julia, this is Eva, where are you?' Her voice is anxious, an edge of impatience to it tinged with worry. 'We're still waiting at the church for you. The priest has done a special favour and cancelled his next appointment. Are you very far away?' My heart sinks right down to my sandals.

Charlie

'Hey, Lopez.' Enrique Lopez has joined me post-op. We're in the wash-up room, I'm pulling my gloves off, wondering where I left my phone. I was just about to call Julia.

'Charlie, my friend. It's good to see you.' I take in Santos's right-hand man. I haven't seen him for a while. We usually only meet at charity functions and society dinners and I don't go to those if I can avoid it. He grips my hand now, pulls me in for the half-embrace of *compadres*. He's a short man but with a powerful frame; a Spaniard built like a bull for a fight, his trousers held up by a pair of old-fashioned red brace-straps.

'Shall we get out of here?' I promised Julia I'd call; I was going to see if I could make the flight back tonight. What's up with Lopez, though? I know Angus mentioned the man was waiting to see me, but I'd put all that out of my head. The operation was more important.

'It went well?' He indicates through the window at the tiny frame the nurses are wheeling out to the recovery suite now. Under the white sheet, all you can see is his head: Ngosi Ontome is wrapped up like a miniature mummy.

'Couldn't have gone better.' I drop my gown in the wash-basket. 'He's a tough little cookie that one. You wouldn't think he was four, would you?' We stand to watch through the window panel as his trolley-bed passes.

'That's Africa for you,' Lopez says, deadpan. 'Thank you for cutting short your holiday to fly back.' I peer out of the window that looks onto Drapers Street. Still drizzling.

'It was worth it to know the boy's going to be okay,' I smile at Lopez. All of our kids are important but some are special.

Enrique bows his head. When he looks up I notice his smile is strained.

'Sure, sure! Look,' he lowers his voice as the last of the team pass out – Angus, I see has got well out of the way, he's nowhere in sight, 'we need to talk, Carlos. Not here. I've got my car outside. We can talk as I drive, yes?'

'As you drive *where*?' I open my suitcase that I dumped in here on the way in. I need a shower, some warmer clothes. He watches me take out a white towel, a clean shirt and a pair of jeans.

'Anywhere you want to go. You came straight from the airport, no? Then we can go on to see Santos.'

I straighten up.

'What, in Cambridge?' I give a short laugh. 'Tonight? I was hoping to catch the flight back out to Spain this evening. Can't you say what you need to say to me on the way back out to the airport?'

'No. Stay over tonight,' he pleads. 'You can catch that flight back sometime tomorrow. It's important, Charlie.' I stop what I'm doing, look him in the eyes. He isn't kidding.

'Right. What's all this about? The rest of them have all gone now so we can stop pussy-footing around.' I've already taken my clothes off. I'm about to get into the shower. Lopez averts his gaze. 'Go on.' The hiss of the warm water as I turn it on doesn't quite drown out his intake of breath.

'It's Baudelaire,' he says quietly, and I find myself straining over the running water to hear him. I turn the power down a notch.

'What about him?' Baudelaire is our man in Nigeria; our chief surgeon out there. He's a French national recruited from the WHO initially, who runs training programmes to help build up

66

the local teams in Africa. 'He's been arrested in Sokoto,' Lopez's voice has taken on a dull quality.

'Whatever for? It's a mistake. It's got to be.' Baudelaire's a top-rate surgeon and a humanitarian of the highest order. 'What's he being charged with, man?'

'Misappropriation of funds.' Lopez has got this nervous habit of pulling at his brace-straps while he talks.

'No.' I need a few moments to take in what Lopez is saying. I don't believe a word of it. Baudelaire's got more scruples than Mother Teresa.

'He'd never do anything like that. Fuck!' The water suddenly splutters out hot, scalding my back and I grab at the dial to cool it.

'He's guilty, Charlie. He admits it.'

'All this is nefarious local politics, isn't it? Someone after a backhander he wouldn't give them, right? What's any of it to do with me, anyhow?'

I turn my face upwards to the shower, the water pelting down my face, wanting to wash his words away because I don't want to hear this right now. I sorted out the boy and I did my job and I don't want to get involved in any more politics tonight.

'This has gotten serious. If we don't sort something out, the Nigerian authorities are threatening to close down the Esperanza Centre in Sokoto. They'll do it overnight if they have to, Charlie. They want a solution.'

'Which is what Santos pays *you* for, my friend.' I feel a surge of anger run through my belly. I've done *my* job. I've done it. What does he want with me now?

I switch off the shower and come out. Lopez is slouched heavily in a wicker chair by the washstand. He's wringing his hands and this man is no shrinking violet. It isn't good.

'Santos wants to see you.' Lopez's eyes narrow as he looks into mine now. 'He believes you can help us. You'll need to back Baudelaire, of course. You'll need to help – cover his tracks.'

'Wait a minute.' The towel I've been using to wipe my face

drops to the floor as I spin to face him. 'You just told me he admitted the charges. He's guilty. I can't believe Louis would do such a thing. But if he's admitted to it . . .'

'It's a little more complicated than that,' the Spaniard admits. 'You'll need to talk to Santos. He's left instructions for me to bring you to him. He'll be in Cambridge first thing tomorrow.'

Santos left instructions. I know him. That's as good as a summons. I won't get anything more out of Lopez if he's been told to keep schtum, either.

'That's why I'm here. It won't be all bad for you,' he adds with a wan smile. 'Lourdes is spending the New Year with her brother, did you know?'

'Lourdes?' She's in Cambridge. Christ.

'She's said she would like to see you too, after your meeting. If, of course, that is all right with you . . .'

'Of course.' I smile tightly at her brother's emissary. 'I'll see Lourdes. It's been a while.'

'She tells me it's been five years.'

'That's right.'

It's been five years, two months and two weeks since I last saw Lourdes. When we last said goodbye I had thought – had hoped – that I would never have to see or speak to her again.

Julia

'You are not ready?' Eva has just popped her head round my bedroom door and she's looking very surprised. 'Abuela is waiting to take you to meet the *cura*. She told you last night that she would. She made an appointment for you to see him, at ten o'clock.'

Shit! So she did. Another appointment to see the priest. When Agustina said last night that she'd reschedule it, I never thought she meant *today*. After yesterday when I had the broken buggy as an excuse, and I had to take a taxi back home. I thought maybe I'd get a chance to talk to them first.

'I'm so sorry; I've slept in too late this morning, Eva.' I glance at the clock. It's twenty to the hour already. 'I'm *really* sorry. I'm never going to make it in time now, am I?' I seem to be digging this hole deeper with every moment that goes past.

'You have to,' she says firmly. 'You left Agustina waiting with Padre Pedro yesterday and you can't make him wait again. If you get up now you can put your clothes on and go. Roberto is already waiting in the car. You cannot cancel this meeting a second time.' She bustles into the room and opens up the curtains and the light falls across Hadyn's face, waking him up at last.

'I'll see to the little one,' she tells me. 'You hurry, now.'

'I can't!' A slow panic is creeping into my bones at the thought that they really mean to make me go. 'Because I . . . I . . .'

'You feel sick?' Eva takes a step towards me, concerned. 'You are not well?'

I nod, pulling a face. With every passing moment it is more true. 'And I have a terrible headache.'

She hesitates.

'You have slept too late, that is all. It will pass. You must get up now.' Eva's face looks strained and frustrated. 'Roberto is waiting,' she repeats.

Hadyn stands up in the cot they have lent me for him and holds out his hands to be picked up. As I walk over to him, seeing him looking so disoriented and groggy, I remember that up to a few short moments ago I, too, had been asleep. I'd been dreaming, I remember now. In my dream it was dark. I walk over to the window with my son in my arms and we breathe in the warm morning air. The sunlight burns bright out of a scorching blue sky. It could be the height of summer. In my dream, the air was cold and damp. I was not in this place.

'I really can't go.' I turn to Charlie's sister-in-law, squinting because the light is hitting my eyes. 'Not today.'

Eva makes a disparaging sound with her lips: *pfffff. You don't go*, she seems to say, *because you don't want to. Because you have slept in late and wasted the morning.*

'Padre Pedro will not make another appointment to see you,' she warns huffily. 'And if he *did*, Roberto would not take you.'

'That's okay.' I hoist my son up higher onto my hip, face reddening. 'I'll have to take my chances with the priest. And when I do go, I won't expect Roberto to put himself out for me, don't worry.'

It *isn't* okay, though. I know it isn't.

Oh why couldn't Charlie just be here?

I have never liked New Year's Eve. Something about all this 'letting go of the old and bringing in the new' just gets to me; what if you're already happy with what you've got? Charlie's gone now and by the time he comes back to us again another year will have begun its cycle. It doesn't feel right somehow that we won't all be together for that.

Eva pulls a little twisted face at me – *as you please*, she seems to say. Eva is kind, but I know she's under a lot of strain right now. The whole atmosphere in this place has shifted – very subtly, but it definitely has – ever since Charlie left yesterday. They're all disappointed he isn't here any more and Abuela is feeling sad. She seems more withdrawn than she did before, when he was around. I can perfectly well understand it. I'm missing him too.

Eva leaves at last and I hear her footsteps fade away down the stairs with relief. Hadyn holds his hand out, pointing towards the place where he knows I have a packet of Marie biscuits secreted away in the drawer.

I'm going to be in the doghouse for a bit. From Eva's reaction that much is pretty unavoidable. And my whole *purpose* in coming here for this holiday, I remember, was to make sure I hit it off with Charlie's family. Maybe I can take Hadyn out in his pram and we can find a flower-seller and buy Abuela a big bunch of flowers to say sorry for letting her down twice? Or maybe some perfume? What would she like?

I crunch on a biscuit and Hadyn jumps down from my arms and onto the bed where the biscuits are. I wonder if it's okay to text Charlie now? I had a brief message from him last night saying the operation went well and he had to go to Cambridge for some reason. He was going to spend the New Year up there. He didn't say why. In theory, he could have got a flight back. Maybe he'll come today?

I need to tell him what's happened. I need to tell him the rest of it, too; *why* we can't be married in the church – about my relationship with Sebastian. As I sit down on the bed, torn between my need to come clean and the knowledge that over the phone won't be the best way to do it, I suddenly become aware of the sound of the women's footsteps returning up the stairs. I know it's them because Eva's tread is steady whilst Agustina's is slow, shuffling. I hear the *click* of her walking stick on each of the marble steps. She is coming up here to see me.

71

She'll want an explanation and I don't know what I'm going to tell her that will stop her from getting cross. I hold my breath as they make their way towards me and every step seems to take an age.

Hell.

The knock, when it comes, on my bedroom door, is soft but not timid.

'Come in.' I turn and they are already in before I call them. Eva is looking flush-faced while Agustina is more a mixture of concerned and cross.

'You are sick?' she inquires. Her faded eyes look me up and down rapidly. She knows I am hiding something.

'I'm not feeling too well,' I confess. I run a hand through my tousled hair. 'I slept badly and I think – maybe I got too much sun yesterday.'

'I could ring the church and see if the padre can see us a little later on?' Eva puts in at last, unwillingly. Agustina pulls a moue, but I can see she's up for it.

No! Not now, not later. What do I say to them? How do I wriggle my way out of this? They both just stand there, looking perplexed. *What is this English girl playing at? I can see them thinking. Why won't she just come to church?*

'Look, I . . .' I pull my hair up into a ponytail and go and edge myself into the wicker chair by the bed. Hadyn has already run to his cot to pick up his elephant and stands there, stroking its back, holding its comforting fur up to his face.

Could you just try being open with her? Charlie's words return to my mind with surprising clarity.

'Heh!' Agustina leans on her stick, watching my son with the elephant, 'my daughter – Conchita – she was just the same as *him,*' she points at Hadyn. 'She used to hold her doll just like that.' She makes a stroking motion with her fingers, mimicking Hadyn's movements.

'She did?' I bite my lip. I stayed on here at Charlie's request

72

mainly so that Hadyn could spend more time with Abuela, I remember. 'He reminds you of her?'

Charlie's grandmother nods slowly.

'He is very like her.' Her eyes well up for a moment and Eva hands the old lady a hanky.

'Abuela would like to have him christened while you're here,' Eva puts in now, 'you are happy with this?'

Well – I hesitate – I could do *that* bit, couldn't I? There's no reason why they shouldn't have their christening.

'Here we do it when they are a few days – only weeks – old,' Eva adds encouragingly, ' . . . just in case.'

I raise an eyebrow. In case – what? In case they die unexpectedly and their unredeemed soul goes straight to purgatory? I don't believe that. But maybe it's what Charlie would want. It's what they believe, and I have to respect that.

'I'd be happy to christen him while we're over here, but . . .' My words run on smoothly now, oiled by Agustina's approving smile, 'there's something I should have mentioned to you before. I apologise that I didn't because you've gone to a lot of bother for me. It's about – the appointment at the church. We need to cancel it. Charlie and I are going to have a civil ceremony.'

The two women look at each other now in surprise. I have to explain.

'It's because – a long time ago – when I was much younger, I was married, for just three months, to someone else.'

'Oh, Carlos never said.' Eva looks embarrassed. 'You'll need the registry office then?' She's taking it quite well but she seems a bit flummoxed.

'That's pretty much it,' I say casually. My heart is thumping like thunder in my chest but they don't have to know that. 'The christening can go ahead, though.'

'I will have to let Padre Pedro know about this.' Eva turns to go to the phone. 'If you had just said so before . . . Carlos never mentioned anything about a former marriage. You will need the

73

divorce papers. As you say, you will not be able to get married in the church.' She looks confused and flustered. 'I will tell Roberto that you won't be ready to go today. He doesn't like to wait.'

'I'm sorry,' I repeat. I feel like such a fool now, for not saying. My first marriage was such an embarrassment, that's all.

'If you or Carlos had just told us,' Agustina says kindly, once the door is closed, 'Eva wouldn't have made all the arrangements. She doesn't mean to be cross. She has so much to do, you see.'

'I know.' I hang my head. 'I should have said.'

'Or *Carlos* could have said something.' Abuela spreads her hands. 'Men always leave these things up to us, don't they?' She puts her head conspiratorially to one side. I feel a lump in my throat. 'He should have known, maybe more than you,' she continues, taking my side, 'what the priests are like here – how they don't like to be kept waiting for no reason.'

'He didn't know,' I croak.

Underneath her indulgence I can sense Agustina's smile is a bit strained. What I've just told them has come as a surprise, no doubt. But not, it would seem, an insurmountable one? Alys was so right. If only I had told them at the very beginning I would have saved myself a lot of heartache.

'*Bueno*, Charlie must have known it would have to be done in the registry. But men – they never *think;* only two days ago my friend Paca promised him she would do the flowers in the church, and he didn't think to tell her then . . .' She tut-tuts, ruffles my son's hair with her fingers. Hadyn looks up, wide-eyed.

'He didn't know, Agustina,' I tell her in a small voice.

'Why not?' she spreads her hands. 'He is Catholic, he knows that if his *mujer* had been married once before she cannot be married by the church again. It is simple. No,' she shakes her head dismissively, 'he should have told us, and that is all.' She's still cross with him, I detect, for going away and leaving her so soon after arriving.

'Agustina,' I take in a deep breath, 'Charlie doesn't know that

74

I was married before. He didn't know anything about it, so he couldn't have told you.'

'How can that be?' A look of pure shock and confusion crosses her face. 'He must have known! You cannot be – how you say it – intending to marry a man without telling him this thing first?' She waits for my confirmation that she has misheard, or misunderstood me.

'He doesn't know,' I confess, 'because I never told him about my former marriage. I meant to . . .' My chest is starting to hurt again.

'This cannot be,' she repeats. 'Do you mean to say that you have *lied* to him? *Dios mio de mi alma!*' She strikes at her chest in agitation.

'I did mean to tell him,' I begin, *it was only a few months, I was worried what he might think,* but it is too late for apologies. Charlie's Abuela flaps her hand up at me in disgust. She cannot even speak.

'What is happening?' Eva is back by the door, her hand over her mouth, her eyes wide.

'What kind of a girl would do this?' Abuela is asking Eva in Spanish. 'She has been married already – but Charlie doesn't know anything about it!'

'Surely that is wrong, Abuela. You have misunderstood. Your English is not so good.' Eva looks at me, questioningly. 'She is mistaken, no?'

'No.'

'*¿Esto como puede ser?*' Eva is perplexed. '*Why* would you never have mentioned to him about this?'

'I didn't because . . .' I bite my lip. 'I thought he wouldn't understand. He'd assume that this other man meant something more to me than he really did.'

'*¿Que estás diciendo?*' Agustina has curled up her lip in disgust. She's seeing me in a totally new light. And it's not a flattering one, either.

75

'If this other man didn't mean so much to you, why would you have married him?' Eva bustles about helping Agustina as she turns stiffly on her stick and leaves the room without another word.

'Mum-mum?' Hadyn is at my feet, gripping tightly onto the elephant. I turn my head away so he won't see my tears of disgrace. It is all exactly as I feared it would be and all because I was too stupid not to have come clean with Charlie first of all. My mum told me I needed to tell him. Alys told me the same, but – because I thought I knew Charlie better than they did – I ignored their advice.

I deserved the reaction I got just now. I know I did. I need to go home. But Charlie is going to be mortified that I have so offended his family.

And I've got him to face yet, haven't I?

Julia

'You can't go home,' Eva tells me when I come down two hours later. I've been trying to get hold of Charlie but his phone's off. 'There is no one to take you to the airport now. Besides, they are saying there are no more flights out today – the weather forecast is too bad for the planes to leave.'

'Are you sure?' I glance up, taken aback at this latest piece of news. I'm not planning on staying out here any longer than I have to. I'll get a flight back today, why shouldn't I? I've got everything packed upstairs already. I'm planning on walking down to the beach front where I've seen a taxi rank and making inquiries from there.

Eva isn't happy, I can see. But either way I'm not staying here. 'I'll . . . I'll go to the beach, then.'

'Too hot,' she warns me. 'And it's too far away for you to walk with the baby. Just wait till Roberto has eaten.'

No way am I waiting for Roberto to give me a lift.

I'm feeling a bit shaken, but also bullish. I know I was wrong, but Agustina sending me to Coventry just as I was trying to put things right isn't going to help anything. Besides, I have to stay strong for Hadyn. I don't want him seeing me upset. I've just got to get us both out of here.

'No, thank you, Eva.' Eva is still trying to be kind and polite, but there's a distance, now, no question about it. I saw the righteous indignation on Roberto's face when he came out of the lounge

77

earlier. There was no mistaking they'd all been talking about me behind my back. My face flushes just to think about it.

'Look, I know I made a mistake in not saying, all right?' I begin pleadingly, but Eva shakes her head a fraction. I know she can't take sides on this, and certainly not my side.

'Don't go to the beach today, Julia.' She lays a smooth brown hand on my arm. 'The day is hot I know, but this . . . this is not right. You should not go alone with the baby.'

'I'm going to the beach,' I say stubbornly, 'not into gangster territory. There'll be loads of families there.' *And maybe a taxi that will take me to the airport,* I think, *a way to get us out of here . . .*

'But the weather is going to change,' she frowns. 'It will be raining hard later, you'll see.'

'I could do with some rain.' I look out over the cloudless sky. I could do with being back in England, if it comes to that. Just standing in the glare of the patio I can feel my skin temperature soar by several degrees. She could be right.

But I can always turn round and come back if we go a little way and find it really is too hot. Hadyn's got his sun canopy. And I've got a water bottle to spritz him with as we go along.

To hell with it, I've got to get out of here.

'Just take care,' she calls after me as we go.

But it is such a relief to be free of the villa enclosure that once I am pushing the pram down the sunny road I almost want to run. All the way down the hill I could run so fast my flowery flip-flops would barely touch the pavement, the front wheels of the pram lifted off the pavement, Hadyn squealing in laughter. I could pretend that everything was still okay. That I wasn't in the doghouse. That Charlie knew about Sebastian and that he was okay with it and that he was still here and that everything hadn't suddenly turned so *shit*. But I can't keep up the pretence for long. It doesn't take me more than a few moments to realise that Eva was right – it really is too hot.

I don't know if I'm going to make it.

As soon as we get to the bottom of the hill at Arenadeluna, I will turn right over the walkway and then we should at least be in sight of the sea. Then maybe we'll get a whiff of the freshness of an ocean breeze, the coolness of the water. The taxis usually wait along the top. So I keep going. I keep thinking, just one more lamppost down, just to the next little house front. But it is taking longer than I thought it would.

Eventually I hear a car pulling up alongside me. Maybe it is Eva come along to rescue us? But I carry on walking. The car moves down a little, catching up with us again and the window scrolls down.

'Hello, *Julia*. Julia, isn't it?' Her Spanish accent sounds vaguely familiar.

'Hi there.' I peer inside the car but I can't see much. The lady inside has dark sunglasses on but it isn't Eva. Is she one of the cousins? I don't care. I don't care who she is. I just want her to give us a lift down to where the taxis are . . .

'Get in,' she tells me. 'It's too hot too walk. Tell me where you're going and I'll drop you.'

Oh, it's that girl Maria who knows Charlie!

When I look inside the car I can see two little girls inside there too. One must be about ten, the other maybe six or so. Are they hers? I didn't guess when we met her the other day that she might be married with kids of her own.

'You get in with the boy. I'll fold up the pram.' My saviour finds the catch and the pram folds down in one neat movement. A second later it's in the boot along with the beach bag and she's back in the driver's seat again, the engine running all the while.

'Where are you headed,' she turns to me casually, 'to the beach?' She doesn't wait for a reply. 'I saw your beach bag. That's handy. That's where I'm headed with the girls too.'

'You are?' I feel a trickle of relief. 'I got the impression only *extranjeros* would be mad enough to go to the beach on New Year's Eve.'

'It's a hot day. I'm taking the girls to the beach and I'm not a mad foreign woman.' She smiles conspiratorially at me. 'Maybe you'd like to join us?'

Should I tell her I'm only going as far as getting a taxi?

'That's very kind of you.'

When we get to the bit at the bottom of the hill where I thought she would look for somewhere to park, she doesn't, but joins the carriageway going west along the E30 interchange.

'Oh, we're not stopping here?' Where the heck am I going to get my taxi now?

'No. I want to see my friend Lupe's new baby. She lives beside the *playa del torro*. There's a better beach there anyway – you don't mind, do you?' She's obviously assumed that I've accepted her invitation to join them. She leans back in her seat, totally at ease. There'll probably be a taxi stand at the next beach too, I tell myself.

'So.' Maria lifts her sunglasses as she drives, taking a better look at me. 'Where do you and Charlie live in the UK?'

'We live just outside Richmond. Do you know it?'

'Richmond,' she rolls the word around her tongue. 'I think it must be nice there. I am going to the UK, too. My boyfriend and I are flying out in a couple of days. It is a place called *Erles Court*, in *Londres*. You know it?'

'Earls Court. Sure.'

'Is nice?' She glances at me in her driving mirror, curious.

'Um – I think so. You're planning on flying out in a couple of days, you say? I heard this afternoon's flight out to Heathrow is likely to be cancelled because of a storm that's coming.'

'It's true.' She checks her own reflection in the driver's mirror. 'If they've got the timing of it right, there'll be nothing in or out of Malaga today.'

Damn. That puts paid to my only other hope, which was that Charlie might yet make it back before tonight. He isn't answering his phone at the moment, either. Apart from that text last night I've heard nothing.

'It'll get rough at the beach today, too. I'm only going because I want to see Lupe's baby. And her husband has contacts in the UK – he might be able to set something up work-wise for me.'

'Oh, you want to go over to the UK to *work*?' I have to drag my attention back to what she's saying. I can't help thinking it might be worth making my way down to the airport anyway, just in case. We could hang out there till the storm passes and then just get the next flight out.

'To work, yes. And you? You are a model, yes?'

I laugh, shaking my head.

'No? I heard you and Charlie met when you were working for a model agency.'

I look at her, surprised. Maybe Eva told her that?

'I heard Charlie went to a party,' she insists. 'Somewhere . . .' She makes a 'far away' gesture with her hand. 'You were there modelling. I suppose it was "love at first sight"?' Maria sighs, a dissatisfied sort of sound.

'I was there taking *photograph*s of models,' I correct her. 'I never worked in front of the camera.'

'Oh.' She considers this for a bit and my mind wanders back to the first night Charlie and I met. We were in Africa, I smile, that much she got right. I remember seeing Charlie coming out of the marquee where all the food had been so lavishly piled up. His hair was shorter back then, sticky with the heat. I remember crouching down behind a bush at the time, hoping desperately that he wouldn't spot me while simultaneously being unable to take my eyes off *him*. It wasn't just his physical beauty; it was the undeniable presence he had.

'And now?' I feel Maria's elbow brush my arm as she drives along, prompting me to continue. 'You still work, yes?'

'No.' I shake my head decisively. 'The hours were too erratic. I realised I had to make a decision or I'd never get to see my child.'

Maria nods. She goes quiet for a bit, processing this.

'Still, you gave up your career to care for Charlie's son. I think

81

it must have been *love at first sight*. That's how it was for me and Diego, too. You became pregnant soon after the two of you met, I hear?'

I flush.

'Gossip *does* travel fast around here,' I mutter. 'And it was three months after we met.' I didn't sleep with him for the first three months; we didn't really get together till after two – but that's none of her business.

'Well then, you are the lucky one,' she says. 'So many women were after Charlie, you know . . . and he chose you. He must have loved you the moment he saw you.'

She glances at me sideways. Maybe she thinks I went all out to get him; that I deliberately fell for Hadyn as a means to ensnare Charlie, but there really could be nothing further from the truth . . .

'Actually, the first thing he ever said to me was: *What the hell do you think you are doing?*' I give a small shudder, remembering.

'What *were* you doing?' Her eyebrows go up in surprise.

'I was sneaking some food out to the families of some of the Esperanza children. My boss had wanted to use some of the villagers in a shoot – which is why Charlie was there in the first place. Anyway, we'd been expressly warned not to feed them. But there was so much food . . .' I trail off, visioning all the canapés with caviar and scallops and creamy gateaux flown all the way out from Paris especially for all the supermodels. It was crazy, really, because most of them wouldn't touch it with a bargepole for fear of putting on weight.

I remember Charlie had taken me for one of them.

I remember his outraged, furious face at the sound of someone puking up their dinner behind a tree not far from the marquee, and then he'd caught me, guilty-faced, doing something I should not have been doing . . .

No: on his part at least, it wasn't love at first sight.

'He was angry because you took food out to them?'

'He was cross because he thought I was making myself sick to stay thin.'

That hadn't been me, though.

Maria shrugs. She goes quiet for a bit, pensive.

'Can I take the baby to swim?' the older girl pipes up now.

'I'm afraid he's too little. He can't swim yet. Actually I . . . I was thinking of taking a taxi down to the airport just in case there were any flights heading out tonight.' I turn my attention back to her mother.

'You miss Charlie.' Her face creases in mirth. 'Never mind. We'll have to look after Charlie's family for him, won't we, girls?'

'Do you know if there are any taxi stands at the beach where we're headed?'

'Perhaps,' Maria is thoughtful. 'But I think you won't have much luck with the planes.' She shakes her head at me. 'I heard the airport is already heaving with people who want to go home. You must not take the baby there if you can avoid it.'

I let out a breath. I am really disappointed. But right now there is nothing I can do.

Maria pulls smoothly into a lay-by. 'You seem very keen to get back home,' she notes. She pulls down the car mirror and reapplies her bright coral lipstick in one smooth movement.

'You find it tough, staying at Roberto's house without Carlos?'

I shrug.

'Agustina's not the easiest person to get along with, is she?' A dab of a sponge on a stick and now her lips are luscious, covered in gloss.

'She can be a bit cranky,' I admit. 'But she's been very kind.'

Maria smiles at that.

'I do feel a bit out of place, there,' I admit. 'I needed to get out of the house. I would have gone anywhere . . .' I stop, because I am sounding too desperate and she will hear it. 'You – er – you know the family well?'

'Well enough. I know her generation, Julia. My abuela, Charlie's

83

abuela, they're all the same. They're possessive of their men. They think women should keep to their place in the home.' She tosses her mane of hair and I get the impression that Maria isn't the type of woman who'd be tied down by family restraints.

'You looked like you were going to cry when I picked you up just now. Has she been giving you a hard time?'.

'Well, kind of, but it's partially my fault . . .'

'Screw her!' Maria puts her coral-covered tissue away in her handbag and shuts it with a flourish. 'It's our turn now. I married the father of my two girls, Julia. But I was only fifteen when I had Talia. They made me marry him. But look at me now! We're separated. I never had a chance to settle in my mind what I wanted from my life, you know what I mean?'

I'm not sure what to say. She's obviously keen to point out all the common ground between us. Maybe it's because she's going to the UK and she wants to be friends? I just nod at her silently. 'We're just waiting here for my boyfriend, Diego, do you mind?'

'Oh, I thought maybe *Blue* was your boyfriend?' The sound of her tinkling laughter confirms she thinks that's a huge joke.

'He wishes! He likes the girls, that's for sure . . .' She gives me a significant look.

Her eyes open wider then and she shakes her mane of hair, all sultry, as a guy with blue chinos, a white top and dark sunglasses saunters over to greet us. Judging by the way he virtually pulls her out of the car and presses her up against it, I'm guessing it's Diego. Her girls in the back seem to take it all in their stride. They're more interested in Hadyn than what their mum is up to.

'Is he still in nappies?' the little one asks me. The pungent smell that I had taken to be the lingering scent of wet beach towels reminds me that he is. I drag my eyes from their mother and back to the girls and my own son. 'Do you live in Puerto Banús?' the older one asks me.

'No.'

'When my mama goes to the UK with Diego, me and Talia are going to live with my auntie Illusion,' the little one says.

'Are you?' I crane my neck round, curious, to look at Maria's daughter. 'You're not going away with your mother, then?'

The little girl shrugs. 'Mama won't be long. When she gets a job she will send for us. And Diego's son will be there with us too. We can help look after him and we like that, don't we, Talia? Diego's wife left him.'

'Illusion isn't our *real* auntie,' her sister reminds her. 'She's Diego's sister . . .'

'Yes she is. And my mother says that Diego's wife is a *puta*,' the little one supplies, 'because she doesn't properly look after the baby.' The older girl gasps in shock and covers her sister's mouth with her hand.

'She doesn't really know what *puta* means,' she tells me assuredly.

My guess is she's hoping I don't either.

'Who's this, *bonita*?' Diego lifts his dark sunglasses and peers into the car at us. His eyes roam appreciatively over my breasts beneath my T-shirt, my stomach.

'This is Charlie's girl,' Maria introduces us. 'Julia. Julia, this is Diego.'

'Hi.' I nod curtly at him. 'Um – thanks for the lift, Maria.' I open the car door and she looks at me in surprise.

'I thought you were staying with us? Where are you going? I have an umbrella you can shade under if you need to . . .'

I hesitate. Where *can* I go? The stretch of beach that she's driven us to is a good half-hour away from Arenadeluna. There is no taxi stand that I can see so I'm probably going to need a lift back now as well. Where can I go in this place, if there is going to be a big storm and the beach is going to turn rough?

When I look out towards the sea the waves seem flat and strangely grey but there are still a surprising number of people dotted about. Some of them are in full-on summer mode, romping about in the water. Others – like the woman with the dark sunglasses sitting all by herself, fully dressed, staring out at the waves – look as if they've stumbled onto the beach by accident. She stares at the group of us for so long as we peer over the sea wall, choosing where to go, that I think she must know Maria or must recognise one of the girls and I am reminded that everyone knows everyone over here, don't they?

This strange woman probably knows all about me and the tale of how I got so quickly pregnant with Charlie's child, just like Maria did.

I feel so very far away from home.

'*Mum-mum.*' Hadyn tugs at me as Talia grabs hold of his hand, smiling at me as she does so. '*Mum-mum.*'

'He's learning Spanish,' she says in her gruff voice, pleased. 'That's what we say here – *mama.*'

It would be good if he could learn Spanish, I think. He should. It will make it easier to talk to his relatives, later.

'Bap-Bap.' He looks at me anxiously.

'Bap-Bap is back at home, sleeping,' I remind him. 'How do you say "elephant?"' I ask her.

'*Elefante,*' she supplies.

'We tucked the *elefante* up in the cot before coming out, didn't we?' I hadn't wanted to risk him getting lost at the beach – that would have been a major disaster.

'Your son wants to go to the water,' Talia informs me.

I'll have to stay and let him have a little runabout now. He's been cooped up in that stifling car all this time.

Pretend it's summer. Pretend it's only two months to your wedding.. I've got to get through the next few hours till I can book us both on a flight back to UK, that's all.

So I paste on a smile and we head down towards a sandy patch that I can spot on the beach, Maria's girls charging ahead of us with Hadyn and Maria and Diego trailing along behind everyone.

Tengo que llevar a mi hijo a casa de me hermana, Diego's telling her. He's got to take his son to his sister's house.

That's *good.* That's a good thing. My spirits rise a little. If her boyfriend has got another errand to run – if I've understood correctly – that means he won't be hanging around. This way I can spend the afternoon quite happily chatting to Maria. When I glance behind me I can just glimpse the swish-swish of Maria's orange skirt as she picks her way elegantly down the shingle after us. But no Diego.

'He's gone off already,' she says to me. '*Bastardo.*' But her eyes twinkle as she says it. 'He's not so bad really. He's an excellent father to his son. He *has* to be,' she mutters darkly.

'He's separated from his wife?'

'He's begged her for a divorce,' she confides. 'But she won't agree. If they're not happy she should let him go. *I* could make him happy. And everybody deserves a second chance, don't they?'

'Yeah,' I agree. Yeah, maybe. I watch Diego vaulting over the wall at the top of the beach, doing a high-five with the mate he meets up there. My eyes narrow as we girls dump all our gear down in our spot. This'll be my home for the duration of my exile for the afternoon.

Maybe everyone does deserve a second chance.

Not everyone gets one though, do they?

Julia

I have resolved to think positively and just be confident that this morning's mess will all sort itself out naturally. I am lying here on the sand, reminding myself over and over that Charlie loves me. He's devoted to his son and we've still got time to work this out. *I might,* I am telling myself, *I might actually be the luckiest person I know* when a wasp lands on my hand. I don't notice it at first because I am watching Hadyn.

You rest, you rest, the girls keep bossing me. We *are looking after the baby.* So I am pretending not to look at them, building their sandcastle, bucket by bucket. Hadyn is in charge of the pebble collection. He picks up the black ones and puts them in his red bucket. The girls praise him to the skies every time he finds one.

I am pretending to listen to Maria, who clearly thinks – as a prospective bride – that I must have only one topic of interest on my mind.

'You have your dress picked out already, Julia?'

'I have a rough idea of what I'd like.'

'Are you going for traditional style? White or – ' she glances at Hadyn – 'ivory? Ivory is very fashionable. If you worked in fashion you must have plenty of friends who could advise you . . .'

I shake my head. In the fashion world things move so fast. Half the people I worked with have already moved on, taken up

posts elsewhere, or moved abroad. That's how it is. I'm not bothered about getting the latest designer gown, anyhow. And I don't
want to talk about the wedding plans. Not today.

'He looks so much like his father, doesn't he?' She gestures
towards Hadyn, strolling purposefully towards their sand
creation, his fists full of stones. 'He is so pretty.'

He *is* pretty. In a boyish sort of way; but pretty nonetheless.

'They're always special aren't they?' She smoothes a long squirt
of sun oil onto her glossy arms. 'The first-born ones?' She smiles
at her friend Lupe who has turned up at last with her three-
week old daughter. 'Don't you think so, Lupe?'

Lupe nods beatifically.

'You two are lucky you get to stay home and look after your
kids. I had to leave Talia after she was born,' Maria is telling me
now. 'When I was fifteen. Did I tell you that?'

I don't know if she's already told me that. She's been telling
me lots of things but I haven't really been listening. I need to
talk to Charlie, that's the thing. He must have finished whatever
he was doing in Cambridge by now, surely? I wonder if there's
a call box here. There's no connection on the mobile and it's
driving me mad . . .

'I took the bus to Puerto Banús,' Maria continues, indicating
over her shoulder, in the direction of her Land of the Golden Sun.
'I thought I could hack it there. I'd work as a maid, a waitress,
anything. I had to leave Talia.' Her voice hardens, remembering. 'I
had no choice, you understand. I was only young. If I'd stayed
with my husband under his mother's roof one more night I think
I would have gone mad.'

'I know the feeling,' Lupe says and Maria laughs complicitly.
She turns to me,

'*You* can imagine what it would be like too, can't you? I only
have to see the way you look at your little boy and I know you
understand.'

'I do, Maria.' I'm tempted to confide in Maria about my

troubles. She's trying so hard to be friendly. I'm sure she'd understand . . .

But I don't say anything. We both lie there and watch Maria's girls for a little while as they painstakingly carve out a moat for Hadyn's sandcastle. Every time the water comes in and fills up his moat his eyes are out on stalks. He knows the water's going to drain away any minute but he can't quite fathom where it's going to.

'Where did you say you work now, Maria?'

'I do clerical work.' She sits up now and rubs some more oil onto her beautifully flat stomach. 'At the local police station,' she continues. 'When I get to go to *beauty school*, in the UK, I will make good money and then I'll only have to do the hours I want, no?'

'I guess.' The beauticians I knew at Brasenose's all worked really hard for crap pay but I won't burst her bubble.

'Maybe you can give me some introductions to your friends that need beauty treatments, yes? I could come to their homes. They wouldn't even have to come to me.'

'Sure.'

'I've got it all planned out.' Maria brings out a comb and starts pulling it through her hair. 'I'm going to make something of my life, you know. I'm not going to be like all the other women in my family who can't think of anything better to do than criticise me . . .'

'For what?' I murmur. I can feel the wasp tickling the top of my hand.

'For going with Diego,' Maria confesses. 'They say because he has been in jail once before – he stole a car – that he's no good. But they don't understand. He has changed. People do. He's had to change all his friends, turn his life right around and that's not been easy; people around here don't like to give you a job once you've got a reputation. And then of course my family object because he is married! But Diego doesn't love his wife. He wants to be with me . . .' She's getting pretty worked up here.

'Still,' I soothe, 'you're working towards fulfilling your dream, now, aren't you?'

I glance at my watch, wondering what time Maria is planning on getting back. Two – no, maybe three hours have gone by since we arrived and a surprising number of people have come and taken up spaces at intervals dotted all around us. I should gather in the toys a bit, I think lazily. The fat German couple who are the nearest to us don't seem too troubled by the mess. The two old biddies with their folding chairs have gone to sleep. The lady with the dark sunglasses who must have walked by our stretch half a dozen times seems to have gone home so I don't suppose I should be too bothered.

The sea smells nice, of watermelons. The last rays of the sun are kissing my back, toasting me a gentle brown. By the time I get back home I might not even be a pasty English girl any more. Maybe it wasn't such a bad thing that I stayed after all.

'Just *look* at them,' Maria laughs, her mood changing as she points towards our children on the shore.

Our trio are traipsing round and round their castle now in a strange slow sort of dance, their hands outstretched, faces and palms turned upwards, laughing. Unbelievably, out of a cloudless sky it has begun to rain, just the faintest pattering of drops on the sand, wetting our heads and our arms.

Talia sticks her tongue out and Hadyn tries to copy her, catching raindrops to drink them as they fall. His cheeks are dusky brown, wet with raindrops, plump as a peach.

I *am* lucky, I know that.

I made a mistake this morning, that is all.

It isn't the end of the world. All I needed was a little bit of distance from the problem – now I can see everything with a much better perspective.

As soon as I get back I'm going to phone Charlie and tell him what happened. I'm going to apologise to Agustina and draw a line under it. At the end of the day, if Charlie accepts it, they all have to as well.

'*Wow. Two pretty ladies for the price of one . . .*'

Diego's back.

I can make him out, even with my eyes half closed, lying with my head along my arms on the sand, because of his unmistakable swagger. The thing that captures my attention most is the ridiculous fluorescent lime-green beach towel with a little purple heart pattern all over it that is flung casually over one shoulder. It looks so camp alongside his macho swagger.

And he's got that other fella with him – the one I thought at first was Maria's boyfriend, what's his name – *Blue*?

'I knew we'd meet again.' Blue winks at me, flops down all wet on the sand right beside me and I get a shower of the sea water that's still dripping off him. I move over a little so he isn't quite so close.

'*Did you see your sister?*' Maria is murmuring to her man, now more interested in personal domestic matters than she is in me. Diego whispers something in her ear and they both laugh.

'Hey move over, man,' Diego calls to Blue. 'The lady doesn't want you sitting so close to her. *Move.*' He aims at Blue's backside with the heel of his foot as he says this and their friend moves good-naturedly along.

'Sorry,' Blue says to me, 'I got you wet.'

'He likes you, eh?' Diego grins, as if Blue's just made some fantastic joke. I want to get up but I can't now because *they* are here. I can feel the sand sticking to my belly, to the tops of my thighs, to my damp bikini bottom. I wish I'd sat down on something like Maria's bamboo beach mat instead of flopping down belly-first onto the hot sand like a child.

The tiny granules are like sugar-coating all over my body and, as I can imagine the comments Blue might make if I get up looking like this, I just stay put.

'No shellfish?' Maria takes a swig of the beer that Blue proffers her. 'No *squid*?' She looks pointedly at the harpoon he's just flung carelessly onto the sand beside him. Blue shakes his head, screwing up his eyes to track their other friends making their way down from the rocks to join us. Meanwhile, Diego leans over and picks up his friend's harpoon and places it in between the spokes of the beach umbrella, out of harm's reach.

This is X, Blue says to me when the rest of their group of friends come down; *this is Y* and *this is Z.* I know he isn't saying that at all but their names are unfamiliar and they're all laughing and talking so loudly I can barely make out a word of his introductions. Besides, I've just noticed that the sun is going down and the long shadow of the mountain behind us is chasing the sun-seekers up to the end of the beach. In a minute the shadow will reach us here and it will turn cold. I'm going to have to get up now; sand-laden bikini top and clammy thighs notwithstanding.

'*Hola, bonitas!*' Diego calls out as Maria's girls spot him. They leave their sandcastle behind and come scampering up to inspect his bag. Hadyn clambers over the sand with them.

'Diego promised me and the girls he'd bring our Christmas present.' Maria's eyes are also glued now to Diego's leather bag. 'He said it cost him a lot of money but he wouldn't tell me what it was.'

'Hey, hey! Leave off! These *women*, eh?' Diego grins at me and I'm not sure if I'm included in the description or if he's appealing to me for some sort of moral support. 'You just wait, okay?'

Blue is smiling broadly. I have the feeling he already knows what's in the bag. The others stand around, drinking their beers and looking on in polite interest.

'What have you got me?' Maria demands. For a minute it's hard to tell her apart from her girls. She looks just like one of them, young and eager and impatient.

'You wait,' Diego tells her. He unzips the bag, deliberately slowly, only partway. He puts his hand in, half covering what he's bringing out so as to prolong the suspense. Then there's the clink of glass as he pops two bottles of bubbly down on the sand. A cheer goes up from the assembled friends and everyone gets poured a drink of champagne and we all have to toast in the New Year before Diego will proceed any further.

'Not drinking yours?' Blue nudges me, as I'm craning my neck round to make sure Hadyn's still okay. I was going to chuck it into the sand and pretend I'd toasted along with everyone else, but this guy had to be watching me like a hawk, didn't he? 'I'll have it, then?' He reaches out with his hand.

'Sure.'

'Want to know what else he's got in the bag?'

I shrug.

Diego puts his hand into the bag again and this time pulls out the gift they've all been waiting for. It's a tiny, cowering little brown puppy who staggers about unsurely on the towel that Diego thoughtfully places beneath it.

There are a few gasps. From the girls, from the friends and from Maria. Blue and I both look at her simultaneously to check out her reaction. The animal looks so little it should hardly be separated from its mother. There is a pause while Maria adjusts her expectations and then the puppy gives out a little yelp and she melts. She puts out her hands to take it from Diego and their fingers touch, as gentle as parents. She hugs the puppy close to her face and Diego takes a photo. Just for a moment she looks rapturous.

'He's *cute*,' she intones in her low voice, 'but I'm not taking him home. Don't even think about it. We're leaving Spain, don't forget, Diego. And Illusion won't have him.'

'You leave my sister to me.' Diego kisses his girlfriend on the lips before she can utter another word. For the minute they look like teenagers; they look young and innocent and impossibly in love. I wonder about his wife for a minute; the woman who won't look after his son properly but who won't let him go either, to be with the love of his life, even though her marriage has foundered.

I wonder why some people are like that. It seems a shame.

'The children will love him,' Diego assures her as he leans down to pick the puppy up, away from the girls who are overwhelming it. I watch him as he takes Hadyn's hand, softly, gently, guides him to stroking the puppy's back. Hadyn laughs his gruff laugh. His face is alight. It's a moment to treasure forever but I haven't brought my camera.

'I'm going in the water before the sun goes down,' Blue calls to no one in particular.

'I'll join you,' Diego shouts as his friend gets up. Good. They're going. Now I can get up. Down on the shore I can see Blue's short fair hair slicked back by the water. The next second, he's disappeared between the waves like a silver darting fish.

'What is *this?*' Diego bends to pick up an all-but-invisible object lurking in the sand. He looks up at me. The others are all fussing over the puppy so they miss it but *he* doesn't. He knows it's mine, too.

'It matches your earrings,' he explains. The diamond ring that Charlie gave me for Christmas. 'Too valuable to bring to the beach,' he admonishes.

'I know.' I hold out my hand gratefully to receive it back. 'I forgot to take it off, can you believe that?' *I'd been in such a hurry to get out, hadn't I?*

'We remembered to leave Hadyn's precious elephant behind so it wouldn't get lost,' I burble, 'and then I go and bring this along. What a fool, eh?'

Diego shakes his head, smiling.

'No. You are a good mama.' Maria slides her arm through his and about his waist; standing behind him, she nuzzles his neck. Talia comes and stands beside them. Diego mutters something in Spanish and they all look at me. They smile.

'He's saying your son is lucky because you will never leave him,' Maria interprets for me. Her eyes narrow then. 'I'm doing what I can, though,' she says to me. 'It's not as if I *want* to leave my girls for a few months while we go and find some work . . .'

I swallow, a little taken aback at the sudden return of her

sharpness. And I have not always been so lucky. That's only what they see.

'I had to go away once, too,' I confess. 'It was soon after I had the baby. It was only for a couple of weeks, but . . . I got post-natal depression, I couldn't look after him, so you see . . .'

'Depression,' Maria repeats. She glances at Talia, who is looking surprised. 'Sí. That is like Diego's wife. She got that too.'

Diego is looking at Hadyn thoughtfully. I see a pang of something – regret, maybe? – and I wonder if he's thinking about his own son; the one he's planning to have to leave behind, to go and make his fortune in the UK.

We look towards the sea where the group of friends have all joined Blue. The shadow has already hit the edge of the water and the waves are a little choppier than they were a moment ago. The girls from Maria's group of friends are screaming and laughing as the men push them out in the little green dinghy. I can see the tops of their heads, bobbing and ducking as the waves push them up and down. They look like little coloured pinheads from where I'm sitting, they've gone so far away.

I glance up at the sky, which has changed in an instant to an unhealthy shade of grey. Now the rain has stopped but a huge cloud has just wandered up from nowhere and alighted on our little patch of the beach. The two girls in their dinghy have actually capsized, but they're still squealing and laughing.

The children have been chasing that poor dog round and round their sandcastle and now it suddenly makes off in a different direction. That's when Hadyn falls over and falls flat on his face in the sand. Talia immediately sets about getting the sand off him with a flannel, but Hadyn suddenly doesn't sound so happy. He looks towards me, flailing his arms in protest.

I'm coming, I'm *coming!* It's got so chilly all of a sudden; he really needs to be dressed. I get up and brush the fine granules off my legs, off my damp bikini bottoms, off my arms.

'I'm coming, honey.'

I *am* coming. That's when I feel the sharp sear of a tiny lancet piercing the back of my hand, stopping me in my tracks.

I fling the blasted thing as far away from me as I can but it's done its job. I can feel the tears springing to my eyes, my skin already beginning to throb.

Shit!

It hurts so much I don't remember feeling a pain like this ever, in my whole life. I can't breathe, I can't see. Oh, *help!*

Julia

'It's going to start raining properly,' Maria says. 'We'd better get the kids back into the car.'

'But I've got to get *this* seen to!' I point at my throbbing hand. My eyes are watering so badly I can barely even see any more. I glance towards Maria who is already pouring herself into her jeans. Hadyn has calmed down, I register through the pain. He will be okay if I leave him for a bit.

'Looks painful,' she agrees calmly. 'Will you be all right to go to the lifeguard station? They'll put something on it for you.'

'I'll go if you look after Hadyn for me? Just for a minute,' I gasp. 'I was going to take him with me to get changed in the Ladies' but now. . . . Look, his clothes are in the bag, okay?'

Maria nods briskly. She's busy shaking sand off damp towels, calling her girls to her. My hand hurts like hell but I don't want to make a fuss and there's other things going on around me at the moment. At the edge of my vision I am vaguely aware that the waves seem much angrier all of a sudden. They're rolling in like big arcs and by the time they break on the shore they must be topping eight or ten feet high. The water rushes right up the beach, bouncing over the stones past my feet and the woman ahead of me shrieks as her T-shirt goes rolling down into the ocean with the backwash; I can see plastic buckets and spades and all sorts headed out to sea at a rate of knots but at this moment I am in too much pain to give a damn. Diego hurtles past me. *I'm getting my body-board from the car, the girls are still out there*, he says. His eyes look wide and strained.

When I glance backwards I get a glimpse of Maria and the gang all huddled over our belongings; Lupe has already left. People are just picking everything up and beginning to run. Maria will have my boy safe – that's all I care about. I can hardly breathe for the pain. I have to get an anaesthetic. I have to get *something* to help me.

But someone with a wasp-sting is not going to be the life-guard's priority right now, I see; two of them dash out even as I reach their little hut, body-boards under their arms, heading hell for leather to the shoreline. An old guy explains to me that one of the girls who was on the dinghy has got into trouble; there's an undertow that's pulling her down. Now I turn back to look at it, the water does look ugly.

In fact the whole outlook on the beach has changed in a matter of less than – what – five minutes? The sky has grown three shades darker. Suddenly, nobody wants to be here any more.

Blue is helping a granny get out of the sucking surf. I can see her eyes white with the effort as the waves keep pulling them back, pulling them down. What the hell are we even doing here?

I meant to get a taxi out of this place this afternoon. I meant to take me and my son home.

I put my throbbing hand to my mouth, sucking it.

Where have Maria and the children got to? I cannot see them now because there is too much of a crowd between me and the place where I last saw them. With any luck she'll have got them all into the car already – I just need to make sure. The lifeguards are waving and calling to everyone, urging everyone *afuera, afuera*! Out of the water! But the girls are still in there, and their friends, Maria's friends, Diego and Blue – who won't give up without them.

The high wail of a siren at the beach-head announces the arrival of the Policia Local to help with crowd control. People need to be

99

taken off the shore, but so many of them are just standing around looking shocked, others just curious, as if the fact that they are recording the whole scene on their mobile phones will make them exempt from the effects of the next wave to come crashing in.

'Señora, *no!*' A policewoman shakes her head at me sternly as I head back down towards the shore. My hand is throbbing like hell but it hardly seems to matter at the moment because I still can't spot Maria. They are not letting anyone go back down towards the shore.

'My son,' I tell her, 'I have to make sure he's okay . . .'

He's okay, of course he's okay. He'll be with Maria. I just need to know where she is and then I'll feel better.

'Go to the *ambulancia*,' the policewoman points at my swollen hand in concern. 'Your son will be taken off the beach, everyone is being taken off, don't worry.'

There are so many people now, being herded up to the top of the shore; where did they all come from? No wonder I can't see Maria. She'll be struggling up with the kids on her own. I should be helping her. Diego was in the water with his body-board the last time I saw him. Out at sea, far, far out, there are heads bobbing up and down. The men row out on their boards, and the waves pick them up like little matchstick men and up, up, up they go in a huge arc and then down again. Nobody is left on the shore-line now. Everything that *was* there has been swept out. And I do not like the sound of the water. There are long periods of . . . *quiet,* as if the ocean has stopped breathing for a bit, as if it is hoping we won't notice what it's up to. Where is my son? I'll be fine, just as soon as I see him and know that everything's okay.

Ten minutes later as the crowd thins I see Maria laden down with bags, her hair whipped untidily across her face by the wind as she struggles up the beach, her two girls trailing behind her, and my heart floods with relief. The little one is holding the struggling puppy. I look to the place where we were set up all afternoon, our 'sunbrella' and our wicker mats all gone.

100

She pauses before she gets to me; looks back. I follow her gaze and I can see that the shoreline looks a heck of a lot further down now than it did a minute ago. 'Excuse me . . . excuse me!' I push brusquely past the fat German man who is standing there gormlessly holding a huge folding table.

'Maria, is everything all right?' She's ahead of the girls. One of them has something on her back – that must be Hadyn, of course, they wouldn't let him walk in this mêlée.

'No. This is not good,' she says. 'We have to wait for the others; Diego's still out there, trying to save the girl, but I'm getting everything into the car . . .'

Maria speaks calmly, taking it all in her stride. Her boyfriend is out there, risking his life 'trying to save the girl' – I'd be having kittens! I don't want to wait, like the gathering crowd by the beach-head, to see if the girls get pulled out okay. I have a really bad feeling that they won't and I don't want to witness their bodies.

'Okay,' I say as I look curiously towards Talia and the little one. Is Talia giving Hadyn a piggyback as I thought? She must be, because I can't see him from here. How odd.

'You want a lift back?' Maria offers. She sounds stressed. She must be worried about Diego but not want to show it.

'Sure.' She hands me my beach bag, the one I didn't take with me. She's managed to save everything, by the looks of things.

'Where's baby?' She pulls her hair back with one fell swoop, into a bun.

'Who, Hadyn?' She can't mean Hadyn. What baby is she talking about?

'Your son,' she says deliberately, looking at me as if I've gone quite mad. 'You were taking him to the Ladies', you said. To get him changed, yes?'

'No I – I didn't! You know I didn't, Maria. I left him with you. *Here*, on the seashore. Your girls had him. I asked you to change him, oh *God!*'

Maria turns, shocked, back to the spot where we'd been sitting.

101

'He ran back after you,' she says faintly. 'I thought you had him. Talia said you had him.'

Talia stands there looking sullen all of a sudden, shaking her head.

'I didn't say that,' she croaks.

We all drop our bags and start to run back down towards the shore. Maria and her daughter are muttering something in Spanish but I can't understand them.

He's here, somewhere. He *must* be here. He's so little; he'll be hiding behind someone's legs. Behind someone's bag . . .

'No!! *Señoras, no es permitido!*' An officer from the Policia Local stops us now before we can get much furthur.

What is wrong with him? He's looking at me blankly, not understanding a word of what I'm trying to tell him. Maria says something to him and he puts up his arms and just pushes us gently but firmly back into the crowd. I can feel the pressure of Maria's fingertips on my arms now, trying to keep me there.

'You can see your son isn't there. You can't go back down now,' she warns.

'But you left him there! *You just left him, Maria!*' I take in great big gulps of air because I don't see any other way I am going to breathe just at the moment. I'm trying to explain to these policemen that they've got to allow me back down onto the shore but they're all just standing around talking in Spanish. I can't make out which one is in charge and *nobody will listen to me* . . .

I look at Maria but she isn't helping.

Oh for the love of God, where is Blue?

My eyes scan the crowd for him like a madwoman. I need him to explain things to them for me. I *need* him to tell me what is happening. Where is he?

'There is no one there on that shore, Julia. There is nothing there.' Maria keeps pulling me back and I shake her roughly off. 'He can't be there. If he had been there, he would have been swept out, just like everything else . . .'

What is she saying? I pull my hair back away from my eyes.

No. This can't be happening. Someone will have him, *dear God*, they must have him . . .

'Have you seen a little boy, a one-year-old?' I ask people as I dash back into the crowd, because this is where he surely must be? 'My boy, have you seen him?'

Maria and her girls are standing in a huddle explaining things to a couple of her men friends who have reluctantly obeyed the lifeguards and come out of the sea. I see their white faces turned, looking shocked, towards me. Blue has joined them now. He looks bedraggled, weary. It wasn't just the waves that have come unexpectedly; the undertow has taken everyone by surprise as well, he's saying.

'My baby.' I grab his arm in panic, because he is the only English person I can see. The only person I feel at this moment who will truly understand me.

'*Blue,* Hadyn's missing, help me find him, help me, please . . .' Blue pulls me in towards him, a sudden embrace, I feel his lips kiss the top of my head roughly, and then he lets me go and I hear his words above the roar of the loudspeakers that the police have now set up, warning everyone to get back, get back, because more waves are coming . . .

'I'll find him for you, Julia. I promise you. Leave it to me.' He squeezes my hand reassuringly. 'Leave it with me, okay?' and then he is gone, disappeared into the crowd.

After many minutes Diego paddles in at last with one of the girls on his board. She's unconscious, but alive after all. No one has seen the other girl for a long while.

'My baby,' I am saying to people, 'my little boy, have you seen him?' Everybody just looks at me with a worried expression on their faces.

'*Tiene el cabello rojo,*' I stutter out. Is that how you say red hair? No, it isn't. '*pelirojo,*' I tell anyone who will listen. '*Mi niño chico – asi de altura,*' I indicate his stature with my hands. '*Esta*

103

perdido.' I can't remember the words properly. I don't know if they can understand me. I think they do, because they look sympathetic. Now a woman officer from the Policia Local takes me over to one side and asks me to write down my name. She wants lots of details: my name, my husband's name, my son's name. She wants to know where I live and where I am currently staying and what is my age and what is Hadyn's age and how long have we been in Spain for . . . ? And eventually I throw down the pen and just scream at her because she is wasting my time and I have to go look for him. He will still be here, somewhere near here. He could not have got too far. Not yet. Someone will have him and I have to find out who.

'Was he in the water?' someone asks me. '*Did you let him go in?*' Then more police are here, pulling the crowds further back, telling everyone to go home because the sea is looking even more strange and no one knows quite what's going to happen, what might happen, any minute. It looks as if the tide has pulled its belly in. Everything's been sucked much too far back, like a tsunami.

Everyone is being evacuated. But they mustn't let the people go home: don't they understand that my son is missing and these people might all be witnesses? They mustn't let the people go home just yet!

'Someone will have him, Julia.' Maria tugs at my hand, pulling me away from the beach. 'The *policía* are dealing with it now. He'll have been taken to a place of safety, be calm. Blue will find him for you. You will see.'

But she does not know.

I have a terrible feeling of *déjà vu*.

'Blue will find him,' she repeats. 'Have faith, Julia. You will get him back.' But Blue will not find him, I know this.

The dark sky. The rain. The water. I have been here before.

Julia

I have been here before, awake in the darkness; alone.

Outside the door I can hear voices, whispering urgently – but my head is too muzzy for me to tell who they are.

Night terrors, they tell me; the dreams that children dream. If I can only get grounded, wake myself up properly, then surely everything will be all right.

The digital clock says 22:20.

Today is . . .

Today is New Year's Eve.

I sit bolt upright and immediately my head feels as if someone's trying to stove it in with a hammer. Did Charlie really leave this morning?

I stretch my fingers out to the place on the bed beside me and it is empty. Charlie did leave this morning. He left as a beautiful dawn was rising. The day was . . .

The day was so hot I took Hadyn to the beach.

I swing my legs out, slowly, my feet taking an eternity to contact the smooth tiled floor, as if I am still back in a dream somewhere, wading through treacle. My left arm is throbbing at the top, and when I touch it the skin is raised and sore as if someone has given me an injection. I shake my head, wanting to clear my thoughts, needing to remember.

The photo of Hadyn and Charlie that I took a couple of days ago is missing.

I'd propped it on the bedside table and Eva had found a frame to put it in for me. I remember that much. Now it's *gone*.

I don't remember Charlie taking it with him.

My mouth feels strange, too. It tastes metallic. I must have taken too much sun today.

Hadyn's cot is empty. Did they take him away so he wouldn't wake me?

The door opens a fraction. Slowly, quietly, Eva puts her head around it.

'She's awake,' I hear her say. Her voice is hushed, reverent.

'Julia, *hija*. Are you awake?' The light snaps on, flooding my room, making me cover my eyes. Who are these people that follow her into my bedroom? Why do they all look so . . .

'Can you remember what happened?' Eva's hand is holding onto mine now. She's sitting on the edge of my bed and I realise I haven't stood up yet.

What happened?

I shake my head dumbly.

I hear her draw in a troubled breath and glance at the long-faced policeman who has followed her in to my room.

'They have to ask you some questions, Julia. Do you think you could help them?' The policeman's face looks familiar. I do not know the woman doctor who is standing behind him (Eva calls her *doctora*, so I know what she is). But I do remember him, the policeman. He was on the beach.

Such . . . a long time ago, it seems.

'She might still be feeling confused.' The doctor speaks in Spanish. 'The shot I gave her earlier on won't have completely worn off yet.'

So, they did give me something.

Why?

I remember it was raining. But should I worry about that? In my dream it is always raining. And I was running, shouting, and the sky had got all dark. This is nothing but my dream isn't it?

106

That's how it always goes. I look up at Eva and I can feel the prickle of tears at my eyes but I don't know why. I feel her hands rubbing the top of my hands.

'Anything you can remember,' she says softly, 'Anything that might help?'

'Where's my baby?' I manage to get out at last.

'There has been an . . . incident,' Eva says. The *doctora* gives her a warning look and she stumbles on. 'We aren't really sure yet. We're looking for him, Julia. Hadyn is missing at the moment.'

Missing?

Somehow I get to my feet. I fling the sheets from his cot, just to make sure. Nothing. His elephant is there, just exactly where I left it when we went out this morning, but Hadyn is not.

'What . . . ?'

'There was a big wave on the beach,' the policeman jumps in now. 'Two girls got swept out, you remember?' Eva is squeezing my hand very hard now. 'We think there may be a . . . small chance . . . that your son has drowned, señora.' The Policia Local officer looks so morose he seems to be in very little doubt of the fact.

'But until we find a body we still hope to find him alive. Someone could have seen him wandering, lost; they could have picked him up . . . this kind of thing happens all the time,' the *doctora* adds. 'And most children are recovered.' She glances around, as if defying anyone to contradict her.

'*Until you find a body . . . ?*' I drag out the words because I can't really take this in. 'I can't remember what happened.' I look from one of them to the other. It feels as if they must be telling me lies, because if Hadyn had truly gone missing I would remember it surely? I would remember *something*.

I slap the side of my head with my open hand. I *must* remember – or I must wake up. One or the other. I have woken up before from just such a nightmare. The details are always different, but this feeling – that some terrible, unimaginable thing has happened – that is constant.

'Julia,' the policeman checks my name on his notepad. 'When is the last time you can remember seeing your child? Who is the last person you remember seeing him with, before you went to get changed?'

But fog has descended on my brain, a horrible fog, and I cannot think. If only I could wake up, just like I always do, then everything would be all right.

'Look at it this way,' the policeman is saying to me, 'at the moment, time is still on our side. The statistics are still on our side. Eighty per cent of all missing children are found within the first two hours. Ninety-five per cent are found within the first twenty-four hours. We're still in the first day period. If the water didn't take him, then chances are that someone else has got him. Do you follow me?' His English is quite good but thickly accented.

'Someone else?' I say faintly.

Hadyn *is* missing.

'You've got to get him back,' I croak at the policeman. 'You've got to.' He nods sympathetically.

'I have children too,' he tells me.

There is so little I remember but I tell him everything, all of it a jumble, about the wasp and the rain and the sea. None of it makes very much sense. When I look, the red numbers on the clock say 23:50 and my heart sinks because I know time is moving on. Just like it does in real life. Just like it wouldn't do if this were a bad dream. My head is less muzzy now, things shaping up into focus.

The lady doctor no longer appears to be in the room. Agustina is here though, I see, and the neighbour Pepi and some other people. They have been bringing me drinks that I haven't touched. They have been closing the windows to shut out the noise and then – because it is so hot – opening them again. Eva is telling someone that Roberto is out with the Policia Local, helping them with their door-to-door inquiries.

Oh no. Oh no, please let this not be real.

I have to get up. I have to get going. I can't stay here doing nothing. But my legs are like heavy wooden poles. What has this *doctora* given me? I didn't need anything to make me sleep. I *need* this first twenty-four hours; this is the most important time, I can't *sleep*. Are they mad?

'Where is Charlie?' I grab at Eva suddenly. 'Have you got hold of him yet? Does he know?'

Eva looks fraught.

'We've been trying to get hold of him these past few hours – but no luck. Nobody is picking up.'

'He was operating on someone, wasn't he?' one of the bodies in the room pipes up now, I have no idea who. 'Maybe nobody is available to pick up the phone – it's nearly midnight.'

'We'll keep trying,' Eva reassures me. 'We'll get him tonight. Don't worry.'

'So you're . . .' I swallow. 'You're still looking for him?' I look at the policeman.

'*No no te procupes*, we'll look for him until we find him, señora. *De una manera u otra.*' One way or another.

Diego phones. At first my heart leaps when Eva reluctantly hands me the telephone. I know he has been out with the others, searching. He was the hero who saved that girl from the waves when even the lifeguards could not. Maybe he is the man who is going to save the day for me, too?

'Julia?' His voice sounds gruff; unbelievably weary. But he has bothered to seek out my number, this must be important. I just want him to tell me that everything is going to be all right.

'*Maria*,' I hear his voice turned away from the phone now, addressing his girlfriend in the room behind him, '*quédate callado.*' Be quiet, he tells her. But I can hear her, howling and crying so loudly it might be her own child that is gone. She sounds as if someone has died! Is she crying because she finally feels responsible for what happened? It is partly her fault, and she knows it . . .

'You've found him?' The hope in my voice is forlorn because I can still hear her weeping.

'No, we didn't find him, señora.' Diego's words come out short, wounded. He has been going on this for many, many hours now, I realise. He has taken on more than anyone could have expected him – really, a mere stranger – to do. *Charlie should be doing this*; the thought sneaks in, uninvited, now. *Charlie should be here, with his family. This is where he should be.*

'But Julia, I want your permission to ask . . . some people I know. To see if anyone has heard anything . . .' His voice lowers a tone.

'Why would anyone have heard anything?' I wail. 'What might they know?'

'Shhhh . . .' he warns me. 'You are surrounded by the others, yes? Say nothing out loud. I know *some people*. If your son was taken by some bad men, they might know something. If he drowned, Julia, then it is too late for him. But if it was something else that took him away from you – maybe it will be possible to get him back?'

'But surely the police will see to that? You think that he—'

'No! *Say nothing.*' His voice hardens, warning. 'I have tried to help you as best I can. You must understand, I cannot be personally implicated in this, señora. I have already been in trouble once before. You know this. This is why I cannot find a job here in Spain. It's why my wife doesn't trust I can provide for her and for my son, and why my whole life has been ruined. It's why I'm going to the UK. I will help you,' his voice rasps into the phone, 'if you want me to make some inquiries, I will do that. But I can't get involved, you understand?'

My breath is coming short and hard. I glance up at the others in the room, all hanging on my every word. Agustina is frowning, trying to follow.

'So you haven't found him?' I say brokenly. The light goes out of everyone's eyes.

'But you have my permission to ask, Diego. Of course, do whatever you have to.'

There is a short pause as he takes in my words.

'I know how much you love your son, señora. As much as I love my own,' he sounds exhausted, broken. 'If I were in your position, *I would do anything to get my child back.* If it is so, that someone has him, I will do whatever I can to get him back to you, but – please – understand me right, my name cannot be linked to any of this, or I risk losing everything all over again.'

'I appreciate what you're doing,' I whisper into the phone. I hand the phone back to Eva, who gives me a curious look as she takes it.

'What did he say?' she asks bluntly. 'Who will know anything?'

'The fishermen,' I pull out of the air. 'He's going to ask the fishermen if they've seen a child hiding amongst the boats.'

Eva shrugs dismissively. She glances at Agustina and I see that brief shake of the head, *it's nothing, the girl is only grasping at straws,* and Abuela pats my hand consolingly.

And then it is here.

The green lights on the bedside clock click onto 00:00 and the boats on the sea far below are sounding their deep horns. The scream of fireworks and the echo of cheering blasts through the windows and somebody goes over to shut them again.

Muted, embracing each other with tears in their eyes, our little party acknowledges the passing away of the old, the coming in of the new. Nobody wishes anybody else a 'Happy New Year'. There is no sense of excitement or joy in our room. There is only a sense of foreboding and fear, as palpable as a clenched fist.

'The statistics are on our side, remember.' The policeman gets up stiffly from the chair he's been sitting on. 'Remember, the first twenty-four hours are the most crucial.'

Roberto comes in and we all look up but he shakes his head at Eva: no news. He ushers his wife out of the room with a slight motion of his head. Once outside though, he does not trouble to keep his voice down, and everyone in the room strains to hear what he's saying.

'We've done the preliminary searches and there's not a sign, Eva. We haven't been able to get hold of Carlos, either. The best thing she can hope for now,' his voice drops a notch just outside my door, but still we all hear him, ' . . . is that sometime soon, she receives a ransom note.'

Charlie

It's the first day of the year; bright and crisp and . . . peaceful, somehow. You could hear a pin drop. Everyone's sleeping off last night's booze, I'll be bound. Maybe Santos will be, too. Lopez rang and left a message on his machine to say we were coming up but we've heard nothing back yet.

Still, I'm awake early, as requested. I'd hoped we'd be here this time yesterday but there were after-procedure complications and I got caught up in London for the best part of yesterday as well. When we got to Cambridge at half-past midnight last night the fireworks were just about dying down. In Arenadeluna the parties would have just got going. Julia and the little one must have had a ball, even without me. I didn't want to miss his first New Year but there was nothing for it. Still, quiet or not, I was out like a light the minute my head touched the pillow. So much for our plans to raise a glass to the New Year! Lopez didn't seem much in the mood, if truth be told. I'd have phoned Spain before I left the hotel this morning but it might have been too early – I didn't want to disturb them.

Santos's place is just a short walk from here, Lopez tells me. If it's not too far from here it must look out over the River Cam. I'll bet he gets a bird's-eye view of all the boat races, too, lucky bastard.

No matter, I've got more important concerns on my mind this morning. From what Lopez has now revealed I get the impression that things are far worse than he originally let on. When I glance at him he doesn't look as though he's had too much sleep.

The Esperanza Centre is currently under a moratorium, he tells me, while an investigation by the Nigerian authorities gets under way. But what else does he know that he hasn't told me yet?

I find it hard to believe that a man like Baudelaire could be involved in embezzlement, but Lopez is adamant that it's so. If it's true, I could throttle the bastard with my own hands.

Santos's apartments are up a little alley just a few minutes down from King's College. There's an entrance lobby, coloured with blue and green tiles, reminiscent of the Mediterranean. Very cool and dark. Not that you need cooling down in the UK in winter. Lopez rings the buzzer and someone – a woman's voice – calls us on up.

Lopez's eyes look sunken, yellowed with worry. I feel a wave of impatience wash over me. If things have really got as bad as they seem, it's his own fault. Seeing as I'm the project's founder, he should have told me earlier if things were going pear-shaped. He should have been aware of Baudelaire's activities himself; that's what the Esperanza project employs him for.

But it's Santos who pays his wages at the end of the day, I remember. Maybe he employs him with other priorities in mind? There are too many fingers in this pie, I'm thinking now. We need to be able to operate this service free from politics and favour.

'If I'd *known* about this . . .' I lower my voice as we climb the white marble stairs to the apartment.

'I know, I know. It was a mistake.' He's mumbling, his voice filled with nothing but regret. 'But . . . the situation in Sokoto is more complicated than you know.'

'So, tell me about it.' I turn on him sharply. 'What did Baudelaire actually do?'

'It's not so much what he's done.' Lopez can barely give me eye-contact. 'The truth is, there's more to our work in Sokoto than I've told you . . .'

'Right.' I rub my face with the palms of my hands. I don't want to hear any more. I can't do the work I do *and* deal with all the political mess that goes on beneath the surface. I'm a surgeon, not a politician.

The door opens and a fresh-faced woman in a maid's uniform lets us in.

'Señor was expecting you,' she says. 'He asks if you would be so kind as to join him for breakfast?'

'Charlie, my old friend.' The pleasure in Santos's voice as at last we are shown into the dining room is genuine enough, but the smile he gives me is measured. 'Enrique,' he nods towards Lopez. 'Come and sit down here, both of you, and may I be the first to wish you a Happy New Year?' He's already pushing his chair out, rising to come and do me the honour of hugging me. Santos and my family go back a long way. He knew my mother when she was a girl. It was he who suggested, when I first approached him for funds, eight years ago, that the centre should take her middle name, *Esperanza* – Hope – in memory of her.

'Please,' he gestures to the chair that catches the best of the winter-morning sun, 'sit. What will you have? Coffee? Eggs?'

'Just coffee for me . . .'

'Enrique tells me you have done me the kindness of travelling down late last night, just to be here?'

I nod, smile at him. 'I heard it was urgent, Santos. I would have spent the New Year with my family, otherwise.'

There is a long silence while Santos considers this. He leans forward on the table, his palms pressed together in prayer-position, against his lips.

'I know what the project means to you, Carlos. I remember when you first came to me . . .' His lips form the ghost of a smile. 'What was it, eight years ago now?' I nod. 'You'd just been taken on by Angus at the Drapers Street clinic. You were surrounded by long-legged lovelies day and night who just wanted their pout improving to increase their perfection and I still remember – ' he breaks into a grin – 'the only thing you were interested in was Angus's little *pro bono* project for the children of Guatemala.'

'Yes, it was Guatemala at the time,' I say, stiffly.

'But it's worldwide now,' he reminds me. 'Enrique tells me we now get children who are potential candidates for surgical reconstruction put forward to us from charities all over the world, isn't that so? We take on those who we feel have the best chance of benefiting in the long term.'

'Which is where Esperanza comes in,' Lopez finds his voice suddenly. 'After surgery they get taken to a rehabilitation centre where they can spend as long as they need learning to do things like . . . like how to eat,' he gets into his stride, 'how to dress themselves. How to wash. How to talk . . .'

Santos leans back now, his eyes hooded. 'The aftercare. That is so important,' he agrees, his dark eyes homing in on me again. 'We'd really like to continue supporting such a worthy enterprise.'

I give Lopez a pointed look here but he seems suddenly very interested in the scrambled eggs on his plate. I could swear his hands are trembling as he lifts the fork to his mouth.

'Well, I hope you will, Santos.'

'You are a dedicated man.' Santos pats my hand approvingly. 'I have always liked that about you, Charlie.'

I incline my head, accepting the compliment. I just hope he's not merely softening the blow he's going to deliver next.

'This whole family . . .' Santos indicates with a wide gesture around the empty table, 'we all appreciate you.' He turns to me again. 'And your people back in Spain – they are all well? Dear Agustina, Roberto and his girls and . . . and your wife?' His dark eyes smile curiously at me. 'I heard something,' he coaxes gently.

'We plan to be married this autumn,' I finish for him. 'Look, Santos . . .'

'I know, I know . . .' he bows his head graciously, wipes his face with his beautiful napkin. 'You want to hear all about the Esperanza Centre. Our friend here –' he inclines his head towards Lopez – 'will have filled you in on the bad news?'

'Some of it. I've heard about Baudelaire's alleged . . . indiscretions.'

'I fear they are more than just allegations.'

'So we do . . . what?'

Santos shrugs.

'That depends very much on you, my friend. I could close Esperanza down tomorrow. I'll be honest with you. I'm under a lot of pressure to do so from my political associates in Spain, and from certain business colleagues who understand that whilst well-perceived charitable causes may be good for the profile, scandals associated with the same are most certainly detrimental.'

'You can't close down the whole centre because of one man's bloody foolishness!' I'm on my feet, the sound of my chair scraping back against the cool marble tiles jarring the air. 'The work we do there . . . Santos, you know what we do. We change the lives of people who have no other means of making things better for themselves. I know that Louis Baudelaire has jeopardised your involvement, but I'm begging you to reconsider. It's still a worthy cause, both for us and for you.'

'I said I would be honest with you, Charlie.' He makes a 'sit down' motion with his hands. 'If it weren't for your personal involvement in this, maybe I'd have abandoned Esperanza a while back. My involvement with the Esperanza Centre isn't just out of the goodness of my heart. I'm a businessman, you know that. I'd like to continue supporting you, but I need to know that I'll have your support too . . .'

'Santos, if you reprieve the centre I will do whatever I have to do – and I mean *whatever*. Even if it means me staying over in Sokoto for a few months till the whole place is settled again – to make it right.'

'You'd do that?' He looks at me with renewed interest. 'Even though you have a wedding to organise, a young child at home?'

'Anything,' I repeat. Lopez is nodding enthusiastically. He's

117

said virtually nothing in this whole meeting. His mission was just to get me here.

'The most important thing – as far as I'm concerned – is that no scandal becomes attached to Santos Enterprises as a result of this indiscretion. If I can get Baudelaire off the charges, you'll be happy to keep him on, I take it?'

'I wouldn't be comfortable with—'

'Burying the charges might be the easiest way to get out of this – I'm thinking of all angles, here. And you'd have to vouch for him, of course.'

'What did he actually do?' I frown. 'What are the charges? Lopez here has been a bit cagey . . .'

Santos throws a glance at Enrique, then directly back to me. 'The truth is – I'd rather you didn't sully your hands with it, Charlie. I'm dealing with it. That's all you need to know. I just need to hear that we've got your support.'

Support for what, though? I shift uncomfortably in my chair.

'You said anything, Charlie. If you want to keep Esperanza you might have to think of the greater good here,' Lopez puts in timidly.

'I meant anything practical that I could in terms of giving of my time and effort. If you mean I should help him get off scot-free, you'd need to be clearer about what exactly he *has* done?'

Santos's eyebrows lift at that and Lopez looks pointedly at the floor.

'The likes of us can talk ethics,' Santos tells me softly. 'But unfortunately not everyone in the world can afford the luxury of them. Well, my friend, my sister is waiting to see you, you know.' He throws his napkin down on the table. 'I have another flight to catch this morning and I think we've kept her waiting long enough, don't you?'

Perhaps Lourdes – much though I baulk at the thought of seeing her again – will be persuaded to tell me more?

Julia

None of us slept the whole night. Roberto went out again with Pepi's husband and they knocked on doors, gathering more and more people, like the Pied Piper, as they went. A fog came down last night after a while, hushing everything except the boats. I heard the sirens *barp-barp-barp* long into the night. The phone rang a few times but it was dead when we picked it up. *The telephone exchange, it keeps doing this now,* Agustina complained, *ever since they dug up the roads for the new works in the town. Nothing that is old works properly any more.*

It will be back on again soon, someone said to her. We couldn't get hold of Charlie. Eva lent me her phone and I texted him, but I've had no reply. The hours went by too fast, even though we women sat there and did very little. They would not let me go out and help with the search. But the clock kept going, the numbers going on and on. I watched them, even though that meant that my first precious twenty-four hours were slipping like sand through my hands and after that the statistics would no longer be on my side.

And so the dawn has come, and with it a silence and a heaviness that was not here yesterday. They don't leave me alone, not even for one minute. Not even when they tell me to sleep, go to sleep. But I am on full alert.

Another policeman comes, one who looks more senior.

'What happens now?' Eva asks him. 'What is next?'

'We're still looking'. He shrugs that heavy shrug that I have seen the others do. 'But if nothing . . .' he pauses, takes me in, '. . . if nothing happens, the British Embassy will be in touch with her in a few days.'

'Is there no word? *Nothing?*' Her sigh is frustrated, tired. The hours are beginning to tell on her. I wish she would go to her bed. I will be fine here. I can stay awake by myself.

'The sea was too bad last night,' he says to her now. 'We're concentrating on the land search. Our best hope is that someone picked him up and in all the confusion . . . hasn't found anywhere to hand him in yet.'

'I heard there was a group of children from a foster home on the beach yesterday.' Eva screws up her eyes.

'We heard that too. We're looking into it. He could have got picked up by mistake. It's unlikely – the children from the home were older than him – but . . .' he looks frankly in my direction. We're all sitting downstairs in the lounge now.

'Does she remember anything yet?'

They keep referring to me in this way, all the officials, as 'she'. As if I were some stupid out-of-touch person who cannot answer for herself. I have to answer them in English, I admit, but everyone so far has been able to understand me well enough.

'Have you spoken to Maria yet?' I address him directly now. 'She says she saw him walking up the beach towards me. What about her girls? Did they recall anything else?'

'We have spoken to Maria, naturally. She came straight into the station after she left the beach, and made her statement. She works for us as a clerk, don't forget. She knows what to do.'

'What did she say?'

'She saw the child running up the beach towards you.' He flips open his notepad and reads her statement out loud. 'She says she thought you'd changed your mind and called him to follow you.'

'Surely she must have known that I—'

'The waves suddenly started getting high and her attention went to the girls on the dinghy for a moment. She says when she looked back both you and the boy had gone. Naturally she assumed you took the boy yourself . . .'

He gives me a long appraising look now as if wondering whether I did, in fact, take him myself.

'Am I a suspect here?' I throw at him.

He looks quite shocked for an instant. Then he throws up his hands.

'We are doing our best, señora! And Maria is . . .' He glances at Eva.

'She's very upset,' Eva supplies.

'She is a good person,' he says simply.

He's right. This isn't Maria's fault. I need someone to blame, that's all.

'She tried to come and see you yesterday,' Eva put in, 'to speak to you herself, but you were asleep. She has told the officers everything she knows, don't worry.'

The police officer finishes his glass of water and I can see the dark lines of strain under his own eyes. Through a chink in the blinds I can see the dull dawn breaking, and I remember the policemen, too, have been up all night searching for my child.

They say that – unless he was picked up by a boat – a search of the sea will only pick up a floating body. They're still going in the houses, further and further away now, widening the net. They're looking in shop doorways and in the archways of stairs, under the boats – in all the little nooks and crannies where a tiny child might have fallen asleep.

He is so tiny. When he curls up and goes to sleep in a little ball, how easily he might be overlooked.

And so, I know, I believe, that he will be found, because he is so small and because he could so easily have been missed. And if last night he has gone to sleep without Bap-Bap – I hold his stuffed white elephant close to my face, drawing in the scent of it, the smell of *him* that still lingers in the well-worn fur – then, by tonight surely, they will be reunited and then I will never, ever let him out of my sight again.

There are so many places a small person might have got to. The thought consoles me because it opens up the possibilities for all the places that he might yet be recovered.

I don't believe he went into the water. No. Eva tells me that many people remember him playing with the girls, building the sandcastle. *Someone* said they saw him walking by the shore before he went missing. But someone else said they saw a boy walking up towards the head of the beach. That one is more likely. It gives me more hope.

What if he managed to cross the road all by himself? Just say – what if someone picked him up who wasn't quite sure what to do with him? They maybe weren't local so didn't know where the police station was, or they maybe weren't all that bright – what if they didn't realise they should hand him back? It could happen. All I keep thinking is: he was so cold, my baby. The image I have of the last time I saw him has become clear. My mind keeps going back to it, again and again. I was going to change him before that wasp stung me and I left Maria to change him but she never did. Wherever he has got to now – *wherever he is* – is he still feeling cold? Is he still wearing just those blue swimming trunks? Is he damp and unhappy?

If no one found him, then once the fog came in and the temperature went down, surely a little naked body like that would . . .

Oh no, it does not bear thinking about.

Many people left once it started to rain. I was happy about the rain at the time but I see now it drove away many people who might have been there to help, to see a toddler wandering off by himself and pick him up.

I have been trying so hard to get hold of Charlie but the telephone exchange in Arenadeluna is still playing up. Pepi's husband says they've got people working on it (his cousin works there). He says we should be able to make our call very soon. It is working intermittently, he says. Apparently *they* got a call from their daughter in the UK to wish them Happy New Year. I texted Charlie from Eva's mobile but he can't have picked that up either – unless he has but he can't get hold of *us* because the phones are down. No good him texting me because my phone got caught in the big wave when the sea came right back up the beach and everything got soaked.

My mind keeps returning to Charlie. What is he going to say? Oh, my lord. Why can't he just get in touch? He was expecting to operate on the 30th, I remember. Then he might have been too tired to travel back to Richmond. He might have slept over at the clinic. But why didn't he ring us at all yesterday? He's got to get hold of us some time soon, surely?

I keep expecting the phone to ring any moment now, and it will be him.

'Do you want to go to mass with us?' One of Eva's girls, beautifully dressed, is at my side. She's holding a little pearl rosary in her hand – it shines and shimmers in that dull way pearls have in the light and for some reason I can't take my eyes off it. The girl has been watching me stroking the elephant's fur and comes up alongside me and mimics my action, her small fingers softly, reverently stroking his fur. For some reason, that chokes me up more than anything else so far. I manage to shake my head. I would like to go, actually. I long for the small crumb of comfort that such an act of faith might offer me but I do not feel it is my place to go there. I cannot make it so just by simply pretending.

'She's waiting for news, Maite. You go for us. You say your prayers for your cousin.' Eva shoos her daughter out. 'They will pray for you,' she tells me tonelessly. 'We will hear something today, you'll see.'

For *you*, she says. They'll pray for me. Why not for him? What does Eva know that she isn't telling me?

'I have to go back down to the beach,' I tell Eva suddenly now. 'Perhaps if I go myself . . .'

I can't just stay here doing nothing. Maybe if I'm out and about I will see someone, or someone will see me and a memory will get triggered. So I go and get washed. Robotically, I pull a comb through my hair. I splash cold water on my face. I rub the toothbrush with toothpaste on it over my clenched teeth.

These are all the things of a normal life. They belong in a time where everything has a place and a structure to hold all the small actions of the day together in some meaningful thread. Where there is, basically, a *point* to it all.

Today feels like the bottom has dropped right out of my life and when I look at the gaping chasm that has opened up beneath me, there *is* no meaning. I do not care about my hair or about my teeth. I do not care how many hours I have been wearing these same clothes – I just need to get out of the house. Because somewhere, somehow, I know my son is out there too, waiting for me to find him.

'Someone is at the door. He's come to see *her*,' Maite's gruff voice tells her mother. They both look at me when I arrive back downstairs again and I feel a shot of pure fear in my chest. Who is it? Another policeman? Good news or bad?

But my visitor is not a policeman.

Blue?

I search his face for any sign of hope. I feel a sob rising in my throat at the sight of him because he *promised* me that he would find my son.

'Julia.' He drops down on the settee beside me and I wonder where he has been all this time; has he been out there on the beach looking? His clothes seem damp to me. He might well have been doing just that. 'How are you?' His fingers interlace with my own for a moment, comrade-in-arms-like, I think. This man is on my side. He's the one who's going to help me find Hadyn, I can feel it.

I don't answer his question because there is nothing to say.

'What news?' My voice is a strangled whisper, nothing more.

'It's going to be okay.' He pats my hand reassuringly. 'Everything will work out soon, you'll see.'

I let this sink in for a minute. In my mind's eye I can see the search party that the police have told me about, all the dozens of people who are out there, still determined to bring this to a happy conclusion.

'But . . . what *news*?' I insist. 'I left him with Maria,' I sob now. 'I left him with her, how could she say I didn't?'

'I spoke to her earlier at the police station,' he nods. 'She was there this morning you know. She's *devastated*.'

I look at him blankly.

'She went in early to see what she could do to help.'

'Right.' What am I expected to say to that? Good on her! I should not be angry with her but I bloody well am, so there. And I have absolutely no interest whatsoever in hearing how bloody *devastated* bloody *Maria* is! I wish I had never met her. I wish I had never accepted her lift to the beach or even gone to the beach at all . . .

'Look,' I pull my hand away from his. Is he not going to come good on his promise after all? 'I appreciate your helping with the search but I've . . . I've got to go out myself right now. He might still be out there – sleeping or something. I might . . . I might still find him.'

'Out there sleeping?' Blue's face creases in compassion. 'Julia, you aren't just going to go out there and find him *now*, are you?'

'What the hell do you know about it?' I scream. 'Nobody else has found him so maybe I will. He's got to be somewhere hasn't he? He can't just have *disappeared*.'

'Christ. You haven't heard, then?' Blue looks mortified. *Heard what?*

'The phone is ringing!' I hear someone saying in the corridor and I fall silent. We have been waiting for the phone to ring all

125

morning and now – now that this Blue is about to tell me something – it rings! 'It's working! Mama shall I get it? It could be
Carlos. It could be the police station. Oh, it's for Julia. Where is
she? Is she still in with the man?'

I take one look at his face and I get up and close the door.
'All right, Blue, exactly *what* is it I haven't heard?'

Charlie

It's been five years since I last saw her. I hesitate for a fraction of a second inside the arched terrace-way. She's looking out over the wide avenue below, watching the people ride past on their bikes. Her expression is peaceful, patient.

'Hey!'

'Charlie!' When she turns at last I see the familiar face hasn't changed that much. She is still beautiful, with the olive-skinned almond-eyed Mediterranean type of beauty that will endure into old age. There are a few lines around her eyes that were not there before. But neither is there any longer that sense of desperation about her, the troubled urgency of youth.

'You look . . . serene,' I tell her. She laughs. The brief, close embrace that we exchange brings back a flood of memories.

'I'm so glad to see you again.' I look away, out onto the sunlit expanse of the wide pavement below.

'Sunny morning,' I say. It seems that Cambridge has escaped the sleety weather in London. 'Lots of people out already, I see.'

She comes and leans over the terrace beside me, just enough for me to be uncomfortably aware of her.

'Beautiful views your brother has here.' She follows my gaze out over the gleaming white towers of King's College, past the college entrance to the square that leads to the magnificent King's Chapel.

'Makes you feel like you've gone back to mediaeval times, this.

I feel I ought to be dressed in full armour, carrying a banner for king and country.'

Lourdes laughs again, touches my arm softly.

'Oh Charlie, you haven't changed a bit, have you? Always the romantic.' She adds, 'How did it go when you carried your banner into battle this morning?'

'With your brother the king?' I turn to look at her.

I could do this without you lot, I think suddenly. The Santos family involvement has made things a lot easier, I'll admit. Not just money-wise. They've opened doors, oiled the wheels of progress for me all the way. But if I had to start up Esperanza all over again, at some other time, in some other place, then I would do it.

'Oh Charlie,' she touches my arm again, reproachfully, and I move away from her. I remember she is like this. Eager as a child, touchy-feely, always clinging on to your arm or running her fingers through your hair.

'He means well. My brother has his own interests to consider too, you know.'

'I know.' I turn my body slightly so I'm out of range.

'You're still angry with me,' she accuses.

'No, Lourdes, I am not.'

'You know I . . . I do a lot for your centre, Charlie. I'm still involved with it.'

'I know that too.' And we've managed to keep away from each other all this time. We've avoided each other for so long that there is no longer any real need to, I realise.

'Do you also know that if it weren't for *your* involvement, Santos would have pulled out his support long ago?'

'He remembers my mother,' I tell her.

'He remembers *you*, and the man that you are. He remembers that he nearly had you for a brother-in-law.'

I fix my eyes on the towers again, slender and white; they reach up into little turrets at the top.

'I hear you're getting married,' she tells me softly now.

'Yup.' I heard she got married, too. 'And you?'

'Separated.' She shakes her head regretfully. Whoever he was, it must have hurt; her eyes are suddenly pained. 'He wasn't you,' she mutters, so low that I might have imagined it. So I let that be. I've got my own family now, there's no going back for her and me.

'Any children?' I ask unwillingly.

'One.' Her smile is suddenly radiant, despite the sadness. 'A boy. He'll be four in August.' Four.

'I'm happy for you, Lourdes.' Truly, I am.

'And . . .' she hesitates, 'you? I heard something – this lady you are marrying . . .'

'Julia.'

'Julia,' she says softly, 'she . . . she has a child already?'

'*We* have a child. His name is Hadyn.'

'He's yours?' She takes in a breath. 'Oh, I had thought . . . maybe the child was hers.' She bites her lip. 'Then, you have found some way to have children after all? You were told you could not.'

'You know my history, Lourdes.'

'You found some treatment?' she probes.

'No.' I look at her candidly. 'I did not. It just happened. These things sometimes do.'

'A miracle,' she breathes.

'It's true,' I laugh softly, 'a miracle.'

'Could it happen again?' she wonders out loud.

'Perhaps.'

'And she *knows*, this Julia? She knows that this child might be the only one? That you were told you could never have any children?'

I give her a hard look. She forgets herself now. She's asking the kind of questions that she might once have had the right to ask. But we do not share that relationship any more.

'Not for you to worry about, that, is it? If I have had one child, I can probably have more.'

'If we had known this, years ago,' her eyes are shining now, filled with regret, 'things between us might have turned out so differently.'

'No, Lourdes. Don't say that. You have a child now too. The child you so desperately wanted.'

'But I have never found a man to match you, Charlie.'

'Lourdes . . .'

'You think that I only regret not marrying you because now I see you can become a father?'

'It doesn't matter now. You have your boy and I have mine.'

Lourdes takes in a deep breath.

'You'll find another man to love you, Lourdes, a beautiful woman like you.'

'As much as you once did?'

'That was long ago and far away. But yes, why not?'

'Will you fight Santos if he tries to close down the centre?' She turns on me now.

'Tooth and nail, Lourdes. You know me.'

'You never fought for me,' she recalls softly.

'You wanted me to fight for you?' I look directly at her now.

'I *wanted* you to fight. I wanted you to persuade me to stay. I needed you to . . .' She runs out of words and just looks at me helplessly. 'When I told you that I *needed to know* I could have children, you just accepted that I was going,' she says at last. 'You never—'

'Don't.' I shake my head warningly. 'This'll go nowhere. I let you go because you wanted to go. I fight for the centre because those kids have no one else to fight for them. That's all.'

'Then maybe you are a knight in shining armour after all?' When she smiles at me now her eyes are accepting of the past, beautiful as I remember them.

'Maybe,' I accede.

'If I can help you I will,' she promises. 'I am so grateful we have met again, Charlie. It's been so hard – not being able to speak to you all these years. For us not to be on civil terms with each other.'

'I've always . . .' I begin, but trail off. 'Look, I could do with your friendship right now, Lourdes. For starters, you could begin by filling me in on all this business with Louis Baudelaire that they're not so keen to tell me about. It's more than just embezzlement, isn't it?' Do I imagine it, or is the colour draining from her face?

'I want to help you Charlie,' she glances towards the door, 'but not here. We'll meet soon. I'm in London in a few weeks' time. We'll speak then, okay? As *friends*, Charlie,' she puts in, sensing my hesitation. 'I know it can be nothing else, but I want you as my friend.'

'New year, new beginning,' I tell her. 'Let's take it from here, shall we?'

She reaches up quickly; her lips against my cheek are soft, compliant. 'That's all I needed to hear, Charlie.'

I turn away from her. 'That's settled then. Now, do you think I could use your phone? Mine's run out of charge and I need to phone Spain. Couldn't get through last night and they'll be wondering where I've got to.'

'Of course.' She indicates through to the living room. 'Close the door after you if you need some privacy.'

I've got a good feeling in my stomach, like I've just unravelled some knots in there that were lying heavily. Like I've closed the door on my past in some way.

The morning of this New Year, I can see through the window, is still peaceful and clear. There's an expectancy in the air, a promise of more good things to come. This is the year that I get married, I remind myself.

I pick up the phone and punch in the number. As I hear it connect at the other end, I wonder if my boy is awake yet. I wonder if Julia will put him on the phone. I close my eyes, hearing it ring for a moment, relishing the thought of hearing his voice again. I am so lucky to have him; Lourdes has reminded me of this. I want to tell them how much I love them. I will be seeing them soon.

But the phone rings and rings at the other end. Maybe they've cut the electricity off again because for some unfathomable reason, nobody picks it up.

Julia

'The phone,' Eva says. She hands it to me, her face white. 'It's for you.' Blue is sitting there, his head in his hands. He hasn't even had a chance to tell me what he came for yet, but no matter. This will no doubt be the news we've all been waiting for.

If Blue already knows it, by his face, it's not good.

'Hello?' My voice sounds crackly and strange. When I put the receiver to my ear I can tell straight off that this is a long-distance call. There's that echoey sound on the line. Oh, could it be Charlie?

'Charlie,' I breathe, 'is it you?'

'Julia,' an Englishwoman answers. Damn it, I wanted Charlie.

I get up and walk over to the window where the blinds are half-drawn and turn my face towards the outside. I can feel everybody at my back, hardly breathing, straining to hear. The dull fog outside is beginning to lift. On the green shutters outside of Agustina's villa window I can spy the lattice-work on an undisturbed spider's web, whitened with dust.

'Julia, this is Didi.' Didi. My housekeeper/sitter. She might be a messenger from another planet. I swallow.

'What is it, Didi?'

'Happy New Year!' she says brightly. She sounds happy. Of course she is. She doesn't know. 'I have a message from Charlie. He couldn't get through to Spain last night and he's been having trouble this morning too. He rang me and asked me to try. He thought you might have tried to phone home.'

'Where *is* Charlie? Where?'

'He gave me a number where he can be reached this morning, he said, but he's going to be travelling back down to Richmond. In all that hurry to get to Cambridge last night he never charged his mobile . . .' She seems to be rummaging about for the number; I can hear her.

'*What the heck was he doing in Cambridge?*' I mutter, half turning to my gathered audience. 'It's my housekeeper in the UK,' I tell them. You can almost hear the relief in the room.

'You have a number for Charlie?' Eva says the minute I put the phone down on Didi. 'You'd better ring him straight away.'

'Yes, I . . .' I take a look at Blue. He still hasn't told me what he came to tell me, yet.

'Perhaps I'd better come back a bit later,' he says.

'No,' I put a restraining hand on his arm, 'don't go.'

'I'm not sure if this is really my place,' he mutters, looking really uncomfortable. 'I thought you knew . . . you should really hear this from somebody else. Someone official.'

Good God, what does he mean? I want to know what he has to say and at the same time I'm terrified to hear it.

'Have they found him?' I stammer. I'm punching in the number that Didi gave me. If this is bad I want Charlie to be in on it as soon as possible . . .

'Not yet. It isn't that. Look – it might be nothing,' Blue starts and Roberto maddeningly pulls him to one side just as one of the aunties comes in and places a cup on a coaster in front of me. I could *so* do with some tea right now. Something comforting and familiar and . . . normal. But it is hot chocolate, not tea. My hands are trembling when I pick up the cup and put it to my lips. What is Blue quietly telling Roberto now? I frown. The number Didi gave me rings only a few times.

'Hello?' A woman with a low, sultry voice picks up. This time the line is crystal clear. I glance at the number I've just written down. Did I dial the wrong one?

'This is . . . this is Julia Fearon. I'm trying to locate Charlie Lowerby. I was told he'd be available on this number this morning.' I can hardly keep my voice from trembling.

'Of course, *Julia,*' she says, as if she knows exactly who I am. 'I'll fetch my brother to speak to you.'

Her brother? I hear her calling someone. That's when my knees give way beneath me. I half sit, half fall into the nearest chair, and Blue scrambles up to help me.

'I think Charlie's there,' I tell the assembled relatives. Thank goodness. Now he will come back. We will do this together.

'Julia? This is Santos.' Not Charlie, no. 'Charlie has just left us. He's gone back to Richmond. I'm sorry. He was trying to get hold of you this morning.' He pauses, noticing my silence. 'I hope all is well, my dear?'

No, all is not well.

I want to tell him but . . . he is a stranger. We have never met, though I have heard about Santos often enough from Charlie.

'Can you get hold of Charlie?' I croak. 'I need him to come home. Now.'

'Home?' He sounds puzzled. 'Have you and the child come back to the UK then?'

'No.' I look at Eva helplessly, tears running down my face. I hand her the phone because I can't speak any more. I cannot say the words.

'*¿Quién es?* Who is it?' She grabs the phone. She knows Santos; all her family does. She starts speaking rapidly to him in Spanish. I catch the gist of it. Hadyn has gone missing. They are still out there looking. No news yet. It doesn't look good.

I glance at Blue.

'I'd better be leaving,' he says.

'You're not leaving here before you tell me what it is you came up to say.'

I remember why the name Santos sounded so familiar now. It rang bells in my head the minute I heard it but I didn't

135

remember – Charlie's former fiancée is his sister. Has Charlie been staying with them? Is she the reason why I wasn't able to get hold of Charlie earlier? Our son has gone missing and he's been off partying with his old flame and her brother over the New Year – while we've been going mad with worry?

My fingers dig into Blue's arm. As he rises to leave, I rise with him. He isn't going anywhere until he tells me what he knows.

'Look, I don't know how true this is . . .' He puts his hand on my arm, as if to steady me. 'I have no verification of this whatsoever,' he adds, 'but I heard a ransom note for your son came in this morning. It was handed into the Arenadeluna police station in an unmarked envelope. Maria told me this morning it was her they handed it in to. Whoever it was who brought it paid a child who was playing outside to actually pass it over, so Maria didn't see the person herself. That's all I know,' he shrugs. 'Perhaps if *she* gets off the phone the police will be able to get through to you themselves?'

Charlie

Finally . . . somebody has picked the bloody phone up!

'*¿Diga?*' My brother's voice at the other end is curt, businesslike. Then, 'Carlos, *dios mío!* We've been trying every which way to get hold of you, man!'

'Sorry about that. I've been wandering about a bit since I got to the UK. How're my two doing?'

There's a long pause. My heart starts to pound. My brother's voice doesn't sound right when he finally answers me. 'Charlie, I'm sorry, it's not good news, *hermano*.'

'What's not good news?' What could have happened, what's my brother trying to tell me?

'You need to get back here,' he tells me tightly. 'There's been an incident.'

I am about to sip from a can of cold lemonade but something stops me. 'What's going on, Roberto?' I pick up on the strain in his voice. 'Just tell me what's happened.'

'Julia took Hadyn down to the beach yesterday,' he says carefully. 'But there was a . . . a bad wave. It took some others – two girls – out to sea. Hadyn is missing. They think it took him out, too.'

I put the lemonade can down on the melamine table with a jolt. Lopez looks at me, sees my face and frowns. I'm gripping his mobile so tightly I'm surprised it doesn't crumble like dust in my hands.

'He's . . . *gone*? We're sure of that?' No. Not my son, a voice in my head screams. It cannot happen like this . . .

'Julia seems to hope there will be a miracle.' My brother's voice is so broken I know he believes there can be no hope of any such thing. 'We have to get you back here. Look, there has been a ransom note – he might still be alive. We were out in force last night – over one hundred of us, searching for him all over Arenadeluna, making inquiries.'

'A ransom note?' My mind is spinning. This is bad, but not as bad as drowning.

'There's still hope, then?' His silence goes on too long for my comfort.

'Yes,' he says at last.

'That's not what you think though, is it?' I press. He's trying to offer me hope but I sense he doesn't believe it himself.

'Maybe, Carlos. Look, I don't want to lie to you. You'd want to know the truth. And I don't think he's been kidnapped.'

'How do you know?' I can feel my own breath coming hard and fast now, my heart beating in my chest. I watch the long line of colourless lemonade that has spilled out of my can. The bubbles fizz up in an orderly line along the surface of the table. In a second the liquid will reach the rim of the table. A split second later, inexorable as the tide, it will spill over the edge and will splatter onto the floor and I am powerless to stop it.

'Why do you say this?' I prompt him.

He doesn't want to continue, clearly.

'I've said enough over the phone, Charlie. There are some things that should never be said . . . over the phone. But I have heard other evidence that Hadyn wasn't taken by anyone. I haven't said anything to Julia yet because we thought it best to wait till you got here. She's taken it very badly, as you can imagine.'

'What kind of evidence?' I insist.

'Evidence pulled from the sea, *hermano*.' His voice is broken.

A body? Bits of a body? Oh, my dear God. There is nothing more that he needs to tell me.

I weigh my head in my hands.

'And Julia, where's Julia?' I need to speak with her.

'She's gone out, Charlie. She insisted. She still thinks she's going to find him. She doesn't know what I told you, remember? Don't worry – she's not alone.'

I look at Lopez, now, whose face remains carefully blank. This is the man who called me away from my family, pulled Tan Yeo off the case when Ngosi Ontome did not really urgently need my help at all. Just so I would speak to Santos for him. This is the man whose mishandling of the Louis Baudelaire affair has led to my life's work being threatened with closure.

I cannot take all this in. Life doesn't suddenly become so different, about-face in every which way – it just doesn't. Things change little by little; things change in stages so you have time to get used to them.

I have to go back to Spain. Dear God, I should have been there. This would never have happened if I had been there.

And Lopez – he looks curiously at me; his expression says – bad news? But he does not say a word, not a word. Which is a good thing because I might just throttle him with his own brace-straps if he does.

Charlie

I picked his blanket up from his cot last night. It is yellow with a row of white elephants strolling trunk-to-trunk across the top. His pyjamas were in there too, beside his Bap-Bap, all folded up, waiting for him to return but I felt . . . he wouldn't be. I don't know why that thought came to me. When I held his blanket to my face it still smelled of the sweet scent of him and that brought an ache to the deepest part of my guts.

All I could think was: I want him back! He was my only one, my little miracle. I want my boy back. How will I ever carry on without him? I do not want to. There is no point. Dear God, let us have something, some good news. I prayed for a miracle. I got down on my knees on the cold tiles last night and begged God, with all my heart and soul, to let me have him back. I could not think of how I would begin to face the days without him. I did not want to think of it. My heart was torn in two with an ache so great, a need so great, that I felt certain God must answer me; that he would not let us continue to suffer like this.

But after all the long hours of the night went by – so many dark hours, so many prayers – I felt not the slightest stirring of hope. It was as if God wasn't listening.

And I have had to face the facts.

I have been everywhere. Looked *everywhere.* My brother and his friends teamed up with me and we went over what I know they have done several times before; we have combed every single inch of this place. We came down to the very spot on the beach where the freak wave came in on New Year's Eve. They showed me the place where the girls were sitting with the children. The waves came up to a new high-water mark on the beach-head that afternoon one week ago.

Everything went. And he – *my boy* – had he been standing in the wrong place at the wrong time when the wave came, I saw that he would have been taken too. I did not let myself envisage it the last time they brought me here, and I do not now. I do not let his face come into my mind.

I think of it only as a likely fact. Anything else would be too much just now. When Rob puts his arm about my shoulders I do not move. I do not cry, even though the world suddenly feels so empty.

My boy. Can he really be gone?

I know it is what the family and the police and pretty much everyone else already believes. Bringing me here, showing me all this – this was their way of breaking it to me gently, that is all.

When someone is gone and you have nothing, the best you can hope to do is fill in the spaces in your head. You take what you know and you colour in the rest with your imagination, drawn with the tools of *the most likely scenario*. I am a scientist. I know how it goes.

So, one week in and we have not had any real positive evidence about what happened that day, other than a load of conflicting accounts about where Hadyn was located when the last person had a sighting of him. But we know that he was on that beach. We know that a big wave came. We know that a young girl drowned because of it. Her name was Salamanca.

They say that if he drowned and his body went out to sea then – with all the disruption in the water, and the unusually large fishes that were dredged up from the depths that day – there would be no evidence left to find. He would be *gone*. In my heart, I already believe this. But Julia does not believe it; she cannot see it.

When I first arrived back in Spain, she clung to me like a thing possessed. She would not let me go. I have had to put on a brave face for her. I cannot let her see my tears. The family told me that there was nothing they had been able to say or do that would comfort her at all, so I just held her. What could I have said?

I do not understand it myself.

When Abuela had a mass said in his name this morning, I went with them and kneeled on one of the pews at the front for a very long time. I have not been to mass in an age but it felt comforting to be there. I prayed for my son, then – that, wherever he was, God might be with him. I wished Julia had been there, but she wouldn't come. She just lay, sedated, on our bed, her eyes as dull as the lead buttons on the wooden church door, staring up at the ceiling.

She has come out with us this afternoon, though. We have just walked the length of the empty beach again. The waves are noisy today, the water overcast and dirty, echoing the overcast Spanish sky. The sea smells of conch shells and the entrails of fish gutted at sea.

'If I had not brought him here,' she says, her face shivering, 'then he would still be with us, wouldn't he?'

'You mustn't blame yourself.' I put my arm around her to draw her in close. 'If I had not left Spain when I did, then maybe he wouldn't have been on the beach either?' I offer.

'No,' she pulls a thin humourless smile, 'because then I wouldn't have needed to get away from your grandma, Charlie!'

I frown. She doesn't mean that.

'Haven't they told you yet?' She's biting her lip, pulling away from me now. No one has told me anything. What could have gone on in those few hours after I left? And what could it possibly signify now, in the light of what's happened since?

'They haven't told me anything, J.' I rub my hands together, blowing on them.

'They haven't told you *why* Agustina got angry with me?' Why is Julia standing there biting her nails, bringing this up now?

'It doesn't matter, J. Surely – whatever it was – it can't matter?' It can't. It won't. The light of my life has gone out. Nothing else will ever matter to me quite so much again. Doesn't she see that?

'Charlie, I've been holding something back from you. And it does matter. Very much.' Her eyes are shining, full of pain. I get a bad hollow feeling in my belly. She's not going to tell me Hadyn wasn't mine after all, is she? No. I hold my breath.

'Charlie, I was . . . I've been married once before.'

I just look at her. The hollow feeling in my innards doesn't go away. I stop walking, grab hold of her arm now, but she pulls back, guilty as hell.

'You can't have been. You'd have told me, surely? Why wouldn't you have told me something like that?' I'm saying these words automatically, but all I can think is: no, it can't be true. That she's lied to me. On top of everything else that's gone wrong in my life, this girl I was preparing to marry – she's *lied* to me. If Julia's done that – how much do I really know her at all?

If she could pretend to love me so much, that I was the only one, and then for it not to be true . . . What else might she be capable of?

'I didn't love him, Charlie. It was a mistake. It was *nothing*.'

'This isn't . . .' my voice chokes, 'just a little thing, Julia. You wouldn't have just forgotten to mention it.' No. Of course not. She deliberately kept it from me.

'*Why?*'

Her voice seems to elude her. She opens up her hands, shaking her head, unable to speak.

'Are you still married to him?'

She shakes her head, standing there hunched, her face looking so thin and white.

'Are you *sure?*'

'No, of course not,' she whispers. 'It was . . . a long time ago,

143

Charlie. And only for *three* months. I thought if I told you, you'd think—'

'Who is it?' My mind is racing now. 'Someone I know? One of your old friends?'

'No!' The tears are flowing freely down her face now. 'Nobody you've ever met. No one you've even heard of. He was so . . . *unimportant* to me . . .'

So unimportant that you kept him a total secret. Right. The look I give her in response to that doesn't even begin to express the dark bile I'm feeling at this moment. It's as though I've got a snake curled inside me that's been waiting my whole lifetime to uncoil and lash out at someone. I can't get my head around this. I thought I'd had as much bad news as a man could take, that it couldn't get any worse; but I was wrong.

'Is this why you didn't accept my proposal straight away?' I had asked her the moment we knew she was expecting, and she'd seemed pleased, but she hadn't agreed to wear my ring until now, just before we booked this holiday to Spain.

'Any other secrets?' I fling at her, but I'm so angry that what I really want to do is slap her.

I don't, of course.

Instead I run up ahead and kick the rickety boundary fence where the boats are tied up into a hundred shards of wood. I smack the posts so hard with my arm I break a couple of them clean in two. Roberto can sort it. This is all his field, isn't it? Making sure everything's neat and tidy for the tourists; improvements and heritage. But *I'm* not going to have anyone to inherit anything that I accrue in my lifetime, am I?

Because every single woman I love betrays me.

'Charlie.' She's caught up with me. 'I'm sorry. I didn't love him; you don't understand how it was. Don't do that. Please stop doing that.'

Love! What does she know about love?

'No. You stop. You stop pretending to be somebody and

something that you're not. You're not the devoted fiancée you made yourself out to be, are you, Julia?' I bite my lip before continuing, but she knows what's going on in my mind.

She puts her hand to her face, her whole body going rigid.

'I didn't *neglect* our son, Charlie. I never just left him on the beach . . .'

'I never said that, did I?'

'No, but it's important that you believe that. Even if you don't believe a single other word I ever tell you,' she hiccups. 'And you have to believe my reason for not telling you about Sebastian as well.'

Sebastian! What kind of fucking stupid, stuck-up name is that?

I stand there with my arms folded, glowering at her as she says, 'It was because I didn't want you to think I'd take our marriage as lightly as I took it with him.'

'That's a comfort.' I narrow my eyes, turn to look out at the uneasy sea. 'So when *we* split, I might just be important enough to be mentioned to your next man?'

'You're taking this all wrong, Charlie. I didn't tell you because . . . Our relationship, having the baby, it's all happened so quickly. I guess I felt rather fragile around it. I didn't know how you'd react. You've always come across as —' she stammers — 'a little on the jealous side.'

No, no, no!

She's lied to me. That's all that I can think of. The thought fills my head till it's louder than her voice, till it's louder than anything, even than the crashing waves that are cascading behind us onto the shore.

'I didn't love him.' Her voice is faint and broken but it doesn't matter any more because, suddenly, I see it. My son is gone. And this woman is not for me after all.

Nothing holds me here.

I have a life that's calling me. People who need me. My work appointment book is full, even though something in the very

145

heart of my life feels now so empty. I had a text from Angus this morning. I need to reply to it, tell him that I'm coming home.

'Charlie,' she's clinging to my arm, rubbing it to get my attention, 'Charlie, you're not listening to me . . .' but her words fall about my ears like all the other words that people have spoken to me since my brother told me of my son's loss. They do not matter.

'I'm going back to London,' I tell her. 'He's not here. You can stay on if you like but we won't find him here now. We never will.'

She has stopped clinging to me now, her misery palpable, but I don't give a damn what she's feeling or what she's thinking. At this moment I feel that she can go her own way from now on as far as I'm concerned.

All is *como dios quiera*, as Agustina says – all is as God wills.

Maybe I was the one never meant to have a son?

And maybe this is all as it was always meant to be?

Julia

I go down to the police station every day. I know the route. I walk it now. From Roberto's house, all the way downhill into the centre, it takes me thirty-five minutes. I go there first thing. The girl who mans the desk in the mornings is the friendliest of them all. She talks to me when she's not too busy, and sometimes, when I've been sitting there for a long while, she'll offer to make me a drink.

'You will find him soon,' she tells me, and then to emphasise her point, she says it again in Spanish: '*Le encontrarás pronto*,' she soothes, her fair hair falling forward as she leans over the worn desk.

I wait for news.

'Where is her husband?' the *jefe* – the boss – of the station asked.

'*¿Ya se fue?*' He's already gone, she told him in Spanish. It is true. Charlie has left. In the end, he stayed for three weeks only. We argued, that day on the beach. At least, he yelled at me when he learned about Sebastian. Afterwards, he apologised, he said he'd never meant to shout, that he was fraught and that was just one shock too many coming on top of all the others. But there's been a distance between us since that day. He hasn't forgiven me yet for my deception. And I can't say I blame him.

The girl in the station told the *jefe* more, but so fast I could only try to imagine the gist of it. *Her husband is a surgeon. They say he accepts the boy is lost. He saw no point in staying...*

I was *mad* at Charlie when he left. I just waved at him from

147

the door, tight-lipped. Even if he was angry at me, he should have had a bit more hope for Hadyn. I know why he has gone. I do understand it, though it tears me in two. I know he has other people waiting on him, and he wanted me to go home with him.

But I feel in my heart that Hadyn is still near. I still go walking along the beach and down all the side-alleys every afternoon, and often Blue comes with me. He won't come to the police station in the morning, but he'll go anywhere else I want him to go. He's a little eccentric, I know, but now I've got to know him more I believe he has a good heart. He says that, ever since that day on the beach when I begged him to help me, he's felt *involved*. It's better than walking along all on my own now that Charlie's gone.

For the last solid week I have been dreaming about Nana Ella. I think she means me to stay close, not to go too far. Maybe I need to wait here to see if another ransom note will come in?

I asked if I would be allowed to see the first one and the girl at the desk said, 'Of course, of course!' and she went inside to where the policemen of the Policia Local sit, drinking coffee and doing their paperwork and asked the *jefe*.

He told her I could not see it because it was 'evidence', if the case should ever come to court. I could not understand that. 'I won't take it away,' I begged her. 'I just want to see it.' I wanted to see it with my own eyes so it could start to be real. Because what is there left that is real, any more? Everything that I thought was real is crumbling to dust in my hands.

I was not allowed to see it. The girl shook her head regretfully, knowing how much I needed it and unable to give it to me.

The *jefe* refuses to talk to me. He always stops for a fraction of a second when he sees me, when he's on his way in or out of the station. His deep brown eyes look directly into mine, a frank, inquisitive look, as much as to say – *what, still here?* And it's always me who turns away first, as if his look overpowers mine.

'Let me see the note,' I called out to him the first time I saw him. But he's never actually spoken to me. And they always come back with, 'No es posible, señora, we have nothing here for you today. You go home now.' Always polite, but firm, and I see what they are thinking in their eyes: *she needs to go home. Someone should come and take this woman away from here.*

I do not know why but I cannot go home. My head says – *go, just go!* And my heart says – *there is no way you are leaving here with nothing.* Because that is all I have managed to garner in the weeks since he was lost: nothing.

How is it possible that there could be *nothing*?

I know every inch of that tiny little waiting area. The floor, a dull sandy-grey colour, remains sticky and none-too-clean, even though the woman always comes with her bucket and mop first thing. The police officers who come and go are mainly in their thirties, I would say, except for the *jefe*, who is rotund, with greying temples. I reckon he must be in his late fifties or early sixties. There's a jovial atmosphere in here most of the time but everyone knows that what the *jefe* says, goes. They don't mess around. One time they brought in a couple of drunken drivers who'd been in a brawl after a smash-up and the girl told me, 'The *jefe* says you must go now, señora. We will call you if we hear anything.'

But where else was I supposed to go?

Besides, I had questions, so many questions, and no one to ask them of except the desk girl who took over from Maria. Not that she ever has any answers for me.

What I can't understand is why they are taking so *long* over things. I know that Roberto has spoken of 'evidence taken from the sea', but it is all very hush-hush. I know they are investigating a big fish because the girl told me that much.

But how long can it take to investigate a fish?

How *big* can the fish be?

Is it a shark?

When I ask her, her eyes go wide and she shakes her head

149

rapidly, *Don't ask me, don't ask! You must make an appointment to speak to the jefe*, she says.

But when I go back that afternoon, she says she cannot give me an appointment. She hands me a small brown packet instead. And when I unwrap it, I find a modern-day version of the *Madonna de Las Lágrimas*. The Madonna of Tears, inside.

'She will help to find those who are lost at sea,' the girl tells me earnestly, as I finger the little figurine, perplexed. This one is plastic. You can see the seams where the mould was set, right the way down the length of her robe. She's been painted in blue and white, with cheeks as rouged as any whore's. But apparently she's going to help me find my baby.

'Only the *jefe* can give out appointments for his own time,' the girl explains haltingly to me. Maybe if I wait, I can catch him as he goes past? She shrugs apologetically. While in bed last night, I put the plastic Madonna by my bed and I dreamed so clearly of my nana Ella that I could have reached out my hand and touched her.

'Look after the boy for me.' When Nana Ella turns from her vigil, eyes closing as she sinks into the high-backed chair, she wants me to see what she sees; so, I look through the bright windows where the wide shafts of sunlight fall and through her eyes I glimpse him.

I see his bare heels kicking up the turf as he runs. The emerald grass is as soft as a breath beneath his feet. The expanse of it flows right up to the limestone edge of the land before it drops away towards the beach, and when he pauses there, his young breath coming hard and short, I see his eyes are focused on the horizon, on distant lands, to all the places he will one day travel to.

When I breathe in I can smell the summer scents that fill his lungs; the clover and the sundew and the rugged wild thyme. When I call him, he looks back only long enough for

*me to see that his blue eyes are full of the deep laughter of
long ago years, and then he leaps down into the dunes and
he's off again, chasing his friends, and I know that he will
not come home until the sun is long gone down.*

*She sleeps now, and the gentle sound of her snoring breaks
the spell. Outside the windows I can see the sky is leaden.
The green fields have given way to a concrete-coloured row
of tenements. And the boy she looked for – I close the
window firmly, drowning out the noise – he's grown up
and long gone from the Bluestack Hills in the county of
Donegal.*

This morning the police phoned Eva and asked her to come and
take me home because they were 'too busy' to have me sitting
there on their bench. I think maybe I made them feel guilty, just
by being there. They were laughing and smoking out back, having
coffee and *churros*.

When I complained, when I cried out that I was *only waiting*,
reminding them that I had been promised that the fish evidence
would surely come in today, the *jefe*'s deputy came out of the
back to see what all the noise was about. I didn't like his face or
his demeanour. Hands on hips, he told me very politely but
firmly that I had to go.

Eva was mortified to be called down to the police station to
bring me home.

She asks the same questions over and over again, they said to her.

But only – I had to bite my tongue – because they will not
answer any of them!

If only someone would explain exactly what was going on, I said
to Eva, I would be okay. But nobody would speak to me. I did not
know why.

After that happened, I swallowed my pride and took some of
Agustina's advice and went and asked Roberto for help. She told
me that without Roberto's help there was no way I was going to

get a meeting with the *jefe*. Without the *jefe*, I was never going to get any information.

'Of course!' Roberto said magnanimously, if not a little wearily, when I asked him. He was none too happy when he found out that I'd been spending my mornings, since Charlie left, at the police station. He'd assumed the women had been keeping me occupied, I heard him tell his wife.

It wasn't their fault if they'd failed in that endeavour. When we'd gone to the church one morning, lighting candles, hearing the mass in Spanish, none of it had given me any relief at all. I didn't want to pray. I *couldn't* pray. God wasn't helping me. Agustina and Eva weren't happy when I refused to stay to hear the full service.

'Come with us to buy some groceries,' Eva offered. As we walked down there Agustina kept repeating to me that she knew what I was going through, '*Te consuelo*,' she kept repeating, thumping her chest. I took care to walk along on the other side of Eva and not beside her. I couldn't stand to see her brimming over with tears all the time. For some inexplicable reason, her tears only made me feel *angrier*.

They took me to the market, but we could not get away from all the people who wanted to ask questions about me. They were curious and friendly for the most part, but several women asked, *Why did she let him go in the water?*, as it had been reported in the paper. At the olive stall, I *swear* I saw one of the people who had been on the beach on the day he disappeared; the strange woman with the dark sunglasses who had sat there in the heat with all her clothes on, looking out to sea. When she saw me, she turned immediately away, and I wanted to go after her and ask her if she knew anything, if she remembered anything; but by then Agustina had already got too hassled and bothered. She had got tired of defending me, explaining to everyone that I had never simply *abandoned my son* to go and get myself changed. Besides, that woman with the dark glasses was *una loca*. Eva dismissed my contention that the poor lady might have been a reliable witness of any sort. She was known locally to be a bit of a loner, maybe a little 'touched' as my nana would have put it. I did not feel like arguing. If she was local, I would see her again. I could check her out another time. So we went home and I asked Roberto to help and once Roberto asked for a meeting with the *jefe* – hey presto, the guy was suddenly free.

Just like that.

So this afternoon we have come down to the station together. Except now that we are here, the deputy guy is shaking his head at me. 'Just him,' he says.

I cannot believe it! Roberto goes through the doors without giving me a backwards glance. 'I won't be long,' he promises the deputy. 'I have to get back to work this afternoon.' I can feel my heart hammering in my chest, watching his back go through that door. I'm the one who should be going in there, not him . . .

When the girl at the desk turns her back for a moment, I take my chance and slip out the back after him. What, after all, have I got to lose? I am scared, oh yes, I am, but I will pretend for the moment that I am not; that I am 'fearless Fearon' as my old friend Naseem used to call me.

I find the *jefe*'s room in an instant. It is only a small station. I can hear Roberto and the boss laughing and exchanging pleasantries like old comrades. I push the door open and the atmosphere becomes subdued in an instant.

'Come in, come.' The *jefe* beckons me in. I see him and Roberto exchange this 'what are we going to do with this woman?' look between them.

'We are,' he places his polished nails towards his chest, 'very sorry to keep you waiting too long, señora.' He smiles thinly at me and says something else to Rob that I cannot understand. 'I understand you are not happy with this?' he turns to me at last.

'I don't . . . I can't find anyone who can speak to me.' I edge

153

away from the door and come and sit down timidly on the metal chair beside Rob. The *jefe* looks at Roberto again.

'This is because she cannot speak Spanish?' he says in his own language. 'She cannot find someone to talk to?'

'No,' I tell him. 'No one will explain things to me.'

'What do you want us to explain, señora?' We both glance at Rob, who's twisting uncomfortably in his chair. 'For this, you have your family, no? They speak to you.'

'But they don't *know* anything.'

'I have explained to her that the matter is under police investigation.' Rob lifts an eyebrow at my raised voice. 'She understands this.'

'But why is it all taking so long?' I lean forward now. 'I mean, to look inside a fish? How can that take such a long time? What is the evidence you are looking for, anyway? Nobody will tell me. *You* tell me.'

Again, those penetrating brown eyes searching mine. A long silence that stretches interminably. Rob bends his head at last and mutters something to the *jefe*. It will be something along the lines of: *you see, this is why we do not say anything to her; she is hysterical, overemotional, a typical woman. But she has lost her child. What else can you expect?*

'He says, there is nothing else to tell you.' Roberto makes up his own version of what the *jefe* says in return. 'He says if they heard anything you would be the first to know it. He says he has been patient with you, but now you cannot hang around the police station, hindering the important work being done here . . .'

'Why can't I see the note?'

The *jefe*'s eyebrows go down now. He taps his fingers in a brisk motion on the desk in front of him, swings around in his swivel chair and pulls open a metal filing cabinet to his side. He takes out a file and pores over some papers in there. I recognise the form that policewoman made me fill out that day on the beach. I see the words I wrote in my scribbled handwriting: 'Blackberry

House' on the place where the address goes. He thumbs through the notes but they're all official-looking documents that I can make out. Then he looks up.

'The note is no longer here,' he says to Rob.

I'm not actually convinced he's gone through all those papers carefully enough. And how could it not be there?

'What does he mean?' I am trying – very hard – not to raise my voice. 'Where could the note have gone?' Is there no accountability around here?

'It could have gone to forensics?' Rob offers.

'*No era importante!*' the *jefe* attests. It was of no importance anyway.

'But . . . it was evidence,' I choke. 'That's what they told me. How can he say it isn't important, now? Well, *have* they sent it to forensics? Is that where it is?'

I see a muscle twitch in Roberto's jaw. Very tactfully, he relays the question.

The *jefe* snaps the folder shut. He puts it back in its place in the metal cabinet and slides the door smoothly closed.

'Who knows?' He pulls a face. 'I cannot know where every single paper in my station is at every single moment, señora,' he says in perfect English. 'We are doing what we can.'

And so I have come home from the police station and I have learned something else: that there are too many hours in every day and too many hours in the night. What do we need with so many hours? The hours are relentless and unending. And each moment of each hour is like a huge gaping chasm into which I perpetually fall, because there is no end to it and no bottom to it. Because after the end of every hour, there are only more hours.

Because there are so many hours to fill, I have brought the watering can down to the geraniums to water them all in their pots on the patio. I have taken all Eva's washing down now that the sun is not pulling the line up too high.

When I look out over the tops of the terraces the view that

winks back at me is the same view that it was on the morning my son disappeared. From here, I can see a little lad drop his pants and pee into a street corner. I can see the rolled-up petals and flower garlands left over from the Festival de las Lágrimas hanging from every door. I can see all the melted-chocolate browns and the orange hues and the yellows of the walls in all the houses, the gaudiness and tawdriness underneath the bright and beautiful sunshine of this land.

But I cannot see my boy.

Julia

It has been only six weeks since my son disappeared and already they have sent me home. Roberto said I could not stay in his house any longer. I could not do any further good staying behind, he said, though I begged him to let me stay on.

At that point Charlie had already been gone three weeks, convinced that there was no further use in staying, but I thought I would stay in Spain forever.

How could I leave? I thought: I will not leave this place until I have solid news of Hadyn's whereabouts; until I know for certain if he is alive or dead.

I thought I could do it – that it might be possible to keep on looking long enough. I might be walking down a narrow street in Arenadeluna, and then he would suddenly be there, holding someone's hand. Or maybe being caught at the bottom of the slide in the leafy municipal park.

But when I went there, the park gates were closed with a sign announcing 'Extensive improvements for the beautification of Arenadeluna.'

So I thought I might find him along the seashore, hidden amongst the hordes of people that came and went. But the sea grew much colder after the New Year, much rougher.

January wore on and all the Christmas decorations were pulled down and every day seemed grey and endless because there were always so many people in every single place I went; so many people to scrutinise, so many children to take stock of, so many faces. I got so weary I could not concentrate.

And I missed Charlie.

The days went by; so many days I could not count them. Then yesterday I walked smack-bang into a lamppost and bruised all the side of my face so badly that Roberto, his own face dark and brusque, said, 'Enough!' and booked me on the next plane out of Spain. When I left the house this morning, Abuela clung to me, a fierceness and a desperation in her embrace that did nothing but leave me cold.

I know full well what the loss of Hadyn has meant to their family. I can see it on every one of their faces. Through it all, not one of them has spoken to me with any recrimination, no one has blamed me. They have been the very face of kindness. I know they want me to go home only for my own good, because I can't achieve any more by being there. And maybe they are right. I can't even *think*. It's as though I've been trapped in some strange cycle of numbness and I can't think what else to do. In her emails, Alys has kept urging me to return home. She's rung me nearly every day. She even offered to fly out but the family said no, they had no space. Everything that could be done *was* being done, they kept telling me.

I just could not see what they were doing. Charlie has put Roberto in charge of everything. He's our first port of call with the Spanish police over there because he knows all the local officers. We are lucky in that. We have a good advocate in his brother, Charlie tells me: the best. He says there is nothing more we could achieve by being there in person ourselves. If we are needed we will be called straight away.

But I know Charlie does not believe we will ever be needed.

In Spain, he tells me, they are still chasing up leads. Roberto is following everything. But whenever I speak to Roberto his voice is always so deadpan, so hopeless. He speaks to me for as few minutes as he can politely get away with, and makes some excuse to get away. All along, they have been looking for evidence that Hadyn drowned, I think. Not evidence that he still lives. They are doing some tests on a large merluza that a fisherman trawled up further along the coast. Charlie won't tell me much about it. They asked me to give them the top that matches the little shorts Hadyn was wearing at the time so they know what they are looking for.

I would have liked to have spoken to Maria again, but she left Spain just a few days into the New Year. Apparently she came up to see me a couple of times but both occasions – so they tell me – I was sleeping. Funny, because I would say I have not actually slept for the last six weeks at all. I must have done, but I do not remember it. But anyway, Maria – she left – and Diego too. I must try and get a mobile number for her. Diego said he was going to ask his 'underground' friends, didn't he? He told me that the night Hadyn went missing. He said it and then he never came back to me again.

Yesterday – before I bruised my face, before they forced me to get on this plane – I asked Eva: what if Hadyn really *was* abducted on the beach that day? Who might have done such a thing? There was that note that Blue told me about, I remember. The one that was handed in at the police station.

But Eva only pulled a face. She looked uncomfortable and sad. Give it up, she seemed to say. I am made to feel it is bad form to think this way. As if there is something distasteful about my clinging on to hope; as if it is all just too pathetically desperate . . .

But what if that note that was handed in *wasn't* nothing? Hadyn could originally have been taken for a ransom but, as we were never given the note, the kidnappers might have decided to use him for some other purpose. Roberto – oh, sometimes I *hate* that man! – dismisses everything so easily. He doesn't want to go there. But I have to look into the darkness, because if I don't, and if he is still there, hidden away somewhere by some evil paedophiles or slave traders or even people who just sell babies on to childless couples . . . then, if I do not look, he will never be found.

Blue agrees with me. We've been seeing quite a bit of each other since Charlie left. It turns out he's done quite a bit of undercover work helping out a friend of his who is an ex-policeman turned private detective. So he might be very useful. Last week we went out to coffee and I made notes on the things we talked about;

    i. *Ex-policeman friend of Blue's (one time private eye) confirms that over 100 children are reported missing along the coast each year. Becoming something of a problem (not something they'd want shouted from the rooftops though).*

    ii. *Most likely scenarios for abduction are: taken by recently bereaved mother; abduction 'to order' – either for childless couple or individual or else by gangs working in the slave trade.*

    More unusually, people (especially with uncommon physical features) may be taken for body parts trade.

    Currently – 35,000 people living in Arenadeluna. 7,000 of these immigrants; 3,500 are illegals. There are people hiding all over the place, all of the time. Most of them in plain view. Maybe that's where Hadyn will be, too?

    Ask why Roberto has not got a poster campaign going? This should be standard procedure.

    Blue's email and mobile number.

    Contact him re. getting Maria and Diego's address in UK

Blue agrees with me that the family aren't doing all they might to look into these things. He was horrified that Charlie left so early. He said if it had been his son, he wouldn't have. I told him off when he said that because I know Charlie loved his son to bits. It's not that he doesn't care, it's that he doesn't know what else to do.

I don't either, but I'm going to find out what needs to be done next. Even if it means I have to keep some of it quiet from Charlie and the family.

Charlie

'Look at this.' Julia's only been back from the relative warmth of Spain for a couple of weeks. She pulls the cord and the curtains part on a grey garden scene. 'The first day of March. It's going to snow later on. Did you know?'

The first day of March, she says. *Two months since he disappeared*, is what she means.

I wince as she turns and I catch a glimpse of what she did to her face; maybe that's her bruised heart that Julia's wearing on her sleeve.

How the hell am I going to tell her the news?

I should say it to her now, tell her about the phone call that came in late last night while she was sleeping. I should put her out of her misery but I know full well that embedded in that misery of not knowing also lies her hope – I don't want to steal that from her too soon.

Julia pulls in her woolly cardigan about her shoulders. She's got a sweatshirt on underneath that I see. She's got jogging pants on, not PJs. There's a slightly red look about her nose and cheeks. I left her sleeping but I've been up well over an hour already – could she have been out?

'Where've you been?'

She shrugs.

'Just looking at the icicles. They look so pretty under the streetlights. Hadyn would love them.'

'He would.' He would *have*, I think to myself.

'Do you remember that time we first met?' She comes and kneels down on the living room carpet beside me. She has to look to find a little space. I'm surrounded by my island of Esperanza papers; *marooned* on it, I think.

'Yeah.' I give a small laugh. 'I yelled at you, right? I got hot under the collar about all the emaciated models posing against the banquet of food in a village full of undernourished kids . . .'

'But you were man enough to apologise to me too,' she reminds me, 'when you realised you'd made a mistake about me.'

'And you were sweet enough to forgive me.' I look at her openly. Is she thinking about how I reacted in Spain when she opened up to me about her first marriage? 'J,' I lean in towards her, 'I meant it when I apologised to you in Spain, too. I was out of order. It was bad timing, that's all. Learning you'd kept something like that from me – coming on top of everything else – it was the last straw.'

She swallows.

'It was a dumb thing to have done, I know that. I got myself into a twist over it.'

'*But?*' I lean in closer, touching her nose with my nose. She rewards me with a very rare smile.

'Charlie, I love you. You know that. I just need to know that we're on the same side. If I knew that, I'd feel freer to be open with you about . . . a lot of things.'

I sit back.

'Is there something else we need to talk about, J?'

She sighs. Runs her fingers through her hair, and then her hand comes back round to stop over her face.

'I don't want to have to pretend to you,' she says at last, 'that I've given up looking for our son. Just because I've come home. Just because Roberto tells you that there's no news, that nothing is happening . . .'

But something has *happened, J!*

'Julia, I need to—'

'I wish I had something as important to me as the Esperanza Centre is to you.' Her eyes are shiny. 'Then maybe I wouldn't have our son in my head *all the time.*'

No, I think, but you'd have other worries. When I look about me at the paper-trail I've become embroiled in, my heart sinks: letters and emails from Lopez and Lourdes; a whole stack of files over there on potential new sponsors for EC, should Santos choose to bow out; still more correspondence on practical stuff – the residential block needs a new bathroom; another asking for guidelines on what to do around the 'grey areas' regarding when people should be asked to leave to make space for new occupants in the rehabilitation suite. She follows my gaze.

'So much work. Where did it all start?' Her hands open questioningly.

I sigh.

'I got involved in the *pro bono* work not long after I started working for Angus,' I tell her softly. 'We were working on a Guatemalan guy. He came in with a great big tumour covering one whole side of his face. He said he'd had it four years. Angus took him on when it got so bad it was threatening the sight in one of his eyes and the pain had stopped this man from being able to work any more.' Julia winces. 'Well, we removed what we could of it – most of it, in fact – and did a bit of muscular reconstruction work so he'd be better able to move that side of his face afterwards. I forget the man's name now. The main thing I remember about it is the boy.' Julia shuffles in a little bit closer to me now and I can feel that she's cold. She looks so quiet and still, almost as if she's holding in her breath.

'What about the boy?' she prompts me.

'I remember it'd been raining that day. I'd come up to Drapers Street in a bit of a hurry. I was feeling cold and I was still at the stage where I wanted to impress Angus. But then out there in

164

front of the railings I saw a little boy. He had that look on his face that you sometimes see on the gorillas at the zoo.'

'What look is that?' Her eyes light up a little but her laugh still sounds sad.

'Like he'd been waiting in one place for a very long time, you know? I called to him and he scarpered but then – the next day – there he was again. Waiting.' I trail off. She won't know what it brought back to me, seeing that lad there. 'That child. It was as if he was waiting for someone to come and rescue him and . . .' I look at her and she's smiling sadly.

'And . . . ?'

'And the one he was waiting for . . . was never going to come.'

'You could tell all that,' she says softly, 'just by looking at him?'

'It struck me as odd.' I avoid her question. 'This boy – so young – out there all on his own. I thought maybe his mother was inside visiting someone who'd had a procedure done and that he'd kept sneaking out, but when he was still there on my way home that night . . .'

'What did you do?'

'I came up behind him quietly, and nabbed him before he could scarper off again. And he felt . . . Julia, he felt so thin underneath that big coat of his. I could feel all his bones. And then he turned in my grasp and looked at me again. There was nothing of him, I swear, but in his eyes there was this huge, powerful determination to . . . survive.'

'That's *good*,' she says, her eyes shining.

That Guatemalan boy, the truth is, he reminded me of me. He reminded me of being in that terrible place of waiting when, in reality, all hope has fled beyond your grasp. The waiting beyond all reason because there is nothing else, because there is nothing you can do but wait. Because sometimes your life is in someone else's hands and you have to concede that, ultimately, we are all in the hands of God.

'She'll come, lad, she'll come. But in her own good time,
you'll see. She's frightened that you won't know her any
more, son. She looks . . . different, now.' We'd stopped by the
place where Dad's green car was parked up against the wall.
I noticed it had rust spots on the bonnet, mud ingrained into
the wheel rims – and that felt unbearably sad because it meant
something big had changed in the world outside; that car had
always been Dad's pride and joy. How would my ma look
different? Had she dyed her hair, I wondered? Would she be
wearing different clothes to the ones she usually wore? Dad
patted my hand in the way he had when he wanted to go. I
grabbed hold of him. I put my arms around his battered leather
coat and wouldn't let him go. He found that hard, I know. 'I
need to be back in Spain with you, Dad,' I'd told him. 'I don't
want them looking after me here. I want you to do it.'

'I am looking after you,' he'd replied. 'Just in a quiet way.'
That's when he gave me the St Joseph medallion.

He put it in the palm of my hand and he just went.

'Turned out he was the Guatemalan's son.' I bring my mind back
to Julia now. 'Nobody had fed or seen to this boy for three days.
He'd been brought in with his dad but when the father wasn't
able to look after him . . .' I spread my hands. 'Anyhow, Santos
was there at the time. He'd come in for a minor op. We got
talking about the need to have some peripheral care for these
cases, family support. Backup, that kind of thing.'

'Who took the child in?'

'While his father recuperated, Santos's sister Lourdes did. She
always had a soft spot for kids.'

'That's how you two met?'

I shake my head.

'No. We met . . . a long time before that. When I was still at
school. She took a great interest in the whole project from the
beginning. It was her enthusiasm that pulled Santos in.'

'Her enthusiasm for the project?' Julia shoots me a glance now. 'Or for *you*?'

I sidestep that question too.

'For her part, Lourdes has always been hugely committed to helping the centre out. She visits them more than I do. She told me – her commitment probably cost her her marriage.'

Julia glances up at me. Will it cost you yours? her eyes seem to say.

'Everything . . . everything seems so huge these days.' She gives a small laugh. 'I used to feel like . . . like Cleopatra, or like Hannibal with his elephants – an organiser of military proportions. When I worked for Brasenose,' she rolls off her knees and sits right up against my thighs, which brings to mind how long it has been since we've touched each other, 'I used to think there was nothing I couldn't do. I don't know what's happened to me.'

A solitary tear rolls out of the corner of one eye and drops off the end of her cheek. 'When I had Hadyn, my world grew very focused in, you know. And now he's not here any more – it's stayed that way. I only know about small things now. Little, detailed things like how many teaspoons of plant feed per litre I should use for the plant in the bathroom; how many minutes it's safe to leave the carpet cleaner on the rug before it starts to bleach the colours out . . .'

'Domestic things,' I say, but she runs on, her eyes looking vague and watery.

'I feel as if I'm a microscope honed right down to the edges of visibility.'

'You could go back to Brasenose, in time?' I suggest. 'Once you're feeling better. He'd jump at the chance. He was that put out when he learned you intended to be a full-time stay-at-home mum.'

'I don't want to go back.' She shakes her head. 'It had begun to lose the meaning it once had for me. Hadyn brought new meaning into my life. I *still* want to be with Hadyn . . .'

167

'Then help me with my work,' I offer. 'It would give you something else to focus on, Julia. You're becoming too insular, that's all. Other people need the kind of support you could offer them.' Helping others would help her too, I know that. I glance at the green folder Lourdes sent me last week. Julia doesn't need to get involved in any of the politics of it – the uglier side.

'In an ideal world it sounds like . . . a very lovely thing to do.' She smiles softly. 'I might be needed back here yet, though. There might be *developments*. It wouldn't be fair to commit.' She picks up the end of one folder gingerly. As if, by feeling the true weight of it, she might have to drop it.

I take in a breath. I've got to tell her. *Now.*

'Roberto phoned me last night.' I take the folder carefully out of her hands. And now Julia's hands are like alabaster in my own. Still as a statue, but her dark eyes drink in the truth. She grips my fingers a little tighter when I do not speak.

'He says they've confirmed a match.' My throat is tight. 'He says the blue material they recovered from the fish – it matches the fibres from that top of Hadyn's that you gave them. They were part of the same set.'

Her mouth has dropped slightly open. 'So that means . . .'

'It means he went into the water, Julia. It means he's gone.' I have to be strong now because I remember that the first cut is the deepest. Even now – as she slides her cold hands away from me – she does not accept it, I see.

But she must.

'What about the . . . the DNA evidence they were going to look for? Didn't you tell me – the fish wouldn't have had time to . . . *digest* everything?' She pulls a face. 'There would have been traces of human DNA in it . . .'

'Roberto says – if we insist – he'll send the samples they have to the UK for further analysis. But the tests that went to Belgium were inconclusive.'

'What do you mean *if we insist*? Of course we insist!'

'Do we?' I look at her significantly. Does she really want to know all the gruesome details of what was inside that fish? 'We will do if you really want to, Julia.' I take hold of her shoulders. 'But you do know that in time you're going to have to accept this, don't you? We need to say goodbye to him, my love. We need to let him be.'

'What about the ransom note that Maria was handed at the station?'

Ah, she hasn't let go of that one yet. I thought she hadn't.

'The police confirmed to Roberto that there was never anything to that story. It was a false lead, Julia, that's all.'

'What are you talking about? Why would anyone send a ransom note if they didn't have him?'

'People pull stunts like that all the time. Nutters and idiots who think it'd be funny to see their actions reported in the papers. If it had been genuine, they would have followed it up with another one, don't you think?'

'What about Hadyn's photo?' she whispers. 'The police took his photo from my bedside while I was sleeping. Eva said they were going to make posters out of it, circulate them so if anyone saw him—'

'No point now, love. Now we know what happened to him.'

'No point?' Her voice is suddenly different. Colder and stronger, somehow. 'You really don't think there's any point? A few posters for our son?'

'Not with what we've heard this morning, no.'

'But before we'd heard it, why didn't they do something then?'

'The fish was discovered pretty soon after, love. They must have had their suspicions back then.'

All this testing of fibres – it's all been a formality as far as they were concerned. And I'm sure Roberto knows more than he's letting on. The DNA tests they did – they probably came up more than just 'inconclusive': he's trying to spare us, that's all. But he's given me to understand this morning, in no uncertain terms, as far as the police in Spain are concerned, it's over.

169

'No. Something is wrong.' She shakes her head. 'I don't buy it, Charlie.'

'*Why* in God's name? I trust in my brother, Julia. You should too. We were waiting for the fibre evidence. Now we've got it. If you got the DNA evidence – more proof – you'd turn round and tell me: "Maybe the fish nipped his finger but he still got away"?'

'I wouldn't! How could you be so *facetious*, Charlie?' She sits up on her knees. 'Do you know the reason why I forgave you for yelling at me that first day we met?' Her tongue goes in her cheek and she looks at me challengingly. 'It was because I could see the passion you had for your work. Your passion is what keeps you going, isn't it?' She indicates the papers about us. 'It's what makes you prepared to fight for what you believe in, bawl out people like Brasenose, even when that's flying in the face of what's accepted . . .'

'That's different. I fight for things I can make a difference to. When will you accept that you're never going to make any difference here?'

'Not yet,' she whispers and her voice is hoarse with unshed tears. She goes over to the curtains and looks out over the grass where a thin layer of ice and snow has fallen since we first began to talk.

'Everything's getting covered over,' she says, more to herself than to me. 'Everything's disappearing. His birdbath, the feeding table. The rose bushes. Soon, we won't be able to see any of it at all. I don't know what it will take.' She turns to me suddenly. 'All I know is, I can't accept it yet.'

'Have you still got that appointment for the counsellor? The one Dr Fraser said she would refer you to?'

Her back is rigid, turned to me again as she looks out over the wide bay windows, out into the grey and dismal garden.

'We were going to make a play area down there.' She's looking at the space beyond the crumbling greenhouse. We bought this house in large part because it had such spectacular potential for developing the garden. We were going to have swings and a slide and – in time – a place where Hadyn could put up a tent and maybe a treehouse.

I'd imagined him sitting in the boughs of one of the trees, eating apples. I didn't let the developer cut those trees down. I'd had plans.

At this moment I can't imagine a time when any of it will matter ever again and I don't know – I really don't know – how such a very small person could have taken up such a large amount of space.

How is it that he filled the whole house the way that he did? It wasn't just his *things* – his sit and ride train that makes such a racket when you press the red button; his collection of assorted and mostly abandoned stuffed animals; the coloured bricks that found their way into every room. It isn't all those things because we've kept those things out till we can best decide what we are going to do with them.

His things are still everywhere but his energy is not. The house feels desolate and I want him back. I want him back so much I swear I cannot bear it.

She's got to put these things away out of my sight now. Put them away or give them away.

Now that I have my final proof I've got to find a place of peace with everything that's happened. And I want to take Julia with me where I'm going.

'Oh I'm still going to be seeing her,' Julia replies tersely, 'for all the good it will do.'

Only trouble is, it's pretty clear to me that where I'm going, my Julia doesn't want to come.

Julia

'So you want me to ring the woman about cancelling the fitting?' My mum Beryl has brought my wedding dress down into the sitting room where she's already carefully laid white crepe paper all over the floor. 'You're *sure*?'

I glance up at her. Ever since Mum arrived two weeks ago she's been doing her best to be of use to me, to try to smooth out the everyday necessities of life, but I can't help but think having her here is a mixed blessing.

'Of course I'm sure,' I reply tersely. Alys and I have been embroiled in a heap of papers for the last two hours, Alys's reporter friend Rebecca from the local rag has just turned up and the last thing I need now is this. I don't want to *think* about the wedding. Can't Mum see that we're *busy*?

'It's just that . . .' my mother hesitates, both thin wrists hovering over one edge of my dress, 'once you put this thing away . . .'

Once I put this wedding dress away I may never go on to marry him. That's what she means. I suck my cheeks in and vow to keep silent. Because maybe he was only marrying me because I'd given him a son: that's what she's implying, isn't it?

The reporter woman – Rebecca – gives me a sympathetic look, jots something down on her pad and I cringe. She's not going to write about the cancellation of our wedding plans, is she? I only wanted her to write about Hadyn. Why did Mum have to bring the dress in here to fold it, anyway?

'Just do it. Please.' I drag my attention back to the folder that Alys brought in to me this morning. She's been very busy while I've been away in Spain, dredging up a whole load of organisations that she thinks might be useful, and Rebecca said she wanted a photo of the two of us poring over them.

'I think we ought to make as much of this locally as possible,' Alys is saying loudly. 'Rebecca says if we can get the right angle, they'll pick it up in the nationals and then, who knows? The more we can get that little face of his out there, the higher the chances are that—'

'It's just,' Mum puts in – she's folding in the silk sleeves carefully, regretfully, unwilling to let the matter go – 'I just . . . don't want to see you dragging it out longer than you need to. I know how much you loved him, but the evidence is all there, love. Perhaps you just need to let him go?'

I look up, my eyes sending 'be silent' daggers at her, but she doesn't take the hint.

'Charlie told me about the phone call that just came in from Roberto,' Mum hisses under her breath, but loudly enough for everyone else to hear. She glances at Alys, no doubt wondering if I've told my friend about the latest news from Spain or not. 'It's over, isn't it?'

'It is?' Rebecca asks innocently. She's got her tape recorder running now, I see.

'It's nothing,' I tell her firmly. 'This is part of the problem as I see it. The Spanish authorities say it's over, but I still have question marks over so many things, don't you see . . . ?'

'You've also got to consider the effect that all this is having on Charlie,' Mum continues, her eyes on the folds of my dress, the white silk and chiffon sleeves, the dream, the beautiful dream that is now never going to happen. 'He's clearly devastated – it can't be easy for him, either, coming home to find you persisting with this research. It must just remind him of his pain . . .'

I don't answer her and she takes this as a cue to carry on.

'If you just accepted that—'

'Mum, please, this isn't the time . . .' Mum's oblivious of the fact that we have a reporter present. *What's wrong with her?*

'Sometimes you've just got to accept that a thing is what it is,' Mum says to the air in general. 'If you could only accept what the Spaniards are telling you . . .'

'If I just accepted that, it would make life so much easier for everyone, wouldn't it?' I put in through gritted teeth. I know she wants me to give up so she can go home and get on with her own life.

'There seems to be some disagreement – even within the family – as to whether your son is still alive or not, do you think it would be fair to say, Julia?' Rebecca advances on me, pen in hand.

I shake my head but Mum blunders on regardless. 'Well . . .' she says awkwardly, 'it *would* be easier on everyone, Julia. It would make things easier for you, too. Maybe that's just what you ought to do.' She's begun folding the edges of my beautiful dress into military style creases now, flattening along the edge of each length with her palm.

'Come in here a moment, Mum.' I take her elbow and pick up the wedding dress box in the other hand, marching us both down the hallway into the kitchen.

'This isn't helping, Mum. Not one little bit.'

'I'm sorry,' she says and her chin tilts up a bit. 'I want to help you and I'm doing my best but you don't make it easy. We're all devastated Julia, it's not just you, even though he was your little boy. We all loved him. And we all – we've just had to accept it, too.'

'Accept it?' I take in a breath. *Just forget about him*, she means. *Nobody has any answers so stop digging. Stop making a fuss and making everybody feel so uncomfortable.*

She nods.

'Just like you did when you left Dad?' I hiss. Whoa! I bite my

174

lip. Where did that come from? 'I'm sorry,' I mutter. 'I didn't mean that.'

'I left your dad because I finally realised that I was never going to get anywhere.' Her eyes widen in surprise that I've brought that up. 'He loved the drink more than he loved us. That's all. If I'd stayed on, I'd only have thrown away my own life into the bargain. Yes, and yours too.'

She's right, I know she's right, but I can't walk away from this situation as easily as she feels I should. I just can't.

I turn round, hugging my arms to my body, go over and stand by the window as Alys comes in with the reporter and fusses around putting the kettle on.

'You've never forgiven me for that, have you?' Mum mutters as she finishes folding my wedding dress into a thousand creases and cramming it back into the box. I would have been better leaving it hanging in the wardrobe, except that I couldn't bear to see it. Then, under her breath, 'You never saw what it cost *me*, Julia. You've never stopped to think how it might have felt to me, that you chose to stay with your dad when I left him, instead of coming away. You're as stubborn and wilful as he was, when it comes down to it.'

'I *chose* to stay?' Is that what she thinks? It was a choice that was no choice, as far as I was concerned. At least it was until the day I . . .

'I think it would make a really good contrast if we could get Mum's side of the story,' Rebecca is saying. 'She seems to have some interesting views on the matter.' I hold my breath and count to ten. *How is this going to help me find my son?*

I don't want Mum here any more. And I don't want that reporter in here either.

And I wonder what Dad would say, if he were still here to say it? Mum's kidding herself if she believes that my dad was all bad, though. *At least he believed in the possibility of things*, I think angrily. *He believed in what might be, and that's something you could never do!*

175

I close my eyes, because the past is getting blurry now. I picture the only photograph I've kept of the three of us: me on a donkey eating candyfloss, standing beside Mum with her eighties-style frizzy hair and Dad in black leather on a motorbike. He had the bluest eyes, my dad. Mum always said he was 'a lad'. He was handsome, that was for sure. You couldn't help wondering, looking at the two of them side by side, how on earth such an unlikely pair ended up together. Her eyes look into the camera thinking – of what? – of the spuds she's going to peel for the evening meal; she's wondering if she'll get home in time to get the clothes off the line before it starts to spit. His eyes, laughing, devil-may-care, promise something else altogether. *I'll be away on this motorbike of mine before dawn*, he seems to say; *I've got the world to discover yet.*

'Am I wrong?' I ask Alys once Mum and Rebecca have taken their tea into the next room. 'I mean, is she right? Am I taking this all too far?'

'You're doing what's right for you. It doesn't mean that it's going to be right for everyone else. They'll be patient for a while – people like your mum, and like Charlie, because they love you. Later on they'll come a point where you have to make a decision . . .'

'*If* I don't find him first,' I remind her. I pile up the folders.

'Just don't be too "in your face" about it,' Alys warns me. 'Now, what's the state of play with this Blue guy? Has he contacted you yet? Has he sent you Maria and Diego's number?'

'Not yet,' I frown, looking at the piles of papers, printouts from the Internet we've amassed on the floor. 'Or maybe he did? I'll have to look again.'

I'm trying to keep a grasp of what does still matter but some days it really seems too hard a task.

Since Hadyn left me, the days have all now merged into one. I get up. The day goes by. I do not achieve very much. I do not know what day of the week it is, mostly. I have no reason to know. On a couple of occasions I have thought that the week must have had two Mondays or two Wednesdays: it's odd. I can't figure it out half the time.

But there are clues that, in fact, the year *is* moving on. The snow-drops underneath the oak tree out back, they had all pushed through by the time I returned, even though we'd had no snow. The crispy autumn leaves that had hung on till Christmas (I remember Hadyn having to step on *every single one* before he would get into the car . . .), they've turned soggy and gone. The mornings are getting lighter as we move on into March. And somehow – I do not know how – I am meant to be moving on, too.

'And you're certain that Charlie wants no part of any of this? You know this is going to work much better if we have him on board.' Alys peeks round the corner where the other two are ensconced in cosy chat with one another.

'Charlie's family have convinced him that it's over. The "blue fibres in the fish" evidence pretty much sealed it for him. He feels the best thing I could do now is agree to see a counsellor . . .'

Alys nods.

'Maybe that wouldn't hurt either. At the very least it'll keep Charlie happy, won't it? You don't want to ignore what he's feeling, Julia. With so much else going on, it'd be only too easy for the two of you to neglect your relationship.' She raises her eyebrows meaningfully. 'In fact, it might be an idea for the two of you to make an effort to get some special time together. To, you know, reconnect. Go out on a date or something.'

I look at her blankly.

'What do you mean, Alys? I see him at home every night, don't I?' And I'm too tired and fed up to want to do anything as frivolous as going out on a date. Whatever is she thinking of?

'You've had to put your wedding on hold.' She puts her hand on my arm for an instant. 'That's a tragedy, for both of you. I know it pales into insignificance compared to Hadyn's dis-appearance. I know that. I'm just saying, don't lose sight of the rest of your life while you go on searching for him. Okay?'

'Okay.'

'But in the meantime you should try and contact that Spanish couple in case Diego ever *did* get any leads.'

Of course I do. I need to take action. I haven't got time to worry about going out on dates or anything like that. Charlie can keep.

I need to get my mind back on track.

I've got to *focus*.

Charlie

'I remember the very first time I ever laid eyes on you.' Lourdes is wearing a sage-green top with gathered sleeves. It accentuates her Mediterranean glow, the colour of her eyes. She's leaning slightly across the table of the little Convent garden café she's brought me to. In front of us, two large cappuccinos, untouched by either of us, cool slowly.

'That would be the time when Roberto and I were having that bicycle race up the Via Alto road that leads up to the cemetery, right?' I remember that day very well, and not without a certain satisfaction. That hill was as steep as they come and my brother had got a two-metre head start on me but he was heavier and I was quicker. I made it up to the top before him, and he sulked for hours afterwards.

'No,' she stifles a giggle, 'that wasn't the first time. The *first* time I ever saw you, you were struggling with your shoelaces.'

'That long ago, eh?' She seems to have been aware of my existence long before I was ever aware of hers.

'You must have been about ten years old. You'd been sent to boarding school by then. The bike incident was later. You'd have been twelve there, and on vacation from Hillstones.'

I frown.

'I don't remember ever having a problem with shoelaces.'

I'm looking out of the window at the people pushing past with their umbrellas through the late winter showers. It's cosy in here. Just the sort of place that Lourdes would choose to come to. I wonder if she ever came here with her husband? Lourdes has always loved London. She's been talking about coming over here to live. I want to ask her about her marriage and about her life since we parted. I want to ask her about one hundred and one things but I don't want her to get the wrong idea about why I'm asking. I don't want to give her false hope; she's made it clear that she's still interested.

'I don't remember much, if I'm honest, Lourdes. I seem to have blanked out most of my misspent youth.'

She smiles sadly at me.

'Don't you remember the time your dad brought your mum and me and Santos with our dad along to see you at Hillstones? It hailed so hard we said we should call your boarding school *Hailstones*, remember?'

'I remember it.' I've often wondered whether my dad did that on purpose. I'd waited so long to see my ma and when he did eventually bring her down – six whole months after she came out of the hospital – he'd brought along a whole bunch of other people at the same time. I often wondered if he did that to dilute the effect of seeing her looking as she did, so changed, after I had waited so long. 'I remember he'd warned me, my dad. How she was going to *look different*, but he'd never said exactly how.'

'People didn't, in those days,' Lourdes muses. 'Nowadays we try and prepare our children for everything. We want to prepare them for how it is . . .' She stops and in her silence I see she's worried because she's just mentioned *our children*.

'It's all right, Lourdes.' I pat her hand. 'I've accepted it, you know. I know my boy is gone.'

'I just meant to say – in those days, adults didn't understand that children had feelings too.' Her hand moves softly to cover mine. 'It must have come as a real shock to you.'

'The way Ma looked after the accident?' I shrug. The back of

180

my throat is stinging so I look out of the window again. This place is very soon going to become too crowded, I realise. 'I could have handled the damage to her face, Lourdes. What I hadn't bargained for was how she wasn't going to be able to cope with it. She was never herself again after that. She shied away from all of us. It felt as if . . . she'd just stopped *loving everyone*, you know.'

'She never stopped loving you.' Lourdes shakes her head firmly. 'She loved you more than anyone, Charlie. You in particular.'

'I'm sure she did. But Roberto got to stay behind with her in Spain and I was the "lucky" one who got to go to boarding school.' My shoulders hunch over the coffee cup. I hadn't meant to sound so bitter about that but it just came out. Why is Lourdes dredging all this up now, any road? She said she wanted to speak to me about costings and about the charity dinner. That's what I'm here for. I don't believe in mulling over the past. My parents did the best they could at the time, and that was that. I didn't do so badly out of it, did I?

'Roberto was the older one. You were that much younger. You needed more looking after, even though you didn't know it.'

'Oh yes? Like someone to show me how to do up my shoelaces?' I offer.

Her eyes take on a shy, almost mischievous glint now.

'The first time I ever saw you,' she repeats now, 'at Hillstones, it was love at first sight. For me, anyway.'

'I gave you a hard time, as I recall.'

'You told me to go away and leave you alone,' she laughs. 'But you were only ten and you were heartbroken, even if you didn't let on about it. You wanted to come home, didn't you?'

More than anything.

'Your father thought you were happy, you know.' She's playing with her cappuccino now, sprinkling more cinnamon on the top, piling sugar in and stirring it with the long wooden stirrer. 'He never even suspected how you felt.'

'Didn't want to burden them, did I? They'd got enough to

worry about. I thought when Ma got better they'd let me go home. That was all.'

She's stroking my fingers gently. Anyone looking at us might imagine we were lovers. I pull my hand away sharply.

'Anyways, what are we here for today?' I clear my throat. 'You said you'd got some inside information for me on the bloke you're inviting to Angus's dinner at Lansdown house – the possible new sponsor.'

Her eyes drop back to her coffee for a minute and there's this slight hesitation while she readjusts to the new topic of conversation. Not without a struggle, I see. Lourdes would always rather talk about personal things than business. But business is what we're here for, after all. And since the Baudelaire incident, Lourdes has become my new funds manager for the centre. I need someone I can trust in charge of the purse strings now.

'His name is Mario Serrano,' she tells me in her drowsy voice. 'He's not currently aware of the Baudelaire situation – and we'll have to apprise him gently of it, of course – but he's a long-term supporter of good causes. It sits well with his religious sensibilities – he's Catholic with a capital 'C', you should know. A good man, strict in his observations. One of his sons is a priest: you get the picture.'

'So we make sure we don't forget to say grace before the meal begins?' I smile. 'I'll remind Angus. Anything else?'

'He's *very wealthy*,' she drawls, her Spanish accent coming through slightly more here as she gives me a significant look – someone with her background doesn't impress that easily. 'So giving to our cause won't be any hardship as long as he's convinced it's a worthy one. He's happy to know that I'm the funds manager – he can't abide corruption.'

'So far so good. Downside?'

'He . . .' Her voice lowers to an uncomfortable whisper. 'Charlie, he doesn't know anything about Hadyn. Angus thought it might be best.'

'Oh?'

'Mario Serrano is very much a family man,' she stumbles. 'Losing a child is tragic but . . . but from what I understand, Serrano can also be a bit . . .' She stops.

'What, for heaven's sake, Lourdes?'

'He can be judgemental. There was some worry that he might judge that the way Hadyn went was . . . *careless*.' She grabs my hands. 'You know that isn't what *we* think, don't you?'

I'm stunned. I don't know what to say to her. How could anybody be so stupid as to think we lost our child through carelessness? Is this what Angus really thinks himself? The hypocritical son of a bitch! I can feel my jaws clenching at the thought. I'd just as soon tell them all – *all of them, including Lourdes* – to stuff it.

But I won't because I've got people at Esperanza relying on me to remain calm and objective about all of this. They need the financial backers. I've got to be the one to find them.

'Lourdes,' I look deep into her eyes, 'we either let this Mario guy know the state of play with my son or I'm not taking Julia within a dozen yards of him. I'll tell him myself. I don't want anyone making any *careless* statements that might hurt her or affect her in any way. She's fragile enough as it is.'

Julia will be at that dinner party because I know that's how it has to be. If any of these South Americans ever plan to do business with you, they always want to meet your whole family. I hold my head in my hands for a moment, trying to stem the flow of unbelievable weariness that suddenly floods through me. I've got to stay strong. For Julia. For Esperanza. For me.

'I'm so sorry, Charlie.' Lourdes looks wounded. I know this wasn't her idea. She was just trying to warn me.

'And there's another thing. I need the low-down on the Baudelaire story. Not the official spiel your brother gave me. The real story. What did Baudelaire do, and why is Santos so keen to support him?'

We both look up as a middle-aged couple breeze through the

doors with three teenagers and a toddler in their wake. They're loud, self-consciously exuberant. Their deliberate and determined joie-de-vivre drills through my skull and I find myself looking daggers at them. Then I catch sight of Lourdes's tragic face.

'*What?*' I nudge her, gently. 'What is it?'

'I just . . . don't know if you're really up for this, Charlie. It's all so hard. Coming on top of what you've already had to endure this year . . .'

The teenagers sitting behind me are jolting my bench with their feet. I'm not entirely sure how I'm going to stop myself from turning back and decking someone in a minute.

'Remind me.' I sit back against the leather seat. I close my eyes. She's right. 'What is it we're really doing, Lourdes? And why are we doing it?'

'Don't you know?'

I shake my head, my eyes still closed. I can feel her come and sit down beside me on my side of the bench. The jolting ceases.

'Then stop,' she says simply. 'Stop doing what you're doing till you know why. You've lost the most precious thing in your life, Charlie. Maybe the only child you will ever father. More precious to you than anyone really knows.'

God, she might as well stick a knife into my heart.

'Except you,' I touch her arm, 'you were always able to see right through me, weren't you, Lourdes?'

'Maybe,' she assents, her eyes hooded. 'But that isn't my place any more, is it?'

'Why are you here then?'

'Because you asked.'

I asked her for figures. I asked her for bits of paper with numbers on them, for a briefing on that Mario Serrano guy. Lourdes arranged the coffee. I didn't ask her to tell me that I should give up the only thing that's still keeping me going. I didn't ask her to remind me that I have lost the one thing that gave the most meaning to my life. Does she think I'm made of stone?

'Do you really think I should stop the Esperanza work, Lourdes?' I ask wearily. 'What will happen if I do? You know full well no one will take it up after me. It will sink. Kaput.'

She stares into her coffee. The bubbles on the top have all but disappeared, revealing the liquid underneath to be a dull, greyish colour. Then Lourdes reaches into her bag and, hesitating for a second, pulls out a green folder which she places in front of me.

'What's this?' I flick it open. It's the Baudelaire file.

'Perhaps this will help you make up your mind about how much further you want to take the Esperanza project. You read it tonight, and you shred it.' Her eyes look pleadingly into mine. 'You promise?'

I bow my head in assent.

'Let's walk.' I stand up abruptly and she gets up after me. The pavements outside are shiny with the rain. They're so shiny I can see the bright red and green of an open umbrella reflected on one of the surfaces. But when I look, I can't see myself. My reflection is a blurry grey blob, that's all it is. The tourists rush past, laughing. Grey pigeons flap onto the road ahead of us. The air smells of wet hair and wet T-shirts and the whiff of buttered popcorn sold by the vendor on the corner. Youngsters jostle past me and the whole world feels solid and up close and *real*.

'How many people are going to suffer if I just give it all up, eh?' She doesn't answer.

Everything feels real except me. I am trying to make a difference in this world but I'm not sure that I can any more. And Lourdes doesn't say anything. She walks along with her hands in her pockets and – because I know her as well as she knows me – she doesn't have to.

I know what she's thinking: *how many people are going to suffer if you don't?*

Julia

'Hello, mad*ame*,' says the generously proportioned black woman on my doorstep. 'I am Winnie Okinosu.'

I blink, keeping most of the door between us.

'Do I know you?'

'Not yet. I have come to see you about counselling. I have been appoint*ed* by Dr Fras*er* to come and see you following your bereavement.'

Oh damnation. It *is* her. What day is it? Wednesday. I meant to ring up and cancel this thing that Dr Fraser insisted on setting up for me. She blackmailed me into it ('No counselling, Julia, then no tablets, understand? I want to see you starting to get to grips with the root of what's keeping you awake . . .').

'I'm not actually *bereaved*, as it happens, Ms Oki . . . Ms Okinsi. My boy is missing. We don't have a body so he might still be alive.' This isn't strictly true. I know it and she does too. We got the 'matching blue fibres' evidence two weeks ago now. 'Quite so.' She glances at her open folder, shifts her weight slightly from one foot to the other, standing on the doorstep. 'May I come in?'

'I don't think that will be necessary, Ms Oki . . .'

'Oki*nosu*. But you can call me Winnie.'

'Winnie. Look, thanks, but no thanks.'

Thing is, I had another email from Blue last night. He sent me through Maria's number in the UK, which is the thing I've been waiting for, for the last two weeks. Only I couldn't ring her last night because Charlie was home. I couldn't ring her till he left for the clinic this morning. Then Mum was hanging around for ages, and I didn't want her to overhear the call either, because she'd tell Charlie. Mum's just gone into the garden and I'd been about to ring Maria when this woman arrived.

Heard the bad news, Blue wrote to me (last night at 11.04pm) *– they're saying in the paper that the police here are satisfied with the evidence they now have and that they have to concede the UK toddler did in fact drown. Just a very brief article quoting the (Andalucian) fisherman who caught the fish, though no real details. That's it. What exactly – if you don't mind me asking – did the fisherman actually find?*

So they didn't actually talk about the matching fibres in the papers. I want to speak to Maria now. I'd travel anywhere in the UK to see her, just to find out if there's anything else she remembers about the course of events that day. I want to speak to Diego again, too. Maybe he heard something but he doesn't know how to contact me? Maybe he's had second thoughts about getting involved?

In the meantime, Winnie Okinosu has been checking in her diary. 'We do have an appointment today,' she affirms. 'I will see you and report back to Dr Fraser on your progress, see?' She points to her file and I can feel my cheeks burning. I am not some bloody kid at school that needs my progress reporting on.

'No. It's not necessary. I'm perfectly fine. Really.'

'But you aren't sleeping. It says here you aren't . . .' she jabs at the file, her voice rising a notch just as Jacob and Louise from next door arrive back on their drive. I can see their smiling but interested faces watching from inside the car. I grab hold of Ms Okinosu by the elbow.

'Look, er . . . perhaps you should come in, Winnie. Take a seat.' I push her into the drawing room, where I remember, thank goodness, I've just opened the curtains.

'There must have been a mix-up,' I continue to bluster. 'I did explain when I saw the doctor that I didn't require any counselling at this point. I'm sorry you've wasted your time.'

Winnie takes her time before replying to me. To my surprise, she seems more engrossed in my garden than she is interested in me.

'You have a truly beautiful garden, Julia.' She turns her head to look at me now and, for a moment, her face borders on the serene. 'Do you mind if I call you Julia?'

I spread my hands graciously. For the next thirty seconds that you are going to be in my life, you can call me what you like, I think.

'Thank you,' I agree politely. 'It *is* beautiful.' It is. I watch without interest as Mum picks at some weeds in one of the flowerbeds. This garden was my pride and joy when first we came to this house, two years ago. I felt so comfortable here, so happy. I could never have imagined how short a time that feeling would last.

'Are you sure that you don't want to take this opportunity to have a word with me?'

'I'm sure I'd have nothing to talk about.' *I mean, what am I supposed to say?*

She hesitates.

'There's something you should know. Your husband did phone in to Dr Fraser at one point and say he was . . . concerned about you.'

'What the hell? Okay, now I really am pissed off.'

'With me?' She looks surprised.

'No.' I frown at her. 'Not with you. With Charlie. He shouldn't be talking about me behind my back like that.' I stop. If I carry on I'm in danger of saying things about him that I probably shouldn't, so I shut up and pretend to look back out of the window. *How could he?* There is nothing wrong with me. Okay, so I am not sleeping well. That is understandable. It has only been ten weeks since my little boy disappeared. And I guess I've been a bit snappy, but that isn't a crime, is it?

Charlie keeps trying to get me to go into his work for a few hours or to get involved with his bloody charity project, and if I'm honest that is the LAST thing on earth I will do. If it weren't for that project and his obsession with it – who knows, I might still have Hadyn with me here right now.

'Look, I'm sorry,' I tell her at last. 'We appear to have got off on the wrong foot. It's been pretty fraught around here recently. We've been getting on each other's nerves a bit. That's all.'

'It's hardly surprising,' she murmurs.

'Well no, it isn't.'

'This has got to be the most difficult situation any parent could be called upon to face.'

I nod. My throat is so tight I can hardly get the words out. 'It's only been four weeks since I left Spain but it feels as if I've been away for ever,' I confess. 'I only came back home because they made me. Part of me couldn't cope with being there any more, either. They said there was no point. They'd let me know if I was needed, if there were any developments. So I came back. Now all I can think of is that I ought to be over there, *doing* something.' She seems to understand but she doesn't answer me.

I turn to look out over the garden. The snow that fell on Saturday has melted already and everything underneath it is a sodden mess. When I look back at Winnie, I see she has been studying me intently.

'You like the birds?' She's nodding towards my bird table. Hadyn's bird table, actually – we put it up there for him – *he* loved to watch the birds. I still put food out for them. I do it for him because he isn't here to do it himself.

'The birds. Yes.' I'm not sure I really care about the birds, if truth be told. All I ever seem to get these days are ruddy great crows that come down off the high trees and gobble up everything in sight.

'So, how long have you not been sleeping for?'

I rustle around the room, plumping up the sunken-in cushions that have betrayed me.

'Since . . . since it happened really. Ten weeks?'

'When we don't sleep,' she tells me, 'we all get tetchy. Everyone does. Don't worry.'

'And I'm depressed,' I tell her suddenly. I don't know why I'm telling her this but I suddenly get an overwhelming urge to confess everything. Like King Midas, whispering into that hole in the ground, the burdensome secret that he had donkey's ears. Howling out of nowhere, there comes this sudden need to unburden.

'And – maybe this is also because I am not sleeping – I'm angry at Charlie. He thinks there's something wrong with me because I can't accept our loss. I think . . . how could he give up so easily?'

'It's going to take a long time, Julia. Ten weeks is nothing.'

'I get the impression some folk wish I was getting on with things a bit more.' I glance out at Mum, then look away. 'They think I should be trying to move on.'

'No,' she says gently, 'it's too soon. It's true some people find these things much easier to accept than others. How is your husband coping?'

'His faith sustains him, I think. But what about me? My feelings can't just be discounted. I don't have Charlie's faith, I'll admit. If I did I'd feel let down by God, not aided by him. Never mind God, I feel let down by Charlie. I feel *furious* at him in fact.'

'Because he's accepted the loss?' she asks me now, playing devil's advocate. 'And *you* feel that there is still hope that – if you carried on searching – Hadyn would one day turn up?'

He might.

'I think he feels he's done everything possible,' I tell her carefully, 'and so it is natural for him to want to let it go.'

'And you feel differently? You have reason to think differently?'

I sigh, now. I feel so tired. Why is it I can never sleep any more when I always feel so tired?

I don't have reason, not really. Reason would point me in the same direction as it has pointed Charlie. It's only my gut feeling that tells me different.

'I'm Hadyn's mother. I'd know if anything had happened to him, surely?'

'We always like to think so,' Winnie accedes. 'But it isn't always so. My cousin's son drowned in a puddle outside her front door. It happened. She never *felt* it happen. She never knew it till they found him.'

I would know it though. We were so close.

'Hadyn doesn't feel dead. Even if he is.'

'What would Hadyn being dead feel like to you, do you think?'

'I can't possibly answer that. I think it's unfair of you to ask me.'

'You might want to let yourself know, though. Otherwise – you could be missing something altogether.'

'Okay. Well, it would feel like . . . he just wasn't there any more. There would be – I imagine – an emptiness in the air. In the world. In my heart.'

'And you don't feel that emptiness just yet?'

'No, I don't.' Just because your cousin never felt it, doesn't mean it's not there to be felt, I think. I know what she's driving at, though, and that – at the moment – I'm not making much sense, even to myself.

'I know . . . sometimes people hang on far too long to things,' I say by way of concession, 'and I may well turn out to be wrong. Maybe he did get taken by the sea and I never felt it. Just like your cousin's boy in the puddle.'

'It's good that you can allow for that possibility, Julia. Keep your mind open and you keep the door open to wellbeing.'

Does she think I need humouring, I wonder now? Does she think that I am grief-stricken and I cannot accept the inevitable?

I shoot Winnie Okinosu a sideways glance while she puts her papers away in her briefcase.

'Would you like to meet with a counsellor again, Julia?'

'No,' I say automatically, but that isn't true so I change it to 'Yes, actually.'

'I'm glad. I think it would help you,' says Winnie. 'It won't be me,' she warns. 'My role has been to assess if you are in a position to benefit from our service. What do you think you would like to achieve from seeing someone?'

'Closure,' I say at once, without thinking.

'That's a good plan,' she beams. 'We can try. And in the meantime,' her eyes grin wickedly, taking in a photo of Charlie and me that's up on the mantelpiece, 'try not to get too angry with that poor husband of yours. He is rather too handsome, you will admit?'

I pull a face.

'You know,' she turns to me now, 'in times of trouble I find it always helps to know that you are not the only one. I'm leaving you a card for the Lost Children's Support Group. It's run by a very nice lady called Elaine Betterton. You may find the support of others who know what you're going through more comforting than you think.'

I take the card and squash it in my palm where she can't see. I've got enough things up and running at the moment with Alys's help.

'Julia.' She turns to shake my hand. 'I am glad we got to speak. And I congratulate you on your remarkable garden. Do you like the crows?'

Do I like the crows? What kind of a question is that? They're carrion, aren't they, harbingers of death and doom (but let's not dwell on that) and just bloody huge and greedy.

'Not really,' I mutter. She's on her feet now and I don't want to open up the conversation again.

'The birds you attract into your garden,' she says 'ga-den', 'that will depend on what you put out for them. If you put out great big lumps of food, the big birds will come. If you put out tiny seed, then they don't bother.' Her eyes are shining, smiling into mine. 'Then the little ones, it will be safe for them, and they will come.'

'Thanks for the tip,' I say. Big bits of bread, big birds. Tiny little seeds, tiny birds.

On the doorstep she stops and turns and shakes my hand. I've got this feeling she knows I know I've only put her off for the minute.

'Someone will come back and check on you again in a week's time, Julia. Take it eas-see. And remember, according to what you put out, that is what you will attract.'

'Got it. I'll remember that.'

I shut the door on her. I go back to the kitchen, where Mum's just opened the side door. She's holding her gardening shoes in one hand.

'Anyone important?' she inclines her head towards the door. 'She looked *official*, so I thought I'd stay out there.'

'You could have come in,' I tell her gruffly. 'It was the counselling person Dr Fraser sent along for me.'

'Oh.' Mum sits down on the edge of a kitchen chair. 'A grief counsellor, you mean?'

I fold my arms.

'Did it do any good?'

I shrug. 'I'll make another appointment, if that's what you mean.'

'I'm glad you're getting some help at last,' Mum begins, examining her nails very closely. 'I'm glad you're not being *stubborn* about this. I know you thought I was speaking out of turn the other day when I stood up and said I felt you really needed to start accepting what's happened, but—'

'You *were* speaking out of turn. You were saying your piece in front of that reporter woman,' I remind her. I watch her put her shoes down on a carefully placed piece of newspaper.

'I just don't want you to suffer needlessly, don't you see?' When she looks up her face is set and determined. 'You really have absolutely no reason to carry on searching any more. *Do* you?'

How can I make her understand this?

'I have . . . my *feelings* to consider,' I tell her after a few moments. 'If I give it all up just to please Charlie – to please *you* – then I'm not being true to myself.'

'Oh I'm not expecting you to take *my* feelings into consideration!' Her eyes go hard suddenly, as much as to say, *Don't break the habit of a lifetime, will you?* 'It's you I'm thinking of, that's all. You were never very good at taking well-meant advice, Julia, and I don't suppose in the middle of a crisis that's going to change.'

I know better than to answer that.

'Well, I'm glad you're getting some support for yourself.' She stands up after a while, all stiff and hurt. 'If you still need me to stay, I'll keep on here for as long as you want me.'

'I think we'll be able to manage okay by ourselves for now, Mum.' There's no point her hanging on any more. We both know it. 'I'm really grateful that you came, but you need to get on with your life, and I need to get on with what I've got to do.' Mum shrugs her shoulders, gives a little *hmmph* sound and then goes to start packing her things. I know it's what she really wants to do, anyway.

The room feels much emptier after she goes upstairs.

I switch on the laptop that's on the kitchen table and pull up Blue's email.

They pulled some fibres matching what Hadyn was wearing out of the belly of a fish, I type in by way of answer to his last question. A logo comes up, informing me that my friend Blue is online at the moment. I add him to my MSN list and I press send.

So what? He comes back almost straight away. *If his shorts had been discarded on the shore, that big wave that came up afterwards and dragged everything down with it would have taken them with it. Everything got wet – all the bags, remember?*

I don't remember, not very well, I type back. But what he is saying does ring a bell. Now I think of it, I seem to think I'd had the impression Maria had started to change him before I went up to the lifeguard with my wasp-sting. But that couldn't be so, could it? *I have to speak to Maria,* I tell him now – *I'm going to try her this morning.*

Is that all the evidence they have? Blue persists. *Nothing more than that?*

Sometimes you are only ever going to get circumstantial evidence, I say. *Maybe there IS nothing else left to be had.*

Maybe, he concedes. *But don't give up just yet.*

Why? I type in. Tell me something, I'm thinking, anything that will keep my hopes alive. And another part of me is thinking – why are you doing this? I'm supposed to be looking for closure.

Speak to Maria, is all he answers. *Got to go. Bye.* xxx

I wander over to the worktop and automatically put the kettle on, even though I don't want a drink. Lists. I need to make lists, I decide.

On the list tacked behind the kitchen door I write the first thing that comes into my mind: *bird seeds, small ones.*

I glance upstairs but it's gone all quiet. I imagine Mum must be packing now and I waver for a minute because I don't really want her to go. Then I pick up the phone, my hands trembling so much I can barely punch in Maria's number. Mum has to go, because I've got to do what I've got to do and she'll only stand in my way.

Maybe Maria holds the answer to all this. Maybe she doesn't. The thing is, it feels like I'm the only one left who is still interested in finding out.

Julia

'Hello, Julia?' It's Maria's voice. I know it is. I can't believe it! Since Winnie visited and Mum left I've left *four* messages over the last couple of weeks for Maria to ring me either at home or on my mobile and she's rung me back just as I've pressed this stranger's doorbell! Hardly the ideal opportunity for us to talk . . .

'Maria?'

'It's been a long time, heh?' Her breathy voice sounds different. Sad, somehow.

'How're you doing?' I glance up at the window where Elaine Betterton from the Lost Children's Support Group has just twitched her curtains back, spotting me outside.

But I want to speak to Maria now! A host of questions tumble into my head at once, and I turn my head away from the door.

'Still here in the UK,' Maria sounds weary, 'but not for long. That's why I've called you back. It's not worked out as we'd hoped, you know? We haven't found work like we'd planned so we haven't been able to send for the children . . .'

'Look,' I swap the phone over to my other hand, 'I need to talk to you *desperately*. There are so many things . . . like' – my mind is racing furiously – 'I need to know if you'd begun to change Hadyn out of his blue shorts before he went missing that day?'

There's a silence as she realigns herself to what I'm talking about.

'His shorts?' She sounds confused. She must know what I mean, surely? What's the Spanish word for shorts, oh hell!

'I can't remember,' she says slowly. She sounds different, somehow. Not quite with it, as I remember her. I'm going to have to take this more gently if I want to get anything useful out of her.

'Look, we can't talk now. I've just rung someone's front doorbell. But let's agree to meet up – you and me. Let me take you to lunch?'

'I meant to come and see you,' she runs on as if I hadn't spoken, 'I didn't know if you'd heard from Diego or not.'

'Why?' I paste on a smile as Elaine Betterton opens the door, point haplessly to the phone, even though it must seem rude. 'Did he have a *reason* to contact me?' I hiss.

'He told me that he would,' Maria says enigmatically. 'I wondered if he ever had, that's all.'

'No . . . No, he didn't. Do you know what that might have been about, by any chance?'

'He wanted to talk to you about what he'd found out before we left Spain, no?'

Elaine Betterton dressed smartly in a floral skirt and high-necked blouse, hangs back a little at the door. She doesn't strike me as the sort of person you keep waiting while you hold a telephone conversation. *I'm sorry*, I mouth, but if people at the Lost Children's Support Group don't understand this, then no one will.

'What did he find out? *Anything?*' My heart is in my mouth. If there was even a crumb of news – why didn't they contact me before this, for God's sake?

'I don't think he did.' She sounds odd; she's holding something back, I know. 'Life hasn't been so good to me since we came over here. It's been hard. That's why I'm going back home.'

'I'm sorry to hear that. Look, we need to meet.' I try to pin her down. 'How about tomorrow, at the Meeting Point, Victoria Station?'

'Tomorrow's not good. I'm a little broke at the moment . . .' Maria's voice is flat. 'Sorry, I'm almost out of credit on this phone.

And I'm about to get onto a bus. Maybe we could meet next Thursday?'

'I'll refund your train ticket,' I bluster. 'Next Thursday morning then. Ten o'clock, all right? Just be there.' When I ring off I see that the lady of house has gone back inside but thoughtfully left the door a little open for me. I spot her in the kitchen.

'Sorry about that.'

Elaine shrugs, 'Don't worry – that's mobiles for you,' wipes her hands on a tea cloth, and makes to introduce herself. 'You must be Julia! I'm Elaine. Do come right in. I am *so* pleased you decided to visit our support group after all. You'll find us a friendly bunch here.' She smiles brightly at me.

'Just as well I saw you from here. I've just come to put the second kettle on and the others are making such a racket in the living room I couldn't have heard the front door even if you did knock.'

'That's okay.' I can hear the noise the others are making. They certainly *sound* like a friendly group. As she potters about with the tea things I gaze out at an older kid's bike leaning up against the side of her house, trying to distract myself from the feeling of sick anxiety that Maria's phone call has brought on. From here I can see a football on the lawn, all wet with the early spring rain and with bits of grass sticking onto it. And the corner of a rabbit hutch. *Diego wanted to get hold of me, Maria said. But he never did. What could he have wanted to talk to me about?*

Nothing, probably; the sceptical part of my brain kicks in. He wanted to tell you he hadn't found anything. That's why he didn't actually *bother* . . .

I need to pay attention to where I'm at. Forget about the call. In fact, I'll ring her back later. I'll ask to speak to Diego himself.

This woman Elaine has got other kids, that much is obvious. There are so many signs of *life*, here. This is what children bring into a house, it strikes me; they bring life.

'I had a phone call through from Winnie Okinosu a couple of weeks back, saying she'd referred you on.' Elaine is smiling at me brightly and I recall I never meant to come here. But when the counselor Winnie had promised didn't show up last week I changed my mind.

'I thought maybe meeting other people who've been through the same thing might help,' I tell her. 'Everyone around me has been great, but . . .'

'They can sympathise but they can't totally empathise, of course,' Elaine finishes for me. 'You'll find we all understand what you're going through here, my dear.' She starts as the doorbell goes again. 'Oh! I have a feeling that might be Jasper. Unless it's the electrics man. Help yourself to coffee and biscuits my dear, I just want to catch him before the meeting proper begins. We've got a bit of excitement going on today.' She sounds both pleased and a little anxious at the same time. 'One of our members has found a – er – rather unorthodox method of gathering information on his missing daughter.'

'Oh?'

'Yes. Some of our members are quite into the *spiritual realms*, if you catch my drift.' Elaine heads out of her kitchen door. 'We're all just through there. Please do come and join us as soon as you're ready.'

Spiritual realms, she said? I'm not sure I'd want to go there with her.

When I take a surreptitious look around Elaine's kitchen, I don't think I am ever going to be ready. I don't even want to be here right now. I want to find out where Maria is at and go straight round to hers. But I can't.

I have a look around at my surroundings instead. From what I can see of Elaine's home, it is small but cosy and efficiently run. The cork notice board screwed to the back of the kitchen door is littered with the paperwork on which this lady must run her life. There are rotas for everything: house chores, school runs, hockey and swimming practice dates.

I pick up one of the fluted cups on the tray. My hand is

trembling so much I can barely hold it. But no, concentrate, *concentrate*! The other bike I saw outside clearly belonged to an even older child so that means Elaine must have, what, three kids? Does that include the missing one? Apart from a snapshot of a young one holding a floppy-eared rabbit that's stuck by a magnet onto the fridge door, I can't see any photos of any of them, but the thing that strikes me most about this household is that the wheels and cogs of its machinery are still going round just fine.

I mean, there's no sense of the world being paused in any way. It isn't like my life at the moment where I feel as if I'm frozen in some kind of holding pattern . . . Hell, I find it hard enough to even get up in the morning. I couldn't even *tell* this woman how much energy it took for me just to drive here today. And yet she seems to find enough to run these meetings, get her other kids to parties and – what's that note? – *Organise the OAPs' jumble sale for Harvest Festival.*

I envy her. How does she do it?

A slim willowy lady – she might be about thirty – in jeans and a floaty wide-sleeved shirt, comes into the kitchen now.

'Hi there. I'm Celeste.' She holds out her hand in greeting. 'I've got my herbal tea bags with me.' She waves away my offer to pour her a cup of coffee. 'I bring my own. Elaine knows.' Celeste smiles at me and I feel instantly a bit more comfortable. Celeste reminds me of some other-worldly creature – a fairy or an elf. She fills up a cup with boiling water from the kettle.

'You mustn't feel afraid,' she whispers to me conspiratorially as we go back down the landing to the sitting room where the noises of jollity are coming from.

'I'm not afraid,' I whisper back. But she knows that I am.

'It's hardest at the beginning,' she says softly. 'It's been four years for me. My little girl Chloe was just eight when she went missing.'

'Oh, that's terrible. Four years. And not a sign?'

200

Celeste shakes her head. She has wide, clear, light-coloured eyes. I can't make out if she still feels sad or not.

'I thought four months was too much to bear,' I say to her now. 'I cannot imagine four years.'

'The passage of time is a funny thing, isn't it?' We're still standing half in the hallway while Elaine busies herself re-organising the chairs in the sitting room (*Jasper always has that seat – does anyone know if he's coming this week, ladies?*). She wants to sit the newcomer – me – next to her so she can do the introductions, she says.

'In some ways, it's better for me, and in some ways it's better for you,' Celeste continues. 'The more that time goes by, the blunter the pain feels. It's like . . . it's like a broken spring in your mattress. You get used to finding ways to avoid it. It's still there but you don't lie right on top of it, but then one night you roll over and there's that spring, digging into your side. At your stage,' she adds, 'only four months, you don't get any respite. It's like an open wound that's there all the time.'

'That's exactly what it feels like,' I agree.

'. . . because you're still hoping that you're going to find your son alive, right?'

'I do still have some hope.' Shouldn't I? I frown at her, feeling uncomfortable. 'But it hurts to keep hope alive, did you know that?' Celeste pulls her handbag to her and peers in to find her special tea bag.

'Don't you all . . .' I glance into the room in front of us where people are starting to settle down and look curiously back towards me, still standing in the door. 'Don't you *all* hope to see your children again?'

Celeste laughs softly.

'The truth is that the nature of hope changes as time goes by. You'll see. It has to.' I want to ask her what she means by this but we're being beckoned in now and Elaine starts to do the formal introductions. 'You've met Celeste already, I see; there's

Ivy – our secretary and minute-taker – and Mel and Lisa and this is Allie. Jasper isn't actually here yet.'

There's a short reading of last meeting's minutes for those who didn't make it last time and – on my behalf – they go round the circle and everybody tells me a brief bit about themselves and then they call upon me to do the same. When it comes to my turn, there seems to be so little to say. Nobody presses me. They just look at me sympathetically, nodding. I see in their eyes they have all been through exactly this same thing themselves.

And then Elaine goes through the rules of the group. Confidentiality, she explains, is paramount. We all trust each other here and we have to keep whatever is said in confidence. You have to agree to come to at least three meetings a year.

A year!

I look at Celeste. I don't intend to be here as long as a year. One way or another I will have Hadyn – or his grave to tend – long before then. This is about 'a commitment to oneself as much as to the others in the group,' Elaine explains. I keep my eyes fixed on her beige carpet as she goes through the rules and regulations. I don't think I should really be here. I don't know why, I can't put my finger on it. I just can't help wondering what *space* is there, in a household like this, for anything as untidy as a child going missing in your life?

It reminds me of Agustina's house – everything is in its place. But how can that be, when the most important thing in the world is out of its place?

'So if you've got any questions?' Elaine is looking directly at me now, just as I was wondering if I could excuse myself and phone Maria back, find out what she really meant . . . and I realise I haven't been listening to the last ten minutes of what she's been saying.

'Um. Yes. I was just wondering what any of the members of the group have done to try and get their child back? And if anybody has been successful?'

'There's a folder we hand out to members with information about all the different organisations you can hook into for support and help,' Elaine reassures me. 'And of course you have us.'

'Actually I didn't really mean emotional support, I meant support to take *action*. To feel you were doing something useful.'

Elaine looks a bit startled at this. There's no immediate answer, though I can feel a couple of the ladies bracing themselves to put their twopenny worth in.

'I'm sure you'll agree that's more the role of agencies like the police and so forth. We try and focus on the quality of life that we have, Julia. And of course, we do what we can, but you will see as time goes by . . .'

Then we're all saved by the clunk-clunk of the heavy brass knocker on the front door and Elaine jumps up happily, announcing that Jasper must be joining us after all. From the male voice that greets her at the door it would appear that she's right.

'Jasper's a real sweetheart,' Celeste leans over and assures me, 'you'll love him.' I can see that the rest of them do, that's for sure. 'Lost his only daughter in Bulgaria – it's all very strange because her mother . . .' She fades to a halt.

'Greetings, everyone.' Jasper blows a random kiss into the room, takes off his greatcoat and sits down on the special chair that's been saved for him. 'Had the damndest time getting away this morning. Didn't miss the reading of the minutes again did I, Elaine? Oh, new member I see.' His eyes alight on me curiously for an instant.

'Coffee please,' he calls to Elaine. 'You know I like it strong, darling. Two sugars. Anyway, I've been in touch with Silas again.' He taps his nose as if this is all some private intrigue they share and I can virtually see the others shuffling forward in their seats. Elaine doesn't move to get his coffee, I notice; she's mesmerised.

'Any luck?' someone says, thrilled.

'Well, you won't believe it, but yes. He assures me she is alive and well and living in Budapest –' cue knowing looks shared around the group. 'I never told him my ex-wife was Hungarian, needless to say. I never let on a *whisper* about that. But it might soon be time for that big celebration party I've been promising you all . . .'

'Who's Silas?' I butt in before I can stop myself. 'Is he a private eye you've engaged to help with the search?'

'He's a psychic medium.' Jasper suddenly recalls the newcomer in their midst. 'A very good one.'

'Oh.' This must be what Elaine was referring to earlier on. I can just imagine what Charlie would say if I brought this up with him! He's not a fan of the 'occult' as he'd think of it. It goes totally against his religious upbringing. It should be against mine, too, as in theory I'm also Catholic – Mum just lost interest in church-going after she and Dad split up, and so did I. I've never mentioned Nana Ella's little quirks to Charlie, either. He doesn't know the full truth about half my family so I suppose Ella's the least of it.

There's a tense silence while they all take a sip from their coffee cups and look around the room at each other. They're all dying to know more about Jasper's encounter, obviously, but they don't feel comfortable with the stranger – me – sitting here, just in case I might judge them bonkers or something. If only they knew!

'Please tell us *everything*, Jasper. You know we're dying to hear what Silas said. Did he give you an accurate description of her? Did he give you any clue where in the capital she actually *was*?'

'He said he could see her in a wide avenue lined with trees,' Jasper obliges. 'He drew me a map. I'm going over to take a look myself next Sunday.'

'Does he cost a lot?' one of the group asks – half-heartedly, I sense. Jasper laughs.

'The main problem with Silas is he doesn't work much any more. You just can't get the appointment, that's the thing.'

The meeting passes quickly enough as Elaine goes round the

group and everyone checks in and then discusses the topic of the month – how they've coped with various anniversaries and holidays without the missing child. They're a good bunch of people, but I catch myself realising halfway through that the one thing they've all got in common is an acceptance of their situation. Nobody – apart from Silas – seems to be talking about taking any action to find their child.

'Will you come back?' Celeste asks me as we file out about an hour later.

I hesitate.

'I'm not sure if this group is going to provide me with the kind of support I want, if I'm honest. I'm still looking for my son, Celeste. These are all good people, don't misunderstand me, but they all seem to have accepted their loss. I haven't. I want to find people who'll support me in my search.'

'I'll support you.' She hooks her arm through mine and walks back with me as far as my car. 'I haven't given up hope of seeing my Chloe either. What did you think about Jasper's news?'

'*He* certainly seemed convinced.'

'He did, didn't he?' She looks at me sideways now. 'Do you suppose . . . there could be anything in it?'

'Possibly.'

'I'd go if you would,' she says, 'to see Silas. We could get answers. What do you think?'

I'm aware of a strange excitement growing in my belly as we stand there, the bright late March sun shining down on us.

'What if we went and he told us something terrible,' I venture after a while. 'What if he confirms that our children are no longer alive?'

'Those are forbidden thoughts!' Celeste shakes her head decisively. 'We don't let ourselves think about failure.'

'No?'

'No. That kind of thinking can erode away at your confidence and your resolve. You have to be strong, that's all.'

'Forbidden thoughts,' I repeat. Think positive.

But for Charlie the notion of going to see a psychic *would* be totally forbidden, I know. He wouldn't take too kindly to me seeing one, either.

I may not have to, though; the memory of Maria's enigmatic phone call comes back to me in a rush.

I may be about to discover something without the use of the spirit world, after all . . .

Julia

On April 8th at 02.25am Koolblue writes:

Sorry not to have replied to you earlier. I've been staying with a friend and I came back to see you have bombarded me with emails! I can see why you'd be excited to hear from Maria after all this time but – to be honest – I wouldn't get too worked up. If she knew anything useful I reckon she'd have been onto you much sooner than this.

To answer your query: Maria's staying at a flat in Earls Court at the moment, address as requested at the bottom of this. Good luck with it but don't get your hopes up too high, will you?

Would you still like me to do a bit of digging for you over here? I got the job in the bar I applied for so I'm free daytimes.

I was talking to the guy I work with sometimes, Todd – you remember, the ex-policeman? – the other night. He commented that if it was a snatch, in Hadyn's case it might not have been totally random. The fact that people would expect your husband to be wealthy might figure. We never did find out what happened to that ransom note, did we? Another thing: he asks if there is anyone who knows the family – yourself or your husband – who might have an interest in a child belonging to you. An ex-boyfriend of yours, perhaps? (Sorry, don't mean to be personal but I did mention to him you'd said the pregnancy was sudden. Could there be someone out there who imagines the child might be his? Just a thought.)

And one final thought for what it's worth: the local rag mentioned that the fisherman had hoped to dine on the fish he'd caught on the feast of Los Reyes – that's Epiphany, 6 January. Therefore I assume he caught the fish around that time – not as early as you seemed to be implying, i.e. New Year's Day? Having said that, we all know that newspapers often embellish a story for the sake of a good 'tale' so maybe we shouldn't read too much into that. Have you been able to obtain any hard facts about when the fish was actually pulled from the sea?

Blue xx

What time is it? I glance at the kitchen clock. Only five. That means it'll be six in Spain. And I've got at least an hour before Charlie's due home so if I'm going to ring Blue I'd better do it now.

I don't want to ring him. But I've waited long enough. It's been days since Maria failed to show up for our meeting and I'm desperate for news.

When I pick up the phone I hold it in my hand for an age before I dial his mobile and, even then, I dial the wrong number *twice*. The second time I don't realise it till someone else picks up the phone and starts jabbering in Spanish and I click her off without trying to explain. Third time lucky. He'll be surprised to hear from me, I have no doubt. I don't want him getting the idea it's okay to ring me back, though. I'm phoning him for information, that's all; not a social call.

'Hey!' When he picks up he sounds more Spanish than I remember him.

'Blue?' I half cover up the mouthpiece so he won't notice me breathing so hard. Charlie doesn't want me contacting this guy. I shouldn't be using the home phone either. I hope Blue doesn't use this call to get my number.

'Hi, it's me, Julia Fearon.'

'Julia?' I can hear his ear-to-ear grin from here. 'This is an unexpected pleasure. What can I do for you, my love?'

'I just got your email. I thought it might be quicker to answer you by phone. Is that okay?'

'Anytime. I'm all yours, as you know. In fact, I'm thinking of coming over to London some time soon. Perhaps we could meet for drinks?'

'Sure. Keep me apprised.' *No, no and no way no!* 'Anyway, what you said about a possible ex-boyfriend of mine thinking it was his – absolutely not. That isn't possible.'

'You'll know best,' he accedes.

'As for the question of *when* the fish was actually caught – that's an anomaly, isn't it? I can't do any digging on that from here, but could you . . .?'

'Anything for you. My pleasure.'

'Thanks so much. I'm in your debt. I mean that. And . . . thanks for Maria's address,' I gush on. 'I haven't been able to get hold of her since she last rung me.'

'I like the thought of Julia Fearon being in my debt,' he teases, but that just buys him my silence so he changes tack. 'You spoke. That's good. *And?*'

'She rang me at the end of March. We arranged to meet,' I hurry on. 'She sounded . . . urgent.'

'A bit like you do right now?' he offers.

'That might be true,' I gabble. And Maria hadn't really sounded urgent, had she? More confused. But I need to impress on him the importance of this to me. 'This *is* a bit urgent, actually. In fact, it might be nothing at all but I was wondering if you had any alternative number I could get her on? She agreed to meet me but she never showed. And now she won't pick up her phone.'

No, and I've been wearing myself into a frazzle trying to work out how I can get hold of the woman.

I'd been so excited anticipating my rendezvous with her after she'd rung. I remember that day I couldn't make up my mind what to wear, whether it was going to be warm or cold; I checked my notes four or five times to make sure I'd got the right place and the right time and I took a train that got me into Victoria one whole hour ahead of our appointed time. When she didn't show I walked the length and breadth of the station, fretting that I'd understood the wrong meeting place; that I hadn't got the right day. Her phone was off the entire time, except for one hopeful ten minutes when she seemed to be using it because it was engaged. After that, it was 'unavailable'.

And I was *furious!*

She's let me down again was all I could keep thinking, over and over. How could I have trusted her to turn up, when I couldn't trust her with the simplest and most important task of looking after my child for a few minutes that day on the beach? The bitch. I wore my heels out walking up and down the station, but then I worried that she'd turned up and – not finding me where I should be – had gone off again.

If it hadn't been for that *something* I picked up in her voice when I spoke to her that day as Elaine opened the door, then I wouldn't have bothered.

'If she said she wants to meet up with you, then she will,' Blue's lazy voice is anything but reassuring. 'They've been having a hard time of it, I hear through the grapevine.'

'No, Blue!' I bite my lip. 'She said they were going back to Spain. But I got the impression that she really wanted to speak to me. I was wondering if it could be maybe – you know – one of Diego's contacts who might have come up with something. I don't suppose you'd have heard anything about that?'

'Diego's been pretty tied up since he got to the UK I think.

I don't know if he would have been following up your case. I think it might be safe to assume, if they'd had anything to tell you at all, they *would* have found a way to make contact?'

'Well, maybe,' I defend. 'But she did ring me, after all. And she agreed to meet me. Someone *could* have rung Diego and told him something, couldn't they?'

Blue doesn't answer.

'Hello? They could, couldn't they? I mean, what on earth would Maria want to speak to me so urgently about?' *She didn't though,* I bat away the thought. *It was me pressing her, really, wasn't it?* Maria had sounded strange, conflicted even. Possibly because she *didn't* want to talk to me?

'I haven't a clue. Maybe she's still feeling guilty,' he offers. 'It's what Catholics do, you know.'

'So you think there's maybe no real reason why Maria would want to see me other than to tell me she's sorry?' I freeze then as the key goes in the door downstairs. Hell. It can't be Charlie, it can't! He isn't due back for ages yet.

Shit!

'Look, someone's coming in now and I have to go. If there's any news you can think of that Maria might have heard and want to tell me, please let me know now.'

'I can ring you back later, can't I? If I think of something?' He's teasing. I can hear it in his voice and he's infuriating me now.

'No. You can't.' *What's wrong with him? Doesn't he realise what might be at stake here?*

'Well I'm sorry, sweetheart. I can't think of anything. Unless . . .' He stops dead, puzzling something out in his mind before sharing it.

'What?' I hiss.

'It's just something Todd said to me the other day. I'm making connections here,' Blue murmurs down the phone. 'Okay. It's possible. Maybe Maria does know something after all. In fact . . .'

211

Is he leading me on or does this man really have something? I absolutely cannot tell.

'Who's that?' Charlie motions. He's dropped a huge bouquet of flowers onto the bed, kissed me tenderly on the cheek.

'No. Don't come to fix the tap tomorrow,' I mutter into the phone. 'I have to go out. I'll ring your offices back, okay?' I click the off button, smile brightly up at him. 'Never can find a plumber when you want one, can you?'

Charlie

'Hey,' she says softly. It's five a.m. She's not used to seeing me awake at this time. When she comes back from one of her night walks she's always careful to be quiet, not to disturb me. I hate her going out at night. She knows this.

'Charlie, it's *okay*.' I watch her as she pulls off her damp jogging bottoms, her wet top. 'I know you think there must be hordes of saddos wandering around in the early hours, but the truth is there is no one. Even the dog-walkers aren't up yet. When I go out in the night there is only the stars and the pavement and the rain – and me. It's easier than tossing and turning . . .'

'You don't disturb me.'

'Of course I'd disturb you if I stayed in bed, not sleeping. Besides, I'm feeling refreshed. I look more awake than you do.' In the streetlight that throws its yellow rays in through the partially drawn curtains, I can see she looks refreshed, alive. I can imagine what I must look like to her, tired and drawn.

'I've missed you, that's all.' I put down the green folder I've been leafing through, pat my side of the bed. 'Where have you been?'

'Just *out*.' She sits down and I can smell the dampness of rain-drops in her hair. I wish she would come and lie down beside me but I know she won't. 'Agustina phoned from Spain again this evening,' I tell her quietly. 'She asked after you. I told her you were sleeping.'

'Well, I probably was sleeping.' She blows a damp tendril of hair out of her eyes.

'Yes you were. Sleeping at eight o'clock. And now – out walking at four a.m.?' She stiffens.

'Your point being?'

I sigh softly.

'It would be good if you could ring them sometime, Julia.' It was Agustina's birthday yesterday, I don't tell her that. She rang to thank Julia for the flowers we sent her as a birthday gift. That was Lourdes' idea. In fact it was Lourdes who sent the flowers as well. From 'Julia and me', because, as she said: '*Your girlfriend will be too upset to think about such little things. I'll do it on your behalf, and that will keep Abuela happy.*' I'd have done it myself but Lourdes seemed so keen to help, and I've plenty enough to keep me occupied as it is.

'Ring them?' Julia is combing her fingers through her hair. 'Why?'

'Because – they worry about you.'

'Who? Your family?' She gives a little laugh. 'They shouldn't worry. What's to worry about? The worst thing in the world that could possibly happen has already happened, hasn't it?' She shrugs and I feel something coil inside me.

'Anyway,' she adds lightly, 'what are *you* doing up at this hour? What's that?'

'It's nothing.' I fold the top flap of the green folder over, put it deliberately to one side.

It's only *everything*. But everything to me, not to her. I don't know what's taken me so long to look into the Baudelaire file that Lourdes gave me weeks ago. I've been busy as hell, of course, there's been that. But maybe I didn't want to know the truth of what's really been happening in Sokoto? But now I do know. And the truth is as ugly as the disease that I've somehow made it my mission to conquer. Reading through that file has made me sick to my stomach. The implications of it are huge. Still,

214

none of this is anything Julia need worry about. I lean back against the headboard, regarding her more closely.

'You've grown thinner, Julia.' It isn't a complaint. It's an observation. 'Have you been forgetting to eat?'

'Sometimes,' she admits. 'But mostly I remember. I'm just . . . busy. I must be burning it off.'

'I was thinking,' I bow my head, 'we need to talk, don't we?'

'We *do*?' She leans forward and kisses me gently on the lips, distracting me, and yes, I want to be distracted, but I've got to say this. I've been waiting for her to come in so I can say it. It won't do, all this dancing around each other that we've been doing for so many weeks now. Whatever's going on between us, I'd sooner just have it out in the open.

'About what's happened. About us. We were a family, Julia. Now we've lost Hadyn, we're . . . just a couple again. I need to know, is that going to be enough for you?'

'What do you mean?' I watch her eyes widening.

'I mean. If we never had another child – would *I* be enough for you?'

'Oh, Charlie! Don't say such things. Don't talk about such things.'

'I have to.'

'Why?'

'Because I have to know. *Would I be enough*?'

'Of course you'd be enough!' She gives me a perplexed look. 'Why do you ask?'

We'll come to that. In time.

'I thought maybe there was something that you wanted to tell me? Something that you just didn't know how to say?'

'Like what?' She looks at me in surprise.

'It's just . . . you haven't come to me in such a long time,' I tell her slowly, 'I thought maybe . . .'

'You thought what?' she shrugs, confused, pulling up her hair away from her face. 'What did you think?' She's tense, I see now; her whole body looks on edge, full of sadness and confliction.

215

'I thought maybe you'd changed your mind about us?' I look at her sideways. 'About the wedding. Your mother told me you've packed the dress away.'

'No!' She shakes her head vehemently. 'I mean yes about the dress, but no about changing my mind . . .'

'I still love you, you know. What's happened – it hasn't changed the way I feel about you.' I pull her face up to mine with my cupped hand. 'You know that, don't you, Julia?'

'You're crazy,' she whispers through her kisses. Oh, but I had forgotten what she was like. I feel the slow ache for her returning, reminding me of what I have missed.

'Maybe.' When I pull her in close again I can hear her heart pounding. 'But if I were a jealous guy, I might even imagine that you were seeing someone else.'

'You're kidding, right? You've got to be.' Her laugh sounds too high-pitched in response. 'I haven't got the time to go philandering! Or the energy . . .'

'Nor the inclination?'

She makes to sit up in protest but then she thinks the better of it, stays where she is; something must tell her that I'm only half kidding.

'No. Not that either.'

'Because – you are good at keeping secrets from me, aren't you, Jules?' I see her swallow. *What does he know?* she's thinking. I can see it in her eyes. I can *feel* it. She's as many-layered as all the clouds in the stratosphere. How can we make a good couple in the long term when we keep so much from each other?

'I'm not keeping secrets from you, Charlie. You know everything I'm doing, even if you aren't happy with it. You know I've been trying to get hold of Maria.'

I feel my eyes narrow.

'Yes. She rang you once and then never showed up when you were supposed to meet. Doesn't strike me as she's all that keen.

She's probably wishing you'd let it all go now. Maybe *Maria* wants to move on?'

She doesn't answer for a bit. Then, 'I know I've agreed to tone down the search. I'm looking for closure, Charlie. That's all. I do *want* life to go back to normal again, you know.'

I wonder what normal is, though? I put my hand to my temple, which is aching.

'Actually I was referring to the fact that you never made the first mention to me of the fact that you'd been married before, did you? You kept that one close to your chest.'

'I *explained* what that was all about.' She struggles free of me and sits bolt upright now, but then seems to subside. 'I was embarrassed about it, all right?' She strokes my stubbled cheek gently, her fingertips conciliatory. She doesn't want us to go down the route of recriminations and heartache right now, I can see that. She wants us to make love again and get back to being the couple that we were before this horrible thing happened in our lives.

'It was just a stupid mistake,' she says now. 'Never a real marriage at all. I told you. I didn't want you getting the idea that I didn't know what a *real* marriage would be like, that's all . . .'

'Yet now you've decided – pretty much unilaterally – that you're cancelling our wedding plans?'

'It wasn't!' she gasps out. 'It wasn't unilateral. And I didn't cancel them, I've postponed them.'

'What was he like in bed?' I ask evenly now.

'Who?' She looks at me, shocked.

'Your husband.'

'Oh, Charlie! *Don't.*'

Somehow, we've moved apart. I fold my arms across my chest as a haunted look in her eyes replaces the desire that was there moments ago. 'I want to know. What was he like?'

'He was crap, okay? Look, we scarcely did it. I told you. It wasn't a proper marriage at all. Anyway,' she looks archly at me, 'you were engaged and you never said.'

'Not the same thing, you'll agree.'

'It nearly is. Let's just drop this, shall we? It's *stupid!* Anyway,' she changes the subject, disappointed, as the green folder with all the Baudelaire papers in it starts to slide off the bed, 'what's in *there* that's so important you're reading it at five a.m.?'

I snatch it up and hold it out of her reach.

'*Don't.*' The edge of warning in my voice should tell her just how important it is. She doesn't care what's in the damn folder, I can tell, but she's disappointed and just to tease me she makes a play for it.

'What is it? Some *charity* papers?' she taunts lightly. 'Let me guess — a list of celebrity guests for the gala dinner? The tally of amazing prizes you've snared for the lucky raffle winners?' She falls over me, laughing, trying to lighten me up, pretending to snatch at it, but I keep it held well out of her reach.

'It's nothing you need to worry about, Julia.'

'Oh,' she lowers her eyes at me, 'now who's the one keeping secrets, eh?' It's a fair point and I struggle to keep my face impassive.

'It's something I promised to read promptly for someone a while back, and I've not got round to it till tonight,' I relent. 'Look,' I bow my head, 'I'm sorry. I didn't mean to come across so harshly. I've had some bad news, that's all. You came in just as I was . . .'

'Bad news?' She holds her breath. What, *more?*

I shake my head. 'It's nothing that should concern you. It's all right. Really. You don't need to worry about it, *Fearless Fearon.*'

'Stop calling me that,' she whispers.

'It isn't true anyway, is it?'

'What do you mean?' She looks at me uncomfortably. 'I wish I'd never even *told you* about the nickname that Naseem gave to me all those years ago . . .'

'All this walking-out-alone-at-night business,' I raise my chin, 'you only do it to prove to yourself that you aren't scared. That's right, isn't it?'

'No it isn't. I'm not scared of *that*.'

'There *are* things that scare you, though. What about the unknown?' I grab hold of her arm as she tries to turn away from me. 'Of course it does,' I continue. 'The thought of what *might* have happened – of what *might be happening* – to our son. That scares you rigid, doesn't it?'

'Yes,' she says through gritted teeth. 'Of course it does. Doesn't it you?'

She's braver than I am, I get a glimpse of the fact that my own fear is the reason why I can't sleep. That's why I can't rest. It's why I believe the official story. It's why I have to.

'I'm scared witless. That's why every time I think about giving up the search I know I won't have any peace, Charlie, until I know the truth.'

'And yet, don't you see,' I let her arm go, 'we may never know.'

Julia

TRAGEDY OF LOST TODDLER SET TO GO ON . . .
screams the front-page headline, with a goofy looking picture of
me and Alys in front of a toppling pile of papers. *See page 2 for
details.* Dear God, what is this?

'I'm sorry,' Alys grimaces. She turns the local rag to page two
for me where there's another picture, this time of me and Mum,
standing by one of Hadyn's toys, and we both read on.

Local mum Julia Fearon is coming to terms with every
parent's worst nightmare – the unexplained disappearance of her son on a Spanish beach during a winter break.
Whilst the Spanish authorities insist they have evidence
that 14-month old Hadyn drowned, tragic Julia remains
unconvinced and is determined to carry on searching for
her toddler

'I've got to keep on looking till I know the truth,' she
said, but it's a decision that's threatening to cause rifts even
within her own family.

'I really wish my daughter wouldn't drag this out longer
than she needs to. We're all devastated and this is just
prolonging our pain,' Julia's mother Beryl told our reporter.
'Her friends are being supportive, but continuing with this
search might be more cruel than kind.' Julia's fiancé and
Hadyn's father, Charlie Lowerby, was unavailable for comment.

220

'I'm so sorry,' Alys apologises again. We've just pulled into the drive at Blackberry House and we're still sitting in her car. 'That bit about everyone being devastated and you just prolonging their pain . . .'

'This isn't what I expected, Alys.' I close the paper and peer out over her dashboard onto the wilting yellow-and-white daffodils at the front of the house. When they first opened out I remember feeling such an rush of hope because it was spring and things always get better in the spring. Now, already, they're drying up and toppling over and things haven't got any better. In fact they've got a whole lot worse.

The tone of the newspaper piece has left me feeling dumb-struck. That reporter has made me look a complete fool and she hasn't helped one jot – she's just opened up the wound all over again.

'I'm sure your mum never said those things. I can't apologise enough. I'm so sorry . . .'

'Don't – look,' I shake my head. 'Let's not go there. She wrote what she wrote. And people are going to believe whatever they want. Perhaps that's what people are already thinking, anyway?'

Alys is quiet for a bit.

'I don't think they are, Jules. Not your *friends*, at any rate.'

'We always think,' my voice is trembling, 'we think that *it will never happen to us*, don't we? We think that we're the careful ones who take all the precautions, who make all the right decisions . . .'

'In fact I think you should put in a complaint to the editor because of the way she's made you look.' Alys digs about in her handbag for her mobile. 'Maybe even sue? I'll get onto my brother-in-law Kurt right away and see what he thinks. You can make a packet out of them and we'll use the money towards Hadyn's search fund. *And* we'll get extra publicity via the nationals if we kick up a fuss. You'll see.'

'No, don't be silly.' I put my hand on her arm and squeeze so tightly that she stops the call.

'Ouch!' My friend rubs her arm where I've just pinched her.

'Do you think she really believes what she's written about me?' My throat is aching when I think of what Charlie will say – *what he will feel* – when he sees this.

'Who cares what she thinks?' She stops and hands me a tissue from her handbag. 'But you could still capitalise on the publicity this could generate.'

'No. No more papers. No more publicity.'

'You should, though. You've been made to look – well, selfish. Here's an opportunity to come back and give all your reasons for what you're doing.'

'No, Alys.' I shake my head. 'I don't want to fight her. I'm not wasting any precious energy defending my good name. I need to save it all for what really matters – and that's still the same thing – finding out the truth of what happened.'

'You've got to defend yourself, Jules.' Alys gives me a strange look, as if she's seeing me for the first time in a new light. 'If you don't, then you're maybe going to come out of the end of this having lost a lot more than just your son.' She stops, realising the implications of what she's just said.

My best friend in the whole world apart from Charlie looks at me for a quiet moment, her eyes filling again before her gaze drops away; she doesn't say a thing. She doesn't have to.

And I know in that moment that she's right; I am losing everything, *everyone* that matters to me over this and yet I cannot stop myself and I'm not going to stop, no matter what anyone says.

Julia

When I walk across the front of Drapers Street clinic this glorious May morning the whole lawn has turned into a carpet of tiny-headed dandelions that yields and then springs back as soon as I've passed. They are so pretty, petals open like supplicating hands to the sky, and I don't want to step on them. I feel sure I must be leaving a path of trampled flowers in my wake – but no. That's the resilience of nature, I think. It all bounces back. We could all learn a lesson or two from nature.

And – maybe – I am. Mum rang last night and she was really glad to hear that I'd gone back to some sort of work. She'd rather I went back to doing a 'proper job', as she called it, but I could still hear the relief in her voice. We may rub each other up the wrong way at times but I know she's been worried about me. I feel I'm beginning to reconnect with some of the small things in life that once made me happy. Nothing too big. I'm not ready to throw my hands in the air and go zippety-doo-dah just yet. But I'm reconnecting with the small things: the creamy bit on the top of a chocolate-sprinkled cappuccino from Starbucks; the sugary-pink of the wide-petalled clematis that straggles up outside our front door; the delicious feel of the gold embossed headed paper they use to send out invoices to clients.

I enjoy being with Charlie's secretary Doreen, too. She may be of the staid, pencil-pleated old school, but in many ways she is a breath of fresh air. She understands me. She doesn't need to be the centre of conversation all of the time. She doesn't mind ordering cream doughnuts for break-times because of being on a diet. And she doesn't talk down to me, or treat me like an invalid because of Hadyn. She talks about him in the present tense, as if he were still here, and I'm grateful for that.

I haven't stopped thinking about my son every hour of the day. I haven't stopped trying to get hold of Maria – though that phone is clearly out of use now. But all the leads I was so fired up about in March and April – trying to get some clarity out of Blue, trying to find another number for Maria – they've all fizzled out to nothing by May. Blue's mysterious comment about 'perhaps Maria did know something' seems to have no basis in anything at all from what I can make out when I finally got through to him after Charlie disturbed our call. He hadn't been able to speak to Todd, so he wouldn't speculate about what Maria might or might not have wanted to say.

And though Blue did claim to have tracked down the fisherman who purportedly caught 'the fish' and the guy insisted that he caught it on the sixth (five days *later* than Roberto's first mention of it to Charlie) – I just can't help but feel that *none* of them is reliable. He described the fisherman as 'illiterate, toothless and about seventy years old' and bragged that even though the man's fifty-year old brother-in-law had claimed to have caught it, and it had been *his* picture that had appeared in the papers, Blue had unearthed that really the old guy had been the one.

He seemed to be very excited about this news. He says it is the 'fatal flaw' in the police argument. But I really can't get so excited. If Roberto 'knew' about the fish before it was caught, Blue argues, then maybe Roberto was being fed false information from the beginning?

This isn't just incompetence Blue is alleging – it's out-and-out conspiracy.

How can I trust any of them? The old fisherman, his publicity-hungry brother-in-law, or the police, with their so-called ransom note? I haven't forgotten the *jefe* at the station: *How can I know where every single bit of paper is in my station at every moment?*

And Blue, I have discovered is so . . . *moody.* If you want a favour from him on a good day, then getting you the sun, moon and stars will not be too tall an order. If you get him on a 'down' day, then he's grumpy as hell.

He seemed very put out that I wasn't going to rush back to Spain to check out the fisherman.

At the moment all I keep thinking is – if I felt either him or Maria were the slightest bit reliable, then I'd get on a plane and fly out to Spain to chase both of them up, find out where she is, what's happening; but the truth is – I don't.

At Drapers Street, I've even been getting involved with Charlie's Esperanza project. It should have been Angus's secretary Merryl's job, but she's been off four weeks with bunions (all those toe-cramming stilettos she likes to wear, Doreen mutters), and I've more or less taken over what Merryl was doing. Only the 'fun bits', though, Doreen has assured me. I've been set the task of searching out a suitable venue for the end-of-summer ball that the surgeons hold for important clientele. Really, it's a thinly disguised excuse for Charlie to drag more sponsorship money out of people for Esperanza, but 'all for a good cause', as he would say.

I've settled on the Savoy this year. I've really been getting into it. Last week I was down there discussing the menu. I had great fun, tasting the puddings with Doreen. We're going to have a photo-board up in the lobby this year with testimonials from all those who've benefited from the charity in the past so people can see where their money is going.

'And with *what's been going on,*' Doreen says in a low voice, 'we're really going to be looking to draw in the big players this year.'

I stop poring through the folder of pictures in my hand. Apart from the *pro bono* patients, it's also been suggested that we put photos of our most 'beautiful' clients up too, so everyone can see just how stunning they (potentially) could look.

'Why? What *has* been going on?'

'Well, I'm sure you'll know more about it than me,' Doreen mutters. 'You'll have had it from the horse's mouth, so to speak. All this hoo-hah they've been having in Sokoto. You know . . .'

'I don't know anything about that.' If Charlie's said anything it must have washed over me. There was that green folder he was worrying about, of course . . . I should pay more attention to his concerns, I think now. I've been so wrapped up in other things.

At the moment I'm supposed to be looking through the files of our previous clients' photos to see who might be most likely to give us permission to use theirs. They keep stacks of photos here. There are literally hundreds of 'before and after' shots – mainly of already beautiful women who want to look that little bit more perfect. Some of them have folders inches thick because they've had so many procedures done.

There's one woman, Adamantine de Ascellas, who's had over twenty procedures done and, as far as I can make out, she's an oddity in that she swapped surgeons a few times. According to the notes, she started out with Charlie (breast augmentation, July 2000), then by 2004 she swapped to Angus for the same again and then requested Charlie but didn't get him for a nose job. And there are no photos of this lady (apart from a little passport-sized black-and-white one) in her folder.

I'm just wondering out loud whether she should be included in the gala guest list for the Savoy when the door swings open and in swaggers Merryl, carrying three shopping bags from Harrods and two from Harvey Nicks.

'I made it!' she smiles at Doreen and me. Doreen rolls her eyes.

'I thought you were due in yesterday, Merryl.' Doreen examines the desk diary in front of her.

'My feet still weren't right.' Merryl looks pitiful. She bends to touch her legs. 'If you've never had it done you wouldn't know, but best not to rush the recovery, that's what the doctor ordered.'

'I'm sure he must have pointed out that wearing the right sort of heels would help?' Doreen looks pointedly at the ultra-fashionable Jimmy Choos that Merryl's currently sporting.

'What's this?' Merryl's caught sight of the folders I've got opened all over her desk. 'You helping out?' She looks at me suspiciously. 'Nobody told *me*. Have you been using my desk?'

She rushes to check that I haven't been into her drawer . . . There were plenty of chewing gum wrappers and empty biscuit packets in there when I arrived a few weeks ago. 'I cleared the empties out but apart from that I haven't touched anything,' I promise her.

'Charlie thought the work would help Julia get back on track,' Doreen puts in. She looks at her warningly.

'Of course. No probs.' Merryl flashes me a smile. 'Oh, you've gone for the Savoy have you? Interesting. You look like you've done a lot of the donkey-work, so I should be glad I suppose. Where are you at with the guest list? Better run it past me before you send anything out. *She's* out, for starters.' She taps her perfectly squared fingernails onto Adamantine's file.

'Not a satisfied customer, then?' I glance at Doreen.

'Oh she's just . . .' Doreen comes over and snaps the file shut. She puts it back in the drawer where it came from. 'She's not really . . .'

'She's a little strange, I heard.' Merryl does a screwing her finger into her head motion.

'We don't talk about our clients like that,' Doreen chides. 'Where on earth did you hear such a thing, Merryl?'

'One of the nurses told me. Stacey it was. She told me . . .' Merryl stops, looks at me, and laughs. 'Oh, but I'm sure you've both already heard all about it. I won't repeat it here.'

'I suppose you had better, now that you've started.' I'm

intrigued now. 'I notice she's the only one with no photos,' I add. 'Why is that? Did she come out all wrong? Is she terribly angry?'

'Not at all,' Doreen corrects me. 'She's quite beautiful, in fact.'

'Why no photos of her, then?' Merryl challenges. 'And why's it she won't be getting an invite to the gala ball?' She already knows why, clearly. This is for my benefit.

'That's not for us to query,' Doreen sniffs. She pulls a face in my direction when she thinks I'm not looking and Merryl goes suddenly quiet. I pick up the folder I've been leafing through, puzzled.

'I'll just take this back through into filing,' I say. Neither of them answers. They're waiting for me to leave, it seems.

'You do *know* that Adamantine had a crush on Charlie, don't you?' Merryl laughs as soon as I'm in the corridor.

My ears prick up.

'Everyone knew it,' Doreen retorts. 'But so what? Lots of women do. It's a natural reaction. Not only is he handsome, he makes all their fantasies of beauty come true.'

'And he's rich.'

I lean back out of sight as the two women discuss my fiancé.

'Oh Adamantine de Ascellas has plenty of resources of her own,' Doreen adds before she can stop herself.

'So what makes *her* any different?' Merryl presses. The sound of the photocopier clicks in just then as she presses the button and I have to strain to hear over it.

'She took it a step further,' Doreen comments. 'But I'm sure you've heard the gossip.'

'Go on, tell us,' Merryl snorts. 'I'm sure I only heard the half of it. Did Charlie actually go out with her?' she breathes.

'No, but . . . I understand she wanted him to,' Doreen admits reluctantly.

'So . . . ?'

'I think she was rather *obsessional*,' Doreen muses. 'Charlie caught a whiff of that and handed her over to Angus for the rest of her treatment. He asked me to get rid of any photos in her file. That's it.'

'*Why?*'

'Ask him yourself,' Doreen sighs. 'If you really must know, she was a little *difficult.*'

'She wanted to have a baby, didn't she, and she didn't have a partner, isn't that right?' Merryl's voice is thick with the intrigue. 'Rumour was going round a few years back that she'd asked Charlie to be a donor for her – no strings attached.'

'Let's just assume that's all hearsay, shall we?'

'Do you think she's still after him, though? Is that why she's banned from the guest list?'

'I should think the poor woman should be left in peace to get on with her life as she chooses. It's not a matter of her still being after Charlie. She's got a young lad of her own, anyway, from what I hear. He'd be about eighteen months old now. I'm sure he'll keep her busy enough . . .'

'Oh,' Merryl's voice goes up with interest, 'she found another male donor, then?'

'She adopted, actually.' Doreen admits. 'She did manage to get one that looked like Charlie, at least. I saw a society photograph of them in one of the glossies. Still . . .' Doreen turns back to her desk and it's clear she's done with the topic. 'Suffice it to say Charlie would probably rather not be reminded of her. So no, don't let her onto the guest list, whatever you do. Now I really do need to type up these invoices . . .'

It takes a while for the implications of it to filter down through my mind. I can't stop thinking about the mysterious Adamantine all afternoon, and all the way home. She wanted his baby. She was obsessed with him. She's extremely wealthy. Now she has an 'adopted' son who's the same age as my son would be. Could *she* have had anything to do with my son's disappearance?

And how the heck could I – *dare I* – broach such a topic with Charlie?

Back home, Alys rings just as I'm rushing around tidying up the bedroom I left in such a mess this morning.

'*Well?*' she asks pointedly. 'How'd your first two weeks at Draper Street go?'

Christ, two weeks? Has the time really gone by so quickly? I feel pleased at that thought. For such a long while, time has gone far too slowly; it has been unbearable.

'Good.' I push the phone between my ear and my shoulder and carry on with the cleaning up – the place has been going to rack and ruin since Mum left, I think.

'Good. That's *all?*' My friend manages to convey her disappointment. I haven't been ringing Alys as often since the newspaper piece. I don't know why, but there's a gap opening up between us. It's what I need right now, but I can tell she's feeling a little rejected by it all.

'I mean, have you met *her* yet? What's she like? Have you got anything to be worried about there or not?'

'Oh, Lourdes, you mean.' I've been thinking about Adamantine all afternoon. I haven't had time to worry about Lourdes. Where's my other pink slipper? I pause, on my knees on my bedroom floor. I need to have a good clear-out under here. There's even a paper that looks like it might have come from the office down here. It says *FAO Charlie* on it. Whoops. I hope it isn't anything important.

'Nah. I think everything's okay there. I haven't actually met her yet,' I admit. 'Well, I thought I might meet her today, except they went out for a business lunch so she never actually came in to the office.'

'*They* did?'

Yes. Lourdes and Charlie did. But that's none of Alys's business. She might mean to help me but sometimes her attempts at help backfire, don't they?

'You two still getting on okay?' she adds into the silence. She always asks me that. It irks me that she asks it.

230

'Of course we are.' I bite my lip. 'We're getting on just fine, Alys.' I say it with a finality in my tone that won't encourage her to ask any more questions.

But we're not. I'm going to have to pay some more attention to what's happening or I'll lose him, I know I will.

'He mentioned that I popped round last Saturday, didn't he?' she adds after a bit, 'with the number for that reflexology lady I told you about. You were out. You didn't get back to me so I just wondered . . .'

'Oh. Sorry I missed you, Alys. You should have warned me you were coming.'

'And what about the guy you met in Spain – Blue?' she puts in now. 'Did you ring him back?'

What does she mean, *ring him back*? I texted Blue today, as it happens. I told him about Adamantine de Ascellas, just in case he'd think it was important. He's not been in contact since he found that old fisherman last month and I told him I wasn't rushing back to Spain to look into it. He hasn't texted me back about Adamantine.

'Why would I want to ring Blue?' I find my slipper, shoved into the corner under the bed.

She sounds a bit sniffy now. 'Well did Charlie not mention that your friend Blue was on the phone to him as I arrived?'

'He was? What did he have to say?' I get off my knees from the floor. What the heck would Blue have been ringing me about a week ago? I've heard nothing.

'I wasn't the one on the phone to him, was I?' I can hear her washing up the plates, the screech of the tap in her kitchen as she runs hot water over the sudsy dishes.

'Let me get this right.' My head feels dizzy all of a sudden; I've stood up so fast. I sit down on the bed and take in Alys's words slowly. 'You're telling me that *Blue* was on the phone to Charlie when you called in to see me last Saturday?'

'I took it to be him. I'm pretty sure he called him Blue. He told him not to ring back, now I think about it. He seemed pretty miffed that the guy's still onto you.'

Blue rang me, and ... Charlie put him off and didn't say anything? I fold my arms, frowning.

'Thanks Alys. He didn't mention that.' And he should have. Charlie has no right to vet my calls.

'He didn't, because he doesn't *want* you to ring Blue, obviously.'

'Alys,' I begin cautiously, as another thought strikes me, 'there's this former client of Charlie's I learned about today. A Spanish lady. Turns out she had a major crush on him. Wanted him to father a child on her – no strings attached – but it just reminded me of something Blue and his detective friend Todd said to him a while back, about *former partners maybe having an interest in the child ...*'

'Do you really think there could be anything in it?' she says dubiously. 'I rather got the impression you were ... backing off the whole search?'

No, I am not backing off the search. I am just backing off depending on Alys to help me with it so much, I remember.

'Well – it's true I've been concentrating on my relationship with Charlie at the moment,' I tell her. 'But this might be worth chasing up, mightn't it?' There's a pause while she considers this. I know she still thinks the best way to go forward would be through massive publicity coverage and making everyone as aware as possible. 'Well, anyway – have you still got that reflexology number?' I distract.

'I'll get it.' She disappears for a bit. When she comes back with the number her voice is warmer. 'If you want me to do anything to help you out, Jules, you know you only have to call me.'

'I know, you're a dear, really you are. I don't know what I'd do without you, Alys.' I stare at the number I've just written on the back of the paper I've just pulled from under the bed. Reflexology. *To relax me*, she says. I'll have to write it down again on another piece of paper. **FAO Charlie.** This one might be important to him.

Then I stare at it a little closer.

It's a note from Lourdes to Charlie. Where the heck did this come from? It must have fallen out of the folder he was reading in bed that night when I came home and found him awake. My eyes stand out on stalks as I read the words she's handwritten there. .

> *Dear Carlos,*
> *I feel so ashamed about this. I didn't want to show you it, fearing what your reaction would be. Whatever else happens, I want to remain by your side in this endeavour, your trusted aide and confidante, from your sincere and loving friend, Lourdes xxx.*

I crush the paper in my palm and then, still not quite believing it, open it out carefully and spread it onto the bed, reading it over and again. She's ashamed about what? *What?*

How could he do this to me? How could he?

Charlie

The kitchen is incredibly quiet. Apart from the frantic tap-tapping of Julia's fingers on the keyboard and the occasional dripping of the tap, the place is lifeless. I wonder what happened to all the red and lilac dahlias she was growing in the patio-pots this time last year. I wonder who arranged all the plastic fridge magnets into the order of the alphabet. They don't look right that way. They look as if they are waiting for someone to come and make some sense out of them.

Like me; like my life.

'I've telephoned Chang's,' she informs me without looking up, 'number forty-seven. Your usual.'

Chang Wu's Chinese home delivery, she means.

'I thought maybe you'd let me thank you for all the work you've been putting in at the clinic?' I come up behind her and kiss the back of her head. It's a beautiful May evening. She shouldn't be stuck in here, still hunched over that computer. 'I thought I'd take you out for a meal, perhaps?' Her hair is scraped back in a tightly pulled ponytail, secured with a rubber band that looks suspiciously like the ones the postman leaves outside the front door.

'No.' She still doesn't look up. I don't know what she's reading but it sure as heck interests her more than I do. 'And I think Merryl is after having her job back, just so you know . . .'

'I'll get Angus to fire *her*,' I offer, 'if you want to stay on?'

'No. It's all right. She can keep the job.' When she turns round I can see the dark lack-of-sleep lines under her eyes. 'I'm the one who needs to go looking for one now. Besides – I don't think I like the idea of being so close to you with all your beautiful clientele all day long. They might make me jealous.' She looks at me coldly.

'Not a hope,' I snort.

'Really? Merryl was harping on about some woman called Adamantine de Ascellas earlier today.' She fixes her eyes on me now. There's not a hint of a smile in them.

'Apparently she wanted to *have your baby*, or something like that?'

'Something like that. I don't want to talk about her, Julia.' God, where in heaven's name did she drag that woman's name up from?

'Why ever not?' she insists. 'Surely nothing ever happened between you? Doreen tells me she was very lovely – but there're no photos in her file, unlike everyone else's . . .'

'No, there was nothing between us. That would have been unethical, apart from any other consideration. And yes, she was quite crazy. She needed psychiatric treatment in the end. So let's just drop her, shall we?' I smile at her but I know it doesn't reach my eyes and my arms around her suddenly feel cardboardy and stiff. 'Anything else on your mind?

'Anything on *yours?*' she challenges.

'Only about one hundred and one things,' I admit. The squeeze that Santos is pulling on me now that he's seen I'm not willing to back Baudelaire. The fax I had in from Lopez this afternoon, telling me that our documents in Sokoto are about to be impounded. But all I have to do is take one look at Julia and I see she's not up for hearing about any of that.

'Look, you can stop lying to me. I found her letter to you, Charlie. It must have dropped out of the green folder that night you were reading it on the bed. I found it when I was hoovering up after I got back this afternoon . . .'

'What letter? *Whose* letter to me?' I stand back, slightly shocked at the look on her face.

'Lourdes' letter, of course.' She gives me an arch look.

'The one where she offers you her undying support and promises to remain forever your staunchest ally and confidante – whatever it was she said. All sounded pretty cosy to me.'

'*What* letter?' I scratch my head. Then it dawns on me which one she must be talking about. 'Julia . . . that's just how she speaks! We're not having an affair, if that's what you think. Don't even *imagine* that. You have to understand how it is. She has to turn her back on her own brother if she sides with me on this case. She's in a difficult position. She just wanted me to know that she'll support me, that's all. Look – we have three weeks to find alternative accommodation for the rehabilitation cases; there's a court appearance for our representative that one of us needs to find counsel for; and they're threatening a moratorium on all further operations until the matter is sorted. Oh yes, and another phone call came in just today from Santos, assuring me yet again that it could all be sorted out if I would only see my way clear to back Baudelaire.'

'I have no clue what you're talking about,' she says dully. Of course she doesn't. She doesn't know what's in the rest of the file, that's the thing. And I can't, by rights, tell her. 'She says in her note to you that she feels very ashamed, doesn't she? What's that about?'

'It's business, love. Her brother – he's been involved in some . . . "difficult" issues – believe me, that's all it is.'

'Sure.'

'Look – let's just go out – I don't fancy a takeaway tonight . . .'

'I thought you liked it,' she frowns. 'You'd like something different?' She grabs the phone. 'I can cancel the pork balls. You can order something else, Chang won't mind.'

I can't understand why she's reacting like this; why she's making such a fuss when there really is no reason . . .

'No . . . I'd like some real food: that's what I meant. Maybe something homemade.'

'You can cook, can't you?' She looks edgy, tetchy.

'Yes. I don't mind cooking it, J. Since your mum left and you decided to dismiss Didi, there's never anything in there to cook.' I make for the fridge but she gets there first.

'What do you want me to buy? I mean, what? Tell me what you want me to buy and I'll get it for you.'

I shrug. For the minute my mind's gone completely blank. 'Fresh, healthy food. Something . . . *nice.*'

'So what I buy isn't *nice*?'

'You don't buy anything any more.'

'I buy stuff. Of course I buy stuff! What did you eat this morning?' She's got the fridge open and she's looking in it, hoping to prove her point.

'Eggs, I had eggs.'

'There you go then, that's healthy, isn't it?'

'I got them at work. I had a breakfast meeting with Angus today, remember?' I go over to the window and open it wide. We need some air in here. We need *something.*

'Maybe that's why I don't need to buy them for home! You're always at work, aren't you? Even for breakfast. Here!' She flings a bag of ready-washed salad at me. 'Food. Okay? *Healthy* food.' She flounces back and sits by her laptop again.

She's not getting away with that.

'Why are you doing this, Julia?' I've caught hold of her hands and I'm holding them off the computer now so she can't type. She sighs exaggeratedly, but I can tell she's getting pissed off.

'I'm doing what I have to do, *Carlos.*' She turns in her seat and looks at me deliberately now. 'Look, I didn't think you'd want that much for dinner. I heard you already went out for *lunch.*'

237

'If you mean with Lourdes, that was only coffee.'

She pulls a face at that.

'Oh. I see. It isn't *what* I had for lunch that rankles. It's *who* I had it with?'

'Don't be ridiculous.'

'When you meet Lourdes,' I tell her, 'you'll see, she's a great person. You'll like her.'

Julia makes no reply to that. She picks up her cup of stale coffee and puts it to her lips, grimacing.

'There is no reason for me to meet *your devoted aide and confidante*,' she says after a bit. 'She's your ex and I'm your current girlfriend. We've nothing else in common.'

'You *will* be meeting her as it happens.' I've got to put this tactfully now as I know she won't be pleased. 'There's a dinner party Angus is setting up . . .'

'She'll be there?' Julia looks pained.

'Yes she will. And so will you.'

'If you say so.' Julia turns away from me and continues typing into the screen.

'Please, Julia, listen to me. He's setting up this dinner so we can meet some people – the Serranos. It won't be just yet – they won't be coming to the UK till later in the summer but, just so you know – we're hoping they might be able to take over from Santos's company in backing Esperanza.'

'Oh, *that!*' She shrugs, infuriatingly uninterested.

'Anyway, who are *you* talking to?' I peer closer at the screen but she closes it down before I can catch who it is. 'It's the bloke from Spain, *Blue* isn't it? The one who wrote to you implying that more could have been done for Hadyn's case. You contacted him?'

'I didn't. He contacted me.' She's breathing harder now and I know she's lying. The irony of this doesn't escape me. She's bothered to bits about me seeing my ex-girlfriend but she doesn't mind going behind my back to speak to this man, Blue. I've already told her he's no good. 'We're in *May*, now – has that occurred to you? All these months that have gone by – if anyone had anything useful to say . . .'

'Maria's disappeared though, hasn't she? Even Blue doesn't have a contact for her.'

I sigh heavily. 'What do you think Maria will tell you that she hasn't already told the police?'

'Blue pointed out . . . she would know if those shorts the police used as evidence were even still on our son when they went out to sea. What if they weren't? What if she'd started to change him?'

'You don't think the police would have picked up on that? According to Roberto she gave them a very thorough statement. That would have included what he was wearing when she last had sight of him. You're clutching at straws, Julia.'

'Blue seems to think it is possible they never asked her.'

'She worked at the police station; she would have known what information they need. For some reason, this "Blue" is trying to keep feeding you tales, and you're only too willing to buy into his stories because you are desperate, don't you see that? Maybe he wants an excuse to keep in contact with you? He knows you want to hear anything that'll keep your hopes up . . .'

She doesn't answer and I continue, 'I thought you'd given up on this. You told me you were keeping yourself busy, occupying yourself so you didn't become obsessed with an impossible dream.' I turn from her in despair. 'You do know what you're doing is going to break us up, don't you?'

'I'm not breaking us up, Charlie.' Her pretty eyes look troubled now. Troubled but still driven. It's been – what – four/five months since Hadyn went missing but she's still acting as if it were yesterday. She's acting as if we didn't already know what happened. And this bloke Blue, I know he's part of that.

'That *is* what you're doing, Julia. You keep pushing me away all the time. I know you're sad, but you won't let me help you. How you're being with me doesn't help me, either. I'm feeling it too, J. But nothing I do or say can make any difference, can it?'

She looks at me unhappily.

'Why don't you carry on helping me with Esperanza?' I push. 'It's given you something else to—'

'Ask Lourdes,' she says shortly.

'If I asked Lourdes to do any more than she already does, I might as well have her in my house living with me.'

'She wouldn't mind that, would she?'

'It's what I want that counts here. I want *you*. And I don't have you at the moment. You haven't un*dressed* already, have you?'

She hoists up her slipping PJ bottoms defensively.

'I didn't need to be dressed. I wasn't going anywhere. Besides. It just wastes time. I have so much to do. I've had leads to follow, this evening. I've had new info come through. *Important info*.'

'*Christ*, Julia!' I pull a beer out of the fridge and open it. She watches me with narrowed eyes as I take a slug.

'I'm still looking for our son, Charlie. I *have* to.' Her voice is more urgent than before.

'He's *dead*!' I don't mean to shout but I don't know what else to do. When is she just going to accept this?

God I am tired.

I am tired and I am hungry and I am not in the mood for a confrontation. All I want is peace. All I want is the woman I used to have. The Julia who was once so excited at the thought of marrying me so she could spend her time looking after our baby. Maybe the baby was the only thing she ever really wanted out of our relationship, come to think about it?

She gets up and hands me a tall glass but I wave it aside. I'll have it straight from the can just to annoy her. She stands back, looking frustrated, hands akimbo.

'What if he isn't dead? I have no actual *proof*, Charlie.'

We've been through this two hundred times before. Five hundred times.

'Well, what if he isn't and you never ever find him? Have you thought about that? What if he is still alive somewhere, perfectly happy, without you? Have you thought about *that*?'

This shocks her into silence for a minute. I drink my beer and I watch her face as she tries to master her expression. She is on the verge of tears, I know. My words have cut deep and I'm sorry for that, I don't want to hurt her. When I see her struggling I want to take her face in my hands and kiss her mouth so deeply that she forgets all about her papers and her search that will never get anywhere. I want her to stop chasing a ghost and to remember me, because I'm still here and by God I still need her; I still want her.

'No, I haven't thought of that. And I don't care either. If he is alive somewhere, I need to know it. If he isn't, then I need to know it too.'

'Sometimes,' I walk up and put my hands on her shoulders, 'you don't get any answers, J. You just don't. I've had patients die on my operating table before now and I've never found out why or how. Oh, you get inquests, you get rubber stamps on death certificates but you never know *why* that person died when they should have lived. Sometimes you just have to accept things, J. You have to learn to *accept* them. I'm not asking you to stop grieving for him. I know that will take many months. But I'm asking you to *start* grieving.'

Her face crumbles.

'I wish – I want to – to do what you've done; put it behind me. How do I do that though, when I . . .'

'You do it by accepting what you have to. Despite your loss, despite the not-knowing, despite the no-ending, you do it by – ' I grab her little, soft hands – 'by putting your palms together and praying, just like I showed you. Ask God for the Grace to let him go, Julia. There *is* nothing else.'

Her eyes are glistening but she does not cry.

'I'm sorry if I've been ignoring you,' she says softly. 'I know that I have. I know it and I know you need far more and deserve far better but . . .'

No 'ifs or buts': I need her to let go of this.

'I need to get to the truth, first.'

'You've got the truth. We know what happened!'

'*My* truth,' she says deliberately. 'And if you won't help me do it then I still . . .' She lowers her eyes here, 'I need Blue.'

'So if I don't countenance your actions then *Blue* is the one to help you do it?' She looks confused, shocked even, at my sarcastic tone. This isn't me speaking; it isn't me at all but something else that has taken me over for the minute: a blind, raging jealousy.

'Blue *has been* helping me.'

'Blue is helping you. Right.' I stop and look at her pointedly for a few moments. 'Have you *heard* anything from him at all just recently?'

'No!' she says hotly. 'And we both know why that is, don't we?' She sits back down at her computer and switches it on defiantly. 'Alys told me about you telling Blue to bugger off that day he rang me. You had no right to do it, Charlie. He's my friend. He's none of your business! What did he want, anyway? Did you even bother to find out before you blew him out?'

I fold my arms. 'He wanted to tell you that he wouldn't be contactable for a while because he's been convicted of petty theft and they're sending him to prison.'

'You're *lying*.' She looks at me, wide-eyed. But she can see very well that I'm not.

'Damn it!' she says. 'I needed him to look someone up for me. I needed him to –' she takes on a sheepish look – 'check someone out.'

I take a step closer. 'Check *who* out, may I ask?'

'Look,' her face colours, 'I know you are going to think I am completely off the wall with this so I'd rather not say.'

'Who?' My frown deepens. 'Just *tell* me?'

'Adamantine de Ascellas,' she says after a while. 'She's a possible suspect. She must be. Don't you see? She has an adopted eighteen-month-old baby now who looks just like you. Blue said that anyone who might have had a very strong desire to parent one of our children could possibly have had the motivation to snatch him—'

'No!' I shake my head ferociously. 'No, no no! This is madness. She might have had psychiatric issues at one time, but they've been dealt with. And her family would never have countenanced any wrong-doing. She's from a well-connected, very well-respected family along the Costa. Do you see the level of desperation you've reached, if you have to pin your hopes on something like this?' I shake my head in despair. 'We have good people on our side, Julia. Trustworthy people. My brother is doing everything that can be done. He *has* done everything.'

'I know he has, Charlie. And I'm grateful to him, believe me. It's just that there are a few bits of the story that still don't quite gel for me.'

'Such as?'

She puts her head in her hands and just sits there for a minute. She doesn't answer me. *Nothing.* She has nothing. No reason to keep this charade going any longer.

'Let him go, Julia. Just let our son go. The problem is no longer the tragedy that has happened to us, do you realise that? It's that you find it so impossibly hard to let things go.'

The doorbell goes then, cutting right through us. It'll be Chang's delivery boy, with a special order number forty-seven. Neither of us moves to get it.

'Maybe the problem,' Julia stands at last, pushing the chair out from under her, 'is that *you* find it so incredibly easy to. Otherwise, if we're honest about it, you probably *would* still be with Lourdes, wouldn't you?'

Julia

On 21st June KoolBlue wrote:

Hi J,

Apologies for taking so long to get back to you, I got sent down for something I didn't do, and they don't run to computers in Spanish jails. I hope you won't think less of me because of it.

I checked out that Adamantine for you. Turns out her family own the Aquavista private beach estate and hotel just down the road from here. She spends a lot of time there with the family in August. That's all I've found out.

To tell you the truth, since I got out I've been pretty eaten up by the fucking awful news of what's happened to Maria and Diego.

Don't know if you heard, but they returned to Spain several weeks ago. She came to see me once, in the clink. They'd been having a lot of arguments, she said. She wanted me to help her. I would have, but . . .

Fuck me, by the time I got out last Tuesday I discovered they'd both been involved in a horrific smash-up on his motorbike. I went to see them this morning in the hospital. It looks bad, Julia. I'm sorry to tell you this, even if they live, I don't honestly know if you'll ever get any information from them, now. Blue xx

244

Even if they live!

What . . . what does he mean, *if they live*? They have to live! They have to tell me what they know – whatever Maria was going to tell me that day she never showed up. I grab the phone from its cradle in the kitchen and dial up Blue's number. Heaven knows if he'll even be at the same place now, if he's been in prison.

I'm going to have to go back to Spain. I'm just going to have to go *now*, look up Maria and Diego and find out what I can before my last chance slips away . . .

'Yes?' the harsh, weary-sounding voice at the other end doesn't even sound like Blue. Is it him?

'It's me,' I hesitate. 'Julia.' I glance at the clock. It's five already. Will I still be able to get a flight out tonight?

'Julia,' he says in acknowledgement. For once, he doesn't sound even the slightest bit pleased.

'I just got your email,' I rush on. 'Is it – are they really bad?'

'I just came back from the hospital, Julia. It couldn't be worse, to say the truth.'

I sit down at my kitchen table. I have to. My legs give out underneath me. There's a long moment of silence. I put my hand to my mouth, waiting for him to say it but he doesn't.

'Are they still alive?' I prompt at last.

'Diego died yesterday.' There is a long, long pause as we both take this in. The sunlight streams in through my kitchen window and it's full of shining motes of dust. Dust. That's what Diego soon will be, and anything he knew has gone to his grave with him.

'Massive internal injuries,' Blue is saying now. 'They said he must have been doing at least a ton. You should have seen the bike.'

I swallow. If I had *known* they were back in Spain, I would have gone there sooner. If Blue had not been in prison, he could have told me they were there. Maybe they are all unreliable and maybe – probably – they don't know anything that will help me at all, but if I don't take the chance now and find out I will have lost it forever.

245

'And Maria?' I croak. Maybe she will recover enough for me to speak to her? She's been through such a terrible time. She will need the space to recover, of course, but . . .

'I wasn't allowed to see her,' he gulps brokenly now. 'She was my *friend*. We had . . . a special bond between us. You know how it is.'

'When things are . . . very bad . . . they only allow the immediate family in,' I tell him now. 'You'll have to give it time. I'll book a flight out to Spain. I'll come over. We'll both go in to see her . . .'

'They said they were waiting for her relatives to come in to identify her body,' he sobs. 'They wouldn't let me in.'

Oh my lord.

'She's dead too then?' I feel the last remaining dregs of my hope drain away as I hear his sobbing at the other end of the phone.

'I'm really sorry, Blue.' I stare at my watch, not taking the time in at all, but realising that it doesn't matter, actually, what time it is at all. All the sudden urgency for action that I felt a few moments ago has ebbed away in a second. I won't need to get on a plane tonight. I won't be going anywhere.

They're dead. The only two people in the world who might have been willing to give me some lead in my search.

'Blue, I have to ask you something,' I stammer out at last, 'did you ever get to speak to your friend Todd on my behalf after all?' I *know* he has just told me the most awful news, but there's something inside me going – what if HE disappears too, and you never get another chance to ask?

'About what?' he says dully. He's forgotten.

'The day I told you that I thought maybe Maria had some news for me – you said you thought Todd might know something?'

'It was probably nothing,' he dismisses my question in an instant. 'I don't remember now, Julia. My best friend has just died. I'm sure you can understand . . .'

'Of course,' I apologise. 'It's just I was never able to contact

246

you again after that. And I still haven't got my son back,' I remind him. 'It might have been something important.'

'No,' he tells me now. 'I never had anything important for you. If I had I would have given it to you, wouldn't I? Seriously.'

He's saying now what Charlie has been saying all along; that nobody knows anything; that if they did they'd have *told* me already . . .

I put the phone down, realising that Blue most likely doesn't want anything further to do with me, after this. My connections with Spain are all dissolving. My connections with people over *here* aren't doing too great, either, I think. I haven't spoken to Alys in a couple of weeks. I'm not getting out much.

I have given up the work at Drapers Street. When Merryl – with all her gossip and intrigues – came back, my concentration just went. The counsellor Dr Fraser referred me on to – after Winnie – looked about eighteen years old and she smiled a lot and repeated back almost everything I said to her, like a parrot. She made me feel even more leaden. So I gave her up, too. I go out for walks with Celeste a couple of times a week. That's the only thing that helps. At least Celeste *understands*.

She's still talking about going to see that psychic but we haven't got round to it yet. Maybe because we're both scared what we'll hear?

All I can think now, as I stare through the hall window at the beautiful midsummer evening, is that, the longer I wait, the more people are potentially accumulating on the 'other side' for me to speak to. I can't believe that Maria is dead!

She shouldn't be dead.

And I . . . I don't know what else I can do, now, to make anything better.

Maybe it's time to face the fact that Charlie's right and there really is nothing left at all for me to do?

Julia

I've tried on five different dresses for Angus's dinner party this evening.

I hate the way I look in every single one of them.

It's only when I peer into the mirror on my dressing table that I realise it isn't the dresses that are the problem, it's my *face*. When I lean forward, looking into my sunken eyes, I see that I look so bloody awful I can't imagine for the life of me why Charlie would even want me there by his side tonight.

I would back out if there was even the slightest chance of it, but that won't make him any too happy.

And then, of course, there's Lourdes, I remember. She'll be there, tonight.

She'll be looking a darn sight more gorgeous than me, too, I'll bet.

For one moment, Charlie catches my eye. He comes over, hugs me lightly about my shoulders, speaking to my reflection in the mirror.

'I know I'm asking a lot of you, coming out to support me and Angus tonight, J.' For one split second, as I feel his breath on my neck, I'm aware of the echo of a long-ago ache for him. But I have been sleeping in the spare bedroom these past few months. I have spent too much time pacing the floor in the small hours for us to share a bed.

He still has to get up in the morning. And I don't.

'But you know what these South Americans are like,' Charlie is saying. 'As I told you before, if they deal with you, they insist on knowing your whole family.'

'I'm not your family yet,' I remind him, twisting my face to look at his.

'You're the mother of my son though, aren't you? And you *will* be my wife.'

'Will I?' my voice is small. The mother of your son. I think: *the one I lost.*

'Do you *still* think that we will ever marry, Charlie?'

Charlie stops on the top button of his white shirt – tonight is black tie – and looks right at me.

'I still want you, Julia. That hasn't changed.'

Do you, I think, *even when I'm permanently miserable? Even when I look like this?* I wipe the edges of my eyes very carefully with my fingertips.

'And I do know how you're feeling right now.' Charlie sits down gingerly beside me. 'It's just that . . . we have to get on with the business of living too.'

'I know.'

I look up cautiously. I want to ask him about Lourdes. I can feel Charlie patting my hand right now, but he seems detached.

'All you have to do tonight is make conversation with people. Everyone knows our . . . situation – so that shouldn't come up. Angus has got these potential Esperanza backers lined up, but they want to meet the team. The main guy's name is Mario Serrano. He's the one to be especially sweet to. From what I hear he could fund the entire annual Esperanza budget from chump change if he'd a mind to.'

Mario Serrano. The Esperanza-Centre-bloody-budget. I am not feeling sweet inside. I am feeling sour.

My carefully made-up face feels as if it's beginning to run. The taxi honks downstairs. It's five minutes early.

249

In the mirror behind me I can still see Charlie straightening his tie. His nimble surgeon's fingers are trembling. I wonder, if Serrano makes approving noises about Esperanza tonight, will this be enough to make Charlie feel happy again?

Part of me wonders if Charlie's nerves are down to the fact that tonight he will be introducing *her* to me? When he says her name I know – I can tell – he still cares about her. What is it she called herself? *His aide and confidante*? I feel a sick hollow feeling in my stomach at the thought. Could Charlie possibly be feeling nervous about *that*?

He picks up my pearl and sequin silver bag from the mess of crushed dresses on the bed and hands it to me with a small smile. And yet, he was engaged to her once and he let her go. You fool, Julia Fearon, I think. He's engaged to *you* now, isn't he? Even if you've had to put the wedding off for now.

Tonight is all about what's at stake with his precious centre, that's all.

I couldn't care less about Mario Serrano and his mountain of chump change.

But I do care about Charlie.

I will sit through this evening with a smile plastered to my face and be as sweet as pie to everyone – including Lourdes – if I have to. Then I will come home and cry whatever tears I've got left, in private.

Lansdown House is tucked into the recesses of a walled garden hidden within the grounds of Hampton Court. It takes the taxi an age to find the nearest entrance to it. In the end we have to come out onto the main road and walk over a straw-littered field and through a wooded area to find it.

It has been raining all day and the ground is muddy beneath my high heels but the beautiful summer evening is just beginning to turn pleasant. A blackbird calls from somewhere just beyond my sight and I wish, for one crazy moment, I could just kick off these shoes and run barefoot through the still-damp grass. I don't want to go indoors and spend a stuffy evening talking about business and pretending that Charlie and I are getting our lives back on track when plainly he is and I am so clearly not.

A girl in waitress uniform opens up the wooden door into the closed-off cottage garden and invites us in. 'Would you like to come into the reception area for drinks, now?' she smiles brightly. 'Thank you.' All I can think is, no; I would not like. I do not want to sit in the eating hall of this medieval hunting lodge and meet Serrano and *Lourdes*.

Charlie, maybe sensing my reluctance, tugs a little on my hand. 'Won't be so bad now, J. Try and put a bit of light into those eyes, will you?' he beseeches.

'Ah, here they are now!' says Angus. 'Mario, I'd like you to meet my dear friend and business partner, Charlie Lowerby and his fiancée Julia.' Mario takes my hand gravely to kiss it.

'Enchanted,' he says sombrely. He wears his silver hair slicked back like a Mafioso hitman. He must be in his sixties at least, but his movements are as graceful and economical as a cat's. His eyes study mine for a moment.

He *knows*.

I'm the first one to look away. He's curious to see how I'm bearing up, that's what it is. I'm like the bear in a cage at a provincial zoo tonight, I suddenly realise. Everyone's going to be looking at me. They're going to be thinking: *How is she coping? How is she holding up?*

I should never have come.

'My dear.' Angus's diminutive wife Katie clasps her hand over mine and draws me almost immediately away to where the 'girls' are sitting. 'We're all having champagne. I've poured you out a glass already. Come and meet Mellita, Mario's wife.' Katie pats the soft white sofa beside her. 'So glad you could make it tonight,' she purrs. 'You're looking really well, my dear.' Last time Katie saw me was when she came to the house about a week after I got back from Spain. My face was still swollen then, from the lamppost. I remember seeing the shock on her face when she caught sight of me; that's all I remember.

'Mellita is such a nice woman,' she's telling me quietly now but I'm more interested in the younger woman I spot standing by the open doorway that leads out onto the garden.

'That's Lourdes?' I indicate towards her with my head, and at that moment, even as I feel my heart thumping in my mouth, Lourdes turns round.

She is older than I had thought she would be, I take her in instantly. Her hair is auburn and shiny and she has the cutest nose. But she has something else – a prettiness and a vulnerability about her – that I know Charlie would find irresistible . . . She knows who I am, too. There is only the slightest hesitation before she holds out her hand to me, but in that instant I know she is equally as nervous about meeting me.

'Julia?' She holds out her hand but doesn't move from the doorway. I leave Katie and go and join her. 'I'm so happy to meet you at last.' Her accent is only faintly Spanish, reminds me of Maria's. Her hand covers mine for an instant; I get the briefest kiss on the cheek. 'I'm Lourdes.' Introductions done, she turns her face out to the garden then, breathing in deeply. 'Isn't this the most beautiful evening?'

'Very beautiful,' I agree. The spicy scent of a myriad of carnations – gilly-flowers, they would have called them in the olden days – wafts towards us. The place is peaceful, but we are both – she and I – very ill at ease . . .

'I've heard so much about you,' she says after a time. 'I wanted to tell you – how sorry I was, when I heard of your tragedy.'

I bow my head in acknowledgment at that, wiping away the tear that springs straight into my eye.

'Forgive me,' she says, alarmed. 'I didn't mean to . . .' She stops, looks over towards where Charlie is still standing deep

252

in conversation with Mario Serrano and then back to me. 'This
. . . is *awkward*, isn't it?' she shares, whispering. 'What are we
supposed to say to one another?'

'I suppose,' I venture, with a tight little smile, 'we should talk
about Esperanza – and all that kind of thing. It's what we're here
for tonight, isn't it?' Stick strictly to business, I think. I'm not
going to get personal with you.

'We are, of course. We are *all* here for that. But between you
and me,' she gives a little shrug, 'it's a little more complicated
than that, isn't it?'

'Why is it complicated?' I give her a direct look. *Because you
are still in love with Charlie?*

'I've known for a long time that we would have to meet,'
Lourdes rushes on. 'That it would be inevitable. And, Julia –' she
looks at me significantly – 'I do so much work for the centre,
it's only going to be a matter of time before we meet *again*.'

'Well, here we are.' If she's saying that we might as well try
our best to be friends, I can't see it happening. I turn my face
back out towards the garden.

'Charlie tells me he's been trying to persuade you to get
involved with Esperanza, too?' she persists.

'No.' I shake my head, barely wanting to look at her. 'I'm not
getting involved with that. I've got enough work of my own to
do.' I sound churlish and I know it. But the harder she's trying
to be friendly, the less I want to stand here pretending to have
polite conversation with her. Because, actually, she is *too nice*. I
don't want to see how nice she really is. It doesn't make me feel
any better; it makes me feel worse.

'Everything in good time,' she says gently. She sighs, then. 'I
love it here, don't you? I sometimes wonder what it would have
been like to live here, back in the old days?' Her voice is suddenly
sultry, just as I remember it from our brief phone conversation
the day after Hadyn went missing. 'Do you think maybe things
would have been much simpler, back then?'

253

I shrug my shoulders and she smiles unexpectedly.

'Did you know that Henry of Monmouth built this house for his courtesan,' she surprises me now. 'When he was still courting her, and before she had . . . acceded,' she lowers her lashes here, 'to his requests.' My face flushes. Is that what she meant when she talked about 'things being simpler' in the olden days? Bloody hell! She could have just been Charlie's courtesan and he could have built her a house of her own, so they could get on with it in peace . . .

I've never even heard of Henry of Monmouth.

'I didn't know you were such a keen historian,' I tell her, dryly.

'There's a lot we don't know about each other, Julia.'

'No,' I seize my moment, 'we don't. I know that you and Charlie were once engaged to be married –' I hesitate – 'and that's about it.'

'You don't know the reason why we broke it off, then?' She looks at me intently and I shake my head.

'Really,' she presses, 'he never told you?' We both look back then, as the assembled party breaks into gales of laughter over some joke that Angus has just told. Nobody is paying us any mind.

I spread my hands and Lourdes gives a little sigh. 'I don't think, if Charlie has never spoken about it with you, that it is my place to say, Julia.'

'You brought it up,' I remind her, annoyed now, and we both look over to where the other women are waiting for us.

'Come over here, you two!' Katie orders us now. 'You haven't even met Mellita yet, Julia. She's dying to hear all about Charlie's girl . . .'

'*Love* your dress,' Katie gushes at Lourdes, the minute we're ensconced on the sofa, 'don't you, Julia? The colour wouldn't look so well on me though – that sapphire blue goes better on younger skin.'

Who cares, *who cares*, I think desperately. You're sixty-two and your skin isn't young any more – so just get over it.

'I'm sure it would look just fine on you,' I say automatically, and at that moment Charlie turns round, spotting Lourdes beside me, and I see him tense up. Then deliberately, consciously, he relaxes. He's telling himself that we girls are going to get on just fine; I can almost hear him thinking it.

But why did you two break it off with each other, Charlie? I glance at his former love by my side. She's crazy about him still, that much is obvious.

She's smiling at him softly, even now, unable to stop herself looking in his direction, unable to *help* herself, and her sadness and her longing are palpable enough for the whole room to feel it, surely? But apparently not.

I feel perplexed.

I feel I have been press-ganged into the most intolerably awkward situation imaginable and nobody in the room – except maybe Lourdes herself – is even vaguely aware of it.

Julia

Charlie seems happy. He's been seated to one side of Lourdes with Serrano on her other side and they've all been engaged in animated conversation all evening. I would be worried, disturbed, except every time I catch the drift of their conversation they're talking about Esperanza and nothing else . . .

'I am so glad you decided to come, Julia.' I drag myself back to Mellita who is saying to me, 'We weren't sure if you would.'

'Charlie asked me to support him, so I came.'

'I was so sorry, my dear.' After three hours of us sitting here, exchanging niceties, Mellita is now looking at me with the same pity-filled eyes that her husband did when we first came in. 'To hear what has happened to you.'

Ah, she's brought *that* up.

'But you will have other children,' she gushes on. 'You will try, yes?'

How could she *say* this to me? As if it would make anything any better. As if one child could compensate for another . . .

I look down at the champagne flute that Katie has pressed into my hands. The little bubbles are still popping on the top. I can feel them when I bring the glass closer to my face. I take in a breath. The wine waitress – who can't be more than fourteen – is filling up yet another glass for me, despite the fact that I haven't drunk the first two, or touched the champagne they've given me earlier.

'Please, don't,' I tell her. I stare at the array of assorted drinks in front of me.

'You aren't drinking?' Mellita smiles broadly at me. 'I notice you are having no wine tonight? This is because of . . . good news?' Her voice goes up a notch.

'No, actually I never . . .'

Katie's head swivels round then, having heard only the last part of Mellita's comment.

'Julia! You *aren't*, are you?' Her face fills with such relief, and she claps her hands together. 'Angus—'

'No!' I choke. 'There's been some misunderstanding. I am not expecting again. I don't drink, that's all. I never drink.' I can feel my face colouring while everyone looks on in embarrassment. I notice Charlie looking concerned. His eyes flicker briefly over mine. I shake my head.

'I hope you do not mind if I say, it is a real pity, my dear, what happened to you both. Such good people,' Mario Serrano addresses me now, 'but you are young, and there is time for you yet . . .'

Suddenly the mood in the whole room has changed. Everyone is looking in my direction and I can *feel* their sympathy flooding towards me. I feel incredibly cold. I keep my eyes on the dinner plate in front of me, the little pattern of green and gold leaves that dance around the rim.

'My dear,' Serrano says quietly, he lays his hand on my arm, 'I hope you do not blame yourself for what happened?'

'No,' I manage to choke out. 'I try not to. It was an accident.'

'No, of course not. And Angus tells me you have been coping so well. Moving on, yes?'

'I think you are incredibly brave.' Where did she come from? The soft voice of Lourdes addresses me from Angus's chair. He's gone somewhere else – everyone has been circulating. When I look around the table I see that they're all sitting in different places except me and Serrano. Charlie has been pulled over to the open doors by Mellita. She appears to be animatedly discussing all the plants she can identify in the garden but she probably just wants to get away from her faux pas.

'Are you seeing anyone?' Lourdes inquires gently. 'Someone to help you with the . . . the process?'

'I've joined a very helpful group,' I tell them now. 'I've only been a couple of times but they're being very supportive.' I only went once, actually, but it's the sort of thing they'd want to hear. I want to pretend everything is okay, that I'm coping okay, because then they'll leave me alone.

'That's good. That's just the ticket,' Angus approves.

'A bereavement group?' Lourdes offers. I watch as Serrano's wife opens the French doors and animatedly leads Charlie outside. An unexpected breeze blows in and I pull my shawl closer about my shoulders. Where is he going *now*?

'The group consists only of people who have had children go missing,' I explain. 'Some of them have been missing for years.' My mouth seems to go on talking all by itself when I know I should really be shutting this conversation down. 'That's the worst thing, I think. Not having any closure. Not having any . . . any body to inter or any grave to . . .'

'It must be terrible. I cannot begin to imagine.' Mario Serrano has thrown his napkin onto the table and is staring at me with huge sympathy in his eyes.

The evening is beginning to lose its focus. I hadn't realised they were all listening to me. When did they stop having their own conversations, and why has Charlie gone out with that woman and left me right at the moment when I need him the most? I don't want to break down in front of all these people. I don't want—

'It must be difficult not to just fall into despair,' Katie comments.

'Oh I don't.' I try and inject a new energy into my voice. I'm remembering my friend Naseem and what he told me all those years back. When you don't feel brave or confident, you just *pretend* you do. It always worked well enough for him. It worked pretty well for me when I worked for Brasenose, too. 'The members of the group are all very positive to one another. They'll try anything, any avenue that might lead them to finding out the truth.' This isn't actually true, I realise, even as I say it.

'So they haven't given up hope then, the members of your group?' Mario Serrano has abandoned his dinner altogether now. He's sitting back in his chair, totally riveted but with a slight frown on his face. I look for Charlie but all I can see is his back turned towards me. Mario's wife is still rabbiting on, impervious, but I can imagine Charlie is no longer listening to a word she's saying. He's got his hand on the door handle, ready to come back in.

'Julia means that *some* of the members of this group have had children go missing who were never recovered,' Angus puts in now, gallantly. 'Most of them are there to help support each other get over their grief. Isn't that right, Julia?'

'What kind of avenues exactly?' Mario suddenly pipes up. 'Surely you and Charlie have already followed every lead you could? I understood that you had lost your child.' He looks confused now. 'I'm sorry if I got it wrong. I had no idea that there was any chance he might still be alive.'

'He isn't,' Angus asserts, as Charlie comes back in with Mario's wife in tow. 'I really don't know that much about the English country garden,' Charlie is telling her. His eyes go straight to me. Lourdes shuffles over and he sits down in Angus's chair.

'I'm confused,' Mario repeats.

'There was a wave, Mario,' Charlie says slowly. 'A huge freak wave that broke onto the beach on New Year's Eve . . .' Mario is nodding at me sympathetically.

'And so this freak wave came, and it took your son?'

'They never found the body, though,' I whisper.

Everyone's eyes become riveted on me when I say this.

'I see that is why you haven't given up hope yet,' Mario says gently. 'That is natural. She is a mother,' he says to Charlie. 'While she has no proof, she hopes yet for miracles . . .' He touches my arm softly. 'Tell me, my dear. Tell me about your group, and what they do. Do they pray?'

I give a little laugh.

'They may do, Señor Serrano. I don't know. They talk about things . . . that might give them hope. Some of them are talking of going to see a psychic medium, for example.' His hand comes off my arm then as rapidly as if I'd stung him and I feel Charlie stiffen in horror. He clears his throat.

'These are the ones who are desperate, though, isn't that right, Julia? Most of *your group* – they are more sensible than that . . .'

Maybe it's when Charlie says *your group*, distancing himself from the Lost Children's club and everything that it stands for, that I realise I just can't stay in this room pretending any longer.

'What *is* sensible?' When I stand, now, I'm aware that the atmosphere in the room has changed palpably, from one of sympathy to one of embarrassed horror. 'I don't know what is sensible any more, do you know that? Maybe you'd all be the same,' I throw at them before I flee for the door, 'if it were one of *your* children who was missing . . .'

'My dear, I thought you knew.' Lourdes has followed me out, damn her. I don't want her here with me. I don't want to talk to her. 'The Serranos are strict Catholics. Any suggestion that you might be involved in activities of a *spiritualist* nature – it won't do much to help Charlie's cause.'

'Oh, right.' I stare up at her in disbelief, my fists clenched. 'You're . . . so *totally devoted* to Charlie and his bloody Esperanza cause, aren't you, Lourdes?' I splutter at last.

I stare at her fiercely. 'If you're the one who's so in tune with his needs and so dedicated to his every requirement, what did you leave him for? Why didn't you just bloody marry him while you had the chance?'

'That is something I have had a very long time to learn to regret,

Julia,' she says quietly. 'I made a big mistake when I let Charlie out of my life. And if you do the same, I know you'll regret it too.'

'None of your business, though, is it?' I spit. 'If you want to know the truth, I wish you would walk out of his life again! You're far too much still in there – aren't you? – getting involved with all his plans. Why don't you bugger off and find some other charitable cause to pour your heart into and leave Charlie's alone? Why the hell *did* you two split up, anyway?'

Her face is flaming and I know I have upset her. She knows there's some truth in what I contest – that she is still too involved with Charlie.

'We split up when I told him that I could never marry a man who would be unable to give me children,' her voice is trembling. 'Because that is what we believed at the time – that Charlie would never have any children; that he couldn't.'

She stops me dead in my stride. She's talking bullshit. She must be.

'But he *had* a child, didn't he? With me.'

'A miracle child,' she breathes. 'Charlie contracted mumps as a boy – it happened in the same month that his mother died, and he was in a weakened state; he got it very badly. He was told long ago that he'd be infertile. When we got together we got it checked out, and it was true – or so they claimed.'

'So you left him because of that . . .' A strange urge to laugh is bubbling up in my throat now, because this is all so ridiculous and crazy. 'And then it turned out he could have them after all?' *Maybe that's why he never mentioned it?* I'm rationalising like crazy – *because it was obviously false.*

'The one,' she says quietly. 'He had the one. We still don't know if he can ever have any more.' She looks back then, at the same time as I do, and there's Charlie at the door of Lansdown House, coming towards the two of us. His face looks like thunder.

That's when I get up and go.

The hell with the two of them.

261

Julia

I wish the earth would just open and swallow me up tonight. I wish I could disappear.

I've done my best to do that. I am sitting on a stone bench I find after five minutes' walk into the heart of Lansdown House's rambling garden. There's a pale moon but I can still see all the tiny little yellow-orange stems of the lichens growing all over the top of the stone.

It's a beautiful evening. I'm only shivering because I can't stop crying; because of all the things I've done and said tonight that I never meant to. I never intended to say those things to Lourdes (and what if she's in there now, repeating all my vitriolic words?). I never meant to bring out the fact – in front of all those people – that I have my doubts about Hadyn's disappearance. And I didn't want to run off and leave Charlie and Lourdes alone together either. I'm just giving him every chance to realise he'd be better off without me.

It can't be true, what she said to me just now about him being infertile. Why wouldn't he have told me about it?

Something tugs at the back of my mind, though. He's never used contraception. We've never spoken about it. He offered to marry me the moment he knew I was expecting his child. I'll never forget his bewilderment – his complete and utter *joy*, when I told him.

What the heck is going on, here?

'You didn't have to do that, you know, Julia.' I don't hear him coming. I'm listening to the sudden gusts of laughter coming from the house. They sound a bit forced, now. As if they're all trying to pretend I didn't just have an outburst. Charlie makes me jump, sitting down beside me, but he doesn't sit very close.

'I know. I'm sorry.' I turn to look at him. He doesn't look as angry as I'd feared he would. He looks tragic. He must have felt I made him look stupid in there – it sounded as if we were both saying entirely different things. 'I'm really sorry. I didn't mean to do that. I don't know why I said what I did.'

'Because you believe it?' His face is half covered by the shadow of the ivy growing on the wall behind us. I can't tell what he is thinking.

'I half believe it,' I whisper. 'And now – you will have even more reason to wonder why you're still with me and not with someone sweet and compliant and understanding, like *her*, yes?'

'No,' he says. He looks so handsome in his tuxedo. And he looks so sad. I wish he would put his arms around me again. I wish we could find some way to melt away all this frost that's built up between us.

Why won't he kiss me? Is it because of *her*? Is she still hovering about somewhere, waiting in the shadows to find some excuse to come out and join us? I shuffle along closer to him, hardly daring to breathe.

'I'm sorry, Julia.' His voice seems to come from a long way away. 'Maybe I didn't make it clear enough how important it was that we got Serrano's support tonight? Maybe I should have shared with you what it really is we're up against?'

'I *know* what you're up against,' I tell him miserably. 'No sponsorship means no more operations and that means all those people have to suffer. Though if Santos says he can sort it out if you let him – I don't know why you don't just do that . . .' I sniff.

'Because Louis Baudelaire was involved in something *really* bad, J.' He looks at the ground.

'How bad?' *How bad could it be?* My mind is screaming.

'He was involved in organ trafficking,' Charlie says at last. 'He took kidneys from healthy donors to help finance their families. He reasoned they had nothing else to sell and they'd have died anyway. I couldn't share that with you, could I? Our son is missing and you still won't accept that he drowned. Heaven knows what sort of scenarios would have gone through your head . . .'

We're both quiet for a moment while I take in what he's just said. This whole Santos and Baudelaire affair has been far more of a disaster for Charlie than he's ever let on.

And if he's virtually infertile, then losing Hadyn would have been, too. I sit up straight as he continues.

'But you're wrong if you think what you did tonight has turned me against you, J. I'm sore at what the likely outcome's going to be, sure. But I don't blame you for reacting the way that you did.'

'You don't?' I breathe. He turns his face so I can see him more clearly now.

'How could I?' His voice is strong, and full of admiration. 'You spoke up for something you believed in. I don't believe in clairvoyants, you know that. And I don't want you to see one. But – you have every right to speak your own mind on that score and no one should judge you for it. And you were right – how do any of them know what lengths they might be prepared to go to, if they were in your position?'

'I'm glad you can see it like that.' I moisten my lips. There is something else we haven't spoken about yet tonight, isn't there?

'Charlie – Lourdes *told* me why she left you,' I say quietly after a bit. 'She told me it was because you'd been advised you could never father any children of your own. Is that right?'

I hear his sharp intake of breath and he doesn't have to say any more.

'It's true,' he says at last. 'It's what we understood back then. But you had Hadyn, didn't you? You proved that it wasn't true.'

'I don't understand though – why didn't you tell me, Charlie? Why didn't you just say?'

'*Don't* you?' He sighs, looks at me intently. 'Can't you *imagine* how the news that you were having my son might have affected me?' Charlie picks my hands up off my lap now, and the familiar touch of his fingers on my skin sends an ache right through me. 'After all those years of thinking I would never father a child of my own? All the sorrow, and shame and the humiliation of that – you wiped it away in a heartbeat. All the pain I felt at losing Lourdes over it. It all vanished. You wiped it all clean in one instant, and I was made – like new again.'

All the sorrow and the shame and the humiliation of that . . .

I feel an ache in my throat at his words.

'Lourdes mentioned just now – you'd got mumps at the same time as your mum died?' Maybe it wasn't just the pain of losing his fertility – and in time, Lourdes – that he associated with that period of illness, I see now.

'I was in the UK at that time.' His voice is quiet and broken. 'And I took so ill I never even got to go to the funeral, you know? I never saw her buried. Just as I will never see my son buried . . .' It would seem he's never really, properly, mourned his mum, either.

'I never saw my dad buried, Charlie.' But I will tell him about that another time, because right now his head has sunk right into his hands. When he sighs it's as if he's trying to unburden himself of the hugest weight. I put my hand up to touch his chest but he still doesn't move.

I had wiped the pain clean, he said.

And then I lost Hadyn and I have brought it all back.

'Why did you never tell me?' I lean in towards him, wanting us to be like we were at the beginning, but I don't know if we can ever go back there again. I kiss him quickly, catching him unawares. He doesn't pull back. He lingers for an instant, tasting my lips. His hands on my hands pull me a little closer.

265

'Because you made it not be true,' he mutters. 'You made me imagine none of it had been real. All that shame I felt for so long – I wanted to believe it was all based on a mistake. Perhaps I was deluding myself?' he whispers. 'I would have told you eventually, but . . . You seemed so unhappy about the whole topic of Lourdes. I didn't want to bring her up. Or the reasons why we separated.'

My thoughts return to how I kept the secret about Sebastian from him. I can hardly complain, can I?

'We haven't been . . . very open with each other, have we, Charlie?'

'No, we haven't.' Charlie smiles sadly then, draws me in closer to him. 'So I will be completely open with you now and say this: I think we have lost our boy, my love. I believe he is gone and we will never see him again. I don't know if I am capable of having any more children. Maybe once you consider this you'll come to the same conclusion that Lourdes did?'

'I won't,' I tell him with utter conviction. 'I love you more than that. That wouldn't be enough to make me leave you.'

It wouldn't be enough to come between us, that much is true.

But Hadyn isn't found yet, and I know *that* is the one thing left which still might.

Julia

I dreamed my old dream last night; it is always the same.

In a place where I am not looking, where I am not expecting to find him, I go round a corner and he is there.

It does not start like that. It starts as the first drop of water comes hurtling out of a darkened sky. It starts with the sound of the rain sloshing into the black water somewhere nearby. I taste the salt tang of it on my tongue. There's a cold breeze and the scent of fear in my nostrils and I want to run. And so I run and run until there is no more breath left in my lungs.

When I look down, that dark stain spreading across my top, I'm scared that it's blood because I don't know what else it can be.

Is he dead, is he dead, is he dead?

But it passes. It always passes; and in my dream, on a day when I turn the corner, not expecting anything, on a day when I do not expect to see him any more – he is there.

Julia

'When I woke up this morning, I realised that my whole life has gone completely to pot.'

Celeste looks at me, mildly surprised. Her blonde hair is hanging in limp strands about her shoulders and she's wearing a thin jumper, whereas I'm muffled up with my coat buttoned right to the top.

'You only realised it *this morning*?' Celeste retrieves the chewed-up stick she's just been presented with by her spaniel and hurls it back along the path. 'This is just to be expected, surely?'

'I guess,' I tell her miserably. 'I just didn't realise that it was my *whole* life. It isn't just part of it. It's everything. It's . . . all the friends I used to have who can't quite look me in the eye any more; it's my mum who won't stop ringing but doesn't help at all when we talk; it's Charlie and me . . .' Maybe that's the worst bit, I realise. 'Things have changed between us and I don't know if they'll ever be the same again . . .'

'They won't be,' she supplies. 'They'll never be the same.' She fishes some thin gloves out of her handbag and they look so ineffectual I wonder why she's bothering.

'Take my gloves.' Reluctantly, she agrees, and we swap gloves while her dog runs down the far end of the park before bringing back her stick.

'I've had a really crap weekend,' I confess. 'I met someone at a dinner party – someone who was once very important to

Charlie – who's just come back into his life. A woman he was once engaged to marry, in fact.'

'Oh.' Celeste looks sympathetic. 'Still. He's engaged to *you* right now, isn't he?' She links her arm through mine and her slim arm feels very cold, even through my warm coat.

'He still feels for her, though.' I don't know why I say this but it's what I believe. Celeste glances sideways at me.

'But he feels for you *more?*'

'I guess. She just . . . told me some things about him that I never knew.'

'He sounds like a bit of a dark horse, your Charlie,' she grins conspiratorially. 'But that doesn't mean there wasn't a perfectly good reason why *they* fell apart. Maybe they realised they weren't in love after all?'

'That wasn't the reason,' I say slowly. I'm not about to explain everything to her but there is something else that's bothering me. 'The worst of it was, I was a real bitch to her, Celeste. I was so nasty I hardly recognised myself.'

Celeste pulls a dubious face.

'No, it's true,' I tell her, 'I'd made a faux pas – some things I'd said at the dinner table didn't go down too well, and I'd gone out for a bit of air to get my head back together. She followed me out to help, but I – god, Celeste – I told her to butt out of my life, that I wished she'd never come back into Charlie's life . . . I said some really horrible things . . .'

'She should have let you have your space,' Celeste asserts after a while. 'You're still grieving, aren't you?' As if this could explain the madness that came over me on Friday night.

'Maybe.' I set my sights along the long line of the pathway in front of us. To the left, there is a verge of grass leading to some very tall trees – conifers and oaks; to the right, a huge open area where several dogs and their owners are enjoying the early start of schoolday quiet time. I used to bring Hadyn here, I remember. We used to watch the birds come out for the breadcrumbs that the pensioners would scatter onto the path.

'Don't be too hard on yourself,' Celeste reminds me gently. 'It's only been seven months. That's too soon to recover.'

I put my hands to my eyes and press my fingers in. There *is* no recovery from this, I think. I look at Celeste. She hasn't recovered, has she? Nothing gets any better. 'You're working yourself up over something that might not even be real,' she continues. 'Why don't you just ask Charlie if he still has feelings for her?'

'No way!' I look at her in alarm. 'I can hardly accuse him when there's no evidence of any wrongdoing, can I?'

'Do you think – after what you said to her at the party – that she will go away?'

'Hardly! She's so up to her neck in this Esperanza project that there's little chance of that.'

'Then get involved in it yourself!' Celeste says decisively. 'If you're so worried. On the other hand,' she adds, 'do you think it's just possible that it's because you're feeling rotten about yourself that you get suspicious? It's natural. It's more about you than about him. Anyway, this woman, what was Charlie actually *like* with her?'

'He was polite to her; attentive; affectionate even, but not over the top. He keeps bugging me to get involved with the Esperanza project as well, so my guess is he hopes Lourdes and I can become best buddies. I don't suppose he'd be encouraging that if he was still lusting after her?'

Celeste laughs.

'Why *don't* you get to know her better then? Then you'll plainly know the truth, won't you? It might not be so bad.' Celeste bends down and scratches Poppy affectionately behind the ears. 'You gave up *your* work, didn't you? Might it help to go back?'

Would it help?

I look at her suddenly. 'I nearly killed myself to get that job at Brasenose,' I admit to her now. 'I won awards for my photography. I made my way right up to the top of my game, but d'you know what?'

'What?' She picks up the chewed stick that's just been dropped at her feet.

'I won the awards because I used my camera to tell the *truth* and they landed me a job taking pictures where the whole point of the exercise was to create a fantasy. By the time Hadyn came along I was already about to look for something else. And I'm still – ' I look at her pointedly – 'trying to get to the truth.'

Celeste smiles sadly.

'D'you want to know the reason I always try and throw this darn stick so far away that she can't bring it back?'

I shrug.

'It's because it reminds me . . .' Celeste rubs at her face with her hands. 'Every time I've tried to push what's happened with my Chloe right out of my life; every time I try and make it go so far away that I never have to look at it again – it just boomerangs right back.'

I sit down on a metal bench; it feels cold on my legs and bottom but I don't want to walk any further.

'Tell me, how *did* you make it all go away, Celeste? Because it's in my head all the time – *all the time* – that's why I can't sleep.'

'I pretended, I guess. I left the Lost Children's Group after two years, did you know that? I couldn't bear it any more. I told you, hope doesn't come without a price. I went away to somewhere where nobody knew anything about me or about what had happened to me and it *still* came back.' Her voice catches in her throat then.

'How?' I breathe. 'Did someone recognise you?'

'No.' Celeste pauses for a long while before answering. 'I just kept hearing these stories all over the place; stories about people who had been missing and were then found. I began to think I had done the wrong thing. That's why I was there in Elaine's house that day in March when you first went there. I wanted to start again. And then Jasper came in and told us what he told us . . .'

'About the psychic, you mean?'

'I got to thinking – maybe this is how I'm going to find out the truth. If this psychic could just give me some proof – some evidence – I might find out the truth.' She looks at me suddenly.

'I know what that would mean to you,' I mutter. Just this morning I received something in the post from Eva. She'd sent me that single photo of Hadyn and myself which she took that day by accident, standing by the washing line. I never did get my camera back, I realise now. In the photo my arms are reaching up, trying to get to the pegs, and Hadyn is mimicking my move-ment, only he's reaching up for me.

Is that what we're both still doing, I wonder? Me reaching out and him reaching out still, in some place very far away? On the back, Agustina has printed *Lo siento, hija*. She is sorry.

Celeste looks at me suddenly. 'Come with me to the psychic? Come on – let's stop talking and just do it. And on another note, if you meet up with this Lourdes person, get to know her better, you'd allay your fears there, too. It's got to be better than the living hell of not knowing for sure?'

'It might be,' I concede after a while. The memory of all the looks of horror when I brought this same topic up on Friday evening floods through me. I know what Charlie will say, too. But I think I'm going to have to go, anyway.

Julia

Why is it uncertainty must haunt me always like a stalker in the night? When I watch Charlie sleeping, the rhythmic rise and fall of his chest, I can only envy the deep peace that certainty can bring. If only I could know so surely, in the way that Charlie can, that Hadyn is gone for ever. It is my lack of faith that's killing me, as Charlie says.

But where do you get that kind of faith from if you weren't brought up with it?

Four a.m. It's always four a.m. these days. I wake – if indeed what I do passes for sleep – and the small hours stretch out endlessly while my brain churns out its unceasing chatter, the interminable arguings to and fro that lead me nowhere.

The truth is, I've been thinking more and more about Silas the clairvoyant. How I want to go and see him.

I have this monstrous need to know, once and for all. I'm beginning to accept that I will almost certainly never see my son again. It's not the fear of loss that keeps me awake any more. It's the fear of not ever really and truly knowing what happened to him.

Charlie sleeps soundly because in his world there is no such problem. God takes care of everything, doesn't he? You do what you can and then you leave it in God's hands, he says. I can't bear it when he tells me that, so he's stopped saying it. Why doesn't He *do* something about this horrible state of affairs then? And if He doesn't, or won't – then why shouldn't I?

'Can't you sleep?' Charlie murmurs, drawing me closer to him, still half asleep. I lie there stiff and unyielding in his arms.

'I can't sleep,' I confess. 'I have too many things going round and round in my head. Charlie . . .' I glance at the clock. It's still the early hours but he's going away tomorrow straight after work. When am I ever going to get the chance to tell him?

He half opens his eyes.

'I need to talk to you.'

He rolls over to kiss me. He doesn't want to talk. Since Angus's dinner party last month there has been a kind of silent truce between us.

'No,' I hold him off after a bit. 'We never talk any more.'

'We talk all the time.'

'Not about Hadyn, we don't.'

His sigh in the darkness is almost inaudible but I feel it rather than hear it.

'Charlie.' I prop myself up on my elbows, facing him as he covers his own face with his arm. 'Do you *have* to go to Santos's place this weekend?'

'You know that I do.'

'No, really, I mean – perhaps we could go away somewhere ourselves . . .'

'I have to go, Julia.'

Okay. *He has to go.* He *has* to because this is an Esperanza-related trip and Esperanza is the only thing that matters.

I draw in a breath.

'I also have to go somewhere.'

'I'll be away till Sunday evening.' He's still sleepy but I can feel the sensuous touch of his fingertips tracing the length of my arms.

'And – *her?*' My eyes narrow as I have a sudden thought, turn to look at him sharply.

'Her *who?*'

'Lourdes, is she going to be there too?'

'Naturally.' He sounds nonplussed. There isn't a trace of guilt in his voice. But the thought of them spending the weekend together emboldens me to say what I need to say next.

'Well. I want to go somewhere with Celeste.'

'You go then, J.' His voice is encouraging. 'Look, this Santos golfing weekend thing – it isn't my idea. But we've lost Serrano so I'm back to courting Santos. After you said what you felt last month – about the psychics . . .' He hesitates. 'Sorry to bring that up, love, but I've got to retrieve the situation now.'

'That's precisely what I wanted to talk to you about.' I seize my moment. 'I want to go and see this clairvoyant with her.'

There's this pause.

'No.' He turns to face the other way.

'Please, Charlie . . .'

'If it weren't for your bringing that whole topic up at Angus's dinner party, I wouldn't even need to be going away this weekend, do you realise?'

'*I'm going to go*, Charlie.'

'We've been through this. It won't help you.'

'I've heard he's very good.'

'If he's very good then he either tells people precisely what they want to hear, or he actually – *he actually* – communicates with spirits. Neither of those things is going to be any help to you. Look – I understand there are many things we're going to disagree about, but this isn't one I feel I can compromise on, I'm sorry.'

'I can't keep on living like this!' I sink my head into my hands. The warmth that was coming from him a moment ago has ebbed away so quickly I could weep.

'It's out of our hands,' he says at last. 'I know you want certainty but . . . you may never get it. Maybe, by God's grace, you'll learn to live with that.'

'God's grace, Charlie!' Why – *why* is he doing this? Why can't he just admit he's not done any better job of grieving than I have?

'Julia, surely you—'

'I've fought, all my life, for control over my circumstances,'

I carry on over him. 'I've made things good if they weren't good. God didn't figure in it. Nothing ever seems to me to have just slotted neatly into place without my best efforts . . .'

'Then maybe you should put your best efforts into making *us* good again,' he suggests. 'Heaven knows *I'm* trying, Julia. I'm doing everything I know how.' He sounds lost, perplexed. Just like he does every time I try to bring up this subject. 'What – what else is it that you want me to do?'

'You could – you could talk to me, Charlie. We could have a conversation.'

'We're talking now, aren't we?'

'We open our mouths and words come out. But neither one of us can hear the other. We *started* to talk – that night in Angus's garden. But since then . . .' He looks pained but I continue anyway. 'I want to talk about this decision that we've made – *that you've made* – that it's all over, just because we've heard, third hand, that some fibres were found in a fish. I don't feel, in my heart, that we've tried every single avenue, for ourselves.'

'You don't always have to do everything for yourself, though.' His voice is sad. 'The family have helped out. You have to trust that they did what they could.'

'I do,' I admit readily, 'but I just don't feel that *we* have. And I need to go back to Spain.' I put the topic of the psychic aside for a while. 'I want you to tell Roberto that I'm coming. Tell him to give me the help that I need. I want to see that *fish* evidence they say that they have. I have to see it for myself.'

There was a discrepancy in the dates for that fish after all. What if there never was any fish? What if it was all made up?

Charlie sighs deeply.

'The case is closed, Julia.'

'Stop treating me like a child, for God's sake. I don't want your *protection* from the truth. *Can't you see* –' I tell him when he just stares at me, distressed – 'all my possible leads are slipping away.

276

Maria is dead. Diego is dead. Blue is hinting that he wants to leave Spain. I've hung about here like an idiot, for far too long, just . . . waiting, and searching out things on the Internet and hoping. But it isn't enough for me, Charlie.'

'Nothing will ever be *enough*,' he begins. 'Because the one thing that would make it right for you – just can't be. It's happened to me too, you know. It's not just you,' he reproaches when I bat his arms away. 'I've had to learn to cope with it, Julia.'

'You know what *I* think? I think you deal with it just *fine* because you don't deal with it at all.' I swing my legs out of the bed and pull on a cardigan even though it is still pitch black outside. 'You sweep it all under the carpet and pretend everything is okay and act as if all I ever want to do is pull that rug out from under you and expose the mess. That's right, isn't it?'

Charlie is quiet for a very long time after that. He is quiet for so long I have to turn around from where I'm sitting on the edge of the bed and look at him before he says anything.

'I'm going to Santos's place tomorrow. I have got to get this sponsorship deal, that's just how it is. Promise me you won't do anything foolish while I'm away.'

Certainty, I think now. You want it just as much as I do, Charlie. You come by it a different route, that's all. The clock clunks onto 4:30 a.m. It is the first of August. Eight months now, since he went from our lives. Eight months. And then it will be nine months. And then it will be ten.

Will I wait forever, hesitating till it's too late, like I did with Maria?

'No clairvoyants: promise me,' he demands again. 'And no flying off to Spain?'

'I'm not going to promise you anything,' I tell him, and my voice is flat and toneless. 'I'm not going to lie to him any more.

'If you do decide to go,' he warns, his voice breaking suddenly, 'then that's your prerogative, but I . . . just understand, I can't support you, Julia.'

'What are you saying?' I look at him, alarmed.

'I'm saying if you insist on flying back out to Spain now, as far as I'm concerned . . . Maybe you just shouldn't bother to come back.'

Julia

Now that we're here this really doesn't seem such a good idea after all. It took us one and a half hours to drive over here and it's bucketing down.

'So, d'you think this guy is really any good?' This must be the hundredth time I've asked her this. If I'm going to *completely ruin* my relationship with Charlie I need to be sure it's in a worthwhile cause.

'Your guess is as good as mine, Julia.'

I watch Celeste as she pushes the doorbell tentatively. She's looking shy. Her long fair hair is caught up in a ponytail at the back. She's so slim she could pass for a fifteen-year-old from here, though she's at least my age.

'If he comes through with Chloe,' I mutter quietly (just in case he's about to open the front door), 'will that be the end of everything for you? Your search, I mean? Will that be it, or will you keep on looking in case he's got it wrong?' Her eyes look large and luminous in the yellow porch light. She's been cheery and chatty all the way up here but I know this means a lot more to her than she's letting on. She's like me: still looking for some kind of evidence that will point her down the next road she should be travelling on.

Even if this Silas says to both of us: *I can see your two children, laughing and happy, joyfully walking hand in hand through the flower-filled gardens of paradise* (and gives exact descriptions of them both), would we believe it, or would we imagine he'd got private detectives working on both our backgrounds before we got here? He doesn't even know our real names. Celeste said she's called us 'Jan' and 'Pat'. He's been given no details about us at all – she even gave him (in case of emergency) a friend's mobile number to call. Talk about taking precautions!

'What will you do,' I press as we wait by the front door; my nerves feel caught up tight in my chest, 'if he sees that they're *gone?*'

'I'll make a "goodbye book",' Celeste breathes. 'I'll go to all her favourite places for the last time. And then I'll let her go.'

So, he opens the door. He looks as odd as I expected him to look. Even worse, he looks as if he's wearing a toupee. And it hasn't been stuck on properly; it seems to be tilting at rather a dangerous angle over to the side. I cover my mouth with my hand and Celeste – horror of horrors – simultaneously does the same.

He might be – oh, forty-something-ish. Difficult to tell. He doesn't look too friendly, either. I thought they were supposed to put you at your ease, but no one has told Silas that.

'Outdoor shoes over there, ladies,' he says, pointing to a wooden shoe rack by the front door. Too late, I think, the whole place already smells of old cat. What harm can a couple of pairs of shoes do after that?

Once we're ushered a little further in I can pick up that there is also the faint whiff of an incense stick burning somewhere.

'Who's going first?' He pauses at the door of what must be his consulting room, nudges the door open with his elbow. 'Ah, you.' He picks on me before either of us can answer. 'I'm getting them in for you already. Don't crowd me dear, don't crowd.' I look at Celeste, but she shakes her head slightly. He is addressing me, apparently.

'You've recently suffered from a bereavement, I see.' *Don't tell them anything*, Celeste has warned me. *You mustn't feed them any clues, or give them any free information. And beware of thinking* that statements of the fairly obvious – like, you've recently suffered a bereavement, since maybe ninety-five per cent of people consulting a psychic might have done so – are gems of wisdom from the great beyond. I go and take my seat at the place he's indicating with a pointed finger.

'You tell me,' I answer smartly, but that doesn't go down too well.

'Ah. A sceptic, I see.' He puts his hands together, elbows on the small table in front of him. The room is dark. Spooky even. A candle splutters in one corner and there are several pictures of the Madonna and various saints up on the walls. There's a Holy Bible in one corner and lots of crystals scattered at various points around the room.

Then he gets up and lights another candle on what appears to be a little altar area. When he comes back, his face is solemn.

'I'm getting the name "Julia,"' he says as soon as he sits down. Could he have heard us talking before we even got into the house? 'Tell me if this makes sense or not. A simple yes or no will suffice.'

'Yes,' I tell him.

'And a white-haired lady with an 'E' name. Emma – no, Ellie – something like that.'

'Ella?' I put in before I can stop myself.

'That's it.' His face is completely deadpan. I have never mentioned Ella to Celeste, so this must count as a 'hit'. His eyes are closed. The little candle on the table seems to be spluttering ominously.

'She knows that you're here.' Okay, fine but unverifiable.

Silence, for a while. The atmosphere seems to be building up inside the room in the strangest way. Almost crackling, I think. Could my nana be here? Or is this just my imagination working overtime because I am half scared out of my wits with sitting in virtual darkness here with this guy? I hadn't even been thinking about Ella, the remarkable realisation hits me now. My one and only preoccupation had been Hadyn.

'She says to tell you that you can't control who comes through,'

Silas relays with the ghost of a smile. Is he picking up my surprise? Is he reading my mind or is she? I can feel tears searing the back of my throat.

'You've had troubles with your car recently.'

I frown. I can't think of any. Does he mean the door of the glove box getting stuck or doesn't that count?

'No,' I say at last.

'You have; the blue car.'

That's Charlie's car.

'Not mine. My boyfriend's.'

'Same thing to them. With the brakes.'

'Yes, he had trouble with the brakes,' I say in surprise. 'Just last week, he took it in to be looked at.'

'And you're going abroad very soon.'

'I'm not thinking of . . .'

'Very soon,' he insists. It's August, I think – and that's the month when many people take their summer break, so this is a general 'cover all' statement he's making here.

'You're looking for someone,' he continues. My stomach tightens.

'Yes.'

'You've been looking for some time. She sends you her love. She says to let you know she can walk very far now. Over the hills and far away . . .' His voice has taken on a softer tone.

'That was her favourite song,' I whisper. 'My nana always used to sing it to me as a kid.'

'Over the hills, along the valleys. Where he went and she could never follow.' My breathing actually stops for a moment. 'He' – is Silas talking about my father now? 'Did she have trouble walking?' Silas inquires. It's more a statement than a question.

'No.'

'She says she did.'

'Not walking as such.'

'But she never left the house, right?'

282

Good God.

'Right. She was agoraphobic.'

'She says she's not frightened any more. She can go walking whenever she wants.'

'Tell her I love her. Tell her I remember her night and day.'

'She knows.'

He's quiet for a long time, then I pull out some tissues from a box and I can hear Celeste coughing quietly in the hallway where she is waiting outside on the chair. I have no idea how long I have been in here. It could be ten minutes or it could be over an hour.

'She's fading,' he says, when I stop blubbing at last. Don't fade. You must tell me what I wanted to know . . .

'She's getting very faint but she's being very insistent about one particular message. She wants you to know that *someone you assume is dead is still very much alive.*'

Oh-My-God! He actually said that.

'What's that?'

'She's gone,' Silas says.

'What did she say?'

'She said – he's alive? Alive?' Silas looks blankly at me. He seems to have returned to his former supercilious, rather sour self. Don't feed him any information. Don't tell him anything at all, Celeste's words return to me, though at this moment I'm just bursting to jump on this man and tell him everything. He never said '*he*' – he didn't mention their gender. He just said 'someone', I remember.

'That's all I'm afraid.' Silas makes to get up. He looks at me with his strange, cat-like eyes and a shiver goes right through me.

'Can you send the next one in, please? Take a tissue by all means.'

Celeste looks anxiously into my face as I go out and she goes in. I plonk down onto the chair she's just vacated and I wonder if she could hear any of what was said in there? Her eyes are as wide as saucers. It must have been hell for her to wait out here all this time. I've been in there at least – I look at my watch – twenty-three minutes.

But could it be true what he said? He gave me names. He gave me facts. The car. The colour. The brakes. He's alive.

But how, and where?

And I can't tell Charlie about this, none of it. He'd go ballistic. Who the hell am I supposed to tell then, apart from Celeste? Everything's been stirred up all over again. I came here for closure and I got – what's the opposite of closure? – it's all opened up again, even wider. The tiny paper-cut of doubt that was left in my mind – tonight has opened up a doubt that's fathoms deep. Ella was here, that's for sure.

But I can't tell Charlie, I remember. Charlie will be on his way to his weekend with Santos and he made his position quite clear with regards to me coming here. The memory of that casts a momentary shadow over my excitement.

Oh, where is Blue? I open up the texting function on my phone. *This* he has just got to hear. Apart from Celeste, he's been the one steady supporter I've had all along. If Hadyn's *still alive*, I may find him yet. But where to even begin?

The stuff I learned about Adamantine in the spring – it might still turn out to be significant. Adamantine was obsessively in love with Charlie. Charlie doesn't have a comfortable feeling about her, clearly. Maybe she really is the one who ordered Diego's underground acquaintances to steal Charlie's baby?

It all fits the profile perfectly.

Blue would understand. I know he's gutted about what's happened to his friends but he's offered to help me so many times. He would surely look into all of this for me if I asked him. And *if* I keep it quiet from Charlie, maybe this time we'll actually get somewhere?

I feel a sudden rush of adrenaline in my belly. The dull, sulky aches and the tiredness that I have been feeling for the last few months – it all burns away.

I've got to go abroad, just like Silas has just predicted I'll be doing. I've got to go to Spain, to enlist Blue's help with a little detective work. I need to leave now, while Charlie is still at this golfing weekend, or I'll never find the resolve to go. I need to be able to present him with some incontrovertible proof. Something as solid and strong as his faith is.

The implications of it all are *huge*. Once Charlie finds out that I've gone to Spain – it'll be all over between us. Our relationship's been hanging on a slender enough thread all these months. And it isn't as if he hasn't got another woman, just waiting in the wings, for me to be history.

But I've got to prove it to Charlie: there's more to this story yet. And in the stillness of the hall, as I press send, I become aware of something else; a quiet sobbing coming from inside the room. What news on Chloe? I wonder suddenly.

And then – as I have learned to do of late – I offer up a silent prayer.

Charlie

Inside St Martin's Roman Catholic church in London, the stained-glass windows let through scant light. Tiers of candles flicker perilously as we open the wooden door to go inside. I go to sit down on one of the wooden benches and Lourdes follows behind me, bobbing in automatic genuflection towards the altar. When she called me to have a working coffee with her this morning, I didn't hesitate. I knew I had to talk to *someone* about what's going on in my life. Lourdes might not be the best person, under the circumstances, but then again, she's a woman – maybe she'll be able to explain it all to me? Julia and I argued again this morning before I left and I said some things I never should have said. I told her if she were so determined to go to Spain, why didn't she just go and not bother to come back?

Christ, I can't believe I said that.

Now she won't pick up her phone, so for all I know she's gone and done it – *left me*. That isn't what I wanted; she must know that, surely? She's right about one thing, though. We talk all right but we don't communicate, her and me.

I watch Lourdes as she tilts forward onto one of the cushioned pads on the floor of the pew.

As I sit there behind her, all I can think of is that Lourdes looks the way I used to feel. She feels comfortable on her knees, praying to her God, just as I once did. But I haven't been able to pray like that for such a very long time; not like I did in the days when I still believed that everything was fundamentally all right with the world.

Every time I tell Julia that *things will come out all right, things are the way they're meant to be*, all I'm really doing is saving her from the way *I* really feel. I'm telling her what I'd like to believe.

I close my eyes. My shoulders feel stiff, my back tense. It's an effort to remain upright on this unyielding bench. I take in a breath, and the familiar scent of the damp bricks impregnated with centuries of incense floods right through me. I want to rest, to find a place of peace, but I cannot. I don't even know if I'm doing the right thing going to Santos's place for this golfing weekend. I can't stand golf. I'm only doing it for the cause. Then next weekend I'll be out again for the annual charity gala evening. And how will I get my head around all the pretty speeches I need to make for that? I can't even think about them. Wouldn't I do better to stay at home and deal with what I need to, with Julia?

Is this what the priests mean when they talk about a crisis of faith? God tests those he loves. It's what I've been taught and what I've always believed.

But I can't pray.

I get up, agitated. I still need help, God. My Esperanza work – I'm not doing that for myself. I'm doing it for others. All those years ago you gave me the vocation and the desire to set that centre up so *why* are you making it so hard for me to continue my work now? I think about the whole mess that's been stirred up by Louis Baudelaire and I press my hands into my eyes now. I need help.

God – are you listening?

After a while I can feel Lourdes standing patiently behind me. She doesn't say a word. She's just there, supporting me in the same familiar way that she always did. I'm grateful to her. Lourdes understands the same rituals that I do. She knows my back-ground, the place that I've come from. She's played in the same sandpits as a child, she's swung from the same swing-seats, and she's sung the same songs, in her time, as I have. A common heritage is a powerful thing, I realise now.

This is something that Julia and I do not share. We share a sense of humour, a love of nature, a taste for the bold and adventurous and unusual; a sense of justice. But we do not share a common heritage, and sometimes – when the winds of change are blowing – it is only your roots that can help you steady yourself, help you find your balance. I look at Lourdes and a sense of gratitude floods through me; that she knows, that she understands, that she isn't threatening to go off and speak to any psychic to get her answers; that she's *here*.

Even if I can't find the words to pray just now, maybe God is listening after all?

Julia

When I think about it now, my insides are lurching just at the sheer stupidity of it. I mean – I've flown out to Malaga for what? To check out a sad former client of Charlie's who once had a crush on him, just because she now has a baby of roughly the right age and who – according to Doreen, looks like him – and because Silas the clairvoyant told me that 'someone who you thought was dead, still lives'? I must be, quite seriously, going nuts.

I do not want to leave Charlie. When I think back on it now, he has been the one true love of my life. He's the one I would have said was going to be 'for ever'. He's the one I was supposed to be getting married to, next month. If I had not chosen to come here now – some will say, on a wild-goose chase – maybe one day we still *would* be getting married.

I made the decision that I had to make, but I know it's one that Charlie won't forgive.

I feel so alone. I'm letting Charlie down; I'm letting his precious Esperanza down because I doubt I'm going to make it back for the gala evening next weekend, either. Assuming that he even wants to see my face again

And yet I can't ignore the burning drive that's inside me. I watch the flight luggage going round and round on the carousel and my thoughts go round in my head.

Oh Nana Ella, *am* I doing the right thing?

But you can't always know that, can you? And I've been wrong before.

'Julia, you should let him crawl home,' Naseem said to me. 'He's your dad and I'm sorry to say it but there's got to come a point where you just say "No".'

'He's at The Crown,' I croaked. 'And they've asked me to take him home.' I wished I'd never picked up the darned phone. I thought it might be Josh Martyn, that's all. I was supposed to be meeting Josh in half an hour, under the clock.

This was one date I was determined Dad wouldn't be allowed to ruin, I told myself furiously. It wasn't as if I got asked out on that many occasions. I was fifteen already and I'd only ever been asked out twice. I didn't count Naseem, who was looking at me sceptically.

'I can't walk with you, Jules, not tonight, you know that. My family's all going out to my aunt's for the New Year. I'm not happy with you going down there on your own.' He stood protectively, arms folded, by the door. 'Especially not looking like that.'

'I want to let him crawl back home, believe me.' But the woman who'd called said he was at The Crown, hadn't she? And that was by the river where the old fool might just fall in and drown himself on the way back home. If he'd been at the Old Queen or the Speckled Hen things might be different, but The Crown was the one where he'd need to walk along the towpath and over the humpbacked bridge to get himself home.

I couldn't just leave it. Even though I was in this beautiful floaty green organza party dress and wearing Naseem's sister's silver stilettos that felt like circus stilts beneath my teetering feet.

'At least get changed.' Naseem had seen the look on my face and he knew it was no use arguing with me. I glanced at the clock on his kitchen wall.

'No time.'

'Jules . . .' He shook his head sadly in that way he has but I only

290

snapped at him – because he was here and there was no one else to snap at.

'Leave it, will you? I haven't time.'

'You've got plenty of time,' he observed. 'Only – if you go fetch your dad home you won't make Josh Martyn, will you?' I didn't like to think there might be a teeny bit of satisfaction in his voice. Naseem and I were best friends in the world but we were never going to be that kind of friend. Not as far as I was concerned.

By the time I came up to the humpbacked bridge about ten minutes later I was wishing I'd brought a long cardi or a jacket with me, something to put over my dress. I was feeling distinctly underdressed for the district. The bridge was never well lit. and the rain we'd had earlier had coated the cobblestones, making them extra-slippery. That route could have been utterly treacherous if Dad had tried to come back this way by himself, no matter what Naseem might say about 'letting him crawl'.

At the end of the day, it wasn't his dad, was it? His dad was respectable and hardworking and dutiful. And I know full well that Naseem would gladly have carried his dad on his back all the way to Scotland if he'd needed to.

A few years before, coming up to fetch Pa from The Crown of a night, I used to think this might be the original troll bridge. You know the one: every time someone tries to get to the other side an ugly troll pops up and says something like, No one here shall pass by me unless he can answer my questions three . . . and if you can't he eats you up, just like that. When I was seven I used to worry about that.

Once I got to fifteen I got more concerned about a different sort of troll who might pop up and surprise me – that's why Naseem often came with me. He'd got a black belt in some martial art or other. When Naseem couldn't come I usually made sure I was wearing some oversized shabby jumper. Just to make sure no loitering trolls would look at me and think me much of a catch.

I wondered how fast I would be able to run if I took the stilettos *off. If Dad could still walk (and maybe he was already past that stage; after all, the landlady had phoned home), how fast would I be able to get him over this bridge and back onto Tumbleweed Avenue, towards home?*

When I got to The Crown I spotted him straight away. He was still sitting there, still on his favourite barstool. Relief to see that he was all right, even tenderness, because I did worry about him, was followed by righteous indignation as I saw he was still drinking. Well, still with one hand cupped protectively around a jar, but his head was hanging down, sunk into his other hand.

'Dad! How could you do this to me?'

My dad did a double-take. He must have thought I was someone else at first. He wasn't used to seeing me dressed up to the nines just to come to fetch him home.

'I asked you not go out tonight, Dad, tonight of all nights . . .'

'It's New Year's Eve,' he protested. 'Ye can't expect a man to stop at home New Year's Eve.'

'But I'm planning on going out too!' I could see May and Bev – the bar-owners – doing their 'drying up the beer glasses' thing silently behind the bar, listening in on every word. I usually took their best customer away without too much fuss. They were used to me doing it. They weren't used to me kicking up a stink. They were probably wondering what had got into me.

'You didn't have to come after me, lass. Why can't ye leave me be?'

'Leave you be?' The straps on my borrowed shoes were really cutting into my ankles by then and I could just feel every drunken bum in the place ogling my backside. My face darkened at the thought.

'Te git home by messell, lass,' he explained patiently.

'Because you'll slip, Dad! You'll fall . . . !' How could he do this to me? I could hear my own voice rising hysterically. 'It's been raining outside, hasn't it? Remember the time you lost your footing? You fell in the stream. If I hadn't been there to rescue you, you'd have drowned.'

292

'Ah, yer just like yer mudder, aren't ye, lass? Tink I'm useless, don't ye? Tink I'd never survive without ye?' His arms opened wide to include the whole of his drinking brethren in our conversation. Some of them nodded sympathetically (with him), whilst the others were too busy drowning in their own sorrows to care about his.

'Maybe you wouldn't,' I told him darkly, hands on hips. I felt like an old harridan, at that moment, like a fishwife, nagging at him to come home quietly. Why couldn't he understand how much this meant to me? Why couldn't he just see that I was a person too?

'Ah, git away with ye,' he'd said.

But I hadn't walked away from him that night. I'd stayed and tried to do the thing I thought I should be doing.

Except matters hadn't worked out the way I'd meant them to, had they?

And I have no way of knowing how things will work out now, either.

Oh Ella, what should I do?

The cab that takes me down to Arenadeluna takes the Costa road and the mountains to the right of us remind me of her once more. 'Over the Hills and Far Away' hums along in my mind as we sweep past the summer turquoise of the Mediterranean Sea. She would have gone looking for her own lad, I know, in her day. If she had not been too frightened to leave her own home. I'm going to be brave for both of us now – for my boy, too.

In my hotel room – which overlooks the Aquavista yacht club – I sit and wait for Blue to arrive and I try not to think about Charlie at home, getting my note. I wanted to speak to Charlie so badly. I've never felt this lonely and this conflicted and this ... *wrong*, before.

I feel all wrong. But what I am doing is surely all *right*? I'm not going to hurt anyone. I'm only going to find out if this boy is – who we think he might be.

Blue's sharp knock at my door makes me jump.

293

'You okay?' he says, the minute I open the door. He walks in without waiting to be asked. He sits himself down on my bed and I take him in. His trainers look dirty, that's the first thing I notice. He looks like someone who's been sleeping rough down on the beach.

'Mind if I . . . ?' He pulls a fag out of his shirt pocket and lights it up without waiting for an answer. His fingernails are bitten to the quick, and his hands aren't quite steady, I notice.

'I'm fine,' I tell him. Funnily enough, compared to him I feel quite okayish, too. 'You look like *shite*, though.'

'Thanks.' He doesn't laugh.

'No, really.' I sit down on the chair beside the bed and watch him carefully. 'I'm really sorry about Maria and Diego,' I say after a while. 'They were good friends of yours I know.' Blue sniffs loudly, as if he's trying to remain nonchalant.

'At least they were together at the end. It's what they would have wanted.'

I nod.

'I'd do anything for that, you know,' he adds after a bit. 'To have what they had together; they were prepared to risk *everything* – just to be together.' That's the romantic view. I look at the ground. Things hadn't been going quite according to plan when last I spoke to Maria, had they?

'You won't believe this but – this is my first time,' his eyes suddenly take on the ghost of a glint, 'in a strange hotel room with a . . . *lady*.'

'Ha-ha. Cut the crap and tell me what's really going on.'

Blue sighs. He takes in a deep drag from his cigarette and looks at me through downturned eyes.

'I'm in a spot of trouble at the moment, my lady.' His usually clear blue eyes are bloodshot. What's he been up to? It's none of my business really, but . . .

'It's not drugs, I promise,' he reads my mind. 'I don't touch them. Not myself.'

I don't even want to know what that means.

I give him a blank stare. He isn't asking me for any money, is he? I haven't got any to give him and I wouldn't give him any if I did because all I have really belongs to Charlie.

'I haven't got any cash,' I say.

'Hey I wasn't asking you, was I?' He seems affronted. He gets up, twitching, unable to stay still a minute longer. 'Nice view you've got from here.'

'Thanks.' I haven't come here for the view.

'Of the Aquavista club, I mean. I recommended you a good hotel, yes?' He allows himself a smile.

I join him at the window. The marina belonging to the Aquavista club is directly below me. Why hadn't *I* noticed that before? They've got their own private docking area and their own private little bit of the beach too; perfect, sugar-fine white sand, quite unlike the other Spanish beaches we've visited so far.

'You might be able to spot them coming out of the clubhouse from here.' Blue lines himself up beside me – a little too close maybe, but he isn't interested in me I see, he's just trying to calibrate which angle would be the best to do my spying from.

'Oh *sweet!*'

'What? *What?*'

'She's here.'

'Who is?' My heart jumps in my throat. I've just got to my hotel. I've barely kicked off my shoes and she's *here*?

'Over there by the fat man with the moustache.' She's standing near the quay. Look, in red.'

I look at the woman he's pointing out and she seems attractive in a fairly ordinary sort of way. She's dressed beautifully, though (lots of dosh, as Blue warned me) and there is a child that she keeps glancing at as she speaks to the man. He'd be about the right age. He's playing with a yellow beach ball, kicking it along the quay (not too near the edge, she seems to be saying to him) but he's got his face turned away from me.

Is this him?

Now that I'm here it seems so unlikely as to be impossible. And from here, after all, I really cannot tell.

Blue hands me a pair of binoculars. Oh, I could kiss him right now for thinking of bringing them! I grab them off him. I fiddle about with the little dials but I make everything go a lot more blurry and then, when I manage to make the view go clear again, it takes me an age to find the right spot because I cannot get my bearings.

'Give it here,' Blue sighs. He takes it back and re-jigs the calibrations; even while he's doing that my heart sinks because I can see the woman has moved off with the boy behind the boathouse and is now out of view.

'Damn.' I feel a huge surge of excitement coursing through me though, as he turns triumphantly to face me.

'Good lookout, eh?'

I give him a high five.

'Time for a drink, I'd say!' He opens the hotel room fridge and rummages around, emerging finally with a couple of gins and tonics.

'Not for me, thanks.' I wave him away. 'Unless there's a diet cola of some sort in there. Maybe we should go after them or something?'

'No need,' he assures me. 'I've had my eye on them for you since they arrived and she always goes to the same spot on the club's private beach at the same time every morning.'

'You have?' I give him an appreciative look. 'That's really good of you to check her out for me.'

'And I'll show you where you can go to get a better look at her tomorrow.'

'Tomorrow?' my voice is wobbly. 'Do we have to wait that long? Can't we just . . .'

'You have another whole four days. I found out she's here till Wednesday evening. Anyhow, they'll be on that yacht, the *Serenity*, by now,' he tells me calmly. He glances at his watch. 'She's a private eye's dream; a woman of habit. This time, every day, they've been going for a spin around the bay.'

'You sure?' I crane my neck to look out as far as I can see and, sure enough, the *Serenity* is just pulling out of the quay.

Blue nods, tipping the bottle of gin straight to the back of his throat without bothering with the tonic.

'Look, if you've been spending this much time staking out this woman for me – doing all this work,' I change the subject deftly, 'I'll have to pay you something.'

'No,' he asserts. 'I did it for you. For your son.'

'Is it *him*, do you think?' I take in a deep breath now. I have little money to pay him with anyway. It doesn't feel right to be using Charlie's cards when I've just left him. I feel so flustered, so exhausted and nervous. So scared. 'The boat has stopped. Are you sure we can't go down there and have a look?'

'You don't want to arouse their suspicions. Better if you observe him properly before you make your move.'

He seems to know what he's talking about but I can barely stand the suspense.

If this is Hadyn, I realise all of a sudden, maybe I won't need to lose Charlie after all . . .

I sit back down on the chair. 'What move do you suggest we make next?'

'That's up to you. If it is him . . .'

'I call the police straight away? I tell my brother-in-law?'

Blue is shaking his head sombrely. 'You won't do any of that, Julia. Not if you want the boy back. If it *is* him, you tell no one.'

'How will I get him back then?'

'We'll have to arrange a . . . er . . . collection,' he says vaguely. 'You won't get him back through the "proper channels", Julia. Her father owns half the real estate in Arenadeluna. She's the only heir he has. To date, this boy is the only heir she has. Who's to say that this boy – her boy – is yours, anyway? You? Even if that is true, there will be half a dozen people prepared to swear blind that he is hers. They'll swear affidavits to that effect if need be. The family couldn't risk the dishonour to their name; they couldn't afford to be shamed in that way. I promise you, you'd never get within a mile of her to do any DNA tests if that's what you're thinking. *You* would be the one criminalised – a crazy, depressed, out-of-her-head woman who isn't even married to Charlie . . .'

He doesn't need to highlight that my status around here in this up-and-coming playground for the rich is beneath consideration. If I'm not connected to Charlie, I am no one, basically.

But I am still Hadyn's mother.

'How am I going to be able to tell for sure?' I look at Blue now. He's the one I must now rely on for everything and, frankly, he's not looking in such great shape himself.

'You're his mother, aren't you? If you get close enough, you'll know.'

That's what I'd like to think. I bite my lip.

'And then?'

'We lie low for a bit. If it's him we won't be able to do it legally, so we'll have to find some other way.'

'Snatch him, you mean?' I am feeling sick, horribly sick. I can't believe I am having this conversation.

'If it *is* him, Julia, you needn't feel so bad about it. You'd just be taking him *back*, right?'

Something about this doesn't feel right to me – but he does have a point.

'You know some people who can help?'

'For the right price, maybe.' Blue looks distinctly shifty for a moment. 'I can't get involved in this myself, Julia. I've already got people . . . watching my movements.'

I'm about to ask *who and why* when I realise I really don't want to know. He's just come out of jail after all . . .

'They won't have followed you here, though?' My throat closes with nerves. I have to focus, here. Whatever his problems are I don't want them interfering with *my* task.

Blue shakes his head; no way, he says.

'So I just . . . find out if it's him and then we . . . come up with a plan?'

'That's about the shape of it.' He shakes his head then. 'I've got myself into some deep water, Julia. But I know how you're suffering at the moment, having lost your boy. I want to do whatever I can to help you.' Then, as an afterthought, he adds, 'Does Charlie know?' He tips the last of the dry roasted peanuts from my fridge into his mouth in one go and gets up to leave.

'Charlie doesn't know a thing.'

'Best way,' he mutters, but he raises his eyebrows just the same. He's thinking about where I'm going to get the money from to pay his 'friends' who might be needed to help out, no doubt.

'He knows you're in Spain, though?'

I shake my head and Blue whistles through his teeth.

'Going it alone then?'

'Of course I haven't told him! He's the *last person* I want to get involved in this. Think about it. I've come out here on the wafer-thin evidence of a clairvoyant's pronouncement and your ex-police guy's assertion that obsessive former old flames can be prime suspects in child snatching. That's all I've got to go on. Do you think he'd risk his entire reputation – and all his precious charity work – on *that*?' *He'd do his level best to stop me if he had the foggiest idea . . .*

'Guess you're right,' he agrees.

'The only thing I haven't yet figured out,' he mutters as he leaves at last, 'is how we are going to get you into that private club so you can get close enough to that child. You'll need a pass. Unless,' he smiles hopefully, 'you happen to be best buddies with the proprietor's family?'

'No I am not,' I tell him disparagingly. But when I think about it, I know someone who is.

Someone – who is the last person in Spain who'll probably want to hear from me. I know this even as I punch her number into my mobile phone. It rings for a very long time before she picks it up. And when she does at last, she sounds very fragile and weary. She sounds like someone who has had all the life punched out of her and I know this is partly my doing.

She will not want to help me.

But she is the only person I know who can.

'Hello?' I breathe into the phone when she answers. 'It's me, Julia. Please don't hang up. I need to speak to you, Agustina.'

Charlie

I am standing in the hallway of Blackberry House and it's bloody cold – there is no central heating on. The lights are all off. All the doors and windows have been closed.

Where is she?

So much for Julia promising to stay here while I went off to the Santos golfing weekend. I needed Julia to be here tonight and she's not.

This house is too big. I glance up at the huge space spiralling towards the top of the stairwell. What do I need such a huge house for? I have no family. I could sell it. I could use the proceeds to put towards Esperanza. I'm going to need every penny now that Santos is out of the picture. Though, dear God, why I am still even bothered about any of it is beyond me. After what I've learned tonight – how he has made a mockery and a sham out of all our work in Africa – maybe I won't bother carrying on with it anyway.

Where are you, Julia?

The lights shining across the white paint in my hallway alerts me to the arrival of a car. Thank God, she's come back – maybe it's not too late to put things right between us? I go over to open up the door before she does. It's ten o'clock on an August evening but it's dark already. The air feels damp. Behind her, as she gets out of the car, the streetlights pick out some of the blackberries on the brambles that still seem to thrive in every corner of this garden.

And when she looks up, it isn't Julia at all.

I look at Lourdes desperately as she waits to lock her car. What is *she* doing here, when Julia isn't?

'Why did you follow me?' I call out, scowling. I turn, half closing the door. She's *known* what Santos has been up to all along. She must have known; she's his sister after all . . .

'Charlie,' she bites her lip, reaching me at the door, 'I didn't know. I *swear* I didn't know . . .'

'You must have known, Lourdes.' I take her in cynically. 'You can't have been totally unaware of the reason why your brother was so keen to support Louis Baudelaire. Why he was so keen for us to cover everything up, pull together as a team and move on seamlessly as if nothing had ever happened.'

'Charlie – *don't*.' She reaches out to touch my arm but I pull away from her. 'My brother is a businessman, first and foremost. Some of the things he's got involved in . . .' She hangs her head, but I won't be taken in by that 'helpless little girl' act this time. '. . . Some of the things,' she whispers, 'are terrible. I don't deny them. It's just . . .'

'*Go home*, Lourdes,' I tell her wearily. 'You shouldn't have followed me home tonight. I don't want anything more to do with your family. Any of you.'

'You're angry.' She straightens, her wide eyes looking directly into mine. 'You feel let down and you can't see any sense yet. But there is too much at stake for you, and my brother knows that. He believes that you will come round. That's why I'm here. It's cold standing outside, Charles. May I come in?' She pushes her way past me into my hallway, into *my* house.

'My, it's nice in here.' She looks around appreciatively, flicking on the small lights as she goes. 'You have good taste.' She looks around then, questioning, 'Where's Julia?'

'You need to go home, Lourdes.' I haven't budged from the open door. 'Your brother deceived me.'

'*I* didn't deceive you, though.' She sidles up to me, her fingers

302

reaching up to my arm again. 'I had no *idea* what my brother was up to. For Christ's sake, Charlie. You can't imagine I would have known about it and not come to you? I brought you the Baudelaire file in the first place, didn't I? You shredded it, I hope?' Her eyes look into mine anxiously.

'That file never made any mention of Santos's part in it,' I hiss. 'His whole interest in Africa was a scam, a cover, wasn't it?'

Lourdes takes in a sharp breath. She's on the verge of tears but she's holding them in, keeping her dignity.

Maybe – she didn't know anything about her brother's shenanigans, after all? She wouldn't have deceived me like that, surely? I turn, closing the door. What should I think?

When I look at her, maybe my very oldest friend in the world, my former wife-to-be, my former lover, my aide for so long in all my Esperanza endeavours . . . how can I believe she knew anything at all about the atrocities her brother has been involved in?

'I learned about it alongside you, tonight,' she assures me. 'Santos would never have involved me in that side of it, don't you see? Why would he have? He keeps all illicit operations close to his chest. I was there – like you – to make things look good. To make the whole operation legit. He's used us, Charlie. Both of us.'

Reluctantly, I pull her in towards me. I don't want her to see the tears that have sprung into my eyes. I don't want her to see the bitterness I am feeling in my heart.

'Everything we've been trying to achieve in Africa,' I say through clenched teeth, 'it's all been for naught.'

'No, it hasn't!' I feel her fingers clasp hold of my back. 'Don't say that, Charlie! We can still make this work. We can do it.'

'We can't do it!' I pull a wry smile at her optimism, turning away from her to sit on the bottom steps of my magnificent stairway. I need time to think. I can't just jump straight from this into my next plan . . .

'We can *do* it,' Lourdes insists, tugging at my hand. 'There's still the gala dinner on Friday night, isn't there? We've got some big names coming this time. We've pulled out all the stops on the promotions side. We could still pull this out of the bag.' She crouches down beside me on the stairs.

'So you're suggesting that we – what? – we start up the scheme again in another location, under a new banner maybe, with new backers?'

'Just do the same work,' she agrees, her eyes shining. 'Just because there's corruption everywhere in the world doesn't mean that good people can't keep doing good.'

'Yeah.' I close my eyes and lean back against the stairs. I've got to carry on. People need me. 'But where is Julia?' I look around, suddenly remembering. I pull my mobile out of my pocket and call her number. 'She's not picking up her phone.' I click it closed in irritation. I hate it when I can't get through to her.

'Are you sure there's nothing on the home phone?'

'Why would there be? She wasn't expecting me to be home this weekend, was she?'

'Maybe her mother or someone got sick and she didn't leave any note because she didn't expect you back yet?'

No, precisely. *She didn't expect me back yet, did she?* I run upstairs and check through the drawer where we keep all our papers and my suspicions are confirmed. Her passport is missing. And there, on the bed, is a little white envelope.

Damn her. I thump the wall behind me. I *know* what she's done.

'Nothing?' Lourdes looks at me expectantly when I come down some minutes later.

'Not a peep. Look – don't even *talk* to me about her right now, Lourdes. She's taken herself right out of my life; her choice.' *Her loss*, I tell myself, but the unremitting pain I feel in my chest tells me otherwise. I scrunch the envelope Julia left behind and the hard metal edges of my father's medallion that she put inside it feel like the edge of a sword on my hand. I promised her I'd always be there for her, didn't I? But I haven't been and she's gone; Julia's gone, and the loss feels like it's all mine.

'Look – I should be leaving.' Lourdes turns to look for her jacket. Outside the evening is dismal. It's raining and it's getting late. She'll have another long car journey ahead of her if she leaves now and, besides, do I really want to be all alone in this house tonight?

'The spare room is made up,' I offer and see her hesitate. My son is gone. Julia is gone. Esperanza might be on its last legs. It's just possible that Lourdes might be the last thing left keeping me anchored in some form of sanity.

'No,' she says flatly. 'Thank you, but no. Even though you know very well that I *want* to stay with you tonight, I'm going to suggest that you do something else instead.'

'What?'

'Go after her,' Lourdes breathes. 'Go and find out where she is and tell her that you still love her. Because you *do*, don't you? If you let that woman slip out of your life now you will regret it for ever.'

'Still looking after me, Lourdes?'

I take her jacket out of her arms, her silver grey scarf, and lay it softly over the banisters. She doesn't move to take it back.

'Maybe I'm not the man you think I am, though? I've done something that I never would have credited myself with doing,' I confess. 'When I went upstairs just now – I started looking through all her papers. I've been leafing through the emails she printed out from her friend in Spain, Blue. She's got them in a folder together with newspaper clippings from Spain, articles off the Internet – all sorts of stuff.'

'And? What's wrong with you doing that? You want her back and she's left you without a word. You were trying to find out where she is, yes?'

'She's gone to Spain, Lourdes. I'm convinced that's exactly where she's gone.' I turn, my eyes skimming over all the photos of Julia and me and Hadyn in the hallway, but seeing nothing. 'She's gone to meet *him*. I don't know what they're planning – the last few emails were too sketchy, they don't really say. But this guy Blue – he's been filling her head with all sorts of lies and false hopes, just as I thought all along.'

'What sort of lies?' Lourdes is standing up very straight in front of me, clasping her hands in front of her. She's looking a little strained.

'He's talking about things like – a supposed discrepancy in timing between when the police say the fish containing their main evidence was caught and what the fisherman, who actually caught it, is claiming. He mentions that we don't even know if Hadyn was wearing those trunks when he disappeared . . .' My voice trails off.

'Could there be any truth in this *at all*, Carlos?'

I shake my head slowly.

'It's nonsense. Roberto would never have let them skimp on the investigation. He has so many contacts in the Policia Local. He would have followed every avenue, Lourdes.'

'But you have to admit,' Lourdes ventures, 'if a child such as Hadyn were to be snatched – let's just say *if* – then it wouldn't look very good for Arenadeluna would it? If there was a big, high-profile case, then that might put the tourists off somewhat, mightn't it? Just like the Louis Baudelaire scandal – if it got out – would put people off being associated with Esperanza.'

'You aren't for one moment suggesting that my own *brother* . . .'

'Look at this objectively.' Lourdes catches my gaze and holds it. 'You need to remember there is an awful lot of European Union "Cultural Heritage" money at stake here. Why do you think they're working so hard to move that Roman fort to a different location and make the beach bigger? If Arenadeluna becomes eligible for the Heritage status that its politicians are after, there's going to be a hell of a lot of cash flying around and even *more* new developments. It's just possible that there might be some people who weren't keen on having a lot of fuss made over one missing toddler. I'm not saying that's what happened. I'm just saying it might have, that's all.'

'No it is not. It is impossible.' I can't believe she's saying this. She knows my family would never have let that happen.

'Even the impossible does happen from time to time, Charlie. You said it yourself. You fathered Hadyn in the first place, didn't you?'

That was below the belt.

She stands now, folding her arms in front of her.

'His birth was a miracle,' I concede. 'It was more than I could ever have hoped for. You know that. But God took him away from me, Lourdes.'

'*God* did?'

'Just whose side are you on here, Lourdes?' I round on her, not wanting her here and yet not wanting her to go. 'I do believe that he died in that storm on that beach. Yes, I do. You're supposed to be supporting *me*, not Julia.'

'I *am* supporting you, you fool.' Lourdes picks up her jacket again and walks to the door. 'I know it's not what I've always done, Carlos. I should never have let you down the way I did. But I'm trying to put that right, as you see. I have to go now. And if you haven't done the sensible thing and got on the next plane out of here to go and sort out whatever mess is brewing in Spain, then – I'll see you on Friday.'

'You know full well I won't be going to Spain,' I call after her, angrily. 'With your brother out of the picture, the Esperanza project needs me more than ever. Friday night may well be make or break for them.' I hold out my hand to her, conciliatory now. 'Stay with me, tonight?'

'I can't.' She casts a half-glance towards the open front door. She steps out.

'You *won't*.'

'No. Not while your heart still belongs to another woman.'

'Try me.' My lips brush against the side of her head as she turns her face away but I can feel her trembling. She feels so familiar. I remember that, once, I loved her.

'Esperanza is the most important thing in your life,' she

whispers. 'But even if you do manage to save it next week, what is the point, really, if you have no life worth speaking of to go home to afterwards?'

'Stay with me, have dinner. Talk to me. Please.' I put my hand on her arm. 'This feels all too hard, Lourdes. What's happening to my family. What's happening to Esperanza . . .'

'The work you do there is vital,' she reassures me. 'What you do makes a huge difference but . . .'

'Does it?' I look at her wearily. 'Ngosi Ontome *died*, didn't he? Oh yes, I heard. Lopez mentioned it tonight.' I give a sigh and it comes out like a huge shudder because that little lad died and it was all for nothing – I lost my son for *nothing* . . . 'I don't want to be alone tonight, Lourdes.' I pull the door closed again, drawing her to me. '*Please.*'

This time she does not resist.

As she reaches up to kiss my mouth I feel the surge of old familiar feelings rush through me. This time they are not tainted by guilt. Julia has left me, after all. I begged her not to go but she has left me anyway. She's made her choice.

'Do you think,' Lourdes murmurs, her trembling hands in my hair, 'do you think it possible that a miracle might happen *twice*?'

I shake my head. This is too much, too soon. I want her to stay. I don't want to be alone, but do I really want to start an affair with her? She takes my hand.

As we go up the stairway I hear the phone begin to trill below and my heart quickens. If it's Julia. . . . I don't care, let it ring. If it's important, then let her leave me a message. Let her give me a reason why she isn't here for me tonight . . .

But it isn't Julia. Another woman's voice speaks into the answer machine now, high and urgent: '*Oiga!* Carlos. This is Eva here. You need to pick up. I have news for you from Spain. Urgent news. Pick up the phone if you're there, *por favor* . . .'

Julia

'I remembered you mentioning the Aquavista club before.' I am sitting on a bench in the shady courtyard beneath Agustina's apartment and we're well hidden from the busy road out front by the beach. I begged Agustina over the phone to come and meet me out here where nobody would spot us, to keep my presence here confidential, and, to my surprise, she agreed.

'I remember you spoke about the owner being German,' I rush on, 'and the fact that he was married to your goddaughter . . .'

'Ah, *sí.*' Agustina is looking at me thoughtfully. She's wearing her floral housecoat over her clothes. She looks . . . different. We haven't seen each other, I realise suddenly, since the day I left Spain six and a half months ago, the side of my face all swollen up and bruised where I'd hit it against that lamppost. At the time we'd all felt battered and bruised, I recall now. But we'd still thought there might have been some hope.

'I'm sorry I never rang you in all this time,' I remember to say. 'I meant to, Agustina. I just . . .' *I just didn't want to.*

She has tried, several times over the past months, to speak to me on the phone after she's spoken to Charlie, but I've always made some excuse and avoided her. I couldn't face her, that's all. I'm not sure where it is I'm finding the strength from, to face her now.

'*Está bien.*' She lays a firm hand on my arm. 'We all know what you have suffered.' For a second the self-assuredness, her erect head, drop a little. I search for some fragment of the hardness I'd seen around the edges of her grey eyes but it is gone. 'We have all suffered,' she adds. 'And Charlie?' I note the sadness that shoots across her face for a minute before she hides it. 'He is well? He doesn't call any more.'

'He's well,' I stammer. When I last left him, he did not look very well. He looked heartsick, worn out to the bone. We argued.

'He's been terribly busy.' I make his excuses and then, my voice hardening, 'He's always terribly busy, isn't he?'

She shrugs, accepting the situation as it is.

'I need to get into the Aquavista club,' I tell her at last, 'because someone I know thinks they may have spotted a child who looks like Hadyn in there . . .' If Agustina is shocked at me bringing all this up then she makes a good job of hiding it, but she closes her eyes momentarily when I mention his name.

'There may be a child who looks like him,' she agrees, 'but it will not be him. He's gone,' she adds after a while. 'Roberto told me, he's gone. We are making another memorial for him this morning. You will come,' she urges me.

No, I will not come.

'I'm sorry,' I tell her uncomfortably. 'I had to come back here. *Someone has seen my son.* Can you understand that?'

'What does my grandson say?'

'Charlie – Charlie thinks I'm crazy!' I stare at her brokenly. I'm telling her the truth because she must be thinking it too. There is nothing left between us but only the raw and un-adulterated truth. 'Charlie doesn't see it. He thinks I should stop all this nonsense and give it up. We had a big argument and I've left him over it.'

'You've *finished* with him?' Her eyes grow wide.

'He thinks the search for Hadyn is all over . . .'

'But not for you,' she finishes for me. 'It isn't finished yet, for you.'

'No.' I hold her hand, entreating, because I don't know what else to do. 'And now I need a pass to get onto the private beach and check out that boy.'

Agustina rubs her face with her hands and I catch the scent of lemon and garlic that comes off her fingers, the hint of fresh fish that she's been cleaning. I have pushed in on a day full of comfortable and familiar tasks to come and stir things up again. Nobody wants that. They want to get on with their lives in peace, and I understand that. I wish I could, too.

But I can't.

'The pass I can get you,' she says after a while. 'But . . .' her faded grey eyes look searchingly into mine for a moment. 'You came out all this way. You quarrelled with Charlie. *What makes you so sure?*'

I pause for a minute.

'You speak good English, Agustina.' I see her brief nod of acknowledgement. 'You never spoke to me much before, did you?'

She smiles softly.

'I have been learning, *hija*. The woman who – how you say it – fixes my hair, she's teaching me, so . . .' she touches my arm with her hand, 'we can speak.'

She's been learning English, just so she can speak to me?

'I thought you must hate me,' I confess. 'I went out that day when we argued. If I had not gone out that day . . .'

I cannot speak.

'Not your fault,' she tells me. '*Mi culpa.*' She leans forward to embrace me. Her tight grey curls rest against my shoulders and I can feel, in the thin arms that cling about mine, the sad fragility of this person who I had taken to be so fierce. She solemnly hands me a plastic bag that she takes from her purse and for a moment, I feel the soft leathery touch of her cheek against my face. Her black walking stick clatters to the ground as we lean together on the bench.

'You never did any wrong,' I reassure her. 'I had lied to everyone. You were angry, that's natural. You had every right to be.'

'Maybe – I did not make you welcome.' She shakes her head, overcome with remorse. Gingerly, I stroke her hair and her scalp feels very small and fragile beneath my fingers.

'I should never have gone out that day, Agustina. I ran away from all of you. *I* did it.'

'So why,' she looks at me, needing to know, 'why you are so sure now? To come all this way – to see this boy?'

What can I say that will satisfactorily explain why I have risked so much to be here today?

'Because he is still alive. I feel it *here*,' I point to the pit of my stomach. There is nothing else.

Agustina smiles sadly.

'You are a mother,' she says at last. 'And if that is what you feel, then you do right, *hija*.' When I glimpse inside the plastic bag she's just handed me I see she's given me back my camera. My fingers run over the familiar surface of it for a minute, and I'm glad to have it back. Maybe I will start taking pictures again one day soon? Pictures like I used to take, of *the way things are*, pictures that capture something of the truth? At Agustina's words a warm feeling is beginning to spread right through me like a smile. The feeling is tinged with sadness, too. Why couldn't my own mum have said that? Why couldn't she just have understood that I have to do what I have to do – even if I turn out to be wrong?

'I will do what you ask,' Agustina says now. 'I will ring Claus, who owns the club. I will ask him to give you a pass for the week. I will say nothing to the others about it. And in return,' she smiles sadly, 'I will ask of *you* one thing.'

'Anything.' Oh my god – she has agreed to my request. 'I will do anything you ask.'

'I would like you to attend the memorial service with the family this morning. As a sign of respect. Will you do that?'

'Of course I will do that!' I heave out a sigh of relief. Is that all? Merely setting foot inside that church – what seemed such an insurmountable barrier before – it is *nothing* now. I'll do it gladly.

'And when you go to the private beach and look,' she asks me after a while, 'what will you do, if it is not him?'

'I will go home,' I say decidedly. 'I will apologise to Charlie. I will give it all up, because I will accept that my boy is gone.'

She nods, acknowledging what I am telling her, though perhaps she is just humouring me. Perhaps she thinks that I am out of my mind with grief. Maybe this is one way of letting me see for myself that they are all right.

What I don't tell her is what I'm planning to do if it turns out they are all wrong.

Julia

When the sun got as high as it was going to get, I figured she wasn't coming.

Adamantine did not go to the private beach where Blue had said she would be, the next day. I was there from 8 a.m. until midday, Sunday.

By that time I'd got quite burned myself, even though I hadn't taken my clothes off. I'd just sat there on the sand but I didn't have any sun cream. I hadn't thought about any of that. All I could think was I was going to see this child this morning and find out if he was mine. I forgot to take a bottle of water and I didn't dare move from my spot because if I did she might come and then I'd lose my chance. The rays of the sun burned right through my canvas shorts and through my cotton T-shirt. By the time I got back to the hotel I was dehydrated and light-headed and I knew I must have looked as pink as a lobster.

I went out to get some Aftersun to put on my burned skin and stock up on water bottles and magazines so I could pretend later that I was reading them and wouldn't stick out like a sore thumb on the beach. I bought myself a two-piece as well (no one else on the beach was fully dressed) and a sun umbrella to sit under. So I went back in the afternoon better equipped and watched the kiddies playing on the shore with their specially imported white sand, but Adamantine never came with her child.

On Monday the weather became a bit overcast. It wasn't a

'beach day' really. I panicked a little bit, walking up and down the length of the beach, over and over again, because I remembered Blue had said she was leaving on Wednesday. What if the weather stayed dull and cool and she didn't come back to the beach again? The pretty yachts that sailed into the quay adjacent to the beach spewed out more people. I wondered if she might be on one of them. Nobody spoke to me – though a few people nodded and smiled in my direction as they walked past. I kept my head down for the most part, wishing I could be invisible. I wasn't really supposed to be here, was I?

I kept trying to contact Blue on his mobile but he never picked up. I phoned Celeste but she wasn't available either. I left them both a message. I never said anything to Alys. Barring Agustina, Celeste is the only person apart from Blue who knows what I've been up to. Silas's reading hadn't been so good for her – though it had been ambiguous enough for her to take whatever comfort from it that she chose. He'd described Chloe, apparently, to a tee. He'd said lots of things about her that he couldn't have known (about how when she was three she'd dropped her mum's car keys down the loo because she hadn't wanted to go out somewhere). Then he'd told Celeste, simply, 'She waits for you.' Whether this was in this life or the next wasn't entirely clear. 'It goes to show,' Celeste had said, 'that there is some part of her that still survives, doesn't it? And she's waiting for me, wherever she is.' The reading had made her sad and happy at the same time. I kept thinking about all that on Monday when I was sitting alone on the beach. I kept going over and over it all in my head.

By Tuesday I'd worked out that if I sat in the restaurant area up on the decking I could sip cool drinks for as long as I wanted and could see pretty much everything there was to see from my vantage point up there. I didn't want to swim or get undressed, and sitting up here as a customer I looked a lot less conspicuous.

Adamantine didn't come though, even late into the evening. I stayed there till six p.m. because I knew my time was running out and my backside felt all achey in the chair. Blue phoned me and said he'd got tied up. He seemed surprised to learn she hadn't been there at all. He'd been there every day since he'd learned she was in town last week: was I going there early enough? he asked.

I started to think maybe what I needed to do was go inside the Aquavista club. You couldn't just go into it, though. Security there seemed to be quite tight. You had to hand over a special card with all your details on it before they let you in. I didn't know if the card Agustina had procured for me would cover it – and I didn't want to attract attention to myself either. Blue didn't join me at the bar on the beach like he'd promised he would. I read all the magazines – in little hurried scraps and pieces – six times over. I was beginning to wonder if Blue wasn't a complete and utter lying bastard who had made all this up and taken advantage of me on the first day (so tired, so eager), when I'd imagined the child he'd pointed out through the window could be mine.

I didn't phone Charlie. The more the days wore on, the less I dared. At the moment I was a free agent. Nobody knew what I was up to so there was no one to come and stop me.

At the same time I was cast adrift. Nobody knew me here. If I disappeared, who would ever find out about it? Who would care? I got into a morose state of wondering if I really mattered to anyone after all.

Then today – on the fifth day of my being here – and with only eight hours left to go, I have broken my habit of settling like a cloud on the beach every morning and I have wandered into the town of Arenadeluna. I don't know quite why I came here. My mind has gone numb and a strange quietness has descended on me. I do not know if this is because I am so tense and tired that I cannot bear it any more, or if it is because I am getting used to the stillness and the feeling of being 'out of place'.

Maybe I will see them here, I tell myself; in the market, buying oranges, or fingering the beaded moccasins that come from Tangiers, the leather handbags studded with bright metal buttons?

I stop and buy some sweeties from the sweet stand. When the man asks me which ones I want, I can't think, I just point to the nearest thing on the counter. Maybe if I find him I will give them to Hadyn? It's a sign of positive intent, as Celeste would say. You have to be eternally positive, she tells me. You have to want the thing that is your desire with every fibre of your being and you have to act as if it is already yours. She reads all these New Age books and they give her hope. As for me, I'm just biding my time.

I look at the T-shirts now. There are T-shirts with fire engines on here and I know Haydn'd *love* these. I'm looking at the wrong sizes though. He'd be bigger now.

How big, though? He'd be coming up to two years old and the T-shirts for two-year-olds look too big. I can't imagine him in that size. It makes me sad. All those sizes he's gone through and I've missed it. My fingers clench tightly around the bag of sweets I've bought. I've got to get out of here. This place is too sticky and too hot and crowded. There are too many people here and each one of them only serves to remind me how very alone I have become.

I was a free agent yesterday, doing my own thing and answering to no one. Today I am without support, and without a friend in the world on a . . . a desert island, that's all.

I walk up the hill away from the market. The Campo Nuevo – the site that's being developed for the Roman fort relocation – is coming along in leaps and bounds. In fact – I can now see – this fort is going to be about three times the size of the old ruin that Roberto pointed out to me, up on the hill. It's going to have all the 'missing bits' added to it, according to the plaque. It's going to be a real up-market ruin when it's completed.

I carry on up the hill and away from the main town and the

roads narrow as I go. The tall buildings lean in conspiratorially towards each other, affording the passer-by the luxury of shade, just as they were designed to do so many years ago. In the old part of the town, Campo Viejo, little has been touched yet. It feels calmer, slower. I walk and walk until, without noticing it, I am at the Church of San José, the place where Charlie had hoped we would be getting married next month, if all had run according to plan.

I go in and sit down on one of the pews. I don't feel out of place like I did last time. I just feel sad. And strangely peaceful, even despite that sadness. And I pray.

There are so few candles burning in the church today. I get up and place a little candle in all of the candle-holders along the top row, and I light them, one by one. And then, because what I'm asking God for is so important that maybe one row of candles just won't do it, I light up the whole tray of candles.

They are leaving today. You must help me now. *They are going from this place and then I will never get my chance again!* As I slot the money into the coin box afterwards an old lady who's been praying at the front of the church comes up to me with wide eyes and says '*No, no, solamente una es suficiente!*' One is enough, she says.

'I've got to be sure God hears me,' I tell her, still digging in my purse.

'He hears you,' she answers in perfect English. 'And you only need one.'

Maybe she's right. God heard me and it's worked like magic because by the time I get out of the church there's a text message from Blue on my phone saying, 'They're on the beach now. I am here watching them. Where are you?'

I take a cab back, my heart thumping all the way. Thank God Blue is there. I don't want to be alone when I see Hadyn up close. What if I can't tell if he's mine? I will, of course I will, but then again . . .

By the time we get back – the crowds are dense, just dispersing from market day – Blue has left me another message. 'Down by the flagpole area. I told you I couldn't stay longer than half an hour. CU later. B. xx'

And I'm on my own.

So I go down onto the beach and watch them. Adamantine is with a friend today. They're sitting there together under a huge umbrella and there's a little baby in there too (is it hers or the friend's?). The two women keep bending over to admire it. The boy – is he my boy? – makes my heart leap. I hardly dare to look at him at first. I have to stuff my fist into my mouth because I want to cry out. Blue is right. He looks so much like my boy . . .

I have to get closer, but I need to take my time about it. I build a little sandcastle of my own, dipping my fingers into the sugary white sand and patting the wet stuff onto the top. If I make a nice enough one I might attract him to my side, I think. I wouldn't even have to go to him to get a closer look.

But he doesn't notice me. He's completely engrossed in his own solitary game. He's collecting pebbles and putting them on the top of his creation, just like Maria's girls showed him to do, once before. He's got the most beautiful hair; lovely, strawberry curls just like my boy. His concentration is intense. I adjust my sunglasses because this way I look as if I'm looking somewhere else.

I edge a little closer, pretending I'm looking for wetter sand.

I stand there by the water's edge for a while, shielding my eyes, pretending to take in the far distant mountains but really looking at Adamantine, her perfect long legs wrapped in a sarong, the immaculate hair pulled up out of the way with elegant clips. She's talking to her friend and then her friend gets up, leaving Adamantine with the baby to see to. Her attention is divided between the two of them, and she is not paying as much attention as she should do to the one on the shore.

As for me, my legs are trembling so hard they're almost

319

knocking together at the knees. The man with the bright yellow ice-cream box parades up and down the beach.

'*Helados, helados!*' He calls out his wares and all the children know exactly what he's got in his box. The boy – *my son*, I'm more and more sure of it by the minute – looks up, now. He stares at me for a minute though I'm still pretending to look at the faraway mountains. I can feel him, looking, just as he can feel me.

I am so close to him now. I turn to him and smile. Will *he* recognise *me?*

He looks at me with those beautiful eyes. His eyes have changed colour a little bit, I think. The shape of his face is a little different too. His nose is . . . more square. But they change, I know that. They grow and the shape of their face changes.

Oh, are you mine? You look as if you might be, but I have to be certain.

I glance at Adamantine and she's not paying any mind to us at all. I still have the sweeties in my bag, I remember. The red gummy bears I bought for him in the market.

Could I lure him away with me for a little bit so I can get a closer look and see if this child is really who I think he is? I have to get close enough to see if he's got that moon-shaped birthmark on his neck.

If it is him I will . . . I will pick him up and run. If I wait for anyone else it may be too late; I may never get this chance again. I feel beautifully focused just at this moment.

I bend down and pat the sand beside him, gingerly, as if testing it for suitability. I put a little handful of it into his bucket without looking at him, easily, naturally, as if I have a right to do it. He doesn't object.

After a while, he puts some sand into his bucket, too. Then he wipes his face with his sandy hands and gets sand all over his tongue. I laugh softly, but in that moment his face changes. He looks perplexed. Far away across the sand a dog starts barking, I can hear it. It's yelping and over-excited to be let loose. I cannot see it. I do not turn my head, but I can hear it. A flash of another dog, a dog on a beach just like this one, eight months ago, leaps across my mind, and suddenly I can feel my heart racing, my anger roused; something within me that has remained quiet for such a long time is stirring.

This woman took him from me. I have to remember this, because what I am doing now is not wrong.

She took him when my back was turned. When the sky had grown momentarily dark, the waves restless. The sound of that dog barking has brought all the blurry bits back; it is all coming back in little cameos and snapshots.

Maria; she's shaking out her towels. The wet sand falls heavily from the brightly coloured fabric. She rolls them up, businesslike, into tight cylinders, and packs them into the bottom of her beach bag.

Her girls; one of them is stomping on the remains of the sand-castle. She flattens it out completely, her short legs moving up and down like pistons. The other one – where is she? She must be behind us, on the shore. Maybe she has joined the crowds that are already gathering to look at the strange waves. People are standing, pointing. The cold rain spits down and their T-shirts are getting soaked and they still stand there, pointing. I can hear a dull rushing in my ears. I don't know what it is. The minutes go by. The lifeguards rush past, their faces surly, set, and determined. I see Blue kicking his shoes off. And Diego, running up to his car to fetch his body-board to help save those girls. Everybody is shifting themselves. Everybody is wary of the strange sea. My hand is throbbing.

The pain.

The pain is setting every nerve fibre in my body on fire. At that moment, nothing else matters. My eyes are streaming, I have to keep wiping them with the back of my hand.

Hadyn is crying; he's cold. He wants to come with me but no, I can't. I can't, my hand hurts too much, so I turn him round and face him towards Maria, and one of the daughters takes his hand and walks him back down to her. He's wearing the blue shorts.

His arms are goose-pimpled with the sudden drop in temperature. I don't wait to watch her put a towel around him. I can barely see; my eyes keep watering. It's as if I've swallowed chilli peppers. I stumble off up the beach but there is no one to help me.

The dog – when I go off it's still there, jumping round and round in little excited leaps, running rings around Maria's girl.

That's when this woman must have done it. When we were all distracted. When there was so much going on that we stopped paying attention for those few vital seconds, that's when she must have snatched him.

The dog on the Aquavista club beach front has stopped barking now. The silence pulls me out of my reverie. If I were to wrap my towel around this child I could just pick him up and walk away with him. I wonder if that is how she did it? Cool as a cucumber; I wonder if that is how Adamantine finally got her hands on Charlie's child? Maybe she got someone else to do the dirty work for her, but I don't have anyone else. I can't afford to pay anyone and I can't afford to wait. They're leaving today, according to Blue. What if I never get a chance as good as this again?

Fortune favours the brave.

When I put my hand on his arm to pick him up, I'm feeling curiously numb about the whole thing. That's probably the best way to be: matter of fact. I don't feel nervous. I don't feel *in the wrong*.

I'm putting things right, that's all. *All this time,* I feel my heart thudding in my chest, *all those prayers the family said at mass this morning for the repose of his soul, and he's been here all along.*

I was right. I told them, but they wouldn't believe me, would they? But he's here! The proof of the pudding. My son. He's surprisingly light. His bones feel small, little chicken bones, underneath my arms.

Hadyn was always so sturdy. So heavy set. Maybe she hasn't been feeding him too well?

He doesn't object at all when I start to move slowly away with him, up towards the head of the beach. He's got his eyes on that ice-cream guy with his bright yellow box. He imagines that's where we're headed.

We're going – oh, dare I even think it? – we're going *home*. I kiss his head and his hair smells different. I didn't expect that. The scent of him has changed.

But that will be because she uses different shampoos on him. She feeds him different things. I look at him curiously, realising for the first time that this child I have retrieved, even though he's mine, won't be the same one that I lost at the end of last year. Because he has lived eight months of a different life. Eight months sleeping in a different cot, eight months of talking to adults who speak a different tongue, who think different thoughts, who go to different places. Eight months – more than a third of his life – shaped by people other than us. They have stolen that time from us, and though I steal my child back now I will never again have that time. My heart swells with anger at the thought, and I cradle him close.

And she? She doesn't even look up to check on what might be happening to him. Not once.

Julia

He feels strange in my arms, this little lad, he feels too light. Something feels *wrong*, I know it does but I . . . I don't know what.

I could make him laugh. If I hear that deep throaty gurgle that is so very typical of Hadyn then I'd know for sure that he was mine. I could just look under his curls, of course, for the birthmark, but I can't bring myself to do that.

If I do that and it isn't there, then . . . what?

I am trying to recall Hadyn's smile. There's something very unique about a person's smile. Last time I saw it – I screw up my forehead now, trying to bring back the memory – it was when Diego produced that puppy from out of his backpack. I remember laughing at Hadyn's ear-to-ear grin. I remember saying – maybe we'll get *you* a dog too, when you're a bit older; you'd like that.

Do you like dogs? I jiggle the lad up and down on my arm a bit but he just stares at me sombrely.

He doesn't look very comfortable, actually. His feet are sticking out at an awkward angle, his toes all curled up. I glance back towards Adamantine and the smallest panic begins to niggle in the pit of my stomach. If this woman really did take my child, then she will surely know exactly who *I* am?

In fact – the thought seeps into my consciousness now – if she did take him, she must be very confident indeed of her own ground if she dares to bring him back here where members of his own family are likely to recognise him so easily?

I need to get away from here, that's what I need to do.

But the further up I travel towards the top of the beach, the hotter the sand feels against the soles of my feet. My purse – and my handbag! – are still in a little pile with the rest of my things; the sweeties I bought him earlier, my magazine, my bottle of water. The sand sinks beneath our combined weight, scorching me, my sandals still in my hands. I dropped my sunglasses when I picked the child up. The glare is so bright. The blue sky goes on for ever.

He's making strange noises in his throat now. He sticks out his tongue and I can see little wet clumps of sand still in there from when he wiped his fingers off earlier. His head is so close to my head I can breathe in the scent of him but he smells salty and damp and strange. He doesn't smell like mine.

I feel so *perplexed*.

The breeze lifts up the curly bits at the front of his hair. I can see his eyes welling up now and his little shoulders heaving and suddenly I realise – he is going to *retch*. I can't stay here if this child is going to be sick. I can stand anything, but not *that*. And this little boy – he doesn't *feel* right, he doesn't *smell* right. What if he really isn't mine after all?

I put him down on the sand but then I realise it is too hot for his feet so I put my hands out as he staggers forward, making a strangling noise.

I look backwards, to where Adamantine is still sitting with the baby, but her head is up now, sensing something's wrong. What am I *doing* here?

She'll know me. She'll know what I'm doing.

The big dog has started up its barking again.

'Help!' I call out to her and she's up in an instant. A couple of other people passing by stop to watch but they don't seem to think there's any real problem. The woman smiles at me sympathetically and I see she is staring at the top of my dress. It's then I realise that the child has vomited all down the front of me.

'I am so sorry, señora, so sorry!' Adamantine is mortified.

I stare at her for a moment. She is well maintained, I see, but she is not young. This is the woman I have been trying to spy on for the past week. The woman who I was so convinced had hatched some sordid and sorry plot to steal my baby from me, but she does not know me. If she had stolen my child, she would know me, surely? When I look at the candour in her eyes I now find it hard to believe that it could be so.

We both look at the dark stain down the front of my dress. She brushes the worst of it off with a towel. I notice she's holding the baby in her other arm even as she helps me. The toddler seems none the worse for wear. I can hear Adamantine apologising to me, consoling him, rebuking him all at the same time, but my ears seem to have closed up in some strange sort of way. I feel battered and ashamed and weak.

She seems to be asking questions of me, but she is speaking Spanish and I can't understand a word of it at the moment. By her face, her fine eyebrows arched up in concern, she wants to know if I'm okay – but I am on my way away from there now.

I bend to pick up my things. My sandals swing from my hands as my bare feet fly across the hot sand. I feel as if I'm choking but I've got to keep running.

I run and run till I get to the head of the beach and then I sit on the wall and catch my breath back. Everybody stares quite openly at me as they pass me by. Nobody pretends that they aren't looking like they would do in England.

This is just like my old nightmare, I realise as I sit there, holding my chest: the stain on my dress, this feeling of terror, this feeling of having to get away as fast as possible. But when I look up the sun is shining hot. The day is bright blue and clear; no darkness, no rain. And this stain – it is not blood, as I had thought.

Nobody has died. I let that thought sink in.

Then I let my head fall into my hands, my breathing coming hard and fast – until I feel the apprehending touch of someone's hand on my arm.

Charlie

The afternoon's getting on. It must be nearly four o'clock by my reckoning. I had urgent work at the clinic and the first flight I could make out of London was late Tuesday evening. I stayed over at a *pensión* last night, not wanting to disturb the household – I've spent the morning with Eva and Abuela, learning more about the situation. Now I've got a bone or two to pick with my brother.

I can feel the sea breeze gusting through my hair as I climb and I keep the pace steady.

Roberto likes to look down on Arenadeluna from a height, Eva told me, and see how all the new developments are coming together; the pieces of his own personal municipal jigsaw puzzle.

'He didn't want me to say anything,' Eva confided over the phone on Saturday night. 'He said – if there's nothing we can do about it, why does everyone have to know? But . . .' she'd wrung her hands, 'there is something I've wanted to tell you for a very long while . . .'

My brother is measuring out the width of a narrow track of road when I come across him. He lets the measuring tape roll back, *snap*, into its metal casing when he sees me. When he gathers his wits together he looks more perplexed than pleased to see me back.

'*Hombre!* Why are you here?'

'When were you planning on telling me, Roberto?'

He raises his eyebrows at that.

For a moment we just stand there: him holding his measuring tape and me with my hands in my pockets. The wind rustles the acacia bushes to either side of us. Roberto's gaze drops back to the road. He seems uncomfortable and I can see he's doing that thing he always used to do when we were kids – scuffing some pebbles with the toe of his boot. I'm pretty sure he doesn't know he's doing it.

'Planning on telling you what?' His gaze levels with mine, now. 'If you're talking about your girlfriend, I didn't even know she was here till I saw her at the mass and even then—'

'You've *seen* her?' Now *that* I didn't expect.

'I glimpsed her yesterday morning,' he shrugs warily.

'And the two of you spoke?' I take a step closer. My brother shakes his head.

'She didn't see me. And, frankly, she didn't look as if she wanted to talk, either. She hasn't been to the house. Look,' my brother sounds embarrassed, 'I don't know what's going on. We heard from Lourdes that there had been . . . difficulties between the two of you. I didn't realise you'd come over with her, Carlos.'

Lourdes mentioned it. That silences me for a bit. I'm not surprised he knows, though. Everyone always knew everybody else's business around here. If Lourdes and I had started an affair on Saturday night, people would soon have been talking about that, too.

'I didn't. Julia came out to Spain by herself. I wouldn't come here and not tell anyone, would I? I've just come from the house, though. Eva rang me at the weekend to say Abuela had needed to visit hospital last week for more tests.'

'She's not actually been kept in—' he begins, but I blast over him:

'*Hombre*, when were you planning on letting me know that

she was dying? At the *funeral?*' I didn't mean to sound this angry. My brother hoists up the tops of his jeans in a defensive motion.

'Abuela told everyone not to say anything, okay? She didn't want you knowing. She says you've suffered enough. It was her idea.'

I wipe my forehead with the back of my hand. Roberto knows – *through Lourdes* – about the troubles I am having with my girlfriend and I am not even told that my own grandmother is dying.

I am not part of this community any more, am I?

I turn away from him. When I look directly down I can see my old birth town of Arenadeluna, spread out like a picnic feast on a tablecloth all before me. Has everything really changed so very much from how I remember it?

When you grow up in a place then – even if you don't go back there for a very long time – the landscape is fixed in your mind. You've got this snapshot in your head: if you go this way you get to the market square; if you take that turn, you get to the *zapatería*, the shoemakers.

Except my map, inside my head, it's all wrong now. There's a boulevard all along the beach front where there used to be nothing but crumbling balustrades and boulders. The place I've just parked my car at before climbing up here (neatly lined bays, five euros per stay) – that used to be the ruins of an old school. Roberto and I used to play there as kids.

'It's gone.'

I turn to face my brother who is now holding his site map in his hands, pointing at a spot that should be somewhere just below where we are now.

'What's gone?'

'The road we used to race up,' he tells me. 'The dirt track. The short cut by foot up to the cemetery. It's gone. Do you remember the time you beat me on the bike up here?' The shadow of a pained smile crosses his eyes for an instant and as quickly fades. 'I saw it all disappear on paper months ago but I thought this bit wasn't scheduled to go till the spring . . .' His voice falters. 'I used to come up here all the time after you left for boarding school.'

'You did?' I turn and observe my brother with new eyes. Is he actually saying that he missed me?

'I used to wish that you'd never gone,' he laughs brokenly. 'Can you believe that? I used to pray that they'd bring you back.'

I put my hand over his. We've had so few moments in our lives like this, I realise, my brother and I. We've been so far apart, geographically and in every other way.

'I used to pray for the same thing,' I confess.

'You did all right out of it, though, didn't you?' he says gruffly. 'Now you're . . . the *big man* – you've got all your high qualifications and your medical practice. You've made a success of your life. It's what she wanted, of course.' He looks down at his shoes.

'I never realised you missed me, Rob.' I feel touched by his confession. 'I thought – I really thought you'd be glad that I was gone. You'd have our mum all to yourself . . .'

My brother's lips form a thin sneering line at the memory. 'Not a chance. To her, I was a man by then – *sixteen*! She never stopped talking about you after they sent you off. You became some kind of a . . . a saint!'

'I was never that, was I?' I try to grin but my brother's words are too charged for me to make light of them.

'No, you were not,' he says feelingly. 'But I had less attention from our mother after you left than I'd ever had before it. Nothing was ever the same here after her accident, *hermano*. You were all right – you were sent out of the way so you didn't have to see . . .'

I didn't have to see what happened *after*. And nobody told me.

331

The light shines off the windows of the cars snaking their way along the Costa road, down past the town. The school we both used to go to – it is not there any more. But there are children there, in the place where the school would have been. They are sitting on a wall, hunched over a hand-held games console. From here they are as small as ants.

'She only had eyes for you, Carlos – *always Carlos* – the baby of the family. She couldn't see anyone else.' His words are bitter, but they form echoes in some ancient cavern, deep inside my memory.

The boys were kicking a ball up against the outside of the school wall when Mrs Eggelston came out. Her look said it all, a mixture of scorn and distaste at the breaking of school rules. No kids and no balls outside of the school grounds. On a normal day I would have just trooped obediently behind the others and gone in. But on that day, for some reason, I didn't. I could see my mama's car steadily moving away from the pavement where she'd just dropped me. It was only for a fraction of a second that I stood there, willing her to sense me there and look at me. When she did I was over-come with joy, because I could see her face in the driving mirror. She was smiling encouragement. I could just imagine her saying, 'You're ten now, that's a big boy. You've got to go in on your own.' I could see her fine arched eyebrows and the proud beauty of her forehead and her beautiful brown wavy hair and she smiled, just for me.

She only had eyes for me.

And so she did not see the back of the refuse truck that was reversing towards her.

She did not see the gleaming bonnet of her car was about to get crinkled up like an accordion in one horrific and inexplicable moment of metal upon metal collision. She didn't see it because she was looking at me, waiting for me to go into the playground where I would be safe.

Does Roberto know this?

Is this why he has spent a lifetime feeling so *angry* towards me?

'I wanted to come home, Roberto! I was ten years old, for God's sake! Do you seriously think it could have been fun for me at Hillstones?'

'They sent us reports,' he defends. 'You were doing well. You had many friends.'

'I had no choice in the matter, did I? But I wanted to be at home with all of you. Do you blame me,' I ask him at last, 'for what happened to her?'

'A truck hit her.' He looks at me as if I must be mad. 'You weren't driving it, were you?'

'No, but . . .' Roberto steps forward then to put his hand on my shoulder. 'Enough, Carlos. We mustn't speak of these things any more. We have to . . .' he clears his throat, 'look forward. That's what I'm doing.'

'Yeah,' I say. I watch him roll up the piece of paper that's been flapping in the wind, the one with all the Arenadeluna plans on it. 'That's probably for the best.'

'And – I'm sorry I didn't tell you about Abuela,' he adds after an infinitesimal pause. 'She didn't want you to know she was sick. Honestly.'

'It's okay. She never did like hospitals. She'll be like a wounded animal gone to ground, eh?' A bit like our mother was, I think.

'Conchita never let anyone in when she was ill, either, did she? If she did, she might have found help . . .' My brother is nodding his head. His eyes are brimming. I have never once, I realise, seen my brother cry. We've never spoken about our mother till this very day.

'And if our mother had asked for help, *if she had let somebody know* how bad she was feeling, she might never have been tempted to take her own life,' I continue. We have not spoken of this before, Roberto and I. Nobody has. It is the great unspoken thing in our family.

But I figured it out a long time ago, when I was just a kid.

My brother looks at me with wide-opened eyes. *Shocked* eyes. His jaw is dropped a little bit, in horror.

'She did not take her own life, Carlos. Whoever told you that?' He puts his hand to his heart now, pained.

Didn't he know? He was older than me. If even I figured it out, I thought that he surely must have too. *Surely?*

'Suicide is an excommunicable offence, Carlos. And our mother is buried on consecrated ground. How could you say such a thing?' His hand slides away from my shoulders in disgust.

'It was never the official line, Rob, but you must know it, surely? She was clinically depressed. She couldn't face life looking the way she did after the accident. She never came to terms with it . . .'

'Who told you this?' he challenges. 'Who did you hear it from?'

No one. I figured it out myself, just as he surely would have if he hadn't been so much in denial about everything that was going on around him.

'I know of no such thing.' My brother goes and stares out over the low stone wall that is all that separates us from a very long drop. When I follow his gaze down to the bottom I see that even the market square has been replaced by bistros and a bloody great amusement arcade.

What is the point of it all? I hate to say it but I see my brother's hand in a lot of this. Bloody beautification of cultural heritage or what-have-you. How can I keep my bearings when everything keeps on changing?

'Do you suppose . . .' I go and join my brother by the wall now. 'Just suppose – if anyone had wanted to take my son that day out on the beach, could it have happened and been kept a secret?'

334

'Why would anyone want to . . . ?' He turns to me, pained.

'Could it, though? Just theoretically?'

'You know Spain, *hermano*. It could have been done. But that fisherman who found that fish just before the Feast of Los Reyes—'

'I thought he found it New Year's Day? That's when you told me about it, remember?'

Roberto looks lost for words.

'*Sí*, on the phone. *Whenever*. He found it, didn't he?'

'Did he?'

'Yes,' he says wearily. 'He did. And our mother died of natural causes, Carlos. And Abuela didn't want you knowing she was sick because she was already worried enough about what you've gone through. There is no conspiracy against you. Do you think there is?'

'Did you ever see the fish, Roberto?'

Roberto throws up his hands in despair.

'Of course not. But Guiliano, the chief of police, did. And the forensics people. That's their job. Abuela fell sick in the New Year. No doubt Eva has told you that. I've had so much else to look out for.'

I feel a sudden lurch in the pit of my stomach. Is he telling me that – after promising me that he was seeing to it – he'd really had his mind on other matters?

'And the modernisation of Arenadeluna. You had that to keep in progress, no?'

'Of course! Do you know how many new jobs my department has created over the last twelve months alone? It's been phenomenal. Young people aren't leaving the town in their droves like they were; they see a future here, jobs for them and their families. Everyone has benefited. So yes, I have been committed to seeing this project through. The young people of this town are our future, Carlos. Even Giorge – he's staying now.'

His mention of my nephew is a bitter pill. 'What about *my* boy, Roberto?'

Roberto shakes his head. He looks at me pityingly. 'The sea had him, *hermano*. I told you this many months ago. It was the most likely scenario. *What else did you want me to do?* His face contorts in a self-justificatory rage for a moment. Then his expression changes to one of reproach. 'First, you say terrible things about our mother. Then you imply that we did not all do everything we could for your boy. We did the best we could, I promise you. The mayor himself forbade that we put up those posters we'd had made. He said it would prejudice our chances of getting the cultural heritage award. There were a lot of people with a lot at stake here at the beginning of the year. Big building contracts for some, yes. For others, just simple things, like the prospect of getting a job again after a long period of unemployment. And all those people matter too, you know.

'But we did make inquiries, Carlos. And I can swear to you,' he holds up one finger meaningfully, 'after that day, no one ever saw your boy. Because he vanished. Into the sea. You are angry because we couldn't help you more. You are angry because we followed Abuela's wishes and didn't tell you she was ill. I understand that. I do. *But you weren't here.* You have to see things from my point of view too.'

I turn from him, my older brother, my oldest rival in the world. I look out over the town again, trying to drink in his words, wanting to see things from his perspective; to have my peace restored again. He's right. I wasn't here.

'I'm trying, brother,' I tell him, but when I look down I see that the old path that we used to race up, it isn't gone at all. It's still there, alongside the new one. I point it out to him.

'It hasn't vanished at all. You just couldn't see it.'

'*Tienes razón.* You're right.' Roberto looks mightily relieved. 'Conchita used to push me up that track in the pram. Just me. Before you were born. *Progress,* eh?' He grins at me with sad eyes. 'Sometimes it entails sacrifices that we never wanted to make.'

I cannot meet his eyes or return my brother's smile when he speaks of these sacrifices. Perhaps it's because I just can't help now but wonder if my boy was one of them?

Julia

'So, what was the verdict?' Blue has been skulking round the corner all along, waiting for me to finish. His eyes skim over the stain down the front of my sundress and his nose wrinkles slightly.

'I thought you couldn't hang about?' I say accusingly. I could have done with the moral support.

'I thought it would look less suspicious if you were on your own,' he mutters, not entirely convincingly.

'Well – he threw up all over me, actually.'

'So I see.' Blue's got a can of San Miguel in one hand. He tilts it towards me now. 'Care to join me?' He's carefully not mentioned Hadyn yet, I notice, though he must be bursting to.

'No thanks.'

'So – was it him?' He caves in at last.

'It looked like him. I could have sworn it was him. I didn't get to check the birthmark because he sicked up before I could get there . . .'

'Jeez, that's . . . If you think it might be him, that's wonderful though!'

'I guess.' I should be ecstatic.

'You're still looking a bit shocked.'

I nod.

'But we look like having a cause for celebration, no?' He nods towards the wooden shack beach bar further up the beach.

'We could talk about your next plan of action. And . . . celebrate this stage, you know?'

'I don't drink.'

'Yeah, I remember.' His eyes narrow in exasperation. 'You wouldn't drink with us on New Year's Eve, would you? God, you middle-class women,' and there is the hint of an edge to his voice now, 'always on detox or low carb or some such thing. All you need to do is let go of that desperate control for a little bit, Julia; that's what might help.' His gaze lingers on me just a second or two longer than I feel comfortable with.

'Help with what?' My voice would normally be frosty here; but I feel so *not like me*. If I were entirely myself I wouldn't have contemplated for one second what I almost actually did on that beach a few minutes ago. I almost legged it out of here with that child under my arm. I wasn't even going to look at the nape of his neck to see if he had the birthmark.

'Alcohol can help when you're feeling uptight, that's all. You don't have to be so bloody judgemental about it, you know.'

'I wasn't . . .' I look at him helplessly. 'I didn't think I was being. I'm not on any detox diet. I don't like alcohol. I never have.'

'Because you don't like the *taste*?' His eyes have taken on a slight glint, challenging me to refute it.

'Because I don't like drunks and alcoholics.'

'Ho! I thought you weren't the judgemental one, though?' He manages to look slightly hurt. 'I'm not a drunk or an alcoholic, Julia.' He puts down his can on the wall. We both look down towards the beach where Adamantine is hastily packing their things away. I won't get a chance to get near her child again today. I should have this huge empty feeling of an opportunity missed, but I don't.

'I just thought we should *celebrate*, you know?'

'That's what alcoholics always say.' I turn to look at him. 'They always want to celebrate everything with a drink. It starts off like that. Then they find more and more things that warrant a celebration. Then they stop needing the excuse of a celebration at all. That's how it happens.'

'Well steady on there . . .'

'That's how they manage to push anyone and anything that ever meant anything to them, away from them. Just like workaholics do,' I add suddenly, thinking of Charlie. 'They let this one thing take over their lives to such an extent that nothing else matters.' I turn towards the sea and wipe a tear away with the edge of my wrist while I'm facing away from him. Christ, what's brought this on? Who am I to be giving a lecture on the moral rectitude of social drinking to this guy, when he's supposed to be assisting me with stealing another woman's child?

'I'm sorry,' Blue says after a while, even though it's me who should be apologising. 'I didn't realise it was like that for you. I thought you came from some privileged background. Daddy's little princess, that sort of thing.'

'Did you?' I almost want to laugh.

'Look, all I'm saying is . . . celebrate the moment with a diet soda.' Blue is standing with a perplexed frown on his face because I'm not giving him the reaction he expects to see from me. 'Whatever floats your boat.' He looks at me, hands on hips, and then he stops.

'It wasn't him was it?'

'You did a really good job,' I say and my voice sounds brittle and strange. 'You really did. I wasn't sure there myself for a while. I thought it was Hadyn, at first.'

'But you never got to check for the birthmark? Babies change, you know.'

I shake my head.

'I knew it the minute he was sick all over me.'

'*How?* Because Hadyn is sick in a different way?' Blue gives a nervous giggle and takes another swig from his beer can.

'No, it wasn't that.' How can I explain this to him? It's because

340

when that child was sick I suddenly got a flash of something else: another time, another place.

And I *realised* something. I'm not even sure quite yet what I realised. It would be more accurate to say that there's this nebulous cloud of realisation just hovering on the edge of my consciousness. Like I'm about to make some connections but I don't know what they are just yet.

'He reminded me of a dream,' I say quietly, and Blue stares at me for a good few minutes, waiting for me to elucidate – and when I don't, he turns his head away, frustrated.

'Your dream of finding your son?' he prompts me at last.

Not Hadyn.

Someone else. Nana Ella knows who. Someone I left behind a very long time ago. Someone I ran away from one night when the wind was blowing my rainswept hair across my face and I could hear the slap-slap of the choppy water of the river bank nearby. One night . . . when it was dark as the tomb.

One New Year's Eve.

'No. The last time I ever saw my father. He reminded me of that.' I take out a tissue and wipe again at the stain on my dress.

It's funny how sometimes a simple look, a bar from a song, the shape of a cloud in the sky, can be enough to jolt a memory out of its hiding place so that something you'd forgotten – it comes tumbling out. It lands right in your lap. You think you forget things but you don't. You just file them away under 'miscellaneous', hoping never to stumble across them again until, sooner or later, you do.

Even if I did see Josh Martyn now – assuming he'd waited for me – how was I ever going to be the life and soul of the party that I'd planned to be? I felt angry and rumpled and cross. I wanted just to spill it all out and tell the very next person I saw what a lousy, good-for-nothing, selfish, uncaring and ungrateful parent I had. I wanted them to tell me – like Naseem had – that I shouldn't put up with it any more.

But first of all I had to get Dad home and out of harm's way.

'You're coming with me,' I said to him in a no-nonsense voice. I put my arm into the crook of his arm and levered him up a bit. Usually that worked. Once his body knew what direction it was being pushed in, he automatically did the rest.

'Yer a real spoilsport, yer know that?' he complained, but the beer had made him sluggish enough not to protest too much.

It was 10.12 p.m.

Josh Martyn might well still be there waiting for me, I thought, looking at my watch. He might even have arrived a little late himself. People always did. It wasn't cool to look too keen.

'Let's get you home,' I said. Outside, the wind was gusting again. It wasn't so easy trying to prop Dad up now I'd got one hand occupied keeping the hem of my dress down and then there were these blasted heels, slipping in every pothole in the road.

I considered taking the long way round. There would be better light and better roads. On the other hand, there would also be more people around to see us. Some of them might be friends of Josh's. I couldn't bear that.

'It's a fine balmy night, so it is.' Dad waved his hands about. He reminded me so much of an insect stuck in a web, waving its legs pointlessly in the air.

'Why do you do it, Dad?' I stared at him, exasperated. 'What's the point?' I wasn't expecting any answer. I didn't get one. 'Oh, let's just go home.' I put my head down and he shuffled in the right sort of direction and together we soldiered on. My hair was getting ruined but I couldn't worry about that just then. He had to be got to somewhere safe so then, and only then, I might get a chance to go out and get some time to myself.

The only problem was, he was looking decidedly peaky. Even in the dim light by the humpback bridge I could see that he looked off-colour.

'You're going too fast,' he complained

'Just walk in the gaps between the cobblestones, Dad. Stick to the side of the bridge. Come on, you can do it.' But he had that stubborn, resisting look on his face – the same look I've seen him use in the past when he really wanted to wind people up.

'No wonder Mum left you,' I breathed at him.

'What's that?'

'No wonder she left you, you stubborn old goat. You're . . . impossible! You aren't even trying to get home for me. I've come all this way to rescue you and you're behaving like a . . . like a . . .'

'She left me because she found another man that better suited her,' he said quietly and deliberately. I noticed he didn't slur his words.

'Well, that wouldn't have been a hard thing to do. Anyone in the universe would have been a better catch than you. What kind of life did you make her lead, fetching you from the pub so many times of an evening?'

'Sometimes I make it meself.'

'Nine times out of ten you don't.'

'Ye've never found it a hardship before,' he complained.

I gave him an incredulous look but, really, what was the point of arguing with a drunk? They made very little sense and whatever they did say they'd always forgotten about it in the morning anyway.

'And if yer going to talk to me like that I tink I'll find my own way home, tank ye very much.' The fresh night air must have given him the impression that he was feeling far more clear-headed than he really was.

'That might be a bit more difficult than you expect, Dad.'

'Oh yes?' He turned and gave me an arch look.

'Well, yes. You're headed in the wrong direction for one.'

'I'm headed back to the pub,' he corrected me.

'No you're not!' I grabbed at his arm and he tried to fend me off. You see, he really was drunk, and not very capable. And the cobblestones were so very slippery and dark. The water went clunk-clunk up against the wooden sides of the troll bridge. It had got so high in the past few hours, due to the rain.

'Don't do that!' I yelled at him as he kept on trying to release my grip on his arm, waving his arm up and down like a demon. When I caught the gleam in his eye I could tell that he was enjoying the fray. 'You'll have us both in the water if you do that. And this time I won't rescue you,' I warned him. 'I'm not jumping in after you again.'

'Let go o' me, ye daft bugger. Ye can't stop me from heading towards me own damnation ye know.'

I was just thinking: he's right. I can't stop him if he's that determined to ruin himself. I was thinking: what am I doing here, what am I really doing, when I saw his eyes go blank and I caught my moment of opportunity. I thought, if I tugged on his hand just then, he'd come with me. So I tugged and I pushed and I pulled him a little more till he overbalanced. Even though I didn't mean him to, he just kind of fell forward, not stopping himself at all. He was so heavy, and the cobblestones, they were so slippery. The water, I thought, my heart in my mouth, it's so high, it's so dark.

And that was when it happened. He threw up all over me, all over my beautiful dress!

It was all over so quickly. It was over in a second.

And this time, oh, I couldn't bear it, because I suddenly

saw that nothing I did was ever going to make any differ-
ence. I couldn't save him from himself.

Sometimes you've just got to give up.

I couldn't bear it and I couldn't bear him so I turned away
and just left him and then I ran, ran all the way to the place
where I knew Josh would still be there waiting for me, under
the clock.

'You're going to need to get near enough to that boy to check
out that birthmark, Julia.' Blue sounds infinitely weary, not like
him. 'It's the only way you are ever going to be sure.'

He says that, but I know in my heart it is over. He wasn't
mine.

And to some extent, I must confess to feeling relief, because
how would I ever have got that child out of here? Could I really
have hoped to have snatched him all by myself and taken him
back, even with the help of Blue's nefarious friends? I couldn't.

No. It is over. I did what I had to do, that's all.

I followed my rainbow to its shimmering and ragged end and
found only a bubble there – that popped upon my touching it.

Julia

'So, what did happen with you and your dad after all?' The sun
has gone down. We've been walking and walking. We walked
right to the end of the Aquavista beach club and up onto the
hot grey pavement above. I could feel the heat coming through
the rubber of my flip-flops. The sick stain on my dress dried up
with all that sun beating down on us.

'I left him, Blue. I called an ambulance as soon as I could, but
I left him. After that New Year's Eve I went back to my mum's
place. I got my stuff together that very night and called her and
she came down with Dick and they took me back to Croydon
with them.'

'And your dad?'

'They told me an air ambulance came and took him into
St Bart's General. He was suffering from broken bones and
hypothermia and – it transpired – all sorts of alcohol-related
stuff.' I've never spoken about this to *anyone*, I realise now.

'Things that maybe would never have been seen to? Maybe
you did him a favour?' Blue ventures.

'I never went to see him, Blue. Not once. Once I left him, I
couldn't go back. Mum and Dick never mentioned a word about
Dad. None of us did. We just blanked him out.'

It was easier that way. The whole topic of Dad became like
the dark corner in the kitchen cupboard where you never want
to look. Whenever something came on the telly – like the cricket

– that he would have watched, Mum just quietly changed the channels over and so we cleverly avoided him altogether.

'I don't know if Mum and Dick ever talked about him in private. Maybe they did. Maybe they just didn't want me to feel bad. Nothing was ever said. Until I was coming up to my eighteenth birthday . . .' I stop, realising that I don't really want to go on. We sit down at a beach bar and he orders some cool drinks and I choose the chair that has a high wicker back to it.

Blue and I do not talk for a very long time. We watch the bathers coming out of the shadowed water; it is getting late.

'Sometimes,' I say at last, 'we just leave things for too long, don't we? We don't do *what* we can, *when* we can, and by the time we decide . . .' I've got this very odd bubbling sensation in my throat. He leans over and pats me sympathetically on the arm.

'Better late than never,' he says after a while.

'Not for me it wasn't.' I give a short laugh.

Blue doesn't say anything to that. He just waits for me to continue. I have never told anyone this. But here, sitting at this beach bar in Spain in this cosy high-backed chair with Blue, I feel suddenly safe enough to speak because I know that – whatever I say to him – this man won't judge me.

I remember Dick was stopped at the lights when I told him. I knew he'd heard me because the lights went green and he didn't move.

'What?' was all he said.

'I thought – it would be nice to invite my dad along to that eighteenth "do" that you and Mum have got planned for me.' Dick had gone quiet all of a sudden so I added, 'I haven't seen him in a very long time.'

The car behind us started hooting angrily then, and Dick did something he never did. He stuck his middle finger up at them!

'She never told you then, love? Well, I'll be . . .' When he

347

still didn't move, the line of cars behind us started snaking angrily past.

'Mum never told me what?'

I watched his face, white, tight-lipped, as he slowly lowered the handbrake down and we moved off.

'Your dad died, love. Would have been about a year ago now. I'm sorry. I thought she'd have told you but maybe she didn't want to go upsetting you, did she? Seeing as you've settled so beautifully.' When he lowered the sun-visor I could see that his hand was trembling. 'She had a lot of bad memories too, love, so don't be too hard on her about it. In fact, best not mention it at all, really.'

He didn't have to ask. We both knew what Mum was like. She coped with things by turning her face away from them, Dick sometimes said, though he loved her nonetheless. Maybe that's why she stayed with my dad for so long when he was drinking – because she didn't want to admit how bad it was. Maybe that's also why, in the end, she left.

'Don't mention it,' Dick begged me as we stopped outside the cinema. 'It'll only upset her, you know that.'

'Christ!' Blue leans over and pats my arm again. It feels strangely comforting. 'It's brought it all back, hasn't it? That's a terrible thing to happen.'

'They meant it all for the best,' I assure him. 'Three years had passed and Dick said they didn't want to upset me because I was getting on so well with my new life and I'd only get all troubled again.'

'Three years,' he marvels. 'You never thought of trying to get hold of him in all that time?'

'I couldn't!' An edge of panic rises in my voice. 'I couldn't risk our old relationship starting up all over again. I loved him, but I couldn't look after him any more.'

'And you and your mum . . .'

'I never spoke to her about it, Blue.' I shake my head. 'Can you believe that? I went to Donegal for a few days that Christmas and I tried to tell his mother, Nana Ella, but I don't think she understood me, either. She was too much stuck in her own world by then.'

'And to think I took you for some kind of daddy's princess,' he marvels. 'I apologise for that, Julia. You *have* had a lot of *shite* to contend with, haven't you?'

I don't like to think of it that way. That isn't how I think.

'I don't feel sorry for myself,' I tell him fiercely.

'I know you don't, girl. You're far too brave for that.' Blue's words are remarkably tender. Brave, he says. He thinks I'm brave and I'm not even pretending to be, this time. Maybe he's right though. And maybe I've misjudged him, too?

'What are you going to do with yourself now, then?'

'I'm going to go back home,' I say to him slowly.

'Your search for Hadyn?'

'It's over.'

'Are you sure?' His bony fingers reach into his jeans pocket and he brings out a packet of fags, a lighter. 'I mean, are you really finished here?'

'I'm finished. And once you've gone there'll be no one here to entice me on any further, will there?'

He smiles into his cigarette.

'I guess not. But life is always full of so many possibilities, isn't it? If I'd been staying on I could have helped you carry on looking. Every day I hear new things – about kids who've been abducted – about the people who might be holding them.'

'You *do*?' I look at him darkly.

'You don't live under tents in coves and beaches without learning a thing or two about the underground world that co-exists beside this very affluent one, my lady.'

'You've been living rough? For how long?' I frown.

'Pretty much since I left the slammer. I've made some enemies who would love to know my address. Safer if I don't have one.'

'Safer perhaps if you leave Spain altogether?' I suggest. I feel a sudden rush of concern for him. He just smiles.

'Look, I don't know where you're going but I've got to go home.' My throat is rasping.

'Will you tell Charlie what's happened?' He looks at me sceptically.

'I'm not going back to Charlie. And I don't want him finding me, either.'

He looks at me knowingly, tapping a finger to the side of his nose.

'You'll let me know if you find Hadyn?' He stands up and I get up with him. Blue gives me a short, awkward hug. I doubt we will ever meet again. We promise that we will keep in touch, of course. But I'm pretty certain he is going to disappear out of my life. He lays out some coins carefully on the table. I see that he's really broke and a twinge of guilt passes over me but I know he has his pride.

I have my pride too, I think. I did the right thing today. Even though I nearly did the wrong thing for all the right reasons. And now I'm going to go home and put something else right that I should have done a very long time ago.

Charlie

It is quiet, here. From this high up on the tor, on a clear day, you can see out over the Mediterranean Sea as far away as Gibraltar. *Gibal Tarik,* Conchita used to tell me, *It means Tarik's mountain – after the Moor the place was named for.* She used to laugh and say that was a fine thing; to have a mountain named after you. I named the Esperanza Centre for her. That was the best I could do. That has been my mountain, which I built in her memory. I built it up as high and as strong as I could. Now it's all going to come tumbling down.

It's Thursday already. It's the Esperanza gala tomorrow, I remember, and I should be there. Only I won't be, because I've come here instead, and without those sponsorship deals I fail to see how we'll carry on. I feel strangely disconnected from all of it, now that I'm here. I thought it was the thing that mattered to me most in the entire world.

I see now that it matters hardly at all.

I've got to *think* – to figure out what's going on in my life. I don't feel I know any more.

It's not as if I'm that old. I'm thirty-six. I shouldn't come back here and find my home town so changed from my childhood that it's beyond recognition. That happens to seventy-year-olds and eighty-year-olds, surely? Why did they have to change everything so much? How can I keep my bearings when everything keeps on changing?

I pause for a minute or two at the top.

I came up here because I wanted to be alone – but now that I'm alone I realise how much I miss my Julia.

And I don't know where she is.

Roberto saw her two days ago, he said. She won't answer her phone. I could trawl the hotels, I suppose. We argued, I know. But I realise now that I want her back.

I can't do this alone so I've come to Spain to find her.

I feel like a complete hypocrite. Everything that I told her not to do – I'm doing it now. I was out yesterday, scanning the beach front, raking through the crowds. I've gone back to all the places where we went with Hadyn, all the places where a small child might be taken; to the carousel in front of the souvenir sellers outside the town hall; to the water fountains that squirt up from the pavement, making all the kids scream and laugh.

I went back to the park. I put his elephant on the swing beside me – daft, I know. It made my boy feel closer to me, somehow. As if I could, by some sympathetic magic, conjure him up. That's the way Julia would think, I know. Some of her must have rubbed off on me, because when I sat there I could feel this really strong pull. It felt as if there were this strange rushing in my heart, like a floodgate of some sort had been opened and I knew I had to get out of the park. I had to get out anywhere, so I came walking up here where I thought I'd be safe.

I brought the elephant up here with me too. Julia was the one who wouldn't be parted from it, not me, but wherever she's gone this time, she's left it behind, and I brought it with me. Just in case. Not that my boy's going to be up here, is he?

Nobody is.

If you go a little way over the tor towards the north side there's a cemetery where my mother's people are all buried. She's there too. I'll go and see her in a minute.

Bap-Bap still smells of him, though that's fading now. If you put the tatty white fur to your face and draw in a deep enough breath, you can catch the faintest trace of Hadyn. Something of him remains – but for how long? Will every molecule of him soon be utterly gone, beyond recall?

Up here the sun beats down relentlessly along the grey stone wall. There's a bird of prey about three-quarters of a mile up: he'll be scanning the valleys for the tiny movements of voles and field mice. The chances of them homing in on the prey they've sighted from that far up always seems to me astronomical, but they do it. Time and again. It only takes them a few short seconds. One fateful swoop and a life is gone. And I was away for one whole day.

'I would have protected you,' I tell him. 'If I'd been there. No wave, no person would have taken you if I had been there. You know that, don't you?'

In the silence that answers me I hear my own thoughts echo back: you weren't there though, were you? You were off some-where else, saving someone else, giving them hope but not saving any for your own . . .

'It's not as if you didn't matter to me, Haydn. You mattered to me more than the entire world.'

The elephant stares back at me, silent. The trunk is slightly bent. I can see the thick black thread where Julia had to sew one of his eyes back on one time. She wanted to make sure there was no chance of it ever coming off again and Hadyn swallowing it. So she sewed it over and over all in the same spot. It looks like a wound. It makes Bap-Bap – if you look at him closely enough – look slightly angry.

I am going to go back home. I am going to go and stop by Conchita Esperanza's grave and watch the tall grass swaying in the breeze by the tombstones and say a prayer and just go home. But when I pick up the elephant and crush him to my chest I can feel the strangest pain. I kiss the white fur. It is the fur he kissed. It still has, hidden in there, the taste of him and his kisses on it somewhere. My knees just give way then and I sink to the gravelled path. I am so alone without him.

And because I am alone no one can hear this primal cry that seems to be rising up from deep within my throat.

I didn't know I felt like this. I have seen other people cry before. I have seen their faces twist and contort, their eyes welling up with tears. I have heard the jagged, stuttering cries of the newly bereaved. I thought I knew what it was – that wrench when one person has to face that a loved one is gone.

But I did not, truly, until this moment, know.

And now I know that I let him go too easily.

I blamed Julia when she wanted to run around looking for hope and I told her to pray for grace. I feel it now, heaving in huge waves of grief coming from my chest, that I have no grace of my own.

When I stagger up and down the other side of the tor where Conchita lies buried I see that everything – here at least – remains exactly the same. I can't bring myself to say the prayer that I meant to say by her grave. I talk to Conchita all the time, anyway. I tell her that it never mattered to me what she looked like, after the accident. I tell her that I've forgiven her for leaving us the way that she did. I've spent a whole lifetime trying to under-stand something of what it must have been like for her, when she found she could no longer accept herself. I deal with women like her every single day. I make people's noses smaller or their eyes bigger and sometimes it helps. Other times the outside form is already perfect and the disfigurement is etched so deep on the soul there is nothing I can do to help.

I let my fingers trace over her name. Conchita Esperanza. I've got to let that go too now, I realise. The hope. The sorrows of the world are far too big, too wide; I cannot be the dam to bridge them all. Maybe that's where faith really comes in. Maybe that's the bit where I hand over and just say – over to you, God, 'cos I sure as hell can't deal with this.

I thought that having faith meant accepting whatever life throws at you – because it must all be some part of God's greater plan. I thought I could get by just believing we're all in God's hands and that must be enough.

But it isn't.

I don't get to escape the pain, the real pain of it. Because I was not there for Hadyn. Because I did not save him. Because I did not believe it might be possible to do anything to save him. Oh and maybe, above and beyond all that guilt, maybe I'm crying because I've lost him, my boy, my beautiful boy, and Lourdes was right; there never was any point putting my heart and soul into my life's work only to wake up one day and realise that I have no *life*.

Julia

I made a mistake cutting Naseem right out of my life all those years ago. At the time I was too taken up with my own concerns to even know, let alone to care. I hope I am different now.

My old home town of Monkswell is certainly different to how I remember it. The steep grey walls that used to enclose it have given way to a modern high-rise building that seems to be some sort of shopping centre. Naseem's dad's corner shop is still there – only it's a lot smaller than I remember it. A Greek family runs it now.

Further along up the road and the tiny Co-op has given way to a giant Sainsbury's. There's less graffiti about than I remember. Smarter cars line the wider-pavement-ed roads and when I venture over the troll bridge, The Crown has morphed into the 'Waltzing Cow' – a wine bar with baskets of geraniums and silver ivy hanging outside.

Naseem is waiting there for me, just as he said he'd be. He's grown plumper. The dark shadow of a beard over his face makes him look that much older. But his eyes – when at last he catches sight of me – still hold echoes of the same young man who used to walk me over the troll bridge every night, way back in the days when he felt it was his job to look after me.

'Hey, Naz.'

'Jules!'

We both stand there grinning, for a bit. I feel I'd like to hug him, but it isn't the kind of thing we used to do back when we were kids.

'Looking good, Jules.'

'You too.' He laughs. He looks at the pavement as if he isn't entirely sure why he has even agreed to meet me here today. It's been twelve years.

I haven't forgotten that I never replied to any of his letters or returned any of his phone calls after I went to live with my mum and Dick in Croydon. I can't explain why I didn't want to, at the time. I didn't want anything more to do with this place. I thought I would never be back here again, after what happened to my dad.

Is it too late to explain all this to Naseem now? And why have I even brought him back into the picture, anyway? When I left here I became someone else; I became the person I always wanted to be, but Monkswell would never have let me. I only know that when I came home last Monday I spent a good while Googling his name before I found the right Naseem Singh. He's a structural engineer now. He has two daughters and a very pretty wife called Nadia and he's a contented man. He lives in Upper Monkswell now, the expensive bit.

'So: how do you like our new-look bridge?' He does a *voilà!* movement with his arms and we both turn to look at it. 'Troll got evicted. They said he was a health and safety hazard.'

'I'm not surprised. I see they've installed proper lights at both ends too,' I marvel, '*and* a high guardrail so nobody can fall in any more.'

'In fact, it's so safe that if you and your dad lived here now you wouldn't have needed me to walk you home at all.'

'You mean if my dad had chosen to frequent the Waltzing Cow?' We both turn to look behind us and laugh at the same time.

'How times change, eh?' He glances at me sideways and I know he's wondering if I've changed too and – maybe – what the hell I've contacted him for after such a long time?

'D'you want to go straight in to eat?' he offers.

'I . . . do you mind if we walk about a bit first, Naseem. I'm not really hungry yet.' The truth is my stomach is one huge knot of apprehension. I came here for a reason but it wasn't just to get reacquainted with my old friend.

'We certainly can. I'll give you the new version of the Monkswell guided tour, shall I?'

'Yes, please.' As we move away from the Waltzing Cow I give him a hug after all. We feel a bit like strangers, as well we might, but I don't want to feel like this with him.

When I grasp his shoulders, he holds me tight, just for that second long enough to let me know he still *cares*.

'You look *happy*, Naseem.'

Naseem nods, his face serious. Then he says, 'I heard what happened, Julia.' He's looking straight ahead of us as we're walking down towards our old school. I recognise the road.

'You did?' My voice is small. Which particular bit of all that has happened in the last twelve years is he referring to?

'There was a small piece in the local paper. About your son.'

I concentrate on the pavement below us.

'Yeah,' I say. What else is there for me to say? I had something precious. I lost it.

'I was so sorry to hear it, Julia. I would have contacted you if I'd known how. And now – you've contacted me.' He pauses and turns to me but I don't want to talk about this.

'Is this our old school?' We've rounded the corner and there it is. Or, should I say, there it isn't. 'What the blazes happened to the Bloomsworth St Margaret's secondary modern school?'

'Blooming St Maggie's was bulldozed down four years ago,' he supplies. We both pause to take in the new building that has arisen like a phoenix from the ashes of our old place of torture.

'It's a bit like Arenadeluna,' I mutter. 'My fiancé Charlie's old town in Spain. Everything's changing so rapidly you can barely find your way about the place from one day to the next.' Naseem looks curiously at me and I return his eye contact but we don't mention Hadyn.

'I just can't believe you're still *here* after all this time,' I say with false gaiety. 'We both always said we would move out of here, remember? We were going to go and take the world by storm.'

'I'm glad *you* did, Julia. You followed your dream. I heard you worked for that fabulous photographer or whatever he was . . .' he smiles sadly, 'but for me, Monkswell is – it's *home*, you know.'

I swallow. I wanted it to be my home too, once upon a time. I didn't want my life to turn out like this. I wanted to have *roots*, just like Naseem does.

'I have a different home now,' I lie. At least, I thought I did. It hasn't worked out that way.

'I heard you were marrying a plastic surgeon?' Naseem looks at me admiringly. You've gone up in the world, his expression says, but I know he isn't envious. He's happy for me.

'We were to be married, Naseem. But when my son – when he *died*, all that changed.' I have said what I have never been able to bring myself to say all this time.

My eyes fill up with tears but we just keep walking along.

Naseem's hand brushes against mine. He squeezes my fingers, briefly but doesn't say a word. He doesn't have to.

We are walking along towards the cemetery now. Automatically, it's the way we are going. As if he knows instinctively what it is I've come to do.

'I don't want to talk about it, Naseem. Any of it. Let's just . . . talk about ordinary things, okay?'

He doesn't say a word.

'The whole of Monkswell . . .' I start up, blowing my nose on a tissue, 'it's rocketed up-market from what I can see?'

Naseem throws me a glance.

'I guess my dad and I wouldn't be able to afford a bedsit above your shop nowadays, eh?' I'm trying for the jovial tone but I know I'm sounding too flat for that.

'Not your father, maybe,' he says quietly. '*You* would.' We are coming up to the T-junction next to Endeavour Road. I know where we are, now. My heart is pounding so loudly I don't know if I can carry on walking any more. Was the cemetery really this near to the school?

'Tell me something,' I beg him. 'Anything at all. About people I used to know. Tell me about them.'

'Okay.' He sighs. 'Remember that poor fella you left behind, heart bleeding, when you left Monkswell?'

What fella? Is he talking about himself? Surely not?

'I didn't mean to leave my dad *bleeding*,' I defend, 'I didn't actually know he *was* bleeding when I left him.'

'I was talking about Josh Martyn,' Naseem looks at me in surprise. 'The boy you were supposed to be meeting the night you left this town forever. You remember him?'

'Well I . . .'

'He went out with Stella Bella on the rebound. Got her up the duff so I think you had a lucky escape there. They had two more kids, then split, and he went to live in Harrogate.' Is this 'ordinary enough stuff' for you, his expression seems to say.

'Stella Bella? Who the hell is she . . . ?' Then, 'The gates of the cemetery – they were around here, weren't they?'

'They still are, Julia. Do you want to go in?'

'Just like we used to,' I say casually. I've got a really sharp pain in my chest. The gate swings open with the same old creaking noise that I remember. My feet feel very heavy and I'm not sure I can actually go in.

'I didn't come back here to find out about Josh Martyn actually.'

'I didn't think you had.'

'I just had to come back because I still feel so bad about . . . my dad, you know.'

'You did what you had to do,' he says quietly. 'He understood.'

360

'Did he, though? I mean – I never saw him again after that. I never even visited him. I thought – if I go back and even visit him it'll be like entering the spider's web again. And I might never escape it a second time. Do you understand that? That's why I couldn't contact you either. That's why I had to maintain my distance from you and from anyone who had any connection with this place.'

'It's okay.' Naseem sucks on his lower lip. 'You don't have to put yourself through this, Jules. It was all a long time ago.'

But I'm on a roll.

'That night, when I left, I *never knew* my dad was bleeding, Naseem. He was sick all over me. That's about all I remember of it. He threw up and he staggered forward and I wanted to help him but I just had to . . . run away.'

'You did the right thing,' Naseem assures me now.

'I did?'

'You did. You left here. It's what was right for you. It's what I always wanted you to do.'

'But I found out later, he got hurt really bad that night, Naseem. And I wasn't there to help him.'

'You called the ambulance didn't you? I still say you did the best thing you could have,' he says softly. 'You *got away* from here. You became the person you always wanted to become.'

'Naseem, I can't even remember *who* I always wanted to become!'

'Someone brave,' he says at last. 'And someone compassionate and someone kind. And you were always all those things, Julia. Even back then, when you didn't know it yet.'

'I need to go and say goodbye to my dad,' I tell my old friend now. 'Will you take me there? I don't know where he is.'

'I have an idea where he is,' Naseem assures me. 'At least, I can point you in the right direction.'

361

I take in a breath and start forward, but what he says next stops me in my tracks.

'You won't be wanting to hang around in the cemetery any longer then?' Naseem gives a small laugh. 'You won't find him in here. It's not as if he's *dead* or anything.'

Charlie

'I've been working with your wife for some time now.' Blue sounds different over the phone from how he does in his gung-ho, upbeat emails to Julia.

'I understand that. You've been giving her reason to believe that our son might still be alive?' My own voice sounds thin, stretched out like a piece of glass wire.

'I think now she accepts that he isn't.'

The piece of paper with this man's mobile number on it crumples now in my hand. Is he saying that Julia's changed her mind? Why would she do that – and why now, after she has come so far and risked so much?

'You've seen her?' The dark sea laps against the quayside by the taverna where I'm sitting alone tonight. She is in Spain, then? I sit upright, jolting the cold beer on the little metal table in front of me. 'Where is she?'

'We parted company the day before yesterday, Charlie. We thought we might have found him but . . . it turned out the child was someone else after all.'

'If you don't mind my asking – you've been helping Julia in what capacity, exactly? As an advocate? A paid private eye? A *friend*?'

'A friend.' He sounds depressed. 'But I don't know where she's gone now. She said something about going back to the UK. And, if you don't mind my asking – where did you get my mobile number?'

'From her emails,' I admit. 'I had to follow whatever leads I could to find her. I've already checked and she isn't staying with my grandmother or my brother.'

'No, she wouldn't,' he says enigmatically.

'You think it might have been a cover-up?' I blurt out now. 'You tried to convince Julia that more could have been done to look for our son?' My words come out like machine-gun fire, accusatory, but I want him to put me right.

'She's let it go, friend. So should you. She's gone home now.'

'I want to meet you,' my voice sounds desperate. 'To hear the whole story, your side of things, from you.'

'Surely it's Julia you should be asking to hear it from?' He sounds uninterested. 'I'm leaving Spain imminently. I gave the fuzz some *information* to get out of prison early – I told you, I was framed – and there are a few people who've got it in for me here.'

'I need to meet with you, come on. You owe me that, surely?' I don't know why I say that because we both know this guy doesn't owe me one thing.

'Please?' I beg. 'Meet me for a drink. Just one. Anywhere you like. I need to hear what you know.'

'Okay. Fine. It's now or never, I suppose. Tell me where you are.'

I wait while he scrabbles around for a paper so he can jot my location down.

'I guess there's always got to be some small chance,' he says before he finally puts the phone down, 'if they never actually found a body, that your boy might still be alive.'

His words filter slowly down into my brain, like the serpent in the Garden of Eden, enticing me to thoughts that I do not want to have.

I wish he hadn't said that.

Is this what he did to her? And if Julia has let it all go now, why should I continue to play his game?

And I do not – oh, I do *not* want to imagine that there are any embers of hope yet to be stirred from this long-dead fire.

Charlie

I'll buy you a drink, I told him, and by my last count he's had five. He's got no money, he told me. Nothing left at all and he's leaving Spain in the morning. He's got himself into some kind of trouble – he didn't elucidate – but he'll be better off away from here.

'I don't know where she is, I've already told you.' He's tucking into his plate of *merluza* with *patatas fritas* and *ensalada mixta* like there's no tomorrow.

'But you say you saw her recently?' I press. 'And she told you she was going back home?'

'Back to the UK,' he corrects me. 'She didn't say where, Charlie. I couldn't tell you that.'

What *can* you tell me, though? I sit back in my chair and observe the man in front of me now. He knows more than he's letting on. This is the man who's been emailing Julia all this time, leading her on – the one who persuaded her she needed to come back. Now that he's sitting in front of me, I don't hate him. He's all nervous energy and nails bitten to the quick. The ladies would all find him attractive, I'll bet.

'She tried her best to find him, didn't she?' he adds between forkfuls. 'She was one determined lady. You've got to admire that.'

'Like you did?' I put in, not without a little sourness.

'I do admire her and I'll admit it.' He looks at me candidly.

'She was prepared to lose it all – everything – just for the chance of being reunited with him.'

I feel a stab of pain run through my guts when he says that and I wince. Blue looks at me curiously.

'What are *you* doing back in Spain, if you don't mind me asking? I thought you two were . . .' He makes a slit-throat motion with his fingers.

'She left me,' I admit. And on Saturday night I nearly blew whatever chance I might still have left with her. I bow my head, remembering Lourdes.

'You been in Spain long?' I change the topic.

'Five years,' he shrugs. 'And you? Arenadeluna is your home town, yes?'

'I went to school in that little stone building just at the bottom of this road.' I clasp my hands together in front of me. I was born here. I was schooled here for ten years. Does that still make it my home town? 'This road – it's been widened now – this is the same road where a truck hit my mother when I was just ten. She didn't die straight away, but she did eventually, from . . . complications . . . that arose from that accident.'

Blue's eyes widen slightly at the revelation. 'I'm sorry to hear that,' he mutters.

'I left Spain and I've never properly returned to it. To tell you the truth I wish to God I'd never come and set foot again in this godforsaken town.' I turn my head away from him. It was here too that Lourdes told me she wouldn't marry me, I recall now. Here where I've lost my one and only son . . .

'Look – I've come over looking for Julia,' I tell him, 'but on the phone you implied that . . . there might be more to be gained?' How to put this? I want to be delicate about it. I know Haydn's gone. But if this man knows something – *anything at all* – then he should be sharing that.

'There might. But then, there are always possibilities, aren't there?'

'Go on.'

'I mean,' he spreads his hands expansively. 'Possibilities aren't certainties. Your son might still be out there. But how long will you be prepared to keep on looking on the back of such a slender hope?'

'Just tell me what you know.' In my heart I don't believe a word of what he's telling me and there's this dull pain in my chest.

'Nothing.' He looks sullen all of a sudden. 'If I knew anything of any use I'd have told Julia, wouldn't I?'

'You must have thought you had something or you wouldn't have called her over here.'

'False lead,' he asserts.

Blue looks at his watch thoughtfully.

'Tomorrow,' he reminds me again, 'I'm getting a lift with a guy I know. I'm leaving for Turkey. Did I tell you that? First thing. I can't stay here any longer.'

'Can we just go for a little walk?' I cajole. I don't know why I'm detaining him. This guy doesn't know anything. He's a drifter. He liked the looks of my girlfriend so he played along with her for a little while. That was all. 'We can go back along the quay-side. Walk off that beer?' I say, even though I know I'm wasting my time. It's like he's got me hooked in, but I can't stop myself. Is this what he did to Julia?

'You mentioned over the phone that you have contacts over here?' I've got him off his backside at last and we're walking along past all the several-million-pound yachts that line the harbour.

'Not really dressed for this, am I?' he grins self-deprecatingly.

'Bugger them. You can walk where you like. No matter if you're not wearing a Rolex.'

'Are you?'

I shake my head. 'Don't need one. There's things I could buy with that money that would put it to better use.'

He stares at me, suddenly more interested than he's been all evening.

'You're talking about your Esperanza Centre, aren't you?'

'Yes I am.' *What the hell does he know about that?* 'And that's exactly what I should be seeing to this evening. I should be back home getting ready for one of the most important evenings of the year, just so I can persuade some of the exceptionally well-off that they'd like to support my Esperanza Centre. Instead of which, I'm here, chasing a woman who's already long gone and – and . . .'

His eyebrows rise curiously. 'Julia's not here. Why didn't you go?'

I couldn't go home. It's not just Julia is it?

Agustina's sick. She wants me to stay on and spend some time with her because, she tells me, this time will be the last time. Next time I come back here, it will be for her funeral.

We've taken a turn down towards the less well-lit path to the beach. It's pretty deserted. Blue's saunter becomes a little more relaxed, away from the crowds.

'I'm hoping against hope, I guess,' I tell him at last, 'that you've got some information for me that'll help settle my mind again.'

'Hey, I feel for you, man,' he says feelingly. 'You've lost it all, haven't you? Your son. Your woman. Your charity work. There's no amount of money in the world that can bring back the things that you've lost.' He gives a short laugh. 'You've put my problems into perspective at least. All *I* need to sort myself out is a little bit of money,' he says unexpectedly.

'You need money?'

'Yes.' He flops down onto the wet sand and I come to a halt beside him.

'You're not expecting me to give you any?'

He smiles then, a slow, almost cunning smile. 'That depends.'

'Stop playing silly beggars with me, man. You either know

369

something or you don't. Which is it?' I take a step closer to him but he isn't fazed in the slightest.

'Certainties, *certainties*,' he says enigmatically. 'I told you, I don't have any answers. There are only possibilities. You have to understand, Charlie, that children go missing around here *all the time*. It isn't just yours. What if I knew someone who knew someone else who can get hold of a boy of the right age that went missing around the same time that yours did?'

'Human trafficking?' I turn to him slowly. 'Is that what this is all about?' I feel the bile rise in my stomach.

'Just how much was Julia paying you?' I growl, sinking to my knees beside him. I catch hold of his collar. 'You've been telling me all evening that you don't know anything and yet now you imply that maybe you do. Just how much were you screwing out of her for all this *non-information*?'

He shakes his head. 'I never asked her for money.'

'What did you ask her for, then?'

Blue licks his lips nervously.

'*What?*' I can feel my grip tighten on his T-shirt, my fists perilously close to his face.

His eyes roll up towards me now and I see the glint of taunting in them.

'Why don't you ask *her* that, Charlie boy? You're the one who's marrying her. *If* you can find her, that is.'

When my blow comes he's not prepared for it. He raises his hand to wipe the blood from his lip and then shifts himself up onto his elbows where I've floored him.

'I never slept with her,' he throws at me sullenly now. 'And I never charged her a penny. She needed someone to take her seriously and you wouldn't do that. I was there for her, Charlie, when you weren't – that's all.'

'Julia doesn't need any help from the likes of scumbags like you. And you *weren't* any help. She could have had closure if you hadn't kept feeding her with false hopes.'

'Hope is hope,' he shrugs. 'It can never be false. It just *is*. That's the nature of it, Charlie. There are no guarantees at the end of it.'

'And what did *you* get out of it? You don't strike me as the altruistic kind.' I want to pummel him into the ground and that's the truth; only part of me knows it's not him I'm angry with – it's *life*.

'Why, I got – *her time*.' He looks at me through narrowed eyes. 'I got the attention of a beautiful and intelligent and decent woman. I'm *nothing*, am I? You've said it. A scumbag. Whereas Julia – she's a princess. And – can you imagine how that made me feel: to be *needed* by a princess? How else could someone like me ever get to pass the time of day with someone as special as her?'

A couple walking their dog along the beach – a huge shaggy black St Bernard – pass by us now. The bloke is carrying a torch so they can see up ahead of them. He shines it momentarily over Blue and me. On impulse, I hold out my hand and haul Blue to his feet.

'She had to go with what she believed in. She wasn't ready to let him go as soon as you were. That's all. And who's to say she wasn't right? Do you have any *idea* how many kids there are out there, still alive but "disappeared", waiting to be found?'

I frown. I do not really want to know. No more than I want to know how many cockroaches live in the bins outside the taverna where we just ate, or how many rats live in the sewers beneath us.

'It's the underbelly of the life most of us see,' Blue assures me now. 'There are a whole load of humans out there with the humanity stripped right out of them. Some are forced into it. Some are born to it. And some come to it completely of their own free will. But then, you already know this,' he smiles weakly at me. 'You've got your *Esperanza Centre*, haven't you?'

I stare at him. He's making too many connections, all far too fast for me.

'It's easier,' my voice sounds lifeless, broken, 'to see what things

371

might be improved over there. To see how I might help ease the suffering over there. It's . . .'

'Far enough away?' he offers.

'And they're important too,' I counter, but something in his words has taken my thunder away. I take in a deep breath. The ache in my heart suddenly stretches out as far and as wide and as black as the beach we are standing on.

'And this – this boy – who you say was taken at the same time as my one. How would I go about finding out if he's mine? Can you arrange a meeting? A *viewing*, so to speak?'

Blue goes silent all of a sudden. His energy seems to change.

'You're game, then?'

'To see him, maybe. What have I got to lose?'

'No, my friend. It wouldn't work quite like that. I haven't got the boy myself, have I? And the people involved – they'd never trust someone like you – too risky. No. I'd have to purchase him outright and you'd have to take the risk. They'd supply a passport for him, that wouldn't be a problem. And, at the end of the day, even if he isn't yours, you'll have rescued the lad from a life of certain horror. You can't lose.'

I can't lose?

'You're a compassionate man, Charlie. I know. Even if this risk doesn't work out, you'll have helped someone.'

'Let me get this right. You are suggesting I should *purchase a child* on the off-chance that he might be mine?' I can feel the hairs on the back of my neck sticking up as we talk.

'The timing is right. There is every chance that he could be. But there are no guarantees. That's how it is, in this game.'

'*Why* in heaven's name would they have taken him, though? If they didn't want him for ransom?'

'Maybe they did and that plan went awry? There *was* a ransom note, you recall . . .'

'That was sent by a joker! They never sent another one, did they?'

372

In the silence that follows, the drunken tones of 'Show Me the Way To Go Home', followed by gales of laughter, reach us from the shore. I stare at Blue helplessly. He's broke, he's not long out of jail. But he knows so much more than I do. In this world where affluence meets abject poverty, moneyed scruples meet depravity, he has the advantage of me.

'If all this is true,' I say to him at last, 'why did you never say anything about it to Julia?'

'She had no money, so there would have been no point. It would have been cruel. You, however, are different.'

I run my hands through my hair and I can feel the sweat on my scalp, hot and sticky. What this man is suggesting goes against everything I believe in. If I . . . *buy* this unknown child, I will be fuelling the economy that led to his abduction in the first place. It's like throwing rupees in the streets of India to those children who have been purposely mutilated in order to make them better beggars; logically, all that does is ensure the mutilation of further generations of children.

The logic of it runs along the same lines that Louis Baudelaire was using when he took out those people's kidneys so they could sell them for some cash on the black market. He should have known better. Santos might have been in it for the cash, but Baudelaire really believed he was doing some good. But it's one little 'right' action that contributes to a greater 'harm'.

'You have to help those that you can,' Blue says after a while. 'It's all you can do.'

'It goes against everything that I stand for,' I tell him. And I feel this huge black anger rising in my belly because we are two men having a perfectly civilised conversation about atrocities. 'This is for you.' When I punch him this time, deep in the stomach, he is completely off-guard and he doubles up in pain on the sand and stays there for a very long time, his breath coming in short, painful gasps.

'You're nothing but scum,' I tell him, but I think what it might

373

be worth to chase the sadness from Julia's eyes, for the chance to hold my boy again.

'I know,' he says softly. 'That's all I've ever been. But your girlfriend saw enough value in me to spend time with me, didn't she? I gave her hope.' There's something in this man I will never be able to punch out of him. And maybe – for all that I despise about him – it's the part of him where he's a better person than me?

'Just tell me,' I call out to him as he turns away from me and starts to make his way back across the sand. 'Just what amount of money are we looking at here? *How much?*'

Julia

I stare at Naseem. How could he not know?

'My dad died, Naseem, *ages* ago.'

My old friend looks baffled, then apologetic.

'God, I'm sorry, Jules. How did that happen? We used to see him up the supermarket, and down the allotments, all the time. He took up growing things, you know. He was always trying to off-load his cabbages . . .' Cabbages? That doesn't sound like my dad at all. I shake my head at him.

'You've really shocked me, you know. I heard nothing about it.' Naseem looks a bit dazed.

'That's okay.' We both stand there, feeling awkward for a bit. There is a low rumble in the distance.

'It's getting very dark, isn't it?' Naseem nods. I feel a spot of rain on my hand.

'I'm sorry,' he says again. 'I swear I never knew a thing. I'd have been there for the funeral, otherwise.' He looks at me apologetically.

'Oh.' How do I tell him this? 'I didn't get to go myself, Naseem. That's how it was, you see. That's why I had to come back here today. I've got to find a way to say goodbye.'

Now Naseem looks embarrassed all over again. What happened to telling me that, 'It's okay, Jules. You did the right thing'? Then again, I remember how close he and his own father were. He'd as soon cut off his right arm as not attend his old man's funeral.

375

'So – where would you like to go now then? I've got to be getting back soonish myself,' he hints.

'That's okay. Just point me in the direction of where he went to live,' I breathe. I've got some vague idea in my head about standing outside my dad's old house and telling him, in my thoughts, that I'm sorry I never came back for him. Later on, when Naseem goes, I'll make my way down to the cemetery and find out where he is. This may be a little crazy; it may be weird, but I've got to do this.

'We'll go round the back of the allotments way, then,' Naseem says. He takes my elbow and turns me around. 'This way,' he directs me kindly.

Neither of us has brought an umbrella. When the downpour starts it's clear from the outset we're both going to get drenched, but I don't really care.

It's five p.m. but the sky has gone as dark as night. The cars on the street have put their headlamps on and I can see the light shining off the rivulets of water on the black road. How strange. This *feels* like my dream feels. When I look down, the dark stain spreading across my top is water, only water. The breeze is fresh in my lungs and when we get to the old wasteground before the allotments, I get a sudden sense of him; my dad.

I've sensed Nana Ella before, but never Dad. He knows I am coming, I tell myself. He knows what I am here to do.

This sense of his presence is familiar and comforting. It's a feeling from the past; from before the time when he started drinking. It is a 'tuck you up safe and don't let the bed bugs bite' feeling. It's the feeling I used to get, standing at the garden gate with Mum after he'd been off on one of his long bike treks with his mates and then we'd hear the sound of his motorbike roaring down the road. I get a flash of joy lighting up my mum's face: she loved him, then. She was young. She had so many hopes for what was yet to come. I remember why it is, despite the years that have passed, that I still love him.

When we turn the corner to where his old house was, Naseem tugs at my elbow and gently inclines his head towards the lone figure standing by the swaying broad beans. My old friend looks at me strangely, sadly, as if he wonders if I have gone right out of my head. When I follow the direction of his gaze, I wonder if it could be so.

I used to pretend. That it was a bad dream, nothing more. I used to think – if I go and stand by our old gate, in the house where we all used to live, if I wait there long enough, maybe I'll hear the sound of his bike again. He will come home. I used to think – if you want something badly enough, if you believe in it strongly enough – you can make it be.

And then, today of all days, when I am no longer expecting anything, on a day when I do not expect to see him any more – he is there.

But – Dick *told* me my dad was dead and I'd believed him. I still believe him.

This, of course, is someone else. Someone who looks just like my dad.

I would be the one to know, wouldn't I?

Naseem is just standing there beside me, scratching his head, looking perplexed.

'Who the hell is that?' I croak.

'Well, I thought it was . . .' He coughs and the cough turns into an uncomfortable coughing fit and he has to bring out his hanky again.

'I'm sorry, Naseem. They told me . . .' My voice reaches out to him, fades away. He puts his hanky back in his pocket.

'I'll leave you two to it, then?' Naseem smiles a sad smile.

And the old man standing by his runner beans, he doesn't know who I am at first, either.

'They told me you had passed away.' When Dad turns to look at me, at first guarded, confused, I see him stiffen his shoulders and draw in a deep breath.

Is this how the things that Silas predicted will come to pass?

'*Someone you assume is dead is still very much alive ...*'

Is this what Nana Ella was trying to tell me, after all?

My dad purposefully shakes the earth off a potato he's just dug up.

'But you're alive,' I accuse. I can see that his hands are trembling.

'I grow me own now, Julia.' I catch the light of pride in amongst the bewilderment in his eyes. Maybe he never expected to see *me* again, either? But why did he never even try to?

'Carrots, cabbages, runner beans. Lettuce. You'll take some wit you afore ye go, now?'

'You grow *cabbages* now?' What else is there to say? 'What about your motorbike?' I ask suddenly.

'Sold that many ages ago, so I did. Couldn't ride it no more on account of me legs.'

'They told me you were dead,' I say again.

'Aye,' he turns away, 'mebbe there's some truth in that, Julia.'

'No you don't!' I stay his arm as he bends to retrieve some more of his vegetables from the ground. 'Just tell me *why*? Did you know what I'd been told?'

'I knew.' My father straightens up and I see he isn't as hunched as I first took him to be. 'We'd agreed that's how it would be. If you ever thought to try and contact me.'

'You agreed it? *With whom*?'

'Your parents,' he asserts.

'You *are* one of my parents,' I remind him hoarsely. 'And I left you here that night. When you fell ... I left you to ...'

'That was the best thing anyone ever did for me, I promise you. I've never drunk a single drop since that day, do you know that?'

I look at him disbelievingly.

'I swear.' He puts his fist to his heart. 'When I saw that you – even you – couldn't abide my ways any more, I knew that I'd got to change them. And I did, Julia. But I only did it because you left me that day.' He leans forward, taking my hand carefully, as if it is a precious thing. 'You saved my life that day, Julia. I didn't want to repay you by ruining yours.'

'So you pretended to be dead. You cut off all contact with me by pretending – like a coward – to be dead!' I can see more clearly all the lines etched by the years onto my father's face. His skin is more leathery than I remember it. His eyes are – they're quieter, I see. They're no longer as wild as they were.

'Not a coward,' he tells me at last. 'Staying away from you was the bravest and most difficult thing I ever did in my life. I freed you, didn't I? The best and most noble thing I ever did was to let you go.'

I didn't want you to, though!

I clench my fists with fury at the thought of all the unmarked years.

'Don't take so, like that,' he says softly.

'I thought I'd killed you,' I tell him through clenched teeth. 'Because I ran away and I wasn't there.'

'Well, you see now, that isn't how it was.' He did the best he knew how; this is what he's telling me.

And who knows – maybe, if I am very lucky, in many years from now my own child will find me and I'll have to explain why it was I gave up the search for him? I ask myself: how will he feel if I stand there and tell him, *The best and most noble thing I ever did was to let you go?*

Charlie

I have been wrong about so, so many things. I wish I could say that to Julia right now.

Upstairs, in Hadyn's room, I have left the bedside lamp glowing. The window in his room is open at the top and the almond scent of the summer's end roses that grow directly beneath, wafts up to perfume the air. I sat in there for a very long time this evening, with his white elephant in my lap.

Was it really only twenty-four hours ago that I stood on that darkened beach with that man Blue and made the most momentous decision of my life?

Twenty-four hours.

But this photo-album that Eva gave me – I've got it open on my coffee-table now – scrolls down the pages of the years much further away than that: *twenty-four years*. There are photos in here of me and my family that I've never even seen. Here's me at ten, standing outside Hillstones: short trousers, brown duffel coat. Suitcase. Dad. Turn the page and here's Roberto (he was chubby then, not chiselled), standing next to Conchita. They're standing in Abuela's sunny patio squinting at the camera, the light falling straight across their faces, shining brightly off their hair. I stare closely at this one of the two of them together because she's had her accident by now. The light picks out the scar line down the left-hand side, a brighter streak across the top of her cheek. But she doesn't look *that* bad. I stare at the photo for a very long time, not comprehending.

If she looked as good as this, then the accident wasn't such a monstrous disaster, then? I turn the page back to me, aged ten, worried face, *scared* face, standing out in the drive in front of Hillstones. I thought she'd never come to see me because she looked so *different* (that was the word they'd always used) that she'd felt ashamed of how she appeared. I'd told myself that she hadn't wanted me to see her like that.

I hadn't wanted to see her 'like that' either, had I? The duality of how I'd felt back then slips in unnoticed. I'd wanted Mum back, wanted her more than anything, and I'd also been scared as hell at the same time, that I would have her back only to find out that she'd turned into somebody else. But she hadn't, had she? So why hadn't she come to visit me?

The answer slips out of the book when I open the next page. It flutters onto the floor like a snowflake. It's a prescription – unused – for morphine, to be administered by a nurse, twice a day. Who kept this? Abuela? Why did she keep it here? It must be hers, I think. But no. The name and date on it confirms that it was written out for my mother.

Roberto wasn't lying to me after all. She *had* been sick. Our mother hadn't taken her own life. Why had my ten-year-old self ever thought that she had?

I rub my face with my hands. I'd felt responsible for what happened to our mother, that was it. I'd told myself a story that fitted in with the way I saw the world at the time; it had made sense *to me*.

It doesn't any more.

And it seems to me that somehow, now that my son's door is open, in some way, my house has begun to breathe again. The late afternoon light that floods through my patio windows has a life to it that was not there before. The birds that call from the tall trees outside, they are different ones. They aren't the huge crows that Julia used to complain about. Those ones have gone.

How much of my life has passed me by, I wonder? How many months like this, with me frozen like a chunk of ice swirled round in a drink at a cocktail party, there but not there, never quite absorbing the details. I mean, *what has been the point of it all?*

Until this quiet moment, sitting in my own house all by myself with nothing but the clock in the hallway making a sound, I have never really stopped to ask.

I have tried to hold tight onto the reins of control for too long, I think. The more they tried to slip through my grasp, the tighter I've held on – and in the meantime both Julia and my son were slipping through my fingers.

I get up, closing the photo album on the coffee table.

I do not know – I still do not know – where Julia is, so I cannot tell her anything. I cannot tell her that Blue offered me the chance – for money – to buy a child that could have still been ours. That I went as far as following him into a disused warehouse on the outskirts of Fuengirola where he said he would be able to make contact with some 'friends' of his. When they came out – two of them, both as much deadbeats as he was – and demanded some money – 800 euros – to 'initiate the search', I took one look at the three of them and turned on my heel and walked out of there. Because I didn't believe them. They wanted to sell me a story I might find more palatable than the truth, that was all. And I realised then that the truth is – not that there *is* no hope, nor that Julia was wrong – the truth is still what I said to her before: that *we may never know.*

When she catches up with me, I hope Julia will forgive me for it.

Julia

'We thought it would be for the best.' Mum's voice is only slightly remorseful down the phone now. I've caught her in the garden. I can hear Dick's motorised hedge-trimmer buzzing away in the background. 'We didn't want you going running after your dad again, getting dragged back down into trying to rescue him.' She sounds defensive.

'But – he wasn't dead!' I breathe harshly. I'm standing in the upstairs bedroom of Naseem's Monkswell home where he's offered me their guest room for the night. I'm not going back to face the music at Blackberry House just yet.

'How could you have made up such a horrible story? You could have said he'd emigrated. You could have said – he'd told you he never wanted to see either of us again. Anything. But not *that*.'

'As if that would have made any difference to *you*,' Mum defends pointedly. 'Once you'd got the idea in your head that you wanted your dad back in your life you'd have stopped at nothing to achieve it. You don't give up that easily, miss, or have you forgotten?'

'I've spent all these years thinking my dad was *dead*, don't you get it? I could have had – some sort of relationship with him, maybe . . .'

'You'd have gone back to spending your life looking out for him. You'd have ruined every chance that you had to make something of yourself.'

'What rubbish! It wouldn't have been like that. I wouldn't have moved back to Monkswell. In fact, I'd been planning on staying with you and Dick, getting a job locally, like you'd suggested I should, just so you know,' I tell her testily. 'I only decided to go to Uni in the end because of that terrible news about Dad. So *you* lost me when you tried to take him from me too!'

'And I'm very glad I did,' she puts in after a while. 'Because going to Uni was the making of you, wasn't it? If you hadn't gone, you'd have never landed that job with Brasenose . . . your whole life would have been – well, it would have been less than it has been. So I'm glad you went to Uni. Even if you only did it to spite me.' I hear the door close behind her and I know she's gone back into the house.

'I didn't say I did it to—'

'And I was wrong to try and cling on to you,' she rushes on. 'I should have been encouraging you to leave, but after those two years when you stayed on with your dad after I'd left him – I felt I'd missed out, too. I just . . . Julia,' her voice breaks here, 'I never felt you understood why I had to let your dad go, in the end. I know you've always blamed me. You've blamed me for leaving him. You've blamed me because you felt duty-bound to stay. You were angry with me when it got so bad you ran away from him . . . I could never win, with you, could I? I never have and I don't suppose,' she says sadly, 'that I ever will.'

But she is wrong.

'I went out to Spain again. I've just come back,' I tell her slowly. 'I . . . saw some things there – I learned some things about myself – that I never knew before. And, just so you know, I see you were right about a lot of the things that you told me. I had to see them for myself, that's all. And as for that fabrication about Dad being dead . . . well, I'm still cross but I can see why you did it. I think I can even empathise with your reasoning, believe it or not.'

'You *can*?' The relief in her voice touches something inside me. She needs forgiveness, and who am I not to give it to her? In the months and years to come I'm going to need so much forgiveness myself . . .

'Yes I can, because this time *I've* had to give it up. My search for my son – I've finished with it. All by myself. You can try your level best to protect the ones you love, but at the end of the day that's all you can do. You can't always guarantee that you're going to get it right.'

'And . . . I didn't always get it right for you, did I, Julia?'

'No,' I agree after a bit, 'but I know you never stopped loving me, Mum. And you never stopped trying. And that's got to be enough.'

Julia

I plucked up the courage to go back to Blackberry House at the end of August, thinking that, even if it was over between us, Charlie and I still had things we needed to sort out.

Blackberry House

My dearest Julia,
When I gave you that ultimatum about – if you go to Spain, don't bother to come back – I never meant it. I have regretted it every day since. I followed you to Spain, did you know? I spoke to your friend Blue. I see now you were more desperate than I ever let myself know. I see how desperation can take a person away from who they really are; how fear and sorrow can twist us into shapes that we would never recognise as our own. It happened to me too, so don't think that I blame you

But it's made me think; maybe being with me is part of what's made it so hard for you? I wanted to do things a different way and you had to do what you needed to do. So perhaps you are right and what we need is some space away from each other? You haven't contacted me and I will be leaving the UK soon for a few months. I see you've no longer got your old mobile but if you aren't here I will

contact your parents on my return. I hope this will be okay
with you?

Love Charlie xxx

He'll be away for a few months, Charlie wrote in August, and he's been away from the UK for *weeks* now. September and October have gone by and already we're into the eleventh month. I fold Charlie's letter up and push it back into its cream envelope. Jacob and Louise came out when they saw my car drive up that day and told me that Charlie was working in France; something to do with his charity, they said. I saw the look they exchanged between them as they realised that I didn't *know*. But they don't matter any more.

And by the looks of it, Charlie's made his plans hasn't he? And they don't include me.

As for me, I scarcely know where the last eight weeks have gone. I spent a couple of weeks at Mum and Dick's, but since then I've been staying at Naseem's place in Monkswell. He and his family have been on an extended visit to relatives holding a wedding in India, so they were happy for me to stay on and house-sit for them. I've seen Alys a couple of times but I haven't stayed over with her. She's glad that I've 'calmed down', as she put it, but she seems a bit wary of the fact that me and Charlie haven't got back together yet. Celeste has gone to the United States. Suddenly and unexpectedly, she just told me one week she was going. She's said her goodbyes to England, she said. I was really sad to see her go. But it's given me plenty of time to sit and think.

Every time I get out Charlie's letter and read it over, it reminds me of exactly what I've thrown away. *I see now you were more desperate than I ever let myself know.*

Blue must have told him everything: our plan to take the boy back, how we staked him out on the beach. *Everything.* He implies that I went to Spain because I felt we needed 'space away from each other' and so he has gone to France and left me no forwarding address, in order to give me that space. But I never wanted it. I don't want it now. But by the time he comes back from France, maybe he will no longer want me?

When I came back to Blackberry House again today (still closed up, dust settling everywhere, radiators off) to pick up some of my things, I couldn't resist listening to the answerphone messages that had come through. That was when I found out that Agustina had passed away.

I sat on the bottom of the dark stairs and cried for ages. When my fingers reached out for the scarf hanging at the end of the banisters to wipe my eyes on, I got another shock. The smell of Lourdes' perfume on it hit me straight away. This was *hers*. That meant she'd been in my house alone with Charlie while I'd been away. I was sad about that but sad about Agustina, too.

I couldn't get out of my mind how fragile Agustina had felt that day, beneath my embrace. I kept thinking how good she had been to me, in the end; how she'd got me the pass for that club beach and how she'd believed in me. She'd never said anything about being sick. Maybe she'd just passed away peacefully, of old age? I hoped that was how it was. I wished we could have had more time together. She'd started to learn English, just for me.

I now know that I will have to go to Spain to her funeral. The message on the machine gave me all the details about time and place.

When I leave Blackberry House, closing the front door carefully behind me, brushing past the shrivelled heads of black-berries on the bushes by the front, I whisper goodbye to my home for the last time. I know I won't be coming back. I've got most of my things out. This time, when I leave, I take Bap-Bap with me. I need him for strength. I've been missing him. Charlie can keep everything else – he's paid for it all, anyway – he's entitled to it. But Bap-Bap is mine.

One week later; San José Church, Arenadeluna, Spain.

After the jewelled brightness of the clear autumn skies outside, the air inside the church is dark and subdued. But it feels peaceful. There are many more people in here than I could ever have imagined, but they don't feel like a crowd. They talk to each other in whispers, walk silently and carefully. From my vantage point, hidden away at the back, I watch them coming in and taking the holy water and making the sign of the cross.

I wanted to come, to say my goodbyes. Even though – and maybe just because – I know that Charlie must be here too. I've already gathered – from letters that came in to Blackberry House that Didi had begun to redirect – that as my neighbours said, he must have gone to France, that he's been working on a new Esperanza Centre. I Googled it, but their website was 'under construction' and anyway, he'd made that excuse about me 'wanting space' hadn't he? I wasn't going to pursue him.

He arrives at last, his family all around him, dark-suited and sad. From my hidden place at the back I peer down the rows as best I can, trying to catch sight of him. When he sits down at last, it's between Roberto and Eva, she with a black lace mantilla over her head; she's holding onto his arm, and his shoulders are stiff, a little hunched. I cannot see his face.

I want so much to run right down to the front and join them all. I want to be the one holding his arm, steadying him, comforting him right now. But – this won't be a good time. I can't just crash in on his family and his time of grief, not with so much unfinished business left between us. So I wait.

The air in here is cool, despite the number of people. For a little while I cannot see Charlie at all because a fat gentleman has sat down blocking my line of view. I look about me at the walls, instead, lined with their larger-than-life saints set into alcoves; the weak sunlight illuminating the coloured-glass windows, retelling the stories of the martyrs. After a while I slide down onto my knees, pretending to pray, but really I'm trying to get a better view of Charlie again. So many relatives! They all have a common look about them. There's something I see in them that Hadyn once had, too.

I once *so wanted* to be part of this family, I remember now. And not just because of Charlie. When I first came to Spain it was all I could think of. But it doesn't matter to me any more: not that side of it, anyway.

I've spent a lot of time over the past few weeks sitting in Dad's kitchen drinking tea with him and talking. The time we lost feels as if it's just melted away. He doesn't want me to be angry with Mum. He wants me to be understanding. She did what they thought was best.

'Just like the day she walked out on me, Julia. She did that for you, too, you know. You just didn't take her up on the offer because of your loyalty to me . . .'

He never saw my running away and leaving him that night as me abandoning him; he saw it as a wake up call. My search for my son has brought me back to my father. It's made me realise that I do have a family. And – for all their faults and mistakes – I don't need anyone else's to fill in the gaps; mine are good enough.

Blue emailed me last week. *I have found a job*, he wrote. *It's the first time I have properly worked in years. I know I was never much use to you and your family in the end, Jules, but I tried to be. I wanted to come good for you. Your faith in me – that meant something. I thank you for that. Wishing you peace, in whatever way you best may find it . . .*

In whatever way.

I can see Charlie only too clearly now. He's turned to say something to his brother and his face, even from here, looks so distraught. It is all I can do, not to go to him. I want to tell him I am sorry. I would, too, if either of us might find some peace that way . . . I get up and begin to edge my way down to the front, heart hammering in my chest. Maybe this isn't the right time? Maybe he will be angry when he sees me and not glad?

But maybe he *wanted* me to try and contact him. It's been my own stupid shame and pride that have prevented me. I cannot go through the rest of my life without resolving this, at least trying to explain, trying to end it amicably. It takes more courage than I ever thought I had, to slip into the aisle behind the family, hesitating like a lost child on the edges, unsure and hurting, not knowing what response I am going to get. Should I do this before the service starts or would it be better to wait till after?

But now I can see properly to the side of him, the woman hanging so supportively onto his arm isn't Eva, as I'd taken her to be, after all.

It is Lourdes.

Julia

The short walk down from the church to the graveyard has been lined with bunches of white flowers. I see them, but I scarcely note them. These flowers are for Agustina. And my tears are selfish tears, more for me than they are for her.

I pause at the bottom of the slope where nobody can see me and turn back, my camera in hand. Click. A photograph of the church where Hadyn would have been christened; it is a photograph to commemorate what never was and what will never be. My legs stumble on down a little further, taking me into the cemetery that houses all the precious ancestors; the ones who *I'm* never going to be connected to, even by marriage.

I know where my dad's own people came from now, though. His dad was Marcus O'Reilly: a respectable married man with five legitimate kids of his own before he met Ella. Fearon was Ella's name. The O'Reilly clan were well-to-do folk, so Dad said. They never acknowledged Dad, though; the bastard offspring of their youngest, already married son: they'd just pretended he'd never existed.

Well he *did* exist.

And so did Ella and so do I. And they're probably all dead now, the miserable git O'Reillys. No wonder Ella was always so precious about her boy. Small wonder that her mind always harked back to her fears for him. She'd had to do it all by herself whilst suffering everyone else's disapproval.

My dad's found his peace now, though. He isn't the angry young man that he used to be. He plants his seeds and tries to grow things and every time the earth rewards him with its bounty that's another reason to make him stay.

José-Maria Hidalga, Jesus Santiago, Dolores Ramón. I walk amongst the gravestones, and the names – some accompanied by red-cheeked photographs of the departed – call out to me as I pass them. *Remember us.*

Is this where the roots of all these families are held? I walk along the little path between the gravestones and the smell of the flowers that people have left behind fill the air with sweetness. Is it here, or is it some place much more intangible than this?

Pilar Moreno, Jaime Moreno, Maria Concepcion Ortega.

Maria Ortega?

My eye goes back to that one. The freshly engraved words on the gleaming stone would confirm – by the date – that this is indeed who I think it is. My God, it's Maria! Beside hers, another gravestone: Diego Moreno.

Shit.

My hand flies to my mouth. That was unexpected. But it is them; of course they would be here. Where else would they be?

A young woman who has been bending over the second grave looks up, startled, as I stop abruptly. She nods at me in acknowledgment, indicating Maria's grave.

'You knew her?'

'I – yes, actually, I did. And you?'

'I knew both of them.' Her small fingers trace the line of Diego's tombstone, a surprisingly tender and elaborate one; he's even got a little cherub sitting on the top. Her eyes well up a little. 'She was my friend, but *he* was my husband.'

Oh, good God; I look at her curiously. It is the deranged wife. This must be the terrible deluded woman who would not let Diego go, to be with his love.

She doesn't look like I thought she would. She is younger and prettier and *saner* than I would have expected. I swallow.

'I'm sorry,' I say. 'I heard – what happened. I only met your husband once, that's all. In fact,' I add after a bit, 'I only met *her* twice.' A meeting that I would give anything, now, not to have taken place.

'It is so difficult to keep it properly clean,' she complains sadly. She has a little bottle of water with her, and a soapy sponge. 'I want it to stay clean. I keep his memory this way, yes?'

Clean; she wants to keep his memory all clean and tidy.

I look down, embarrassed.

'How you knew him?'

I can hardly tell her that Maria introduced us, can I? Yet she said Maria was her friend.

'I met Maria first. She introduced me to him. He picked up my ring that day I dropped it on the sand and he gave it back to me.' I remember that day now. I remember Diego's face, quizzical, amused, handing me back my ring. He must have thought I was a real dummy, bringing that thing to the beach, but the only comment he made was that I must be a good mother because I'd remembered to leave Bap-Bap behind. He tried to help me, too, after his own clumsy fashion, just like Blue did. I take in a deep breath and she sees the tears that have welled up in my eyes.

'I think I know who you are.' Her eyes are screwed up thoughtfully now. 'You are the English lady, no? Maria told me what happened your son.' *She did?*

'*What* happened to him?' I look at her challengingly.

'I know people said bad things about you,' Diego's wife continues. 'They said you let your son go in the water that day. The waves were very high. Maybe you let your attention slip for one minute . . .'

'No, I—' I shake my head.

'But I don't listen to everything they say.' She wrings out her

394

cloth and applies the soapy water to her husband's gravestone again. 'Sometimes they don't know everything so they make up stories.' She follows the line of my gaze down onto the two gravestones. She sees what I'm thinking. They buried Maria and Diego side by side.

'Were these two *related*?' I ask innocuously. I know full well they weren't.

'They were friends. They died together so we buried them together. Some people have said that they were – *going together* – you know.' She lowers her eyes here. 'But that's just spiteful words. It's not true. He was giving her a lift that day. She was a friend of both of ours; that's all. We were going to start a new life, Diego and I. Did he ever mention that?'

'You wanted to start a new life? *He* went to the UK didn't he? Did you . . . ?' I look at her carefully. How much does she know? Nobody ever mentioned this lady having gone to the UK after her husband. I'm confused.

'No. I never got there. It got – complicated. Diego went ahead of me and our son. He was going to find a place for us, get some work, first. But he couldn't get the job he wanted that would support us all. He stayed there many weeks but nothing came up. Maria had a dream of living there, too. They took the same flight out – but they were in separate parts of the country,' she defends. *That's what she thinks.* I look at the ground.

'How come . . .' I know this is none of my business, but curiosity gets the better of me now. 'If *you* didn't go out to the UK with Diego, he was talking about taking your son to his sister's house before he could go abroad, himself?'

She looks at me blankly for a minute. 'He spoke of this, when you met him? Well – I work as a back-up tour guide. Sometimes I'm called out at short notice to go on a cruise ship for two weeks at a time, but Diego wasn't working. He was the one mostly looking after our boy. Perhaps this is what he meant?'

'But you never did join him in the UK, did you?'

'God did not want it to happen,' she says feelingly. 'He takes back those he loves the most. My Diego was a good husband. He loved his family. Sometimes, I can feel him around me still, you know. I feel his *presence* . . .' She swallows hard, here. 'If it were not for *my Angel*,' her fingers brush softly over the cherub on the head of the gravestone, 'I would not have coped.'

'I wish I had your faith,' I tell her honestly.

'I think you have,' this pretty lady tells me before she stands to give me a brief embrace and let me go on my way. 'You just don't know it, yet.'

Julia

I have taken 108 pictures today. Of these I will delete 96, leaving just the 12 that I will choose and these, which are all pictures of pretty much nothing, I will paste into the last three pages of Hadyn's photograph album. And then it will be done.

The pictures are of the truth, because they show what my quest has brought me to; they show what I have left. They are pictures of nothing: of the deserted beach on a cold autumn day; of the papers blowing around the market square on the day after market; of the views from the hilltop of the gaping square of excavated rock where the Roman fort used to be – nothing.

'Make your goodbye book,' Celeste said. 'Go and get little scraps and memories from all the places you went together, of all the things you felt and saw and did. It was only when I did that for my Chloe, when I ordered everything onto a shape onto the page, that I finally began to get it together inside.'

So; I am doing it – but it hurts. They all feel like pictures of *nothing*.

There are no bitter-sweet memories to grab hold of. Nothing here to put my unquiet mind to rest.

'*¿Buscas a tu hijo?*' The woman with the frizzy red hair laced with grey startles me. Are you looking for your son? she asks. She's noticed Bap-Bap, which I've got tucked under my arm, that's why. She thinks I'm looking so lost because I'm rounding up my children from the park or something. I watch her as she turns and indicates a little group of eight-year-olds kicking a football around a little way further along, on the path. Apart from them, and this woman and her charge, the Parque del Rosario seems pretty deserted.

'No,' I pull a smile at her, 'I am not.' Not any more, I think.

The woman plonks herself down heavily on the park bench and bends over her straw bag to fetch out a snack. She looks vaguely familiar.

'Didn't I see you at Agustina's funeral this morning?'

She looks up from delving in her handbag.

'I was at the cemetery,' she admits in laboured English. 'I went to tend my brother's grave. I saw you there too.' She peers at me more closely now. '*Si*. I remember you. You were talking to *her*.'

'To whom?'

'To his widow.'

'Oh!' Of course I did. I spoke to Diego's widow. 'You must be Diego's sister then?' I sit down gingerly on the bench beside her. 'That's a coincidence, isn't it?' It's a small town.

'You know her?' The woman looks at me suspiciously now and I see she hasn't even moved up one fraction despite the fact that her ample behind is taking up most of the seat. '*¡Ten cuidado!*' she barks at the toddler she's keeping her eye on in the sandpit. Take care! He's been flicking the sand everywhere with the tip of a big yellow spade.

'No. I don't really know her.'

'That's her son.' The woman indicates her charge with her head. She crosses her arms against her chest now and leans back in the seat.

'You're Illusion, aren't you?' Her name comes back to me in a flash. 'I remember Maria and Diego speaking about you . . .'

'Ah!' The woman's eyes open wide in understanding as it dawns on her who I am. 'And *you*, you are the English woman. You were looking for your boy.' She looks at the ground. 'You never found him?'

398

'No. I never did.'

'Forgive me, I don't live here any more. I don't keep up with all the local news. I only come once a month to tend the grave.' Illusion leans over and touches Bap-Bap reverently now. She understands what this means to me.

'This was *his*, was it?'

'It was his.' It still is his, I think. He just – can't – reach it. The gate at the far end of the Parque del Rosario opens now. We both look up as the group of young lads file out. The lone man waiting by the gates looks familiar. Once they've gone he lets himself in and goes and sits on a park bench. I crane my neck round to get a proper look at him; oh, is it . . . ?

'I am so sorry, *hija*.' Illusion touches my hand. 'Maria spoke to me about you a lot. She never got over what happened, you know. She blamed herself . . .'

'Did she?' I never knew that. I hold Bap-Bap tight to my chest. Does it still smell of him? I can't be certain, any more, that it does. 'I came to say goodbye to this place,' I confess to Illusion half-heartedly. 'I came here to try and . . .' Grab something, I wrinkle up my nose, some essence, I don't know what. How do I explain this to her, though? She's looking at me sympathetically, waiting.

'Never mind. How about you? Are you still looking after Maria's girls?' I glance back at the man but he's got his face turned away from me.

'No. After she died her mother came and took them both away. Now I only have Angel, my nephew.' Illusion goes back into her bag and brings out a bottle of sugary lemonade, which she puts to her lips and drinks.

'You help out Diego's widow? That's kind of you. I only just met her this morning. She told me that she's sometimes called out at short notice. We spoke briefly. She seemed – like she took it all very hard.'

'No, I do not help her out!' Illusion snorts through her lemonade.

'I do not speak to her at all. She is – *cómo se dice* – not a nice person. You wouldn't like her.'

'She *seemed* nice.' The woman's ferocity takes me aback. 'She just seemed – very overwhelmed by everything that had happened to her.' I remember she had believed that Diego was bringing her over to the UK to start a new life. He must have told her that so she'd hand over her beloved son to Illusion while she went to do her work. But Diego never really had any intention of making a go of it with his wife, I recall now. I remember Maria telling me that day on the beach – how Diego had tried and tried to make it work with his wife but she '*wasn't well in the head*'.

'If she really loved my brother,' Illusion leans over and whispers in my face now – 'why did she never come back for their son?' She indicates the little boy in the sandpit. 'She's got her job, hasn't she? She pretends he doesn't exist. She's never once come to me asking to see him. That's what kind of a mother she is.'

I shake my head, confused. This can't be right. Diego's widow seemed so convincing just a short while ago when she told me she '*could never have coped without her Angel*.' Now it seems as if she's just as delusional as they warned me about in the first place, if Illusion's been looking after him all along...

'And you – you *know* what I'm talking about,' Illusion continues. 'You never stopped looking for yours even though he was drowned...' She stops awkwardly, realising that she has revealed she thinks she knows what happened to my child all along. 'Maria told me,' she adds for good measure, but I'm not listening to her any more. I don't care what she thinks. I twist my head to look behind me but the man has got up and is walking towards the roadside. Maybe it isn't Charlie after all? He'd have gone back to the house with the others after the funeral, surely? I turn back to Illusion.

'She seemed genuinely sad when I spoke to her this morning.' Diego's wife believed him when he told her that they still had a chance together. Maybe she was just a woman with very bad judgement, a woman in love and desperate. I don't believe she ever had any inkling about Diego and Maria. But – none of that is my business.

'Not all mothers are as devoted as you,' Illusion says solicitously. 'Some of them just don't care. My brother knew it. He didn't want her to have Angel back, either. He *told* me that when he went off to the UK.'

'Mama, *bebida!*' The toddler has spotted the lemonade bottle she's holding and he's come over for his share of it. He's a pretty child. I could have mistaken him for a girl, his hair is so long. And red, like hers. When he turns to me, eyes sparkling with mischief, and offers me the bottle, I see it isn't red all the way down though.

'You dyed his hair?' I ask her in surprise.

'As a precaution.' Illusion dismisses me with a waft of her hand. 'In case his mother came looking for him. I told you, Diego wanted him to stay here with me.'

He *wanted* Angel and Maria's two girls to go over to the UK and join him and Maria, I recall.

I look at her curiously now. I know full well that Diego had intended that his son should join him in the UK. Did he tell his sister otherwise? Did he lead her to believe that, his wife being so incompetent and uncaring, he needed Illusion to look after the child for him for his own safety?

'So, the plan was – you look after the child until . . . when?'

'Until my brother came back from the UK. He said it would be for a few months.' She pulls out a packet of jelly beans now and passes a handful of them to the child.

'What did he tell his wife?'

Illusion snorts. 'She thought she was going to be joining my brother. That's what he told her. He told her, when they were settled, they could have the boy brought over and they'd start up a new life.'

'So he lied to her?' *He lied to you too,* I think. *He never meant to leave the boy with you either . . .*

She shrugs. 'How else could he have got her to give up Angel? She would never have given him up if she'd thought Diego was taking him away for good, would she?'

Why not, if she cared as little about him as they claim?

'She had to work though, didn't she? Why *wouldn't* she have been prepared for you to look after their son if Diego was going to the UK?'

Illusion pulls a face, now. 'She wanted *nothing to do with my family* from the start. I never even saw my nephew till that day Diego brought him to me – do you know that? She didn't like us and we didn't like her. That's it.'

'Yet she never did go to the UK with him in the end, did she? He took Maria instead. How did he square that with his wife?' I say to her. We watch as the little lad carefully picks out all the sweeties he wants and throws the others of the wrong colour onto the sand. She doesn't tell him off.

'You are very *curiosa!*' Illusion admonishes me now. 'My brother delayed her, that's all. She thought she was still going to join him, that she would as soon as he found work. She accepted what he told her – that Maria and he were not together, even though she knew they had both come over at the same time! Because she's stupid.'

We're both silent for a while and she wipes the boy's face with a cloth. Then she pulls her big cardigan on and I see that she means to be going. The boy sees it too, and he runs off, screaming with laughter, to the play area.

'His father was always naughty, just like that,' she says indulgently. But something is still eating away at me.

'You just told me that his mother never came looking for him. *If she had,* would you have handed him back to her?'

'At first I would, *naturalmente.* Then when I saw how little she really cared, I hid him for his own protection. The fact that

402

she never came looking for him after his father died – that shows that she couldn't care less about him.'

I look down at the white elephant in my lap. Does that mean what Illusion says it does? Maybe it just shows how easy it is, to hide a child in plain sight.

But no, I'm not going down that route. Not any more.

I've come here to say my goodbyes, that's all. To take my last photos of the places where we once came together. This is it. The last place I've got to say goodbye to. Then it's done.

I take Bap-Bap up to the top of the slide and balance him there. His white fur looks grey and well worn against the bright blue of the sky.

Let this be it, then. I pick up my camera. One last memory to put to bed. One last picture of this place to complete that photograph album with *nothing*. I shall not come back here again. I shall not stand with my sandals filling up with play-sand, smelling the clean ocean air that blows in off the shore, the late morning sun making me squint up into a bright empty sky, the sound of the vacant swing squeaking beside me as it rocks all by itself.

But when I look through the lens to line up my shot, fingers trembling, asking myself why I am really bothering – Bap-Bap is gone.

Julia

I should just let him have it, Diego's boy. He holds the white stuffed animal just the way Hadyn always did, possessively, close to him, tucked right under his arm. It makes me happy to think that someone else will love Bap-Bap again. Some other little fella will go to sleep with the feel of the well-worn fur tucked safely against his head. Some crazy sentimental part of me can't help but feel glad about that. Bap-Bap deserves to be loved again. And maybe once I know Hadyn's elephant is in safe hands, *I'll* get a whole new lease of life, too?

I watch the lad climbing backwards step by step down the steep rungs of the slide. Sturdy little thing, he is. He shoots me a mischievous glance.

Which month of the year are we now?

December. The year is beginning to draw to a close. I shall soon leave the year which I began without my child. But it is so hard. I do not want to leave behind what I had. Something in this little boy's look tugs at my memory. Maybe it is because I see his father in him, I don't know, but perhaps his father connects me to the day I last saw my own child.

I can feel my legs buckling, and I sit down on the bottom sticky-out bit of the slide.

I fought for Hadyn, oh I did. I fought with every last ounce of strength in my body but it was all to no avail in the end, I couldn't get him back. And this beautiful, healthy lad has a mum who's never even come looking for him. The world is full of strange anomalies and injustices and none of it makes sense to me.

Illusion is telling him off, now. I can hear her, berating him for taking away my elephant, because she knows it is all I have left. '*Dáselo para atras*,' she's urging. Give it back. I feel the soft warmth of Angel's short legs brush by mine as he sits down beside me on the slide, waiting for me to look up again. When I do, my eyes brimming, he gives a gruff little laugh. The sound of his voice makes me smile.

I can't help but wonder about Diego's wife; here was her child right under her nose all the time, and she never even bothered to come looking for him.

Why wouldn't she look?

Because maybe – the possibility rears its head – she never lost her boy in the first place? Maybe she's still got him – *her Angel* – and he is tucked up somewhere safely in his bed, back at home.

What if the child that Diego brought to Illusion that day was my son and not his? The thoughts surging through my brain right now feel like a fever. What if Diego – *the opportunist who told me he was prepared to do anything to be reunited with his son* – what if he took my boy that day amongst all the mayhem on the beach, when no one was looking? What if Diego – *the saviour on the beach whose cast-iron alibi was his heroic deed in saving the drowning girl* – was the man who took my child?

He could have hatched some hare-brained scheme about ransoming him and then – after Maria reported the note at the police station – maybe got cold feet? Was Maria in on this as well, then? The thought sends a shiver right through my spine because both of them are dead now and I will never get to know the truth.

I try to imagine Diego going to Illusion and saying, let me take my boy back, still letting her believe that it was his son, her nephew. And Illusion, standing firm, solid in her housecoat,

405

shaking her head, saying, your wife is not well, Diego, she is not capable of looking after this child. *First* you come begging me to take Angel for you, *now* you want to take him back to her. Are you mad?

And I imagine Diego thinking: *I suppose, it is done now. I have taken the boy and his parents are wealthy enough to pay well for him* and maybe by then he'd have been in contact with me, telling me that he had underground friends, people who 'knew people' who could help me, egging me on to believe his lies . . .

Yet – the girls – Maria's girls: they would have known he was mine, surely?

But they could have been told lies, too; that Illusion was looking after him for me because I was not well, just like Diego's wife – just as they all had heard me say, that day on the beach, that I had been before. Maybe Diego said – *change of plan, folks; my wife has decided not to hand over our son, so Illusion is looking after this guy instead,* but don't tell my sister he's not my nephew *– if she knew, Illusion would get angry, and the rich English lady is paying us well for this. And the more money we have, the sooner we'll all be together.*

This could be how it happened. What if it was?

But these, as Celeste would tell me, are all forbidden thoughts. They are the first steps on the long road to perdition. They are the first drops of alcohol after long abstinence to the alcoholic. They are the spit-spots of rain that run so harmlessly off plantain leaves down the mountainside only to gather such strength in streams and rivers that their force can never be spent till they've emptied themselves all out into the ocean.

And I have no strength left to engage in that struggle all over.

That man! He's back in the park. He's given the boys their ball back and he *has* seen me. Oh Charlie; you look – so different. Your hair is longer than it was. You have grown thinner. But I would know that walk anywhere. When he walks towards me now, his eyes bright with sadness, I see he's got the chain that he gave me last Christmas – the St Joseph medallion – dangling from his hand. *I always said one day I would give it to the woman I would marry* he said to me so long ago.

And I left it behind. What is he doing with it here now?

A sob catches in my throat; I came here for endings, didn't I? Will he tell me now that Lourdes and he are engaged to be married once more? Will he tell me that he has got his life back on track, wish me much love, and release me to get on with the rest of mine?

Angel is talking to me again, pulling on my sleeve.

'*Luna*,' he says. He's pointing out the faint outline of the translucent moon in the sky. I close my eyes and my son dances for a moment in my memory; a huge tree filled with baubles blots out the ceiling in the arrivals lounge; we look through the windows at the moon that sails high. *Moon*, Angel says, in his own language, and nudges against me, but I am lost in a vision of Charlie as he picks Hadyn up and carries him on his shoulders because there was a time when I believed his shoulders were so broad, and so strong, that there was no burden he could not carry. I know that I love him even now when he is not so strong. Agustina; I hear her faintly; *you do the right thing*, she says, and then she too moves on and the flickering image behind my eyelids becomes that of Naseem and he is telling me what he always told me: to be brave.

Then, for the smallest fraction of a second, I see *her*, my nana Ella. She is smiling. I am a child again, feeling everything all so unbearably raw and up close and real just like children do. And Charlie has reached me. I know because I feel the feather-light warmth of a kiss as he bends down to greet me, on the top of my head. The solid chain of his medallion slithers down into my lap now. And I know it is still mine.

And this time, when Angel nudges against my arm, I put my hand out to reach for him, my fingers curling around his shoulders, the skin warm at the nape of his neck.

This could be Hadyn. Deep in my heart I know this child is so like him. But this little boy could be one of many hundreds of thousands who I will now go through the rest of my life thinking is just like him.

And I have let him go, my son. I consign his fate to a lifetime full of possibilities and what-ifs and maybes. But I will never know the truth.

Not unless...

My fingers brush against the soft hairs at the back of his neck.

Slowly, not daring to look, I lift up his dyed red curls. And now unexpectedly, unbelievably, I hear Charlie's strangled gasp.

'*My God*, Julia.' His face looks so shocked and bewildered that seeing it sends a tremor right through my own body. And then I look down. The child has the same crescent-moon birthmark our Hadyn was born with. He has it.

When I look upwards, crying out to thank God, *thank God*, the tears are streaming down my face. The blue morning shines down like a gentle blessing. The moon is huge and full. And I know that we've come full circle, back to the beginning, just like we always do.

Acknowledgements

The first inkling of what this book would be about came to me early in February 2007 during a reiki healing session with my friend Fran Smith. In fact, what came through that day was so vivid and real that it formed the backbone of what would become *Little Miracles* – so for that, and for all her other good work, I thank Fran.

Thanks go again to my really good editor Maxine and the great team at Avon, Keshini and Sammia; to my agent Dot, for putting suggestions so nicely, and to Jan Sprenger who was such good company on the writing retreat where I got a quarter of the book done. Thanks to all the great folk at the RNA who have helped me celebrate all the highlights of my year so far. There are so many people but I will mention Pia and Catherine especially. Thanks to my mum Yolanda once again, and to Imma for helping me with the Spanish bits I wasn't sure of (any errrors that remain I claim entirely as my own). And last but in fact most importantly, thanks go to Eliott and to all my lovely boys

If you loved *Little Miracles*,
don't miss Giselle Green's gripping novel

A SISTER'S GIFT

THE BABY
SHE HAS ALWAYS
WANTED, COULD BE
TAKEN AWAY...

A
Sister's
Gift

GISELLE GREEN

Two sisters. Best of friends. Worst of enemies.